Before the Dawn

A NOVEL

Before the Dawn

A NOVEL

DEAN HUGHES

DESERET
BOOK

SALT LAKE CITY, UTAH

Library of Congress Cataloging-in-Publication Data

Hughes, Dean, 1943-
    Before the dawn / Dean Hughes.
        p.   cm.
    ISBN-13: 978-1-59038-788-7 (alk. paper)
    1. Relief Society (Church of Jesus Christ of Latter-day
Saints)—Fiction.   2. Mormon women—Fiction.   3. Christian fiction.
I. Title.
    PS3558.U36B44 2007
    813'.54—dc22   2007026702

Printed in the United States of America
Publishers Printing, Salt Lake City, Utah

10   9   8   7   6   5   4   3   2   1

For Jim and Bonnie Parkin
and George and Anne Pingree

Chapter One

LEAH SORENSEN LEANED backward, pulling on the leather lines that were wrapped around her shoulder. "Whoa," she called, but her horses didn't have to be told; they had already stopped. She twisted the plow onto its side, right handle on the ground, and then guided old Betty and Barb as they looped back to the furrows they had already plowed. She tugged the plow upright, held the handles high, and leaned a little forward, loosening the lines. She felt the blade dig into the earth as the horses pulled forward, but the steel struck something hard and jerked Leah off balance. She caught herself, winced at the pain in her tired neck and shoulders, but set out again, walking slowly, keeping a loose hold on the horses' bits, mostly letting them take their own pace. It had been a long day and they were surely as tired as she was.

Leah had trudged halfway back across the field, south toward her house, when she saw a Model A Ford turn into her lane. She watched the red dust billow behind the car, and she wondered who this could be. A salesman, more than likely, trying to convince her that she needed some implement she couldn't afford. She didn't want an interruption right now. She had to get this field plowed while the dry weather held.

The car stopped by her house and a little man got out. He was wearing blue denim overalls and a worn-out felt hat—not a salesman, she told herself. It wasn't until he pulled his hat off and waved that she knew who it was—knew him by his bald head and his big ears. It was Keith Bowen, her bishop. The truth was, he was just about the last person she wanted to see at the moment. But he was still waving, and she couldn't pretend she hadn't seen him. She finished the row she was plowing, then turned the horses and dug in the plow, ready to start a new furrow. She pulled the lines off her shoulder, tied them to the plow handle, and then spoke softly to her horses. "You wait there now, Betty, Barb. I'll get rid of the bishop quick as I can."

"Hi, Leah," Bishop Bowen shouted as soon as she looked his way. "How yuh doin'?" He plopped his hat back on his head and took a few steps toward her.

She walked to the fence and said, "I was doing fine until you showed up. What's on *your* mind?"

The bishop grinned. "What kind of talk is that?" he asked. "You're s'posed to tell me how glad you are to see me."

Leah laughed. She liked Keith Bowen—had especially liked him before he'd gotten himself called as bishop of the Richards Second Ward. She'd been friends with him and his wife for many years, since back in the days when she'd lived in town. "All right. I'll say it. Glad to see you, Keith. Just don't stay too long. I've got to finish this field before dark."

The bishop was a sturdy little man, round in the chest, with stubby legs and arms. He ran a gas station and garage in Richards, Utah, nearby, and could never quite wash the grease out from under his fingernails. "Ain't that ground a little wet for plowing?" he asked.

"It is. But I couldn't stand to wait any longer. I'm afraid, any time now, the heat'll set in and we won't get another drop of moisture all summer."

"I know what you're saying. That's how it is some years."

But he had something on his mind and Leah could see it—mostly in the way he wouldn't look at her straight on. "So, what brings you out here, Bishop?"

"I need to chat with you for a few minutes if you can let them horses take a rest."

"Well . . . actually . . ." She stopped and gave him a careful look, tried to show him with her eyes that she'd meant what she'd said about the plowing. "Two minutes. That's about all. But I need a drink of water anyway. Let's walk to the house." She bent low and pushed down the middle line of barbed wire. The bishop grabbed the upper wire and pulled it high, and Leah stepped through. When she stood straight again, she was close to him and she felt like a beanpole, her nose about even with the brim of his hat. She turned toward the house, but after a few steps, stopped and looked back. "Hey, Keith, I've got some coffee left over from breakfast." She laughed. "You want me to warm you up a cup? I'd never tell anyone back in town."

"I'll say this much, Leah. There's nothing I'd like better. But I've given that stuff up for good now. I'm a righteous man at last." He was grinning again, showing the space in the corner of his mouth where he'd lost a tooth.

"What about tobacco? Did you give that up too?"

"I haven't chewed for years. Never did smoke."

"Well, don't ask me to give up my coffee. Some days that's the only thing that keeps me going."

She was actually joking about the coffee—mostly. She hadn't really made any that morning, and rarely did. But there *were* days when she wondered how she could keep putting one foot ahead of the other. Twelve years back, in 1920, her husband had been kicked in the head by his favorite saddle horse. He'd lived for a few days, but the bleeding in his brain had finally taken him. Such a strange thing—a man who'd spent his whole life around horses and loved them so much, to get himself killed that way.

Leah had been on her own since then, had raised two children by herself, kept the farm going, and learned to do what she had to do. She'd actually grown up on a ranch, but she hadn't really loved that life, so as a young woman she'd gone to college and become a teacher, and that had seemed to fit her better. But she'd learned things as a girl that came in handy now—as much as anything, just the will to get up early each morning and stay at her work all day.

She walked ahead of the bishop to her house—a little white frame place her husband's parents had built when they'd first come out to the Uintah Basin. She stopped on the porch and tugged the laces loose on her muddy boots, then struggled a little, balanced on one foot at a time, to pull them off. She dropped her gloves next to her boots, opened the door, and stepped inside. Looking back, she said, "Come in, Keith. How about a glass of water—if you won't have any coffee?"

"Sure. I could use a drink of water."

Inside the house, she felt more self-conscious about her ragged old striped overalls, which were patched in the knees and in the rear end. But she didn't apologize. She got a couple of glasses from her cabinet and dipped him a drink from a bucket she kept in the corner, and then she dipped one for herself.

"Sit down," she said, motioning to the kitchen table. "Just don't settle in and get too comfortable."

He made a loose little sound in his throat—his way of laughing—and he set his hat on the table, pulled out a chair, and sat down. In the same wet voice, he said, "How are you holding up, Leah? Ain't this place a little much for you sometimes?" He glanced around as though he were referring to the roomy old kitchen with the pine cabinets, but she knew he was talking about the whole farm.

"I don't know. I don't build time into my schedule for feeling sorry for myself. If I did, I'd probably give up the place. But I don't know what else I would do."

"Well, I admire what you done. I didn't think a schoolteacher woman like you could make a go of it out here, but you've held on when plenty of folks've long since went broke."

"That's only because Wayne inherited the farm from his dad, and I haven't had payments to make. This last year it was all I could do, after I sold my turkeys, to pay my taxes and my water assessment. Everyone talks about the Depression like it's something new, but times have been hard for farmers so long, we don't know anything else."

"Would you ever think about teaching school again?"

"Tell me where there's a job, Keith. And if I got it, tell me what they'd pay me. I'm better off here. At least I can grow something for the kids to eat. And you know what we say every year: Prices *must* have hit bottom. They've *gotta* start going back up." She laughed at the thought of it—how many years she'd been repeating those words.

"So what's Rae going to do? Isn't she about finished with high school?"

"One more year. But Bishop, you haven't been out this way in a long time. I doubt you dropped by to talk about my kids and the price of corn. Tell me what's on your mind. My horses aren't going to stand out there all afternoon."

He laughed again, reached over, and took hold of his hat as though he were getting ready to leave. But he only fiddled with its brim. "Well, now, that's true. I did have something I wanted to talk over with you."

"Don't start telling me I don't go to church enough; I figure I can decide that for myself. And don't tell me my kids haven't made it in to Mutual much lately, because I'm the one who has to pull into your place and pay you twenty-five cents a gallon for gas—if my old car will even start in the first place."

"You ought to bring that car to me. I'll have a look at it for you."

"And what would I pay you with—turkey eggs?"

He let go of his hat and leaned back. "I take eggs and bacon, anything like that. I do it all the time." He gave a little nod, maybe to show he was serious.

"Well, I might do that some time. But I've got so I know all that car's bad habits. I can probably fix it about as well you can."

"I don't doubt that. You always could manage things about as—"

"Come on, Keith, tell me what it is you want."

"All right. We'll get down to business." He took another drink of water and set the glass down, still acting like he had all day. "I've had an awful lot on my mind lately—lots to worry about—and that's how I come around to thinking about you. I don't know how much you keep in touch with ever'body around here, but there's not a single family that ain't been hit by these hard times. You might think someone like the Willises, they would be all right, but Jim's store ain't doin' much business. He told me just a day or two ago, he might have to close the Emporium, and if he does, he's got no way to make a living."

"That might be good for *his* family."

"Now why do you say that, Leah?"

The softness in the bishop's tone made her own voice sound brassy. She hated the hardness she felt in herself these days. So she leaned forward, with her forearms on the table, and she spoke more gently. But still, she said, "Bishop, there's no one at the high school who lords it over Rae more than LuAnn Willis. Rae's come home crying more than once because LuAnn didn't ask her to one of her parties, or made some remark about what she was wearing. Maybe the girl needs to go through some hard times—wear a secondhand dress just once, to know what it feels like."

"I know what you're saying, Leah. Bad times teach us all some lessons. But Jim Willis has worked hard for what he's got. It's a sad thing to see a man lose everything he's worked for, the way he just might."

"I know. I've known Jim as long as you have, and I'm not saying anything about that. But his wife keeps her nose in the air when I walk by, like she's afraid she might smell a little manure on me. I don't like that woman—and I don't like her daughter."

She watched the bishop's eyes, saw him react to her harshness. She thought of taking some of it back, but she didn't do it. "Well, I'll tell you something," he said. "When you get to know folks, what they're thinking and what they've gone through in their lives—all those kinds of things— you feel a little different about 'em. That's the main thing I've found out from being bishop. We all have our good points and bad points, and some people who seem mostly bad, they're just folks like the rest of us."

"I know that. Lord knows, I've got more faults than most." Leah felt a little chastised by the bishop's words. And surprised. Old Keith was changing—thinking a little deeper than he ever used to. Leah could hear the kitchen clock ticking. She placed her palms on the table. "But Keith, come on. Now we're talking about the news and weather again, and you said we were getting down to business."

"All right. I know. I was just trying to show how I come around to what I've got to say to you." But that sent him reaching for his glass of water again—and he was still only sipping at it. "I'm just saying, lots of folks are going through things they've never dealt with before. Even Clark Evans is having a tough go of it. No one's getting their teeth filled now. And he's got rent to pay on that building. Fred Miller at the drugstore says he—"

"All right. You made that point. Let's get to the next one."

The truth was, Leah didn't feel very sorry for any of those town people. During the twenties, when she had been working herself ragged, she'd watched them act like they were better than she was. They'd had it good back when farmers were the ones going broke. Sometimes Leah didn't go to church because she couldn't start the car, or because she needed to plow or maybe cut hay—but sometimes she didn't go because she wanted five minutes to herself and didn't need to sit down with a lot of people who considered her and her children beneath them. She and Rachel—the daughter she called Rae—each had one dress they could wear to church, and it wasn't easy to show up in the same one every time, especially when some women could trot out a whole closet of nice things. Her son, Wade, had a pair of dress pants that were too short on him now, and a white shirt that was frayed at the cuffs even though Leah had already turned them once. She kept telling the kids that maybe after the harvest they could get some new clothes, but chances were, prices would be as bad as last year—or worse.

"Okay, here's what I want to ask you." Bishop Bowen sat up a little taller, as though he wanted to take on some authority. "I'd like to call you—or actually, the Lord wants to call you . . ." But he stopped, as though he had lost his courage. "Leah, don't just answer right off when I say what I've got to say. Give it some time and think this over."

"Not if you're calling me to some Church job. I don't have time for it."

"I'm telling you, it's the Lord who wants you. You have to take that into consideration."

"Wants me for what?"

The bishop drew in a long breath. "Well . . . he wants you to serve as our Relief Society president."

She heard the words, but she didn't believe them. She laughed a little, then studied him over. He was trying to look solemn as a judge, but he had to be joking. She let go and laughed hard. But Bishop Bowen was still waiting, and that slowed her down. Just in case he really did mean it, she said, "The answer to your question is no, I won't serve as Relief

Society president. But you know that. I think you just wanted to scare me and then offer me something that won't sound half so bad."

The bishop didn't say anything. He waited until Leah had stopped laughing entirely, and then he sat forward and looked directly into her eyes. "The first time I got some feelings that you were the right one, I told the Lord what you just said—that he must be kidding. But he wouldn't let go of me. He kept telling me over and over, so I told him I'd come and ask you, but I warned him that it didn't seem like you'd say yes."

"I'm glad the two of you are clear about that much, at least."

"Maybe I am. But I'm telling you, Leah, this is the Lord's call, not mine. He still thinks you ought to be our new president, no matter what I tell him."

"Don't shake my faith, Keith. I can see where you might get a wrong idea in *your* head, but I don't want to find out that the Lord has no more sense than you do."

She saw him wince at that one, and she knew she'd gone too far, but he needed to know she wasn't the right kind of person for a job like that. All the same, he was still looking her straight on, his eyes not wavering.

"Listen, Bishop, that's just about the worst idea I've ever heard—me trying to be a Relief Society president. What in the world would people say?"

"I don't ask *people* what I should do. I ask the Lord. I'll admit, my counselors reacted about the same as you did—you know, at first—but I told them what the Lord had told me, and they accepted it. Now I want you to do the same. I'm telling you, if you turn me down, you're turning down the Lord. I don't like to put it that way, and I usually don't, but in this case it's true, and I'm dead sure of it."

Leah stared at the man. Was it really something she could do? But the idea didn't merit a lot of thought. "Bishop, I can get up in front of people and speak if I have to, and I can teach a pretty good lesson, but that's about as far as my *aptitude* for a call like that goes. The truth is, I don't like to go to church. And I don't like half the women in our ward. That's not a Christian attitude and I know it, but it's the way I feel. I never could be an example for the sisters, and no one knows it better than they do. They'd all vote against me if you put my name up—and I'd vote with them."

"But you haven't thought about the most important thing."

"What's that?"

"You lost your husband and you didn't give up. You've gone through falling prices and hard times, and you've kept things together for your family. You know how to survive hard times, and some women in our ward don't. I'm not looking for a sweet little church lady right now. I'm looking for someone with some grit, and that's what you've got. It was the Lord who put you in my mind, and once he did, I seen it was right. So I'm not taking no for an answer—not until you talk to the Lord about it, the same as I did. I'm asking you to get down on your knees tonight and ask whether he isn't the one behind all this. Will you do that much?"

Leah folded her arms, leaned back, and looked at the ceiling. She didn't want the man to leave this house thinking there was any chance she would say yes. "How do you even know I pray?" she finally asked.

"Do you?"

"Not as often as I should. I just fall into bed some nights and don't bother."

"I'm guessing you haven't forgot how."

Leah shook her head and started to laugh again. "You're like a bull-dog, Keith. You've taken a bite on my ankle and you're not about to let go. But I don't think you've ever bit into anyone as tough-skinned as I am."

"Do you believe in Jesus Christ, Leah? And Joseph Smith, the prophet? Do you accept the restored gospel?"

Leah took a breath. She let her eyes go shut. She didn't want the bishop to start into all that. But she said, "You know I do. I'm just not the kind of person—"

"What about President Heber J. Grant? Do you believe he's called of God?"

"Sure I do, Bishop, but I don't think that's the point."

"It is the point. Do you believe the Book of Mormon to be the word of God?"

The truth was, Leah read the Book of Mormon almost every night of her life, and she loved that book. It was also true that she rarely missed a night of saying her prayers. But the daily labor of working this farm had turned her into someone about as deep-thinking as her workhorses. She farmed and washed the kids' clothes, kept a garden and cooked, fed animals—filled every minute of her day that way. Some people had it way too easy, didn't appreciate what they had—and then, by some trick of logic, managed to look down on her for not having what they had.

"Bishop, I'm just not suited to the job. When my horses act up, I swear like a man, and the danger is, if I have to deal with some of those town ladies, I could end up using some of that language on them."

"Come on, Leah. You wouldn't do that."

"You don't know that. I'd probably talk back to you, too. I don't like people telling me what to do."

"You wouldn't have to worry about that. I pretty much let the Relief Society run itself. I just get out of the way. You have your own budget, your own handbook, everything. The truth is, the women are the ones who make my job a whole lot easier."

"Well . . . none of that matters. You've got my answer. I won't do it. I *can't* do it."

"Leah, I'm going to leave now, and you go back and plow your field. But look me in the eye first." She did. "The Lord is in this calling. I know it like I know I'm sitting here. You get down on your knees tonight and turn the Lord down—to his face. Once you've managed that, then you can turn me down again."

Leah didn't say a word. But she wasn't going be the Relief Society president. She let him grab his hat and walk to the door. She could see him trying to look taller than when he'd walked in, but she knew Keith. He was younger than she was, and he never had been the smartest chicken in the coop. Now he thought God was talking to him like the two of them were a couple of old pals.

The bishop got to the front door, but then he turned back, returned to the kitchen door again. "There's something else you're forgetting, Leah." He pointed his stubby finger at her. "I know you. You put on this act like you're a hard-nosed old mule skinner. But I knew you when you was teaching school. I remember how much the kids in town loved you—all them Shakespeare plays you put on, and everything else you done. You've got a good heart. The Lord knows that, the same as I do. So when you talk to him, don't try to pull no wool over his eyes, the way you just done to me."

Leah didn't say anything. She just let him go. But she sat for another minute or two after he was gone. She thought of the young teacher she'd been, right out of college, when she'd first come to Richards. It was hard to remember what she'd been then, and she was almost sure she could never bring *that* Leah back, even if she wanted to.

So she got up and walked back to the field. She plowed that afternoon until the horses couldn't go any longer and she could hardly see the furrows she was turning up. And all afternoon she got angrier at the position the bishop had put her in. Why should she have to tell the Lord no when the bishop should have done it for her?

She finally unhitched her horses and walked them to their corral, where she pulled off their harnesses in the dim light. Then she checked on her other animals—which she found Wade had already taken care of. He'd milked the cows, too. When she walked into the house, she was ready to cuss out Rae for not fixing dinner. As it turned out, though, Rae *had* made a start on that. Leah wished she hadn't—she needed to yell at someone.

After dinner she told the kids to get their homework done, and she slipped off to her bedroom. She didn't tell Rae and Wade that the bishop had been there, or what he'd asked her to do. She pumped up her coal-oil lamp and lit it, and then she sat in her chair—her one place of peace—and picked up a novel that she'd put down a couple of weeks back and hadn't gotten back to. She liked to read the textbooks her kids brought home, or the novels they were reading in their English classes. Once in a great while she would borrow an old British or American classic from the lending library in Richards. But lately she had gone back to the few books she owned, mostly from college. Right now she was reading *Vanity Fair.* She liked Becky Sharp much more than she had when she had read the novel the first time. Becky, for all her faults, was a survivor, and Leah liked that.

But Leah's reading didn't go well. She kept thinking about the bishop, and she kept making up little speeches, telling him that putting all this on the Lord didn't wash with her. She finally decided she would go to bed early. She was even more tired than usual, and if the weather held, she had another day of plowing ahead of her. She had heard on her old car-battery-powered radio that another storm was expected, perhaps late the next day.

What Leah didn't do was read her Book of Mormon that night. She didn't want to hear old prophets spouting off about obeying the Lord. The bishop had dosed her up with enough guilt for one day; she wasn't going to swallow any more.

Leah drained off some hot water from the reservoir on the side of her kitchen stove and carried it back to her bedroom. She pulled off her overalls and then stood and washed herself in front of her dresser. She wished she could fill up her big galvanized tub and take a warm bath, but she heated enough water to do that only once a week. Sometimes she wished she lived in town, where people had electricity and indoor plumbing, but she was used to what she had—and what she didn't have—so it wasn't something she ever dwelled on very long.

For the first time all day she was thinking of Wayne. She wondered what he would say about this. He had always said it was wrong to turn down a calling—and never would have himself. That was all well and good, but he hadn't stuck around to plow the fields she now had to plow herself. Men weren't supposed to die as young as he had—for no good reason. And she shouldn't have been put in this position, forced to work like a man. But she told herself she wouldn't let all that run through her head again—the resentment she'd lived with all these years. What she knew every day of her life was that she had been forced to take on a life she hadn't chosen. Couldn't the bishop understand that? Couldn't he see that her way of life just didn't fit with the job he wanted her to do?

She looked into the mirror on her dresser. Some years back it had cracked, and she had gotten used to looking at her face that way—always a little distorted by the break that ran across her forehead and down her right cheek. Tonight she leaned left, away from the crack, and took more time than usual to see what she looked like. She thought she had been fairly pretty at one time. In 1905, when she'd been fifteen, she'd moved with her family to the Uintah Basin from a farm in Heber Valley. That was back when some of the former Ute Indian lands had first been opened for homesteading. But at eighteen she'd gone off to the Brigham Young University, in Provo, happy to escape life on the ranch. Still, when she'd sought a teaching job, she'd looked back to the basin country she remembered, and found a job in the elementary school in Richards. She'd taught there three years and thought maybe she was destined to be a teacher all her life, but then Wayne Sorensen, a bachelor in his thirties, had begun to take an interest in her. He had been a quiet man, not really very good-looking, and certainly not sophisticated, but he'd wanted to marry her, and no one else ever had, so she had become a farmer's wife and had returned to the life her mother had known.

Leah had married at twenty-four, had two children, and then lost her husband when she was thirty. She was forty-two now, and hardly the same person she'd once been. Her face seemed nothing but bone and leather now. It was a stranger's face, and when Leah really looked at it, the image hurt. She washed her hands hard every night, but the dirt was almost as ingrained as the grease in the bishop's fingernails. She turned her hands over now and looked at the calluses, the splits in the skin on her fingers. She had cut herself across the palm of her hand once, cleaning the blade on her plow, and a scar was left—a slice through her life line as though it were a symbol. Her life, in her own mind, had ended twelve years back, and now something else was happening that she knew was necessary, but it was not what she had wanted. She knew she was not really Leah anymore, never would be again, but it was the old Leah who would have felt more pain about it. This second Leah didn't have the luxury.

Her focus, every day, was to get her children raised, educated, and in a good place, and she had a secret that pertained to that. Wayne had left her a life insurance policy. She had received $2,000, which she had used to bury him and to pay for some other necessities—like the Model T Ford she had bought so she wouldn't be stranded on the farm. And a telephone line, for almost the same reason. But the money had dwindled to about $1200 before she realized that she had to stop spending it or she would never be able to send her kids to college. So she had stopped using it and had never told Rae and Wade—or anyone else—that she had so much. She only told her children that their dad had left them a little nest egg that they could use for college—and that couldn't be touched for anything else. When she watched her children go off to school in worn-out clothes, she wondered whether she was doing the right thing, but if she spent the money and they couldn't go to college, she would hate herself forever. She held onto that money fiercely and lived on what she could get out of her farm—and lately, that had been only the food she could extract from the ground itself.

So what would happen once she got the kids through school? She almost never thought about that, but she took a look at the question tonight. What would she do then? Would she keep this farm going? Could she sell it for enough to live on for a while? Could she teach again? But the real question was the bigger one: What would she live *for*? She had cut herself off from virtually everyone, and she had focused on this one job she had to do. After that, old age was next, she supposed, and she hated the thought of it.

It was not like Leah to look at herself so long. But she was still trying to remember who she was—or who she had been. She had liked her hair once, light brown, soft, and thick. When she was a girl, people had always told her how pretty it was. She had been gangly then, taller than any of the boys, and not a beauty. But she hadn't been homely— and she thought maybe she was now. She didn't look like a woman anymore—didn't feel like one either. She had no pretty clothes, no jewelry, not even rouge or lipstick. And worse was the thought that it didn't matter.

But Leah was thinking too much. She put on clean underwear, pulled her nightgown over her head, and walked to her bed. Then she made a decision. She would not pray tonight. The bishop knew he could make her feel ashamed if she had to tell the Lord why she wouldn't accept the calling. It was a trick on his part, and she hadn't thought Keith Bowen knew any tricks. She'd been pleased when he'd been called as bishop, since he wasn't the kind of man who would ever get it in his head that he was more important than other people, but he was picking up strategies from somewhere, and she didn't like that. She decided she would call him in a day or two and tell him *she* had had a vision. She'd tell him an angel had appeared in her bedroom and told her she was the last person in the ward the Lord would ever choose for Relief Society president. The thought made her laugh, and she slipped into bed. But a bit of a prayer came into her mind. "I can't do it, Lord," she said. "You can understand that, can't you?"

Chapter Two

SLEEP WAS RARELY DIFFICULT for Leah. Most nights her head would start to nod as she was reading. She'd turn off the gas lamp, twist onto her side, and be asleep in seconds. But tonight she had a little more trouble. She found herself trying to imagine it: her conducting meetings in front of the women, calling on them in their homes, organizing bazaars and ward dinners. She didn't have the time; she knew that. That was such an absolute that other questions didn't matter, but she did wonder whether she was capable of doing the job. She concluded again that she wasn't, that she would be like a sheepdog nipping at the ladies' heels. She didn't have a single trait that would make her beloved. There was a certain kind of woman who did those things, and Leah didn't fit. All this stuff about grit and toughness was the bishop's idea of what was needed, but it wasn't what the women would want.

The bishop thought she had a good heart. Maybe that had been true once, but Leah felt none of it in herself now. These days she spent half her life angry at one thing or another, and, as often as not, she took it out on her kids.

When she did finally go to sleep, she slept deeply, but sometime in the night she had a dream—a long, involved dream that seemed to fill up her head for hours. Still, when she awoke she couldn't remember it. She went back to sleep and it started over, but it was gone again when she woke a second time. Then, toward morning, she awakened suddenly, knowing what she had just said: "All right then, I'll do it." She had spoken to the bishop, either in her dream or just awakening, and she had the feeling he had heard her, that she had accepted the calling. She wondered whether she could turn it down now. But that was nonsense. It had been a dream. She hadn't really committed to anything.

There was also something else in her head. The face of a woman. A young woman. She couldn't think who it had been or whether it was anyone she knew. But it had been important in some way. The dream had been about the young woman.

But Leah wasn't going to think anymore about this. Dreams were dreams, that's all. They never made much sense.

Leah got up, did her morning chores, made breakfast for the kids, and then harnessed Betty and Barb again and spent her day plowing. Thin clouds in the morning were turning thicker, darker by afternoon, but the rain held off, so she worked until after dark, said little to Rae and Wade when she finally came in, and went to bed early. She didn't say it to herself, but she knew what she was doing. She was getting ahead on things; she had to. Again and again, she told herself that it was silly, that she wasn't going to accept the calling, but she couldn't get rid of a feeling that she had already given her answer. She didn't pray until Sunday morning, and then only to plead that she not be bound to anything she had said in a dream.

Leah had no idea what was happening to her. She wasn't like this. She didn't have dreams—not like some women who stood in testimony meeting crying and carrying on. She'd scoffed at such "visions," thought that people who had them were a little off balance. And now here she was going about life as though she'd accepted a call when she hadn't, even asking the Lord to release her from her promise.

Leah got Wade up early on Sunday morning, in time to help her milk the cows before priesthood meeting. She returned to the house before he did, cleaned up and dressed, and then fried bacon and eggs for him, even fried some bread in the bacon grease, the way Wade liked it. He had taken his bath the night before, but he washed up quickly when he came in, then dressed in his white shirt and dress pants. When he hurried into the kitchen, his hair was dark and wet, slicked back. Leah saw what she always noticed in him when he did that: He looked like his father. He was tall, like both his parents, and strong, with a man's shoulders, but his face was a refinement of his father's, with a clean jawline and dark eyes. He smiled more than anyone Leah knew, even if he wasn't smiling now, and he had fine teeth, straight and white.

"Where are you going?" Wade asked.

"What do you mean?"

"You've got your dress on." He sat down at the table but didn't start eating. He was the one in the family who always made sure they said a blessing.

Leah nodded to him, and after he had prayed, she said, "I thought I'd go to Sunday School today. I'll get Rae up in just a minute."

Wade sometimes walked the mile into town, and then Rae did later, in time for Sunday School. Leah, more often than not, drove in only for sacrament meeting in the evening. Wade gave Leah a curious look, but he didn't say anything. He had told her at times that he thought she ought to go, so she knew what he was thinking now—that he'd better not say too much and get her upset. Leah knew how grouchy she could be; the kids often seemed wary of saying the wrong thing to her.

But Leah didn't explain. There *was* no explanation—except that she needed to talk to the bishop. She didn't know yet what she was going to say. She tolerated the same careful, curious looks from Rae, and said almost nothing to her at breakfast or after, driving into town. And then she suffered through the adult Sunday School class. Aldon Toliver was the teacher, and the man had cow plop where his brain ought to be. No matter what the lesson was supposed to be, he had to tell his experiences from his mission in the deep South. She'd heard every one of these faith-promoting stories. He had told them in sacrament meeting talks, testimony meetings, or anywhere else he could get an audience—always in a tone of great piety. He was also convinced that the Depression was part of the great winding-up scene, and the Second Coming was "even at the doorstep." That was what he was preaching today.

Leah didn't say a word. She kept noticing glances in her direction from the time she'd walked into the chapel—as though she'd broken some rule by showing up. Old Brother Burns told her it was nice to see her, but he didn't finish his sentence, which was probably, " . . . because you need to start coming all the time—and repent of your sins." He had a few sins of his own, though. This was a small town. People knew things—and remembered.

She held her tongue, even when Brother Toliver said that it was obvious the moon was gradually changing, if you watched every night. It was taking on a hint of red. *That's your brain starting to decay,* she wanted to tell him.

As soon as class ended, Leah went looking for the bishop. She found him near his office. He was talking to Harry Edwards, one of his counselors, but Leah wanted to get this over. She put her hand on his shoulder and told herself, even then, that she was going to say, "Sorry, Bishop," but she knew better. She knew what she had to say; she just didn't know why. "All right then, I'll do it," she said, then turned to walk away.

"What?" she heard behind her. "Leah, what did you say?"

"You heard me," she said, and kept going.

But he was coming after her, and when he caught up, she stopped. "Could you step into my office for just a minute?" he asked.

There were lots of people in the hallway, and she had the feeling they were all looking at her. "I don't want to right now. I'm still too mad. I don't like the way you went about this, Keith."

"But you'll do it?"

"Not very well, I won't. You'd know that if you had a brain any bigger than a pea."

The man was laughing, and for some reason, Leah couldn't hold back a bit of a smile of her own. "You got your answer, Leah," he said. "I knew you would."

"I don't know what I got. When do I have to start?"

"Please. Just walk back to my office for a minute."

So they went into his office, and he stepped behind his desk, but Leah didn't sit down, so he didn't. The old First Ward building hadn't had a bishop's office, and people had had to visit the bishop in his home or simply talk at the back of the chapel, but this new building had not only an office but a Relief Society room, which would be helpful. At the moment, however, Leah was feeling awfully hemmed in, and the pictures of all the prophets on the back wall made her feel guilty. She didn't want to stay there with them very long. "Do you know what the job involves, Leah?" the bishop asked.

"No. I guess not. Is there a book or anything?"

"Yes. There's a handbook. I think Sister Milsap has it. She'll have lots of materials you can read. I'll get all that from her and bring it out to your farm. You can study up on the procedures. I know you haven't been to the meetings much lately, but over the years you must have . . . you know . . . gotten the general idea." He tucked his hands into his pants pockets. He was wearing the same brown suit he wore every Sunday, and the same tie—maroon and cream colored in a jumbled, ugly pattern. He smelled so strongly of Old Spice, she wanted to gag. He was trying to act relaxed, but the poor guy was clearly as scared as she was, now that she'd actually said yes. "I guess you're a *member* of Relief Society, aren't you?"

"I paid my fifty cents last time they came around asking for dues—if that makes me a member. But I haven't been to a meeting since last fall. Maybe they've kicked me out."

"No, no. They wouldn't do that. I'm sure you're still on the rolls. And you know what? I feel confident, you're going to do just fine."

"If I understand the job, I'm supposed to act like I'm holier than any-one on earth, and then go around poking my nose into everybody's business—whether they want me to or not." Then she added, in a syrupy voice, "And I have to sound like I'm the sweetest lady in the ward."

The bishop laughed. "No. None of that. Just be yourself. You're going to be real good at this. You really are. As soon as you grab onto this thing, you're going to be a doozy of a president."

"And you're full of the same stuff I use to fertilize my fields, Keith—right up to your eyeballs. You'll release me in about a month, if you can stand me that long."

He waved his hand, as if to say, "That won't happen," but what he said was, "You need to choose two counselors and a secretary-treasurer. Have you thought about that?"

Leah had *not* thought about it. She felt her head filling with a buzzing noise, the idea finally setting in of all the fuss she would have to deal with. "I thought you picked those people for me," she said.

"No. You choose the women and suggest them to the bishopric. Then we approve the names."

"Why don't you just choose some sisters and tell me who they are. The only women I'd choose, you won't want, and the ones you'll want, I don't like."

"No, no. This is your organization now. You make the decisions. There's no job in the ward more important—including mine—so we'll support you every way we can."

"Do I have to look after that old Relief Society building, or does that belong to the First Ward?"

"It doesn't belong to anyone now. It's in bad shape. I talked to Bishop Jenson the other day and we decided to tear it down this summer."

"So where do I store food and all that, like we used to in that old place?"

"There's some storage space downstairs. And lately more people have been paying their tithing in eggs and bottled fruit, even some fresh vegetables. I've just been keeping those things at my house, out in the shed, when I have to, but nothing ever stays long. There's too much need."

"Are there really people who don't have enough to eat?"

"Yes, Leah. That's what I was trying to tell you the other day."

Leah was astounded. She just hadn't realized things had gotten that bad. She wondered again what she was getting herself into. But she said to Bishop Bowen, "So when do I give you these names for my presidency?"

"We'd like to sustain you in sacrament meeting next week. So maybe I can stop by at the farm in the middle of the week and find out what you're thinking. Then I could get the other ladies called before Sunday."

Leah shook her head. "All right. But don't come until Thursday. I'm going to need some time to think about this. I'm not sure God's going to drop by my house and whisper in my ear the way you claim he's been whispering in yours." She turned toward the door.

"Leah."

"Yes."

"I'd be a little careful about acting like you're all put out about this. The Lord's given you an answer. Now let him touch you with the spirit you're going to need."

Leah turned and stared at the bishop. He'd said he wanted her for her grit; now he was already telling her she needed to change. She thought of telling him that, but she wanted to get out of his office before she grabbed him by that ugly tie and strangled him right in front of all the prophets. So she grabbed for the doorknob instead.

"Leah."

She looked back at him again.

"I came back from your house pretty sure you wouldn't accept, but when I woke up the next morning, the Spirit told me you *was* going to take the job. Just as clear as a bell ringing, I heard a voice say to me, 'She's softening up out there, and she's going to take that calling.'"

Leah was surrounded by religious nuts, with the moon turning to blood and the bishop hearing bells. But as far as that went, she was acting just about as strange herself. So she didn't comment; she simply left.

Leah found her kids, who were clearly wondering why she had been talking to the bishop, and she drove them home, but she still didn't tell them about the calling. She didn't know how to explain any of this to them and didn't feel like trying. But she did go back to sacrament meeting that evening. She sat at the back and spent the whole time looking at all the sisters, asking herself which ones she could work with.

The attendance seemed a little sparse, some of the men probably taking advantage of a dry day to get their crops planted. But most of the sisters were there, all with hats perched on their heads—the "nicer" ladies wearing the stylish ones that fit tight around their heads, ugly as a swim cap. Leah didn't like hats, and she wouldn't wear one. They were a silly waste of money. And she didn't like dress gloves and purses and all the other things the town women thought they had to tote around with them.

She scanned back and forth, thinking about each woman and feeling a little sick about all of them. Then she noticed old Belva Stone, who was nice by nature and had seen all the hard times here in the basin almost from the beginning. Leah had seen her, little as she was, pitching hay onto a hay wagon, working alongside strong men and keeping up with them. That had been many years back, and the woman had to be around eighty now, but she was a person Leah respected. When Leah had first come to town, Belva had more or less adopted her, had often invited her home to dinner with her husband on Sundays. Belva liked to talk, and Leah had been lonely in those days, so the two had always enjoyed visiting, as different in age as they'd been. Once Leah had moved to the farm, she hadn't really seen much of Belva, but she still liked the woman more than anyone in the ward.

What would the bishop say if Leah asked for an eighty-year-old woman as her counselor, another widow like herself? Belva knew all the skills women used to know: cooking from a garden, quilting, canning, mending. Still, the idea probably wouldn't go over very well, no matter what the bishop had promised her.

The most obvious choice was Marjorie Evans. She was serving in the current presidency, and she was a town woman, the dentist's wife. She knew about all the things that had to happen, and she knew all the sisters. She was the one the bishop should have chosen as president, really. In fact, that was exactly what would have happened if Keith hadn't gotten himself all "caught up in the spirit." But Leah couldn't abide the woman. Marjorie had grown up in Salt Lake or Ogden or some big city, and she thought she was the fashion queen of Richards. Her son was good at sports and something of a hero to all the kids at the high school, but he had made Wade's life miserable. Wade could have strengthened the teams at the high school, being good at sports himself, but he never had tried out. Leah knew why—knew that he felt the responsibility to help his mom on the farm—but Tommy Evans took it as disloyalty and never would let Wade forget it. Or maybe he was jealous that Wade showed him up sometimes. Tommy was the varsity star, and yet Wade, at least according to his own report, could hold his own with the kid in gym-class games.

Tommy's attitudes came straight from Marjorie. There wasn't much of an upper crust in a little town like Richards, but Marjorie obviously thought she was as fancy as Nadine Willis, and the two of them, along with five or six others, considered themselves superior to everyone else in the valley—and the ward. Marjorie always acted nice enough, greeting everyone, wishing everyone well, but Leah saw no sincerity in any of that. The woman didn't bother much with the farm women, and she was especially distant with Leah.

Leah put Marjorie's name aside and looked around at the other women. She liked a young woman named Betsy Chase whose husband farmed on the other side of town. She was really just a girl, maybe twenty-two or twenty-three, and she had a little baby, which might be too much to work around, but she was a good person—Leah always felt that when she was around her—and she didn't put on a false front. She might have had two dresses, not just one, and she had probably bought those before she was married, but she and her husband were struggling to make a go of things, the same as Leah was. She was someone Leah could work with. Maybe if she called an older woman and a young woman, with herself in the middle, that might give each woman in the ward someone to look to.

Leah decided she liked those two choices, and felt stronger about them as the week went on. One of the things she liked best was that she was sure Keith would turn her down, and then she could tell him to do what she'd told him first: make the choices for her.

On Thursday, as promised, Bishop Bowen showed up—but in the middle of the day, not when she had expected him. Still, she had stopped at noon and warmed up some stew she'd cooked earlier in the week, so this was as good a time as any.

"Come in," she said. "I've got some soup on and some fresh bread, if you want a little dinner."

"That'd go down good. I like the smell of that bread. I figured I wouldn't find time to eat dinner today." He stepped in, took off his hat, and looked for a place to set it. Leah took it from him and for some reason found herself smiling. She knew she had him going, running scared of what she might say or do. She also knew he was in over his head a little as bishop. That was something she could relate to. Still, she couldn't resist saying, "Well, I've got two names for you, but you're not going to like either one of them, and I can't think of anyone for secretary. You know better than I do who could do that."

He didn't say anything. She stepped into the kitchen and set his hat in an empty chair at the table, then motioned for him to take a chair. She dipped him a bowl of soup from the pot on her woodstove and cut off a couple of slices of the bread that was already sitting on a breadboard on the table. The kitchen felt cozy, warm on a day that had turned cold and windy after more rain earlier in the week. She'd stoked up the morning coals in the stove and added some wood and a lump of coal. "Feels like another storm coming in," the bishop said.

"Are you talking about me or the weather?"

He smiled but didn't answer.

"You can go ahead. I already blessed this food. You probably figured I didn't."

"I'm not surprised at all. Not now that you've found religion." He made that wet noise in his throat again instead of laughing out loud.

But Leah liked him joking with her. She laughed too. She ate a little of her stew and chewed on some bread—just to make peace—and then she said, in a softer voice, "I'm thinking Belva Stone and Betsy Chase. I know that sounds strange, but it gives the women in the ward three different ages, and they're both women I like to be around."

The bishop nodded, then slurped a little as he took in a spoonful of his stew. "I think Belva's a great idea. I thought about her for a while when I was trying to choose a president. I'm impressed that you would come up with her. Sometimes we forget about the older folks in the ward."

"Belva can teach these women a lot more than I can."

"I don't know about that. But she can teach them plenty. And I think she'll be thrilled. She's not someone who wants to be put out to pasture."

"Is she okay with you, then?"

"With me, yes. I need to talk everything over with my counselors, but I'm sure they'll agree."

"You didn't say anything about Betsy."

Bishop Bowen nodded, ate some bread, looked past Leah. "I don't know, Leah. It might be asking too much of a girl that age. She might feel that—"

"But I thought about most of the women, and I know darned well they won't want to work with me. They'll be mad you called me instead of one of them."

"Some people figure I pray about these callings and get an answer. They even try to support what I do."

At least he was smiling.

"But people question, all the same. You know they do. And I don't blame them one bit if they think you've run off the track with all your cars—calling someone like me."

"Which other women have you been thinking about?"

"You know very well."

"What do you mean?"

"You know that Marjorie Evans is the right sort of person, but she won't support me. She doesn't like me in the first place, and more important, she could never respect me. She'd be thinking the whole time that she ought to be the president."

"Are you sure she doesn't like you? Or is it you who doesn't like her?"

"Both."

"I think you can only know half of that."

Leah let her breath blow out in a long gust. "Okay, ask her if she'll do it."

"Is that who you want, or are you—"

"No. I don't want her. But the Lord probably does."

The bishop made that little noise again. He had a smudge of grease by his ear. She knew he had washed up before he'd left his shop, but he'd missed a little patch—which seemed right. The Lord had cleaned him up some, but he was still old Keith, automobile mechanic. "So is she your choice?"

Leah thought about saying no, but that would only complicate matters. She'd known last Sunday it would come to this. So she just said, "Yes," and let it go.

"You're starting this job right. You three are gonna be a strong presidency."

"Could Betsy be secretary?"

"Why didn't you just give me those names, the way you've got 'em now? Isn't that the answer you got?"

"Let's not start into all that. Let's just call it good. See what the rest of the bishopric thinks."

"All right. But I'm pretty sure we'll go with this. These are some of the same women we talked about. And I think this'll work out good for Betsy—a chance to learn from women with more experience." He nodded at Leah. "Some folks might actually figure something was going on here. Inspiration, maybe."

But Leah wasn't sure about that. She hadn't heard any whispers.

On Sunday evening, at sacrament meeting, the bishop stood before the congregation after the opening prayer. "As you all know," he said,

"Sister Verla Milsap has served long and well—over nine years—in her position as president of the Relief Society." The congregation hushed, clearly sensing what was coming. Leah knew what everyone was wondering, and what they would soon be thinking. She stared straight ahead, dreading the moment her name would be announced.

The bishop asked the ward to release Sister Milsap and her presidency with a vote of thanks, and they did, their arms rising in unison. Leah was sitting in the back, as usual, where she watched the motion. It seemed a little quicker than usual, as if the members really did appreciate what Sister Milsap and the others had done and wanted to show it.

"Would the following sisters please stand as I read off their names?" Bishop Bowen took a breath and looked around. "We've called Sister Leah Sorensen to serve as Relief Society president, with Sister . . ."

There was a gasp. It seemed to slip from every set of lungs in the room.

The bishop hesitated—only for a second, but it emphasized the sense of shock. Leah stood as he continued with the other names. "All those who can support these sisters in their callings, please manifest it by the uplifted hand."

All the hands went up again, but Leah felt this motion, too—not quite in unison, spreading more than bursting. Leah was still staring at the bishop, not returning the glance of those who were twisting to see her.

"Any who are opposed, please indicate it by the same sign."

Leah had imagined some votes against her, even knowing that people almost never did that, but now she realized, no one would have the nerve. They would wait until they got home, and then all week the telephone party lines in town would be abuzz with the talk. "Leah Sorensen? How did the bishopric come up with her?" She had run the conversations through her head all last week as she was working.

At least it was over. She sat down and waited. She refused to look at Rae or Wade or anyone else. "Mom! What's going on?" Rae whispered.

"Just what you heard."

"How are you going to do that?"

Leah knew Rae was asking several questions, not just one, but she didn't answer any of them. She glanced at Wade, who was looking at her, smiling, obviously more pleased than Rae. Leah ducked her head as the sacrament prayer was said, and then she waited for a little deacon to step up to her, his shirttail half hanging out, and she took the bread, ate it, then shut her eyes and tried to pray. She hadn't really thought enough beyond this moment. She was still a little angry about this happening to her, but she was mostly just scared. She had no idea how she was going to carry this off.

When the meeting ended, Leah tried to avoid making eye contact with anyone, but actually that wasn't difficult. People were moving out of the pews, working their way out of the chapel, and no one approached her. Finally, Brother Parker turned around in the pew in front of her and said, "Well, Leah, that's a fine thing. Congratulations."

He seemed to mean it, but his wife couldn't hide the strain in her voice when she said, "Yes, congratulations," and then couldn't seem to think of anything to add.

A few others said the same thing to her, politely, but they appeared embarrassed, as though they were worried that Leah would know what they were actually thinking.

Leah said nothing except for a mumbled "thank you" each time, and she shook hands with those who offered, but she was trying to make her way to the door without doing more than that. She knew she ought to seek out Belva and Marjorie, but she thought she'd rather do it later. For now, she just wanted to get to her car. When she reached the door, though, Belva was waiting. She reached for Leah, who had to bend low to embrace the squat little woman. Belva's hand patted Leah's back a few times, and she said, "Oh, Leah, thanks for thinking of me. I'm just thrilled as I can be."

"You'll have to help me a lot, Belva," Leah said. "I don't know what I'm doing."

"Don't say that. You'll be wonderful. You're just what we need."

"What's that? Someone who never knows when to keep her mouth shut?"

"A strong woman—and a good one. With a heart of gold."

Leah was amazed by the description. Belva was seeing what she wanted to see; she wasn't seeing Leah. "Can we get together this week?" Leah asked.

"Sure."

"Okay. I'll call you and we'll figure out a time. I need to talk to Marjorie and Betsy."

But Betsy was there, reaching out with her hand. It was Marjorie who didn't appear. Leah shook Betsy's hand, glad Betsy didn't expect to be hugged, and then she saw the bishop walking toward them. "I've got a couple of things I need to take care of right now," he said. "I was wondering, could we set you all apart one night this week—or even next Sunday morning?"

"I think you ought to set me *way* apart, and leave me there," Leah said. But the bishop paid no attention. He talked to everyone, and they agreed to meet after Sunday School the following week.

Leah walked to the parking lot and saw some little groups of ward members standing about, talking. She was pretty sure she knew what they were saying. Old Sister Christensen called out, "Congratulations, Leah," and Leah nodded to her but stayed on a straight line to her car. Rae and Wade had walked out ahead of her. Wade waited in front of the car, let Leah set the spark, and then cranked the old engine three times before it started. When he got in, the three were packed together close, as always.

"Okay. Now would you explain this to me?" Rae said.

"No. I can't. And I don't want to talk about it. I plan to drive home without saying a single word. I'd appreciate it if you two would do the same."

"Hey, I'm happy for you," Wade said.

"That's words. We're not going to say words."

So home she drove, and the kids didn't speak. The sun had set, with only a little brown glow left behind on Leah's side of the car. She kept glancing that way, thinking that she too was sinking into some kind of darkness, someplace she couldn't see.

When they reached the house, Leah went straight to her bedroom. She pulled off her church dress, put on her overalls, and headed outside to milk the cows. She thought she'd been quick, but Wade was there ahead of her. She still didn't talk to him, and after they had finished with the cows, she returned to her bedroom, pulled on her old flannel nightgown, and lay down on her bed. She had expected the reaction—the gasp, the awkwardness—and she thought she had prepared herself for it. But it had still hit her hard. What had she become, that people would feel that much doubt about her? There had been a time in her life when the calling wouldn't have been a shock to her or anyone else. She realized now, she really had hoped that someone besides Belva would find something in her that was acceptable. But they hadn't—even the ones who had tried to be nice—and she understood their reaction. They were right about her.

Leah didn't cry. She hadn't cried for years. But she felt the humiliation so deeply she wished she could reverse time and go back a week, and this time give the bishop the right answer. She'd had a nightmare and had taken it for something else, and now she had to live with the answer she had given.

Chapter Three

L EAH GOT UP BEFORE five o'clock the next morning. That was a little earlier than usual, but she couldn't sleep. She got a fire going in her kitchen stove, dropped in a couple of lumps of coal, then gathered eggs in the dark chicken coop, feeling under the hens, telling them to shut their mouths when they squawked at her, but feeling at home in the musty, dry smell of the place. She fed her kitchen slop to the old sow that had a litter of pigs to nurse, threw some hay over the fence to the horses, and dropped feed into the turkey pen.

Leah still had not finished her plowing, but the weather had cleared, and she hoped to get back into the fields before long. She needed to harrow the soil and get her spring corn planted. That was a big job, so she needed to get her Relief Society work started before all her farm hit her at once. She wanted to call her presidency to see if everyone could meet that day, but she doubted any of them were out of bed yet. So she heated water on the stove, filled her old gasoline-engine Maytag on the closed-in porch behind the kitchen, and put a load of wash in with a couple of lumps of lye soap she had made the previous fall. The engine vented outside through a tube, but when she started it up, the smell of the gasoline filled the room all the same.

Leah let Rae and Wade sleep until six and then rousted Wade out first. "I fed the other animals. It's just the cows you need to milk. I'll be out to help you in a few minutes."

Leah and Wade milked twelve cows every morning and evening of their lives, and Leah knew how tired both of them were of doing it. But Wade rarely complained. He rolled out of bed, looking disheveled, and said in a tired voice, "Thanks for feeding the animals." Leah walked back to the kitchen, but only a minute or so later Wade stepped from his bedroom, which was off the living room in the back of the house. Leah looked up to see him pass the kitchen door. He had dressed in his overalls, boots, and an old red-plaid mackinaw jacket. She watched him walk to the front door and knew he was heading to the outhouse.

She waited a few more minutes before walking to the bedroom door next to Wade's. The two rooms had once been a single bedroom, but a few years back Leah had built a divider and had even cut through the living room wall herself and hung a door for the new room. She tapped on the door, then opened it a crack. "I'm sorry, Rae, but it's time to get up. I'm going to need some help with this wash before you catch your bus—either that or you can make breakfast."

Rae moaned but didn't say anything—and also didn't move. The girl never liked to get out of bed. She stayed up way too late, using up gas in her lamp, reading until all hours, and then woke up grouchy and resentful.

"Just roll over and stand up. Get that much over with and you've done the worst thing you'll have to do all day."

Still no reaction.

"Come on."

"Why do you have to start the wash already?"

"You know why. I've got to get it done early today. I need to meet with my presidency, if I can. Things are going to be a little harder around here now. I'm sorry, but that's just the way it is."

"I don't understand why you—"

"Get up, Rae. I mean it. Right now."

Rae finally dropped one foot onto the floor. But she stopped there. Rae was tall, like her mother, with skinny legs and hardly any shape. She could look pretty when she took a little time to fix herself up, but she had stopped smiling these last couple of years, and her smile had been her best feature. Her skin had been a problem, although it was clearing a little now, but it was her confidence that had taken a beating. She had thick hair, a pretty shade of light brown, like Leah's, but she didn't do much with it, and she had hazel eyes that had been bright and wonderful when she was a little girl—but not so wonderful now.

Leah couldn't stand to watch any longer. She mumbled as she walked away, "I don't like getting up either—but I do it." Behind her, she heard grumbling, probably something sarcastic, but she didn't pay attention. Rae's reaction to getting up was part of the daily routine, and Leah didn't want to get upset by it today.

She checked the water heating on the stove, which was almost ready, and then she checked on the washer, which had a way of vibrating its way across the floor. She tugged the thing back a little, away from the wall, and then stepped back into the kitchen. She could hear that Rae was moving, pulling on some clothes, but a few minutes later, when she walked by the kitchen door, she was looking even drearier than usual. Her hair was scattered and her face creased. She hadn't really dressed; she had only put on a pair of rubber boots and her winter coat. She tromped out the door, obviously also heading to the outhouse. Leah felt a pang of compassion, knowing how dark and cold the place was on these spring mornings, but the feeling didn't last long when Rae returned and said, in a loud voice, before she even shut the door, "You spend your whole life complaining about all your work, and now you take on another huge job. It doesn't make sense."

"And good morning to you, Merry Sunshine."

Rae stomped into her bedroom and was gone for much longer than Leah thought necessary. When the girl did finally come back, she had on one of her three school dresses—a gray dress with shoulder pads and a rather short skirt. It wasn't really what the girls were wearing anymore, but it was what Rae had. Actually, it was made over from a dress that Leah had worn during the twenties.

"I'll fry some eggs," Rae said, "but I don't want to fuss with that old washer and get myself soaking wet."

"That's fine. Put on some bacon first, and make some toast."

Rae shot a sarcastic look back at Leah, and Leah knew what she meant: *Isn't that what we do every morning?* Leah had to admit to herself, it had been a silly thing to say, but Rae had sounded final, as though she were saying, *Eggs, and that's it.*

"You haven't answered my question," Rae said.

"What question?"

"Why did you let the bishop talk you into something like that?"

"He didn't. I told him no."

"Well, it didn't look like 'no' when you stood up in church. And why didn't you tell us?"

"Because I wanted to put off *this* little scene as long as possible."

"Just tell me what sense it makes, Mom. That's all I'm asking. We can't keep up with things as it is. Wade works from early until late every day—and I hardly have time to get my homework done. I don't see how we can help you any more than we do, and I sure don't see how you're going to do everything *you'll* have to do now."

"Say the rest. You don't think I'll be a good president, do you?"

Rae turned around, put her hands on her hips, and stared at her mother. "Do *you?*" she asked.

Leah didn't answer. She headed for the back porch. She needed to wring out the first load of wash and get it hung on the line—even if there was still frost. The sun was coming up and a breeze was blowing; the clothes might freeze, but they would still dry in time.

"Well . . . do you?" Rae called from the kitchen.

Leah was hoisting the wet clothes from the washer, getting ready to run each item through the wringer before she carried everything outside. The lye and bluing, mixed with the exhaust, was a smell she'd learned to hate. She turned her head away from it for a moment and said, "I think I'll do a terrible job, Rae." She grunted as she lifted again, and then she added, "I'll do my best to live up to your expectations."

"I'm not saying that. I'm just saying that it's not the kind of thing you like to do. And you don't have time."

"And you're worried you might have to work a little more. I just don't happen to think you're so picked on as you pretend. You'd have plenty of time for homework if you didn't spend all your time reading those silly romance novels you love so much."

"*You* read novels."

"I read *classics* when I have the time. You read those trashy love stories you borrow from Nedra White. I thought you'd get over that once you passed thirteen."

But this was an old topic, and Leah looked into the kitchen to see Rae's face burn, exaggerating her pimples. She turned away from Leah and walked to the cabinet, opened a door, and got out a frying pan.

Leah let herself breathe for a time, to calm down. She'd been way too cranky with her kids lately, and she could feel it this morning, as if she were almost eager to start a fight. But she'd prayed the night before that she could develop more patience, and she knew she had to start at home. "Listen, Rae, I'm not happy about this any more than you are. The bishop asked me to do it, and . . . I don't know. I just feel like it's something I have to do. I haven't worked much in the Church for a long time.

This time I just . . ." But Leah had no idea what to say. She wasn't going to tell Rae about the dream.

"I'm not even sure you believe in the Church," Rae said. "You always say the members are a bunch of hypocrites."

Leah stepped back into the kitchen, even walked halfway across. "Honey, listen. I know how I talk sometimes. I say things I shouldn't. But I do believe in the Church, and the bishop felt like he needed me right now. He says our family's been through some bad times, so he thinks maybe I can help the women who haven't been through so much."

Rae was holding the frying pan in front of her, as though to guard herself from Leah's approach, and she was staring again. "You mean all those ladies in town who look down their noses at us?"

"Rae, I'm not so sure they do. I know I've said that, but maybe that's me more than it is them. I have to change my attitude now." Leah wasn't sure she even meant what she was saying, but it was what she had been trying to tell herself.

"Mom, I heard LuAnn and Sharon when we were walking out of sacrament meeting. They were whispering and giggling and I heard LuAnn say something about a bull in a china shop. I know she was talking about you."

Leah nodded. "Well, she probably was. And she's not far off, is she?"

"They won't *let* you do the job, Mom. We don't meet their standards. How are you going to go to all those meetings wearing the same dress every time?"

Leah had been thinking the same thing, of course, but she didn't say so. "I don't know, Rae. I'll just get by the best I can. It's what we always do."

"Well, I'm tired of it. It's not fair. We pray and pray, and God never lets up on us. It's always 'next year's crop,' and 'when things get better,' but nothing ever does get better."

"Rae, listen to me." Leah stepped a little closer, but Rae was still grasping the frying pan against her chest. "You're the smartest girl at the high school. You know that. Is that fair? Why didn't God give LuAnn or Sharon the brains you have?"

The door opened and Wade came in. He'd taken off his boots on the porch and was wearing only stockings—tan ones that Leah had mended a time or two with black thread. Leah felt what Rae was saying, saw it in the toes of those socks, but she was not going to let her kids feel sorry for themselves.

"God gave you a good mind, so if you want things to be fair, use it. Work hard in school and get that scholarship we've talked about. Your grades aren't bad, but you know they could be a lot better."

"Maybe they would be better if I could come home after school and do my homework instead of having to cook and do dishes and clean house."

Leah saw where all this could be heading: back to their discussion of Rae's reading habits, and she didn't want that. But Wade had started to laugh. "You don't have enough homework to last an hour, Rae. You're just lazy. You put it off, and then you do as little as you can. I get better grades than you, and I do lots more work around this place."

"Oh, aren't you wonderful, Wade? Aren't you God's little gift to us all?"

"Okay. That's enough," Leah said. "I don't need this right now. Just get some breakfast on, and Wade, don't brag about your grades. With your brains, you should have all A's, and you don't come close to that."

Wade smiled a little—which was how he responded to most things. "I don't want to show my sister up too much. That's all."

"Shut your mouth, Wade," Rae barked. "You know you were saying the same things I was last night—that Mom shouldn't take this calling."

"The first thing I said was that she would be great. And I think that's right. I just think it'll be a strain on her. That's all."

Leah looked at the floor—the worn hardwood that had needed

sanding and sealing for at least five years. "Look, I *know* I shouldn't have taken this calling. No one knows that better than I do. And I'll probably get fired before half a year goes by. But the bishop asked me to do it and I said yes. Please, just help me all you can and I'll try to find a way to make everything work."

Leah's voice had become pleading, and that did seem to affect Rae. Her face softened and as she turned toward the stove she said, "You're already doing more than any woman I know."

Leah nodded her appreciation. There had been a hint of respect in Rae's voice, and that was more than she had heard from her for a while.

Leah waited until eight o'clock before she called Belva, who said she could meet that day or any other day that week—and that she was excited to get started. So Leah took a deep breath and twisted the handle on the telephone again. "Brenda, could you put me through to Marjorie Evans, please. Six-one-two, I think it is."

"Sure, Leah," the operator said. "Say, what's this I hear about you getting called to be Relief Society president?"

"Is that the hottest item on the lines this morning?"

"Hey, watch it. I don't listen in on conversations. Someone told me—first thing this morning."

"If you'd go to church, you could've heard it yesterday."

"You should talk. I told LaRae Putnam, if they can call Leah to something like that, I might be the next bishop." She laughed in a series of squeaks, and Leah found herself smiling too. "But LaRae said she thought you'd be real good and not snooty or anything. After I thought about it, I told her that's right. I'm glad they called you."

Brenda had a little voice, usually sort of flighty, but she had said this with sincerity. It pleased Leah to think that *someone* thought she could do the job. "Well, thanks. But I'm afraid you two are the only ones in town who think so."

"Who cares? You know how some of 'em are. Anyway, I'll put you through to Marjorie. She's probably the one wondering why *she* didn't get called."

"I'm sure you're right about that."

By then the phone was ringing—one short ring, one long. After that sequence had repeated three times, Leah heard, "Good morning. This is the Evans residence."

"Hi, Marjorie. This is Leah. Are you back on your feet yet?"

Marjorie didn't answer, didn't laugh.

"I thought maybe the bishop knocked you off your feet, telling you that he had called me, of all people."

"Not at all. I'm certain you'll do a wonderful job." This was way too polite.

"Is there any chance we could get together right away? Belva said she could meet just about anytime."

"Certainly. When did you have in mind?"

"Today would be best, if you have some time. We've got our first meeting with the sisters tomorrow afternoon."

"Well, this is a busy day. I work as a volunteer at the library on Monday mornings, and I have a Reading Circle presidency meeting right after lunch."

"What about three or so, this afternoon?"

"That would be all right—if we don't plan to meet for a terribly long time."

"We'll just meet long enough to get ourselves organized a little and talk about that first meeting."

"I'm sure Mayrene has her lesson prepared, Leah. It's our day to study literature. We'll be all right for tomorrow."

"I know. But we probably ought to say a few words to the sisters—you know, before the lesson starts."

"That would be fine—if that's what you want."

Leah was stopped for a moment. All she knew was that she had to say something to the sisters—if nothing else, to clear the air. They were surely still in shock. "Well, anyway, you need to instruct me a little. I have no idea what I'm doing. I guess it's easier if I come into town, since you and Belva aren't too far from each other."

"You're welcome to meet here."

"All right. That sounds good. Three o'clock, then?"

"Yes. That will be fine."

Leah had been leaning against the wall next to the phone. She stood straight now, drew in some potent-smelling air—mixed with bacon grease—and then waited for a moment. She wanted to find just the right tone of voice. "Marjorie, look, I'm sorry about this. I know you would make a better president than I will. It's not something I thought I'd ever get called to do."

"I don't know why, Leah. You're an educated woman. You've taught school. I'm just a housewife—and never have desired to be anything else. I'm sure the bishop knows that."

Leah heard the nastiness just under the surface, and she was a little surprised—even though she had known all along that Marjorie wasn't going to be happy about this. "Marj, I'm going to need your help. You're used to working with the women around here, and organizing things. I've been out here on my own all these years, and I . . . well, do you know what I mean? I really need you."

"That's fine. I'll try to do my best for you."

"No. I don't mean for me. We just need to work well together. I know it seems like the bishop doesn't have a brain in his head, calling me. But he did say that he prayed about it a lot—and he felt like he got an answer. For all I know, it was just something he ate, but he's calling it

44

inspiration, so I think we have to take him at his word. Do you know what I mean? I'm just saying . . . I can see where you might not like this whole situation, but . . ." Leah knew she was doing it—saying the wrong things, as usual. "Anyway, I just hope we can get along all right. He made the call; I didn't."

"I'm sure we'll work together just fine." But the ice hadn't melted—not a drop. So Leah thanked her one more time and then called Belva, who said three o'clock would be all right, and then Betsy, who said she would have to bring her baby. Leah hoped that would be all right with Marjorie, but she didn't want to call back and ask. What she really hoped was that while she was working outside that morning, lightning would strike her dead. She pictured a little vision. She would keel over out there in the west field, and then, as she was being carried up in the arms of an angel, she would shout to the bishop, "Call Marj. Make her the president. The Lord needs me on the other side." But that didn't seem likely. The Lord probably had enough problems without calling Leah home.

Nothing had changed when Leah met with her presidency that afternoon. Belva was warm and excited. Betsy was quiet and unassuming. And Marjorie was icy and all business. She explained many of the workings of the Relief Society, read out loud some of the policies from the handbook, and suggested some changes she had always thought Sister Milsap should have made. She was especially concerned about the fundraising bazaar coming up that fall. "We've usually done a lot more by this time of year," she said. "We've got to get the women going or we're not going to have enough money to operate next year."

"But it's getting harder for the women," Belva said. "They can't afford to buy material or thread. We pieced two quilt tops, and those two are ready to be quilted, but Peg told me she doesn't have enough material to do any more."

"What do we do with the money we earn from the bazaar?" Leah asked.

Marjorie slowly turned her head toward Leah. Her look seemed to say, *Don't you know anything?* But what she said was, "That's where we get our operating budget."

"Sister Milsap always asked me to pay fifty cents for dues each year."

"We don't keep that money, Leah. A quarter of a dollar goes to Salt Lake, to the main office, and the other quarter goes to the stake, so they have a little money to operate. We have to raise all our own funds in the ward."

Leah kept watching Marjorie, trying to guess what she was thinking. They were sitting at the dining-room table. It was a beautiful piece of furniture, dark walnut with ornate legs. The house was as nice as almost any in town, a two-story home with fine woodwork and elegant, violet-colored draperies. Marjorie was sitting straight, her hands folded in her lap. She was a plump woman with short, soft arms and rounded cheeks, but she had pretty hair, almost blonde, and dark blue eyes. Leah remembered her when she and her husband had first moved to Richards. She had been a beauty then, much thinner. But something else had changed. She had been talkative and enthusiastic about everything. She had joined the local clubs and charities, even started a little community theatre group. Leah, back when she was teaching, had accepted a part in one of Marjorie's plays—*The Merry Wives of Windsor*—and Marjorie had directed the play and acted in it. In Leah's mind, Marjorie had always been possessed of too much self-importance, but she had made up for it with goodwill. What Leah had watched over the years was a sort of slow death as Marjorie seemed to lose all that spark she had brought with her.

Marjorie's husband, Clark, was the only dentist in town. He was a big, likable man, attractive in some way that had nothing to do with good looks. He always seemed on the edge of a smile, no matter how seriously he was speaking, and he knew things. Leah had always found him interesting to talk to. So many people in town cared little about anything beyond their own noses, but Clark read everything he could get his hands on. He had no use for Herbert Hoover in a town that, until lately, had been mostly Republican. Leah wasn't sure that the Democrats would come up with anyone better to run this year, but she liked talking to Clark about his hopes for a change. He seemed to know what was going on in both parties.

Leah knew that Clark was struggling to make a living these days, but she never saw that in his face. It was as though Marjorie had taken on all the worries for both of them, and the weight of it all was dimming the light in her. It was true that Marjorie and Leah had clashed a time or two in Relief Society meetings, usually because Marjorie took the most orthodox position on any question of doctrine, whereas Leah enjoyed "unsettling the settled" now and then, saying something no one expected. She had told the ladies once, "Multiplying and replenishing is all well and good, but maybe we've done enough of that for a while—since we can't seem to feed all the children we've brought into this world."

Marjorie had said, with controlled anger in her voice, "I consider our children our greatest blessing. Tell me, Leah, which of the children in the ward would you like to send back?"

Leah should have let it go, and she had actually only been joking, but she'd said, "I could nominate a few. Should we call for a vote on it?"

Most of the women had laughed. Marjorie hadn't. Both women had probably known that one candidate in Leah's mind would have been Marjorie's daughter Sharon, who was as bad as LuAnn Willis when it came to speaking painful little darts to Rae.

"I guess I still don't understand," Leah said now. "What do we need a lot of money for?"

"For all our needs, Leah. And it's not so much for dinners and socials anymore. It mostly goes to help people in our ward. The bishop doesn't get much in from fast offerings now, so we're the ones who have to raise money."

"What about the visiting teachers? They're always hinting around that I ought to make a donation."

"Not anymore. Clark drove me down to Salt Lake to Relief Society conference last year, and Sister Robison . . . do you know who that is? Louise Y. Robison?"

"Yes. Of course I do." Leah actually did read the *Relief Society Magazine.* She knew Louise Robison was general president of the Relief Society, and Leah liked some of the things the woman had to say in her editorials. She seemed smart, and modern, and she believed that women ought to be listened to.

"Well, Sister Robison told us to take donations when they were offered, but not to pressure the sisters or make them feel guilty when they can't give. Times are just too hard. Still, though, some women give every tenth bottle of fruit they put up, or donate vegetables from their gardens. We just don't get a lot of cash."

"Who ends up with these bottled goods you're talking about?"

"The poor, of course. The suffering. The unemployed."

"So we ask people to give what they don't have, and then we give it back to them?"

Marjorie looked ready to strike back hard when Belva jumped in. "Oh, Leah, some are so much worse off than others. Those of us who are managing to get by need to give what we can to those who don't have enough to feed their families."

"That's fine, Belva. I see no problem with that. But there are too many around here who've never learned to make do with what they have. I don't think we ought to be feeding people who won't bother to plant a garden and work up a little sweat pulling weeds." She was noticing the nice rug on the dining-room floor. She felt like telling Marjorie she could sell that and feed a few families for a month or two.

"I don't think that's the case anymore," Belva said. "Maybe it was a few years ago, but people are doing whatever they have to do now."

Leah had heard her own harshness when she had spoken, and she felt it even more deeply as a contrast to Belva's good spirit. Still, she doubted that Marjorie had ever pulled a weed in her life. She knew that Clark had always kept a garden. Back when she had lived in town, she had walked past the Evans's place on her way to school, and she had seen Clark out in back many times, before he'd gone to his office. Somehow, it didn't seem likely, however, that Sharon had ever helped, or even their son, Tommy. Maybe they weren't the ones asking for food, but Leah suspected that some of those who were hadn't done all they could to feed themselves.

Still, Leah softened her voice a little and said, "I know, Belva. But maybe we need to teach the sisters some of the skills women are forgetting. The bishop told me that when he called me."

"That's exactly right," Belva said. "But we need to look out for those who get sick, or the ones who've lost their jobs and—"

"That's what Relief Society *is*," Marjorie said. "If you don't believe in helping the poor, you shouldn't have this job."

Leah sat back in her chair. She waited for a moment, swallowing a couple of sentences that came to her mind, and then she said, "I guess I need to meet some of the ones who are suffering. We all do. We need to figure out what we *can* do. I guess we want to have a bazaar, but the first thing, as far as I can see, is to see what our needs are. Maybe we fuss too much with making quilts when people need shoes."

"We sell the quilts so that we can buy shoes," Belva said.

"I know. But there aren't many around who can afford to buy a quilt. It seems silly to give the cloth and then buy it back. The first thing I want to do is assess the needs. Tell me what families are in the worst trouble."

"We already know more about that than you might think," Marjorie said. "It's what the visiting teachers do. Each pair calls on twelve families. They report the needs they see."

"But I still need to see it for myself."

"That's fine," Marjorie said. "You ought to visit the sisters. But you need to look at the information we've already collected. Do you know who Amy Brown Lyman is?"

"Yes, I do. She's in Sister Robison's presidency."

"That's right. She's the second counselor. I also heard her talk at conference. She believes in *scientific* social work. And that's what we're trying to teach our visiting teachers. They're trained, Leah. They go into houses and ask a set of questions. They *analyze* the needs of poor families, and then they train sisters in budgeting and the other skills you've been talking about. We have all the notes from those visits."

"Well, then, I guess I can do my job by correspondence."

"I'm not saying that. The handbook says you should visit every sister once a year—preferably toward the end of the year. But you don't have to start from scratch. You can look at the reports and learn a great deal."

"All right. That makes sense. I'll do that as soon as I can. But I want to get to know all the sisters. There are too many I can't even call by name."

"Well, of course."

Marjorie pressed her mouth shut and crossed her arms. She looked disgusted. And Betsy was too shy to say anything. When her baby began to fuss, she excused herself and slipped into another room, saying only, "I need to nurse her." Leah had no idea why she couldn't do that in front of the others, but she didn't say so.

It was Belva who listed the families that had the greatest needs. "Most of the farm folks are managing," she said. "They have their animals and their gardens. They don't have much, but they're eating. But quite a few men in town are out of work, or they've been cut back on their hours." She named off six families, and Leah was embarrassed to realize that she didn't know some of them and had had no idea that the others were in such desperate straits.

"I'll tell you who worries me as much as anyone right now," Belva said. "Nadine Willis. No one has seen her for the last couple of weeks. Lily Placer says that she's had a nervous breakdown and she's staying in bed night and day. Jim's store is about to go under, from what everyone is saying, and the Willises could lose everything."

"We're not exactly talking about the *poor,* Belva," Leah said.

"We could be. If Jim loses his business, I don't know what he and Nadine will do."

Leah could work up plenty of concern about a man who had lost his job and couldn't feed his kids, but she found little pity for Nadine Willis. "Well, they haven't gone broke yet. Maybe that's all just talk."

"It could be," Belva said. "But someone needs to see how Nadine is doing. Would you like me to go over and visit her?"

"I talked to her on the telephone last week," Marjorie said, "and she said she wasn't feeling well. But it was just a little stomach upset. I don't think it's anything serious. People spread too many rumors."

"Well, then," Leah said, "why don't you check on her—and let me know what you find out."

But Belva said, "You know, the more I think about that, maybe you ought to visit her, Leah. You said you wanted to meet everyone and assess the needs. Nadine might be a good person to start with."

"I was thinking more of the—"

"Leah, you need to get to know *everyone.* I know that you and Nadine have had your differences, but it seems like it might be time for you two to draw a little closer to each other. You're both such lovely women. And Nadine is one woman who can help us a lot if she's on her feet and supporting us."

Leah was still laughing about being called "lovely." "I'm about as lovely as a prickly pear, Belva, and Nadine is pretty much the same, if you ask me."

"Prickly pears have pretty flowers in their season."

Leah shook her head. "Well, all right. I'll go by and see her, but I don't have time to run home and come back later. I'll stop by there right now."

"I think I would call her on the telephone first," Marjorie said.

"No. I'd rather just show up. Maybe I'll get the straight story that way."

Leah watched Marjorie take a breath and then not say anything. But she obviously disagreed. That was not likely to be the last time.

Chapter Four

LEAH KNOCKED ON Nadine Willis's front door and then waited, scared she wouldn't know what to say to the woman. No one answered, and for a few seconds Leah was relieved. Maybe she wouldn't have to deal with this situation quite yet. But if Belva knew what she was talking about, Nadine was staying home all the time now. Maybe Nadine was just choosing not to answer. So Leah tried the doorknob and the door opened. She stepped inside. "Nadine?" she called out, but she got no response.

Leah had been in the house a few times, long ago, but it had all been redecorated since then. The living-room walls were covered with a flowered paper: deep rose with shades of green. The windows were draped in maroon velvet, and a big couch and chair matched the drapes. But it was the lamps and end tables, shelves and paintings that made the room look like something out of a museum. Leah sensed that this was a showplace, not a room where the Willis children had ever played or where young people lounged about with their friends.

"Nadine? Are you home?"

Leah was pretty sure she ought to back off now, but she was almost certain that Nadine was hiding out somewhere, and Leah might as well find her now as go through this again later. She walked on through the living room to the cherry-wood stairway. She knew that the bedrooms were upstairs. "Nadine, I'm coming up. Are you all right?"

There was still no answer, but Leah thought she heard some sort of movement upstairs. She kept calling, kept climbing. "Nadine, it's Leah Sorensen. You might as well say something now or I'm going to start pulling doors open."

Leah heard a faint response from the back of the house. "What?" she called out.

"I'm fine. I don't need a visit."

Leah followed the sound to the last door on the right, then opened it a crack, but didn't look in. "Nadine, I'm a little worried about you, that's all." But when that sounded just a little too sweet, she added, "You know me. I'm the dear church lady—out doing good." With that, she pushed the door open.

Nadine was sitting up in bed, leaning back against a dark headboard, with pillows stuffed around her. No one had ever accused her of possessing much in the way of beauty, but she had always made an impression, mostly from her presence—her considerable size—and partly from her clothes and her piled-up hair, the glow of her rouge, her bright fingernails. But now she was shockingly diminished. Her face seemed flabby and gray against the white pillows. Her hair was falling out of its pins, and her nightgown let her body droop into an inelegant mound.

"Leave me alone. I didn't invite you here," she said in a low, throaty voice. And then, like a child, she pulled one of the pillows over her and held it just under her nose. "You have no right to barge into my home like this."

"Nadine, you're not well. I came to see what I can do."

"I'm fine. I—"

"No, you're not. You look like you got thrown from a horse and dragged a few miles. Have you been eating all right?"

"Get out of my house, Leah. You have no right to talk to me that way."

"I just mean, I can tell you're sick. Would you like some of the ladies in the ward to bring meals in until you're back on your feet?"

Nadine pulled the pillow down a little, but kept it at her chin. "I'm not sick. I've had . . . *allergies* . . . or maybe a cold. I'll be up in a day or two."

"You told Marjorie you had a stomachache. Which is it? You need to get your story straight."

Leah walked toward the bed and stood at the foot of it. She had meant to tease a little, just to show that she knew Nadine's problems were more emotional than physical, but she saw the effect of her accusation. Nadine was livid. Color was coming back into her face. "Don't try to pretend that you care about me. You never have liked me, and this new calling hasn't changed that."

"I know what you're saying, Nadine. I guess I haven't liked you much. But then, you haven't liked me, either. Once people get to know each other a little better, though, they usually get over some of that."

"And why should we suddenly want to know each other? Because you think you have to act like a Relief Society president?"

Leah put her hands on her hips. She felt funny wearing her church dress on a weekday. It was an old tan thing, out of date and shapeless from so many washings, but it was the best she had—and still not satisfactory in this house. "Okay, fine, Nadine. Let's not pretend. But here's the thing. You're sick, and I came to check on you—and I never would have thought of such a thing if I hadn't gotten myself stuck with this job. So I'm checking. Is there anything anyone can do for you—or do you just plan to lie here and feel sorry for yourself?"

"Leah, get out of here right now. And don't think I won't tell the bishop how you've treated me."

"I haven't *treated* you any way at all. I asked what we could do for you. We could bring in meals until you're doing better, or—"

"I don't need meals. I've never asked the Church for anything and I'm not going to start now." Nadine had been steadily slumping deeper into the bed, into the pillows, as though she wanted to disappear. Her eyes looked more desperate than angry, as though she feared being found out.

"Look, I know these are hard times for you and Jim. And I know you're worried. Worry builds up until sometimes it just seems like the only answer is to go to bed and stay there. After Wayne died, I did some of that myself. But there comes a time when you have to get up and do whatever can be done."

"I told you, I've been a little sick. That's all."

But the power had gone out of Nadine's objections, and Leah saw how much fear was in her drooping face. So Leah said what she was thinking. "In the end, we're all just little kids. We never do grow up. When bad things come, we just want to hide."

Nadine didn't speak. She stared at Leah, maybe softened by her change of tone, maybe feeling the rightness of what she'd said, but apparently not ready yet to admit to anything.

Leah felt awkward, so tall, standing above Nadine like one of those gawky sandhill cranes that landed on her farm sometimes. She looked about the bedroom, another place that seemed a parody, some sort of royal bedchamber. She spotted a tall chair with a needlepoint back sitting next to a mahogany nightstand. She walked to it but, feeling its closeness to Nadine, pulled it back a little before she sat down. Nadine was watching with obvious discomfort, but again, with no verbal resistance.

"I know you don't want any advice from me, but I have some." Leah felt the sharpness in her tone again and tried to think how she should say what she wanted to say. She really did need to start speaking more gently. "When Wayne died, I didn't think I could run a farm. I'd been raised on a ranch and I'd done my share of the chores, but I didn't think I could plow and plant and all that sort of thing. So for a while, I just sat in my house and tried to figure things out. But I couldn't come up with a single answer. My kids kept watching me, scared as two little abandoned birds in a nest. They needed to know what was going to happen next—but I didn't know myself."

Leah stopped and gave Nadine a chance to say that she didn't want to hear this—if she really didn't—but Nadine was still watching Leah, looking tired and sad and gray, and still skeptical. She was breathing like a bellows, pulling in air in long drafts and then letting it ease out in gusts, even making little grunting sounds in her throat.

"The only thing I had was my land. I couldn't sell it because no one was going to pay me enough to live on for very long. I thought I might like to teach again, but the pay was so bad I had barely gotten by when I'd been a single woman. I didn't know how I would ever give my kids a leg up and get them to college—and that was something Wayne and I had always talked about. So one morning I told myself that I had to go on with things the way they were. I'd have to farm the land, milk my little string of cows and sell the milk, raise some wheat and corn—just pull in enough to pay the bills and, I don't know . . . keep living my life. It didn't feel like a life to me, but it was all I had. I don't know if I'm happy. If I ever stopped to ask myself that, I'd probably have to say not very, but I'm still hoping to get my kids through college, and I feel like Wayne's going to be proud of me if I do that."

Again, she waited. Nadine certainly knew what Leah was trying to tell her, but she didn't say so.

"I guess you're afraid the store is going to go broke, and you won't—"

"No, I'm not. What makes you say that?"

"I've heard people say that your business is about to go under and Jim might have to close it up."

"People talk too much in this town. The more that kind of negative talk goes on, the worse things get. We have a good business. We just have to get by for a while until this Depression lets up a little. Then we'll be all right."

"I hope you're right. But I've got a feeling we're not going to be out of the woods for quite a while yet."

"That's the kind of talk I mean. Everyone holds back and won't buy anything, and that only makes things worse and worse for anyone with a business."

But that was a little hard for Leah to take. "Well, that's all fine to say, Nadine, but a lot of us around here farm, and we're lucky to get our taxes paid. We'd be more than happy if we could shop at your place and keep you living like this . . ." She waved her arm in a sweep, gesturing vaguely at the furniture and wall coverings. " . . . but we're only eating because we keep our gardens going and kill some pigs to get us through the winter."

"Get out of here."

"Okay, fine. But I'm going to leave you with one piece of advice—whether you want to hear it or not." She stood up and leaned over the bed, looking Nadine straight in the face. "You need to get off that big rear end of yours and go down and help Jim at the store. The more you lie around in this bed, the sicker you're going to get. So get up and do something. Jim could save a little on overhead if he had you working for him, and you'd feel better about yourself if you weren't a 'kept lady' all your life. I don't know if you've ever worked a day in your life, but I'll tell you what—it'd put more steel in your backbone than anything else you could do." Leah turned and headed for the door.

"President of the Relief Society!" Nadine said. "What a *disgrace* it is, even to call you that."

Leah stopped. She was looking at the door, not at Nadine. "I know. No question about it. But what you just heard was *Leah*—not the president of the Relief Society. And what I just told you is right, even if I said it wrong."

"Don't come back here again."

"Don't worry. I won't. You don't need me. You need to start acting like a grown woman, not a spoiled little girl."

Leah kept going, out the bedroom door and down the stairs. It wasn't until she shut the front door behind her that she started to feel regret. And it wasn't until halfway home, in her car, that she told herself she'd messed up her first chance to do the right thing. But it wasn't until evening, after she'd worked off some steam, that she admitted to herself that she would have to go back to Nadine someday and try to patch things up. She really couldn't go around talking to people like that anymore. All the same, she was still disgusted with the woman, so she said what she really felt to her bedroom wall—said it in a voice that would knock any angels in the vicinity flat on their backs: "She *does* need to get off that big rear end of hers. And boy oh boy, is it *big!*"

By morning, Leah had calmed down. She was not only worried about the things she had said to Nadine but scared to face the rest of the women that afternoon. She had gotten off to a terrible start—and Nadine would probably soon spread the word about that—so she had to do a better job with the other sisters. What she hoped was that she could be honest with them, express her self-doubts, and admit that she knew they had their own doubts about her. Maybe that would ease some tension. But she had to be careful how she said things this time, so all morning, as she worked on the farm, she practiced what she would say. She didn't write anything down, but she pretty much memorized the words that came to her.

And then, that afternoon at 2:00, she stood before the sisters in the Relief Society room and forgot everything she had planned.

The room was comfortable, with a rug on the floor and nice chairs, but Leah felt the awkwardness as the women entered and took their seats. They filled in from the back, sitting in six rows, all of them wearing church dresses and most wearing hats. The colors they wore were brightening with spring, but the women seemed solemn. They didn't talk as much as usual—as though they were all waiting to see what Leah would do. The numbers were also small, with maybe forty sisters there. Leah seemed to remember a bigger attendance in the past. Maybe some had stayed away because of her.

But Leah stood and welcomed everyone, and she tried to use her best schoolteacher's voice. She knew she had spoken with more refinement at one time and had slipped into a rougher style over the years, but she wanted to be a "lady" today, and she tried to sound like one. She was conscious that she was wearing the same dress as always, but she had borrowed some lipstick from Rae, had put on just a little—then blotted most of it back off—and tried to curl her hair, even though it was almost too short to do anything with.

"Sisters," she said, after the opening song and prayer, "I hope you'll be patient with your new presidency—or especially with me. Belva and Marjorie know all the procedures, but I'm rusty on some of those things, so I might not do things just right at first."

That much she had remembered from the little talk she had prepared, but the rest of it had left her, and now she was standing in front of everyone, lost in the quiet, the neutral faces, the thick smell of lilac perfume hanging like sweet dust in the air. She suddenly found herself trying to explain.

"I know you're wondering why I was called to this position, and so am I, but the bishop seems to feel that I can be of help to you. These are difficult times, and I've worked through some of that, and I guess he feels I can teach some of what I've learned." She wondered, now that she had said it, whether she should be revealing what the bishop had told her. And she didn't like so much seriousness. "Of course, you know Keith. He's used to fixing cars, not choosing Relief Society presidents. He might have gotten this whole thing wrong." She laughed, making a breathy little sound that pinched off quickly in her nervousness. She heard the squeak of wooden chairs as some of the women squirmed in their seats.

She tried to keep smiling, but very few smiled back. "I guess I shouldn't say things like that, but I've known him for such a long time and I always tease him." She hesitated, getting at least a few more smiles. "And I'm just, you know, joking. He's not just a car mechanic. He's really, you know, a good man and everything. And he told me he prayed hard, and he felt like it was what the Lord wanted, you know, to call me to this job." She smiled at Liz Bowen, the bishop's wife, to let her know that she really had been joking. Sister Bowen, a pleasant little woman with dark, wavy hair, smiled a little too, but not nearly enough.

"But anyway, I do feel kind of like a goldfish trying to swim with whales. Or maybe that's the wrong comparison. I didn't mean . . . well, anyway, I'm a giraffe or something, and you're all . . . I don't know. But you know what I mean. I'll need a lot of help from all of you. Since the day the bishop called me, I've been thinking a lot about the pioneers." She picked up a line of logic from the talk she had planned—but she couldn't think of the words she had practiced. "If you think back to those women who walked across the plains and then later, the ones who settled this valley, they all pulled together and helped each other, and I think that's what Relief Society should do. The problem is, now, we've had things a little too easy—or some of us have anyway—and I think some women have forgotten what it takes to get by on a little less. What was it they used to say? Use it up, wear it out, make it do, or . . . something. Whatever that is."

She stopped, tried to remember where her thoughts had been heading. "Well, anyway, we buy too many things from the grocery store these days and don't cook from our gardens as much as we could. Instead of baking, we eat that nasty white bread they wrap up and sell in the stores."

But now she was looking at Glenda Poulson, whose husband ran the market in town. He sold plenty of that kind of bread. Leah could see from the look on Glenda's face that she didn't appreciate the remark.

"I mean, we all have to decide about things like that. But I'm just saying, people used to make their own soap and put up all their own fruit and vegetables, sew their own clothes—then mend them and make them last a long time—and if some of us don't know how to do those kinds of things and we can't afford all the store-bought things, and we don't know how to teach our daughters how to . . . of course, my daughter never pays any attention to anything I ever try to tell her anyway. Do you have that problem?" She tried to laugh again.

Belva and Marjorie were sitting behind Leah and to her right, facing the sisters. Leah glanced back to see that Marjorie was staring at the floor, but Belva was looking up, smiling, as though she thought Leah was giving a fine little talk. And then, mercifully, she raised her hand.

"Yes, Belva."

"I think most of our sisters keep gardens and do quite a lot of bottling and baking. And we have some wonderful seamstresses in our ward. But I agree with you so much that we need to share those skills with each other and then pass them along to our daughters. I also know that some of us are better at one thing than another. Belinda, for instance, can look at a pattern and see how much material is called for, and then she can find a way to cut her cloth so she saves half a yard every time. I think that's the sort of thing we can teach each other, and it's just what we all probably need to do now—make the most of what we have."

"I agree with that," Leah said. She turned back to the women. She longed to see another hand go up, but the room was unusually quiet, no chairs squeaking now, and Glenda's face looked hard as marble. She was usually a talkative woman, opinionated, and someone Leah had always had fun sparring with, but clearly, she was seeing no humor in any of this now. Leah knew she had to change the mood. "I know Belva's right. I shouldn't talk so much about people not having skills. I didn't mean to say that you don't have them. Lots of us do what we can around the house. I sew—you know, because I have to—but nothing I do ever looks as nice as it ought to. I'm getting so I think I'm plowing when I sew. I give the machine its head and figure the only thing to do is swear at it when the seams don't run straight."

Leah laughed, but this time her throat emitted a little screeching sound. She ducked her head and swallowed, took a breath, and tried to smile again. "Now, swearing, that's something I could teach all of you. I'm good at it." A few of them laughed, sort of nervously, and she was worried that they didn't know she was just having some fun. So she took a deeper dive. "I'll bet some of those pioneer ladies could curse a blue streak after they drove their teams across the whole country. I never met a team of horses—and it's probably the same for oxen—that didn't understand cussing better than soft words."

Quite a few women laughed, but way too many looked embarrassed for her.

"Anyway . . . I'm just joking. You'll have to get used to me. I mean, I have been known to let loose with . . . well, here's the thing. I think way too many people are feeling sorry for themselves these days. Everyone talks about hard times and suffering, and how the government ought to step in and help us out—and all the rest of that. I just think we're better off to figure out what needs to be done and do it. These aren't the first hard times to come along. Some people have been living in the lap of luxury and they might have to figure out, things just couldn't keep going on that way forever."

Mayrene Johnston, a young woman from town, was sitting on the front row. She raised her hand. Leah was glad to see a reaction. She knew a little about Mayrene: The girl wasn't thirty yet and had five children. Her husband had some sort of government job—Forest Service, Leah thought.

"Leah," Mayrene said, "I heard last week that unemployment in Utah is above twenty-five percent. We don't see quite so much of that here, with so many farmers, but the man on the radio said these are just about the worst times ever, and the country could fall apart, the way it's all going. If it keeps getting worse, we might see more people, even in Richards, going without food—and I just think we have to look out for them. I don't think it's good enough to tell them they have to buck up and not feel sorry for themselves. We might have to feed some families. It seems like that's what the Church is all about."

Leah didn't really disagree with that—and she was suddenly aware that all this time she'd been standing in front of everyone like a flagpole, waving her own flag. She knew that a discussion would be so much better. She walked back to her chair next to her counselors, sat down, and said, "Okay, let's talk about that. What do the rest of you think? What should we, as sisters, be doing for each other?"

When no one else said anything, Mayrene said, "My husband doesn't make much, but he has a steady job, so I know I can feed my kids. Some families in our ward get a little relief from the government, and I'm afraid that people make them feel bad about taking it. What makes it worse is that it's not really enough for a family to live on. Some of us take over a sack of flour or a dozen eggs once in a while. I just think we need to do that. Those who are out of work don't need to feel ashamed to take some help. Maybe later, they'll be the ones helping some of us."

"Lots of people are trying to help," an older woman in the back said—a woman Leah didn't really know, except that her name was Mildred. "There's people in this town who would be going hungry right now if others weren't looking out for them."

"I've got to tell you," Leah said, "I didn't know that. But I'm glad to hear what you're doing. I've told my counselors, I've got to get around the ward now to meet everyone and find out more about the needs. There's no doubt about it, we have to look out for those who are destitute." She hesitated and waited for someone else to comment. When no one did, she added, "I wasn't talking before about people who've lost their jobs and would give anything to get back to work. The ones that bother me are the people—you know, across the whole country—who got rich during the twenties when a lot of money was coming in, and now they lose some of their money in the stock market, and maybe see their businesses slow down some, and suddenly they want the government to bail them out, or they cry their eyes out that their wives can't buy new dresses every time they see one they like. I don't like wearing this old thing I have on all the time, but you know what, as long as I keep it clean, I'm not ashamed to wear it. I don't know why we think we have to have a closet full of clothes and fancy furnishings, or even indoor plumbing, as far as that goes. The pioneers were probably happier than any of us, and look how they lived. There's nothing wrong with a simple life, working hard, and using good old homemade, home-crafted goods. I don't feel too sorry for people just because they have to start living a little more like the rest of us."

Somewhere in the middle of her ramblings, Leah had realized that some faces were hardening. She also realized that she really ought to stop and backtrack a little, but she had continued to roll on through, and now she was guessing that she had offended several more of the women.

"But I'm sort of saying that wrong. There's nothing bad about setting out to do well, starting a business and making it prosper. That's the

American way. I'm just saying that when you get into something like that, and reap the rewards, you have to save and be ready for the days when things turn another way. And maybe if some people have gotten away from basics, and homespun goods, it's a good time to relearn those things. Maybe it's time some people stop holding their noses so high in the air, and we all accept one another as equals. That's how it ought to be in the Church. It's the only way we can stand side by side and help each other. Do you understand what I'm trying to say?"

Leah could hear the buzz of a fly against a window behind her—the room had fallen that quiet. She looked around for a hand to go up, even for someone who looked ready to speak, but lots of arms were folded, and lots of colorful hats were holding still. Leah felt something close to desperation.

Belva finally said, "I think we all understand exactly what you're saying, Leah. I've heard you express your love for the sisters and say how much you want to bring unity to the group. And I'm sure that's what you'll do. We *are* all equals, and I think the sisters know that."

Leah let her eyes scan the faces. There were more who refused to look at her than who looked back. But Glenda was now taking Leah on with her eyes, staring at her defiantly. Leah had to say the right thing before it was too late. "Belva's an awful good woman," she said. "But she's telling a white lie right now—a pretty big one. I've never said anything like that. She's telling you what I should have been saying instead of what I have said. I'm not a very good woman. I'm judgmental and harsh, and I've gotten used to doing what I have to do on my farm, and pretty much ignoring all of you. I don't know your troubles or your needs, and I'm afraid I've often thought the worst about some of you."

Glenda nodded, and then said, "I think we know that, Leah. I've heard it in everything you've said today. Maybe you see noses in the air just because that's what you want to believe about some of us. Maybe you have your mind made up before you even know the situation. And let me say this: I've never advised anyone to buy their bread at our store. We only stock the things that people come looking for."

"Oh, I didn't mean—"

"I don't think you know what you mean. You just want to harp at us and get some things out that have been festering inside you all these years."

Belva stood up quickly. She was wearing a little gray hat, as squatty and round and old-fashioned as she was, a darker gray dress with billowing sleeves, and a long string of pearls. All the women tried to dress nicely for Relief Society, but clearly, Belva had thought of this as a special occasion. "Oh, sisters, let's not do this. Leah is new, and she—"

"And she thinks she knows everything." The room was suddenly silent again, even the fly no longer making a noise after the big, deep voice had rung out. It was Suzanne Oberg, a stout, older woman whose husband ran several large herds of sheep in the area. "Some of us have worked hard to get ahead just a little bit, and I don't think we have to be ashamed of it. If Leah knew what was really going on around here, she'd know that we're the same ones who are the first to look after those who need help—and usually don't say a word about it. We don't come to Relief Society to be criticized and accused."

But Jean Watkins, sitting up front, was quick to say, "Oh, Suzanne, get off your high horse. Leah's dead right. There are people in this town who like to lord it over everyone—act like they're too good for the rest of us. We're *all* willing to help our neighbors, so don't act like you're the only one."

Leah had to stop this. "Sisters, I didn't mean—"

"You have no idea what people do in this town, Jean," Suzanne said. "I know who donates to charities around here, and you're not one of them."

"Some of us give all we *can,*" Elizabeth Call said. "And some give their time. Jean's always helping someone. She just doesn't *brag* about it—the way some people do."

"Sisters, please. I didn't mean to get anything like this started."

"Well, you did, just the same, didn't you?" Glenda said. "And it's not the first time. You resent anyone who's managed to make anything of herself. I talked to Nadine Willis this morning, and I know what you said to her yesterday. You couldn't even wait twenty-four hours to drop by on her and tell her everything you don't like about her."

Leah's temper flashed. "I did no such thing. I went there to check on her. I knew she'd been sick."

"Yes, and you insulted her every way you could. I knew better than to come over here today, but I told myself I'd give you a chance. Now I know I made a mistake." Glenda stood up. She was a tall woman, strongly built, with a hard face, except for the rolls of fat under her chin. "I don't know about the rest of the sisters, but I don't plan to come over here and listen to any more of this." And with that, she began to work her way out of the row, bumping over women with her long, awkward sidesteps. When she walked out, she wasn't alone. Leah counted six sisters who stood, looking just as stern, and followed: Suzanne Oberg, June Lewis, Doris Berg, Nelda Carlson, Evelyn Brewer, and Janice Ingersol.

"Oh, sisters, please don't leave," Belva was pleading the whole time. "We can talk this out."

But Leah was speechless. She had no idea what to do. She had planned to let Marjorie take some time at this first meeting to start organizing the annual bazaar—make assignments and plan the monthly work meetings through the summer. The only thing she was sure of was that she had better sit down herself, so she said, "I'm sorry. I've made a mess of this. I'll try to make things right, but please, the rest of you, come back next week."

"Let 'em go," Elizabeth said. "They came here looking for a fight."

That wasn't the answer—Leah understood that much. But she wasn't going to give any more opinions. "I'll turn the time over to Marjorie, and then Mayrene will continue her literature lessons on the American short story." She sat down.

But nothing went right after that. The sisters had little to say about the bazaar, and Marjorie clearly had no heart for it herself. Finally, Lily Placer said, "I'm not sure there's much point in it this year. Who's going to buy anything?"

Marjorie gave a halfhearted rebuttal, but she left the bazaar up in the air, not trying to determine whether it would even be held. Mayrene then led a lackluster discussion on Sarah Orne Jewett and Willa Cather. After the meeting, women didn't linger and chat, but left quickly.

Belva tried to tell Leah that things hadn't turned out as badly as she thought, that tempers would cool, but Marjorie told her that she had offended half the women and would need to start making amends. "No," Leah said. "That's not going to work. What I need to do is go see the bishop. I can't do this job. That's obvious. Can you put things up around here?"

"Of course," Marjorie said, one eyebrow arching, disgust showing in the firm line of her lips.

Leah didn't care. She was quitting. She would go back to her farm and stay there.

Chapter Five

LEAH LEFT HER CAR at the church and walked down the block to the bishop's garage. If she resigned now, everyone would be relieved, and someone could work quickly to get the sisters back together. Belva was probably the one, just as the bishop should have known from the beginning. When Leah reached the garage, she found the bay door open and saw that a Chevrolet was parked inside with the hood up, but she didn't see the bishop. Just then, however, he stepped out of his little office. He was wiping his hands on a rag. "Oh, Leah, thank goodness," he said. "God must have sent you. You're here just in time."

"Actually, Keith, I need to talk to you about something. I—"

"Clyde Dibble's shot himself."

"Shot himself? You mean on purpose?"

"I don't know yet. But he's dead, and he's left Mary with seven kids. We need to get out there right now. Why don't you follow me out to their farm in your car?"

The bishop walked past her out of the garage and then stopped to wait so he could close the door. Leah followed, but the bishop needed to know what was going on. She said, "Bishop, I'm not sure I should go out there. I need to talk to you about what happened today."

The bishop turned around and looked at her. The pain in his face stopped her, changed everything.

"No. That's all right. I'll go," she said.

He nodded and turned away.

"My car's down by the church."

"You know where they live, don't you?"

"Sure."

"Just meet me there. I need to hurry." He turned and trotted around the building to where he always parked his car. What lingered in Leah's mind was his expression, the solemnity of it.

Leah walked back to the church, but she was thinking about Mary Dibble now, and the idea was sinking in—the realization of what she was going to have to deal with. She understood this kind of pain. She knew what Mary was going through right now, and knew what it would cost the poor woman to come back to life. Leah wasn't sure she could reach deep enough to pull the woman back—especially now, the way Leah was feeling about herself. But by the time she made it back to the church, she told herself she had to do what she'd told Nadine: She had to quit feeling sorry for herself and do something. She hurried into the Relief Society room and found Belva and Marjorie still there. "Clyde Dibble has . . . died," she said. "I'm going out there right now. We're going to need some things—some meals brought in, I guess. Maybe you could start on that. I'll let you know what else we have to do."

"Oh, Leah, what happened?" Belva asked.

But Leah couldn't say it. "I'm not exactly sure. But Mary's going to need all of us." She took only a glance at Marjorie, but she saw the recognition in her face. Maybe it was what Leah was feeling: that their job had started now, no matter what Leah had said a few minutes earlier.

Leah drove out Main Street and followed a county road to a country lane west of town, then up a rutted road to the Dibbles' farm. Clyde Dibble was around the age Wayne had been, not yet forty. She hoped he had been cleaning his rifle when this had happened, so this would be the same as Wayne's death—just one of those things, an accident.

The bishop was not that far ahead of Leah. She could still see the red dust from his car hanging in the air along the lane—with not so much as a breeze to blow it away. Leah let off the gas, slowed almost to a stop. She wanted to let Keith have a little time with Mary before she arrived. She let the car crawl on down between two rows of tall Lombardy poplars. After she parked next to the bishop's car, she waited a couple more minutes. But she was feeling it all—that day when the life she had known had ended.

She'd been expecting Wayne to come in the house that day, had been a little put out that he would linger out back so long after she'd called him to come in to supper. Finally, she'd walked out back, hadn't seen him, called a couple more times, and then walked to the corral where he kept his horses. She hadn't seen him at first, hadn't thought to look at the ground, until she noticed Tony, his young saddle horse, tied to a post and stepping nervously, pulling at his halter. Then she had seen Wayne, lying in a heap, his face in the dirt, his arms folded under him. She had run to him, turned him over, and she'd heard him take a breath when she did, but there was no life in his limp face, and she'd known immediately that he wasn't coming back to her.

Leah had sat by Wayne's side for two days, waiting for the pain to set in so she could start to deal with it. Old Bishop Jenson had stayed with her for hours, and Relief Society sisters had come in shifts. They'd sat with her, prayed, promised, tried to feed her . . . and she had hardly known they were there. And then Wayne's death had come late in the night, when she was with him by herself, her kids asleep. She'd heard his final gurgling breath. Then she had walked out to the kitchen, sat at the table in the dark, and waited for morning so she could get on with whatever it was she had to do. That had been the worst, just waiting, feeling nothing, knowing nothing.

Now, as she sat outside Mary Dibble's house, that emptiness returned. She had no idea what she should say to the woman. She knew better than anyone that nothing helped very much. God would take Mary in his arms for a while, and people who loved her would do what they could, but Leah didn't want to tell her the truth. Mostly, Mary would have to do this herself, and nothing about that was going to be easy.

Leah got out of the car and walked slowly to the front porch. The weathered little house was sun-dried wood more than white paint. The porch was sinking into the clay, and the grass out front was mostly dead. The drought had done some of that, but all the other signs of defeat were there: a broken windowpane stuffed with a yellowing rag; a paintless rocking horse in the front yard, one runner broken off; a rusty tractor next to the porch, all the tires flat. Leah had heard for a couple of years that the Dibbles might lose their farm. Spider mites had gotten into their corn and eaten up most of their crop last year, so Clyde hadn't been able to feed his cows and had had to sell them off, thin and weak, worth almost nothing.

Leah tapped on the door and then opened it herself and peeked in. "Come in, Leah," the bishop said. He was sitting on a faded green couch next to Mary. Her hands were folded in her lap and she was staring ahead, not seeming to notice that Leah had come inside. An older daughter, Constance, who was fourteen or fifteen, was sitting on a chair, positioned like her mother. Her eyes were red and glaring. Her faded cotton dress was too large for her skinny body, the worn fabric hanging limp. "Where are the other kids?" Leah whispered. She knew the pain she had caused her own children when she couldn't think clearly enough to watch out for them.

The daughter glanced up at Leah, seeming to notice her for the first time. "My aunt come and took 'em over to her place," she said.

At least that was something. Mary did have a sister who lived not far away. Old Brother Barrett, Mary's dad, was dead, but Mary's mother could help a little, too. She lived in Neola now, not too far away, and she wasn't very well, but Leah hadn't had that much: a sister and a mother she could turn to. Leah had only brothers, and all of them had left the basin, gone to college, and never come back. Leah's father had died young, only fifty-four, and her mother had gone to live with Leah's oldest brother in Logan. She wrote a letter to Leah once in a while, but Leah hadn't been very good about answering over the years, and she now had far too little contact with anyone in her family.

Leah walked to Mary, knelt down in front of her, and took hold of her hands. Mary looked at her for a time and then said, "You went through this yourself, didn't you?"

Leah nodded.

"But your husband didn't do it on purpose."

"No."

"Clyde ran out on me. I *hate* him for that."

The bishop put his arm around Mary's shoulders and said to Leah, "He told her last night, she and the kids would be better off without him. The government would give them relief. He went out this morning, like he was going about his usual chores, but when noon came, he never come in for dinner."

"I didn't think anything about it," Mary said. "He's been doing that sometimes lately. He would just skip eating—I guess because he was worried about not having enough to feed the kids. So I didn't even check on him 'til after two o'clock. Then I went out to the old shed out back, and there he was, leaning against the wall, still sitting up, this little dribble of blood running down in front of his ear. His eyes was open—wide open—like he'd surprised hisself by pulling the trigger."

Leah was nodding, gripping Mary's hands. She didn't want to hear this. But if it was what Mary needed to do—say such things—she would let her say them.

"He was more than happy to make all those babies," Mary said. "Now where is he when I have to bring 'em up by myself? I don't have a nickel. I can't even bury him. And this farm belongs to the bank."

"I told you, Mary," Bishop Bowen said, "you can't worry about all that. He'll be buried, and I'll make sure that's done right. And people around here aren't going to let those kids of yours starve. We're going to stand right with you and make sure you're all right."

But Mary was still staring at Leah, and her eyes said, *Nothing's ever going to be right again.*

Leah, of course, knew that was true. "Mary," she said, "we're going to bring some meals out. Belva Stone and Marjorie Evans are working on that right now. Will you have some family coming?"

"I guess so. I've got a brother down in Heber Valley. He'll probably come out, if he can. I've got some cousins around here who'll come to the funeral, I guess."

"What about Clyde's family?"

"I don't know. They're mostly from Sanpete County, down around Moroni. Maybe his one brother will come out and bring Clyde's parents, but I doubt any of the rest of 'em can afford to come this far."

"We'll see to it there's a place for everyone to sleep if they need to stay over for a night."

"Some can stay with my mother and sister. We'll probably manage that part all right."

Mary was staring at Leah but not seeming to see her. Still, she was obviously starting to think what had to be done.

"Do the kids have clothes they can wear to the funeral?" Leah asked.

"Not anything nice. They got what they wear to church. But it's old things that make them ashamed."

"You'll want them to be fixed up a little that day, Mary. It's something they'll remember, too. I'll see that they have something better. It might be hand-me-downs. You know how it is. No one has lots of nice clothes these days. But I'll make sure they have decent shoes they can wear, and something a little newer to put on that day."

"I don't want charity, Leah. Just about everybody's broke now, and I don't want them digging into pockets that are pretty near empty as it is."

"Mary, you've done plenty for other people. Now it's our turn to do a little for you. That's how we'll all get through."

"I'll work my head off, night and day, if that's what it takes. But what'll I do with my little ones? I got two still wearin' diapers." Mary ducked her head, and Leah could see that she was fighting not to cry. The bishop was still holding her around the shoulders, but he was watching Leah. Leah felt the responsibility, knew that he was depending on her to do this right.

"Mary, look at me."

Mary did look up.

"I've been where you are. I know what it takes. And mostly, it's a matter of taking one day, even one minute, at a time. Don't try to figure *everything* out just yet. For now, let some of us do what we can to support you—until you get some strength back. At first it feels like you can't get your feet back under you. But you will."

"I got enough strength in me. I'll manage one way or another. But I'm going to hate that coward for all eternity. When I get to the other side, I want to see him jist long enough to tell him what I think of him, and then, never again." She turned toward the bishop. "Is there a way I can divorce him now—after he's dead?"

"Give this time, Mary," the bishop said. "I know it's hard to understand right now, so don't try."

"It ain't hard to understand. Not one bit. He lost his nerve, that's all.

I don't respect him, and I don't want the kids to respect him either. He don't deserve to see any of 'em in the next world."

Leah glanced around at Constance, who sat without moving, still staring ahead. "Mary," Leah said, "I don't have a lot of advice for you, but I will say this: Bishop Bowen is right. Just let all that part go for right now. You can try to sort it out later. It's not going to help you to—"

"It's helped me more than anything else so far. It makes me mad, and it feels a lot better to be mad than to feel sorry for myself. If I could box his ears right now, I would, and that would make me feel even better."

"Well, maybe. Maybe not. All I know is, you'll go through a lot of different feelings in the next few weeks. If you want to tell some of them to me, that might be good. And if you don't want to talk, we'll do it that way. I just want you to know I'm going to help you in whatever way I can."

"I know that, Leah. But I need to do for myself. That's how life is."

Leah knew better than to tell Mary what she ought to feel. Maybe the anger really was what she needed right now. Being mad at God hadn't worked out very well for Leah, but it had seemed the most logical thing for a time, and she had clung to it. "I'll tell you what we need to do. Let's make a list of your kids, and you remind me how old each one is and what sizes they wear. Then you and the bishop can talk about the funeral, and we can just keep doing that—taking the next step."

"I don't know, Leah. I don't want you to go into town and start begging all them town ladies for things for my kids."

"Mary, people will want to help. They'll all be asking me what they can do. That way, I'll have an answer for them. Just think what you would want to do if something like this happened to one of the other sisters."

"We have quite a lot of clothes stored up for situations like this," Bishop Bowen said. "All the sisters in Relief Society try to give one item a year. We've used a lot of things up lately, but we still have some pretty nice things—made over mostly—but we even have new things that haven't sold too well down at the Emporium. Nadine Willis turns them over to us."

Leah had known that the Relief Society asked for clothing items each year, and she'd given things her kids had grown out of, but it was hearing what Nadine had done that registered with Leah, and she felt guilty for things she'd been saying. Maybe Suzanne had a point.

"I haven't looked through what we have yet," Leah told Mary. "But it's surely not a matter of begging people for things." She got up, and then she helped Mary stand too, and they walked into the little kitchen with its ancient coal stove and pine cupboards, once varnished, now worn to gray around every handle. Mary found a pencil and a scrap of paper. As Mary named off her seven children and their ages and sizes, Leah wrote everything down.

The bishop stood behind Mary and listened. When the list was finished, he asked, "Is there someone you'd like to have speak at the funeral?"

"No one who's going to say what a good man he was. This wasn't the first wrong thing Clyde Dibble ever done. I don't even want to tell you what he's said to me lately, or done to me either."

"Mary, I think the worry has been hard on him," the bishop said. "He wasn't always like that."

"More than you know. Every bruise I've ever had hasn't come from banging myself on a door or something, the way I always told people."

The bishop nodded, his big ears making a comic sort of silhouette against the bright light from outside the window. "You should have told me about that, Mary."

"Why? What good would it do? But it's not worth talking about now. You be the speaker, and you say he was a good man, if that's what you want to say. But don't ask me to say anything, because I'll tell the truth. And there's way too much my kids know, so don't lay it on too thick."

"All right, then, I'll speak, and if some of his family comes out, maybe we can get his brother, or someone like that."

"His brother's a better man. He's no coward. Maybe he'd be the best one."

Bishop Bowen asked her about hymns she might like, but she only said she didn't care. He finally stepped to the table and tore off some of the scrap of paper Leah had used. He wrote down a few things in a print like a little boy's. Leah watched his steadiness, his quiet kindness, saw how much all this hurt him. She could feel what his spirit was bringing to Mary. Things had happened to this man since he'd received his calling. Leah hadn't had any idea who he'd become in the last year.

Mary's mother arrived after a time. Fred Grant, Mary's brother-in-law, had driven to Neola and brought her back. She was a frail woman, taller than Mary but bent, with bony, twisted hands. "Oh, Mary," she said, "I never thought anything like this would ever happen. Did you see it coming at all?"

"I don't know, Mama," Mary said. "He said lots of things. I got so I never could believe him about much of anything. I've never told you half the things I've put up with from that man."

"Oh, my. Oh, my. You should have said something." She took Mary in her arms. "It seems like you still ought to be wearing pigtails and coming in from school, and now all this to deal with."

But Mary pulled back from her mother. "I'll get by," she said. "Don't let it worry you into the grave. I'll figure things out."

"Oh, honey, don't try to sound so hard. I know you. I know what a soft heart you have." She took Mary in her arms again, and finally Mary cried. Leah thought that was what she needed: her mother, and some time to cry.

Fred said he'd go watch his own kids, along with Mary's, while his wife came back to be with Mary and their mother. "The three of them together, I think, need some time," he said.

"Then me and Leah will head back to town," Bishop Bowen said. "I'll get things set up for the funeral, and Leah here will see to it you have a meal out here tonight. Is there anything else you can think of?"

"I don't think so. The bank's about to take this farm away, but Mary and the kids won't be out in the street. We'll all crowd into my place, if that's what we have to do."

"You can't shoulder everything, Fred," the bishop said. "Let the rest of us help."

Fred was nodding, but everyone knew this was going to be more difficult than the bishop was making it sound. "Well . . . we'll see."

Bishop Bowen walked outside with Leah, and while the two stood behind his car, he said, "Belva and Marj probably have the meals worked out, and you can look into those clothes. I think Mary can stay in the house for a while. Glen Whiting, down to the bank, told me a couple of weeks ago that he wouldn't throw 'em out until they had somewhere to go. And the thing is, I don't know that he can get anything out of that farm anyway, so he won't push the matter too fast, especially after this. Poor Glen's going to feel like this is his fault, but he was getting pressure from higher up."

"But how's Mary going to feed those kids?"

"I don't know. They'll get some government relief, once we get all the paperwork taken care of. But I don't know where she'll get a job, or what she'd do with the children while she was gone all day. The Church will have to help; that's for sure. Those relief checks ain't near big enough to take care of a family like hers. So there's a lot to figure out, but like you said, we'll just take one step at a time right now."

"How do you do this, Bishop? You must have worries on your mind every minute."

Bishop Bowen pulled his hat off, ducked his head, and ran his hand across his eyes. She could see that the emotion was finally getting to him. "Well, let's just say, I wouldn't have applied for this job if the stake president had put up a 'help wanted' sign. But the pay's not too bad." He grinned, showing his ragged teeth, and then set his hat back on his head.

"Really? Wouldn't you be glad to hand the whole thing off to someone else if you could?"

"No. I'll let someone else take it when the Lord figures I've done my share, but I'm a little better man than I was a year ago, and I got feelings running through me now that I never knew nothing about before."

"Mostly just *worry*, I'd think."

The bishop pulled his hat back off, as though he were about to say something sacred. But he rubbed his eyes, then his bald head, and he waited for a time. "Well," he said, "I'll tell you this much. In case you've ever wondered, there *is* such a thing as the Spirit. I guess I've believed that for a while, but I never knew until lately that it could come to you the way it does—tell you what you need to do, or just fill you all up inside until you can't talk."

It was hard for Leah to believe she was talking to the same man she had known for almost twenty years. "Bishop," she said, "I came over to your shop today to tell you I was quitting. I made a mess of things at our Relief Society meeting today. I popped off just the way I told you I might, and I made a lot of people mad. We had a blowup. Some of the sisters walked out and said they weren't coming back."

The bishop took a long look at Leah, and she thought she saw disappointment in his eyes again, but he only asked, "Well . . . do you still want to quit?"

"I do want to. But I won't. Not now."

"Maybe God knew about Mary. Maybe he knew she was going to need you right now."

"Yeah, I was thinking that. But it's the kind of thing I don't understand. If God wanted to give Mary some help, he could have slapped that gun out of Clyde's hand—not waited until the mess was made."

"I know what you're saying. But Mary had too much to deal with long before Clyde went and done this. She would have needed you, no matter what."

"I still think someone else could do it better. But I'll try to straighten out what I've already fouled up."

"I saw exactly what I was expecting from you today, Leah. You knew enough not to say too much. What you did say was what she needed to hear. And it meant more from you than anyone, since you knew what you were talking about."

"See, that's fine. I'm glad I could help a little. But why didn't the Lord tell me what to say this afternoon in our meeting? I planned out the right things to say, and then all the wrong things came out of my mouth."

The bishop put his hat back on and shoved his hands into the pockets of his overalls. "I don't ask those kinds of questions too much, Leah. The Lord lets us make our own mistakes most of the time. But then, sometimes, when we really need the help, all of a sudden the words are there, or you know right what to do. That's what I keep finding out."

Leah looked out across the fields, the sagging fences. She thought about all she still had to do today, just to keep her own life moving ahead. And now there was this new worry. "I've got Nadine Willis so mad at me she could kill me," she told the bishop. "And after today, some of the rest of the sisters are willing to get in line to help her do it."

"I know about Nadine. She told me what you said to her."

"What did she say?"

The bishop couldn't help smiling just a bit. "Well, she said you come over to her house yesterday and walked right in like you owned the place, and you climbed up her stairs and hunted her down in her bedroom. And you told her she ought to get out of bed and go down and work in the store. She said you were rude, too, and you insulted her, and I don't know . . . quite a few other things." But by now Bishop Bowen's smile had grown into a grin.

"Well, it's all true. That's exactly what I did. So what are you laughing about? It's not funny." But Leah had begun to smile herself.

"You know where I talked to her?"

"*Where?*"

"Down to the Emporium. I was in there this morning. After you told her all that, she got up today and went down to that store. She said she'd made up her mind to start working there, regular."

Leah was astounded.

"So it sounds to me like you done all right. She's up and around."

"And madder than a wet hen."

"Well, sure. But you told her right, and she took the advice, whether she's giving you any credit for it or not."

"I think I gave her good advice, Bishop. But I said it all wrong. I *was* rude. I told her to get off her big rear end."

The bishop laughed, swallowing the sounds as usual, but he couldn't stop himself for a while. "Well," he finally said, "you shouldn't have said that. That's for sure. But I don't know of anyone else who could have gotten her out of that bed. I'd already tried myself, and I told her something just about the same. So maybe rude is what was called for in that case."

He started chuckling again, and Leah knew he was still thinking about the words Leah had chosen. "I *am* glad she's gotten up," Leah said. "But I doubt she'll ever speak to me again—along with half the other sisters."

"You'll learn to work with everyone in time. You just need a little practice."

"Don't expect any miracles."

"Oh, but I do. You asked me about my pay, and I'll tell you what it is. I've seen a few miracles. And I've got so I expect to see more. That's honest pay for an honest day's work, I'd say."

Leah thought so too, but she was more of a skeptic than the bishop. She wasn't expecting miracles. She knew herself too well.

"Well, I guess I'm glad I was here today. I'll say that much. I'm glad you brought me out here, Bishop." But it wasn't until Leah got back in her car and was driving back into town that she realized something. She would never call the bishop "Keith" again. Not after today.

Chapter Six

WEEKS HAD PASSED, and summer was coming on. Leah had never been so busy in her life. She had finished her planting and worked hard—but always with her sisters on her mind. She tried to get things caught up around the farm by putting in long days, and then she would set aside a whole morning or afternoon when she could visit the women in her ward. She tried to visit the ones she had heard were having struggles, and that tended to be the ones with husbands out of work. She knew she also had to visit the sisters who were "better off," but she kept putting that off. The ones who had walked out during her first meeting had not come back, and there were others of the town ladies who were not showing up at meetings. Leah knew she had to do something about that, but she feared she'd only make things worse if she started calling on them before they calmed down.

Belva was trying to get people out to the monthly work and business meeting, which would continue through the summer even though weekly meetings stopped in June and didn't start again until October. The problem was, the confusion about whether they would hold a bazaar had made work meetings seem less important than usual. Leah thought it might be good for the sisters to get together and work, but so much of the financial burden would fall on the people who were getting by all right, and they were some of the ones most upset by the blowup that had occurred in Leah's first meeting—so where would the support come from? Leah was realizing, the Relief Society had depended on those women more than she had ever known.

What Leah was learning, too, was that her ward was full of hard-working women. Over the years, she had come to think of everyone else as having easier lives than her own. Most had husbands, and they didn't have to plow and plant, but burdens came in lots of shapes, and she was seeing them all. These women were simple in a lot of ways, but they weren't as simple-minded as she had suspected. Maybe at church they weren't quick to reveal all their challenges, and sometimes their solutions, in Sunday School, could end up sounding too rose-colored for Leah's taste, but that was part of their hope, their faith. Leah was embarrassed that she had been so judgmental about the discussions she had heard in those classes.

Leah had visited Mary Dibble as often as she could, every few days, and Mary was holding up without her husband better than Leah ever would have expected. Her government help wasn't coming yet, but food—from Relief Society, but also from anonymous sources—kept showing up on her porch. The bishop was checking on her quite often, and so were Mary's sister and brother-in-law. The bank had sold the farm to speculators who were buying up foreclosed farms, but Glen Whiting had talked the buyers into letting Mary and her kids stay in the house for now and keep their garden going. Leah wasn't sure how long that arrangement would last, but it solved the problem for a while.

School was going to let out a couple of weeks earlier than usual this year, the school district having run out of money. Leah hated that; she wanted her kids prepared for college. On the other hand, it meant that

Wade would soon be able to put in full days at home, and he had been telling Leah that he would take over the farm this summer. She knew that it made him feel like a man to make that promise, and she appreciated it, but it was also hard for her to let him do it. She worried that he had never had a chance to be a boy, always working so hard. Beyond that, she also found it difficult to let go of some of her duties. She had her own way of doing things, and she thought Wade sometimes cut corners just to get a job finished. Besides, the first crop of hay would have to be cut soon, and they both would have plenty of work to do until it was raked and dried and hauled. Still, so far, she had done much better at balancing her time than she had ever expected she could.

One afternoon in late May Leah came into the house with some new potatoes she had dug. She thought she might prepare supper, just to give Rae a break. Wade charged through the front door ahead of Rae, as usual, having walked faster from the bus down the lane. He said hello but headed straight to his bedroom, as he always did, so he could change his clothes and get his afternoon chores started. When Rae came in, she stepped into the kitchen and said, "I'll bet Wade didn't smile at you, did he?"

"What?"

Rae leaned against the frame of the kitchen door. She was wearing that same gray dress she wore to school two or three times a week. Leah could see a place where the hem was pulling loose. She wished that Rae would try just a little harder to keep things up, even if the dress was worn out. "Make him show you his front teeth. He broke one of them today."

"Broke? How?"

"I don't know. He said it was during his gym class."

"Wade," Leah called. "Come out here."

But it was a minute or two before he did, and by then Rae had gone to her own room. Wade was snapping the shoulder strap on his bib overalls when he came out. "Rae told you about my tooth, didn't she?" He stepped into the kitchen, then leaned back against the wall.

"Yes. What happened?"

He pulled his lips back in more of a grimace than a smile to let her look, and he said, "Me and another guy just ran into each other, playing basketball. But it doesn't matter. I can still chew, and it doesn't hurt or anything."

The break ran on a diagonal line, with almost half the tooth gone—like a carving in a jack-o-lantern. "Oh, Wade. It does make a difference. You've always had such a handsome smile."

"Now I'm *ruggedly* handsome." He laughed, raised his arms, and flexed his biceps. But he seemed to see Leah's frustration, and he added, "Mom, there's not one thing we can do about it."

"I want to get it fixed. Let's drive in and see what Clark Evans says. I'll bet he can put one of those caps on it." She had just put her apron on, but now she pulled it back off.

"Think about it, Mom. You know that's going to cost a whole lot. There's plenty of guys at school with a broken tooth or two, or even some knocked out. Let's wait for now. One of these years things will get better. We can fix it then."

"Get in the car. We're driving to town. Let's find out what it *would* cost. We can at least do that."

So Leah told Rae to pick some peas in the garden to go with the potatoes, and she and Wade would be back as soon as possible. Rae agreed, but managed to mumble that Mom wouldn't even bother if something like that had happened to her. Leah was trying to ignore that kind of stuff from Rae these days, so she said nothing. She walked outside ahead of Wade, set the spark and the throttle on the Model T, and was about to crank it when Wade stepped up and did it for her. It started on the first crank, but it ran rough until Leah adjusted the choke. She waved for Wade to climb in, and then headed out the lane. Wade complained all the way into town, but in a quarter of an hour he was sitting in Dr. Clark Evans's dental chair.

"Well," Clark told Leah, "we can certainly put a crown on it, if you feel like you can afford it."

"What would it cost?"

"I'm afraid it would be about thirty . . . well, let's say twenty-eight dollars."

Leah let out more of a gasp than she meant to, and she saw Clark's face redden. He looked like a man who ought to be a lumberjack, not a dentist, and his big hands always frightened her when they came toward her mouth—or maybe it was just that drill of his. She never had liked dentists and she was lucky that she hadn't needed them much. "I guess I hadn't realized it would cost that much," she finally managed to say.

Clark tucked his thumbs into the back pockets of his trousers and rocked back a little. He was a big man, tall and sturdy. His features were too emphatic, too strong, to be handsome, but he did have kindly eyes, even if the color was more gray than blue. And what she liked best was his smile that came easily and so often that it was hard to talk to him without smiling back. "It's the gold that makes a crown cost so much. I don't charge much for putting it on."

"Gold? Would he have a gold tooth in front?"

"No. It's enamel on the outside, so it would match up pretty well with his other teeth, but it's gold on the inside."

"Thirty bucks."

"I said twenty-eight would be okay."

"Mom, it just isn't necessary," Wade said. He sat up in the chair, as though he thought it was time to leave. "Lots of people have broken teeth."

"Wade, it looks terrible. I don't care what other people do. I don't want you walking around like that."

"I'm the one walking around with it, not you, so let me decide."

"Go sit in the waiting room, Wade. I need to talk this over with Clark, and I'm not going to do it with you chiming in all the time."

"Fine. But he can't fix the thing if I won't come back and sit in this chair." Wade slipped out of the chair, worked his way past his mother, and walked out.

As soon as he was gone, Leah said, "He worries about money more than I do. But I guess I've taught him to be that way." She took a closer look at Clark. "I'm wondering what we could work out to get this done."

"Well, if you could pay something down, and then pay a dollar or two a month, we could handle it that way."

"But how much do you have to have to start with?"

He looked at the floor. "Well, maybe fifteen. I have to pay for the materials, and my cash flow isn't very good these days."

"Oh, I know." Leah stood for a time and tried to think. "Maybe we better let it go for the summer. I hope I get enough off my farm this year to come out a little ahead for once. Maybe I could come up with the whole thirty by then."

"Do you see any sign that farm prices are going to be better this year?"

"Not really. But maybe someone besides Hoover will get elected this fall, and something will start to change."

Clark grinned, showing his big teeth. "So you've come around to agreeing with me about that?"

"Who hasn't? Hoover doesn't have any idea what's going on in this country. He's got his head in the sand."

Clark was standing in front of Leah. He was one of the few men around who didn't make her feel like she was way too tall. "What do you think about this bonus army, marching on Washington?"

Leah had read all about that in the newspaper and listened to reports on the radio. A group of veterans of the Great War had started in Oregon and were picking up supporters across the country. Congress had voted them $1.25 a day for the time they had served in Europe, but the pay wasn't scheduled to start until 1945. The vets, many of them unemployed now, planned to fill up Washington, D.C., with protestors and convince Hoover and Congress to pay them now.

"I don't know, Clark. What do you think? I guess it bothers me a little when they start making demands like that. Everyone's suffering. Why should the government help them more than anyone else?"

"Because they fought in that miserable war. What kind of help is it to vote them some help in 1924 and not pay them for twenty-one years?"

"But they get the money with interest. That'll help a lot of them retire."

"Yes, and how do they feed their families now?"

"The same as the rest of us, I guess."

"Well . . . I know what you're saying. But Hoover doesn't want to do one thing to get the economy moving. Someone's got to do something."

But Clark was smiling by now, and Leah thought she knew why. He seemed to like talking to someone—maybe especially a woman—who could talk politics. She had the feeling he even liked that she would disagree with him. Leah was smiling, too, and she thought maybe she was blushing a little.

"Well, let's hope for better times," Clark finally said.

"Yes, let's hope. And we'll see about that tooth in the fall. I just can't raise that kind of money right now."

"I could maybe take—"

"No. You have to get paid. I've heard Marjorie say how much work you do without ever seeing a red cent for it."

Clark nodded. "Well, all right. But we can work it out so it won't hit you too hard all at once."

Leah took a step toward the door before Clark said, "So how are you feeling about Relief Society now?"

She looked around at him and then shook her head. "I don't know.

I'm trying hard. I've still got half the town mad at me. Your wife puts up with me, but I know darn well that she'd do a better job if she were the president."

Clark laughed. "Marj puts up with me, too. She'd probably be a better dentist than I am, if that's what she wanted to do—or better than me at anything else."

"She's a strong woman. She and Belva are the ones keeping us in business right now, and I'm sure they feel like they're dragging me along, dead weight."

Leah actually hoped that Clark might say that Marjorie had gained a little respect for Leah in the last couple of months, but instead, he said, "Sit down for a minute, Leah. I want to tell you a little about Marj. I think it might help you understand the way she is."

"Don't you have appointments coming in?"

"I wish I did. But I don't. Marj used to come over and work as my receptionist, but these days, I just handle the whole thing myself. Some days I don't have a single patient." He gestured toward a chair, and Leah sat down. Then he walked out front and came back with another chair he could sit on. The room was so small that they ended up sitting across from one another at the foot of the dental chair, almost knee to knee.

"I don't know whether Marj has ever told you much about her background."

"She told me she grew up in Salt Lake. I think she said her father was a doctor."

"That's right. We met when I was down there at the university— before I went back to Baltimore to dental school. She waited for me while I was gone."

"Sure she did. You were a 'catch.'"

"I think she thought so then. I'm not so sure she does anymore. Marj grew up in a nice home. She had pretty much everything she wanted, and her family was well connected around Salt Lake. At the U, she was involved in all kinds of things: music, acting, sorority. She was even one of the attendants to the homecoming queen."

"She's a beautiful woman, still."

He nodded. "Yes, she is," he said.

"And then you brought her to Richards."

"Yup. I'm afraid so." He folded his arms across his chest. Leah heard more sadness than she wanted to.

"Why did you come out here?"

"I grew up in the basin, so it was home to me. When I found out Richards needed a dentist, I wanted to come, and she was fine with the idea. You remember how she was when we first got here. She was all set to make the best of things—start a book club and an acting society and all that. It kept her going for quite a while. But I've never been able to make the kind of money she was used to, and now, with things turning so bad, I'm watching the heart go right out of her. She'd like to move back to Salt Lake, but how could I start over? Dentists down there aren't doing very well either."

"Maybe things will turn this next year and people will start getting their dental work caught up after letting it go so long."

"I know. That's what I tell Marj. But she knows as well as I do, we might not make it through the year. I've got a pretty steep mortgage, payments on my equipment, and monthly rent to pay on this office. We've also bought some other things on credit—our car, and a fancy new electric refrigerator Marj thought I needed to shell out eighty-eight dollars for. It's all coming home to roost now, and Marj is so scared that it's almost the only thing she thinks about."

"Aren't you scared?"

"I don't know. I'm certainly worried. Marj tells me I have to stop taking eggs and vegetables for payments—you know, because we need cash to pay our bills. But she doesn't have to look at a kid with a toothache, and she doesn't have to tell the kid's mother that she has to pay cash—when the poor woman doesn't have any.'"

"Or a woman who says, 'I guess I better wait on getting that tooth fixed.'"

"Sure. But you don't have twenty-eight dollars. And the truth is, I ought to be charging thirty-five or even forty, if I'm going to stay afloat. But I saw your face when I said thirty. How can I ask for forty?"

"Oh, Clark, I'm sorry to hear all this. I knew things were tough, but I didn't know you were in quite that much trouble."

Clark turned a little so he could stretch his legs past Leah. He leaned back and smiled. "I figure things'll work out. The bank will probably work with me until better times come. Somehow, we'll be okay. But that's not why I'm telling you all this. I just want you to understand Marj. It's not her fault she was raised the way she was. I guess some people would say that she's spoiled and that she thinks she's better than other people. But you know, it's only natural that she expected life to go on about the same as it always had for her."

Leah had sort of known all this, and yet it was clearer to her now—even what it must have meant to have Leah called as president instead of her. Leah was having a hard time looking at Clark, who was obviously hurting much more than he was admitting. The room was getting warm, and there was a smell of medicine, or something—one she always noticed in a dentist's office—that she didn't like. She thought she ought to go, but she said, "Things aren't turning out the way any of us expected right now, Clark."

"I know. But I made promises to her; I told her how great her life would be in a nice little town like this. So it's pretty tough for her. She's trying to deal with everything, but she's tired of the worry. And all the clubs and everything are dying out, with everyone running so scared."

"I know it was a blow to Marj that the bishop called me and not her to serve as president."

He smiled. "Well, let's just say it's another opportunity for her to acquire some humility. But you know what? She's saying some pretty good things about you now, and she's trying her best to play second fiddle, even though she's never done much of that."

"I know she shakes her head sometimes when she hears the things I say."

"Maybe. But I think she envies you a little, too—the way you say what you think. She came home pretty hot under the collar after that first meeting you held. But I told her you were right. We *can* cut back on our expenses if we make our own soap and some of those kinds of things. And I'll tell you what. Marj has started saving our cooking fat. She's going to make a batch of lye soap—if she can do it without burning herself up." Clark suddenly laughed hard, his voice booming off the walls of the little room.

"The trouble is," Leah said, "in a town like this, everyone's life affects everyone else's. I've stayed to myself too much. You can't tell people not to buy store-bought bread without getting Glenda all stirred up."

Clark was nodding. He sat up straight again. "But here's the thing, Leah. We're all finding out, no one's really above anyone else. And I think that's good for all of us. Marj is a good woman—probably better than you think she is—but she needed some humbling and she's getting it. We all are. You start thinking about what the Lord said about the meek inheriting the earth and all that sort of thing, and maybe this Depression will turn out to be a good thing for all of us."

Leah had been thinking a lot about that lately—had even read the Sermon on the Mount over again, with exactly those thoughts in mind. She liked that Clark had been thinking about the same things. "Clark, I'll tell you something," she said. "Maybe Marj needs some humbling, but I need it more than she does. I've had it in my head that I was just about the strongest woman around—that I could handle whatever came.

But these last ten years I've gradually been turning into *nothing.* Do you know what I mean?"

"No. Not really."

"I just keep going, working all day every day, and I get so I don't know my own emotions. I thought I didn't need anyone—but getting back in touch with people is like freezing your fingers and then warming them back up. It hurts, but at least it feels, and I haven't *felt* much for a long time."

Clark was nodding. "Okay. I do know what you mean. There are times when I wonder what it was I was expecting out of life, and whether it's too late now to . . . I don't know . . . feel more satisfied. There's something very lonely about the way . . . ." But he stopped, as though he realized he had started into a sentence he didn't dare finish.

Leah was suddenly aware of how long she had been in the office, how long Wade had been waiting, how much she liked this man. "Well, I better get going," she said.

"What kind of a guy was Wayne? I never got to know him very well."

There was a hint of logic in the question that made Leah nervous, although she didn't try to fill in any blank spaces. She stood up, to remind him that she needed to go, but she said, "He was quiet. He didn't like to talk much. I always wanted to talk about the things I'd learned to love in college. He'd listen to me—at least at first—but he never had anything to say about things like that." She stopped and laughed at herself. "I probably am the most boring person in the world when I get rattling on."

"What things did you try to talk to him about?"

"Literature. History. Just thoughts about life. I would read things and I'd try to tell him what I'd been thinking about in the house all day while he was out working. But eventually, he wouldn't even try to pretend he was interested."

"Why did you marry him?"

"Because he asked."

Clark laughed, but then neither said anything, as he seemed to realize that her answer was at least partially true.

"I think I was mostly afraid I'd never marry."

Clark got up. He pushed his hands into his back pockets again. "I took a lot of literature classes in college," he said. "And I did some acting. That's how I met Marj. We were cast opposite each other in *Taming of the Shrew*." He laughed, as though he saw some irony in that. "Sometimes I think, if I had it to do over again, I'd be a professor of some kind. Drilling teeth just doesn't excite the mind very much."

But now Leah was hearing another possible step in Clark's logic, and she felt her face warming. "Well, anyway, I'll think about getting that tooth fixed one of these days. And when I do, I'll pay you what it's worth. Forty."

"Naw. I'll do it for the price of the gold—if you'll come back and chat with me again. The funny thing about Marj is, she acted in lots of plays, but it's like she never paid any attention to the ideas in them. I try to talk to her about those things now, and she's about like you say Wayne was. 'It's just a play,' she'll say. 'Why do you have to *analyze* it so much?' But I've read some things lately that maybe you've read. We could—"

"Oh, I hardly ever read anymore, Clark. I don't have the time." Leah was suddenly feeling self-conscious. She was moving by then, and as she stepped out of the office, she saw Wade standing up, looking at her curiously. Maybe he was wondering what she had talked about with Clark so long, or maybe he had heard through the door—heard what she had said about his father. Leah knew this was another time when she had been a lot more frank than she should have.

On the way home, Leah told Wade that she'd try to get the tooth fixed in the fall. "Or maybe I can find the money sooner than that. I'll have to do some figuring about my seed costs and all that." But that wasn't the truth. Leah was thinking about the $1200 she had in the bank. She didn't want her handsome son going back to school in the fall with a broken tooth, looking like a country boy. Maybe she could take that much money from the bank. But if she did, it would be at least thirty-five, not twenty-eight. She would pay what a person ought to pay for something like that.

When Leah and Wade got home, Rae was not happy that they had been gone so long, but she had done more than pick a few things from the garden. She had made supper, and Leah was pleased by that. The girl showed some signs of growing up every now and then.

After supper, Leah did the dishes and let Rae do her homework, but later, alone in her own room, Leah read her Book of Mormon. She decided to read the version of the Sermon on the Mount in Third Nephi, and she thought again about humility and about the things Clark had said.

And then, when she went to bed, she did something she had been trying not to do all evening. She thought about Clark.

He was a married man, and she knew she shouldn't take anything from the things he'd said, but hadn't he meant something by comparing Wayne and Marj? Hadn't he been saying, "What if you and I had met? What if we had married each other instead of those two?" It certainly seemed as though he had let the thought pass between them, bringing up the possibility that they could get together and talk again. She found herself wondering, what if he had been a professor, not a dentist, and what if he had married someone who could talk to him about the things he liked to talk about? And of course, that led to the other thought—the one she always tried to avoid. What if she had met a man in college, someone who liked to talk and take walks and listen to music? What if she had lived in a city where she could have gone to symphonies and good plays—and had had a husband who liked all those things? She had imagined a little scene many times in her life, and she allowed it to come back to her now. She was sitting in a nice living room—not fancy, but comfortable—with a fire burning in a fireplace, and she and her husband had spent the evening reading, and then talking, and then after, they had gone to bed together, and he had held her as though she were precious to him.

Wayne had wanted her, plenty, but he had wanted her the way men want a big meal of meat and potatoes. She had always wanted to be savored, and he had never seemed to have the slightest inkling of what that would mean. She certainly had never dared say anything. So many nights she had lain in bed frustrated, longing for the part of love he never understood.

But maybe all men were like that. Clark was nothing special to look at, and just because he liked to chat, that didn't mean he would be all that different from the way Wayne had been. Maybe there were men who understood, but she would never know. And so she lay there now, tense with the longing that she tried so hard never to think about, and for a few minutes she did feel sorry for herself, even though it was the one indulgence she hated most.

Chapter Seven

THE SUMMER OF 1932 turned hot and dry. Leah watched her corn wither in the heat, never grow to full height, never produce much. Irrigation canals dwindled to almost nothing by August, and every farmer was placed on short water turns. The drought, all across the Midwest as well as in the West, promised to help farm prices a little, but what difference would that make if crops failed? It would be another bad year; that was already certain.

Democrats had nominated Franklin Delano Roosevelt, fifth cousin of Theodore, and the new candidate was saying all the right things, promising a "new deal" for Americans. Leah knew she would vote for him, just to see if something might change, but she had a hard time trusting such promises. Hoover was trying to convince Americans that somehow this "correction" in the economy wasn't nearly so bad as people were letting on. Leah had begun to lose faith in Hoover the year before, but now, through her Relief Society work, she saw what the Depression was doing to people, and she wondered how the man could be so blind.

Leah had stopped by the Emporium twice now, and she had tried to be pleasant with Nadine Willis, but the woman didn't hide her distaste for Leah. Leah could pretty well guess what she was thinking: "All right, you told me to go to work and I did, but don't gloat over seeing me here."

Still, things seemed to have bottomed out for the store, and even though Nadine and Jim were working long hours themselves, they were apparently staving off bankruptcy. Certainly, though, Nadine hadn't been expressing to her friends her appreciation for Leah's advice. What had gotten back to Leah was that Nadine had told lots of women, not just Glenda Poulson, about Leah's "rudeness."

Belva had been working hard to bring back some of the sisters who had been avoiding Relief Society meetings, and two had started to attend again lately, but the others were staying away. Glenda was still angry and had announced her opinion of Leah all over town—and had said some things about Bishop Bowen, too. She was no longer coming to church at all. Suzanne Oberg hadn't gone that far, but she'd told Belva she wasn't coming back to Relief Society until a new president was called. Nelda Carlson, whose husband owned the local creamery and a dairy farm, had never been back either. She'd told Belva that she had always kept a garden and canned every fall of her life. She didn't like Leah's accusations. Some others were saying similar things. They weren't as well off as Nadine or Glenda, but they attended some of the same clubs, where women were undoubtedly comparing opinions.

Pearl Street, whose husband also ran a big-time sheep operation, lived in one of the nicest homes in Richards. She hadn't attended Relief Society on the day of the big argument, and never had come all that regularly, but she was telling people she would never go back—after talking to Nadine. Leah had also heard that Pearl didn't like Marjorie, either. They had met with the same book club for years and somehow had rubbed one another the wrong way. Leah knew now why she had avoided all those kinds of groups, but she had no idea how to fight against what was being said at their meetings.

What Leah was starting to understand was that hard times could bring out the best in people, but also the worst. Some people saw others struggling and felt compassion; other sisters seemed to hide away in their homes, as though afraid that someone might ask them to help. Leah heard comments that implied that those who were out of work were somehow responsible for their own misfortune. She thought that was wrong, but she did understand that it was hard enough for people to feed their own families, without trying to figure out everyone else's problems. The truth was, she had been hiding out for a long time herself, so she understood the impulse.

All summer Leah had been meeting sisters and hearing their stories. What she couldn't do anymore, at least in most cases, was blame people for their problems. Her challenge was that the needs were so great that she felt overwhelmed.

Still, Belva never lost confidence, and Leah had learned to take Belva with her on most of her visits. Marjorie was willing to go, and she usually had advice for people—or advice for Leah after the two left the houses—but she didn't do much to show her concern, and Leah wasn't good at that either, so Belva was always better to have along. She hugged the women, listened to them, cried. Leah wished sometimes she could cry, just once, or say such sweet things, but she usually ended up asking questions, probing for answers, when many times there really was no practical answer. It was easy to teach patience and faith—and to provide some food in the short run—but families needed to get back on their feet and overcome the emotional struggles they were going through. The trouble was, as long as the Depression continued, unemployment and bankruptcies were going to continue.

In Washington, the thirty thousand bonus-army men had set up a shanty town and waited out Congress most of the summer, only to have their appeal voted down. A skirmish had followed, with a couple of men killed, and then the government had come down hard. General Douglas MacArthur had led a cavalry charge on "Hooverville," as the vets called their camp, burning the shacks and driving the men out of the city. Leah had not felt much sympathy for the protestors back in the spring, but now she wondered what was happening to her government, for it to treat veterans that way. It really seemed as though the whole nation could explode if things didn't get better soon. Even in Salt Lake City, there were long lines at soup kitchens, and protest marches had begun.

One afternoon in August, on a day so hot that cattle were all huddled under any tree they could find, Leah and Belva parked in front of Pat Hyatt's farmhouse and walked to the door. The Hyatts milked a small string of cows, like Leah, and kept a big garden. The farm wasn't producing much this year, but the family was still eating, and the kids were neat and clean—even if they didn't have more than one change of clothes. But Will had gotten sick a few weeks back and he wasn't getting better. He had never stopped working, even when he was burning up with fever. Now the fever itself had passed, but Pat had told Belva at church that he was so weak he could hardly pull himself out of bed each morning. He kept doing it anyway, and she was worried to death about him.

"Hi, Patty," Belva said when the door opened. Leah saw the weariness in Pat's face. She had lost weight even though she had always been tiny, and she was pale, even her hair seeming to have lost its color.

"Oh hi, Belva." The late afternoon sun was at Leah's back. Pat shaded her eyes and looked up to see who else was there. "Hi, Leah. Come on in. I appreciate you coming by."

Belva stepped aside and let Leah walk in first. Leah thought of bending to hug Pat, but she couldn't get herself to do it. When Pat reached out to shake her hand, Leah recognized the effect she had on people, how awkward the poor little woman felt around her.

Belva did take Pat in her arms, and she held her for a moment. "Is Will doing any better?" she asked. "We just came by to ask about him."

"Sit down," Pat said, motioning toward the couch. It was covered with a faded Indian blanket that looked out of place in the drab little room. There was a big rag rug in the center of the hardwood floor, but it was worn to shreds, and the floor hadn't been varnished for years, the shine holding out only around the edges.

Pat sat on a chair that was covered with another blanket. "I don't think Will's any better," she said. "He always says he is, but I watch him when he doesn't know I'm around, and sometimes he has to hunch over with his hands on his knees and just hold on for a while. I think he's hurting in his kidneys, but he won't say so."

"Has he been to the doctor?" Leah asked.

"No. He says this is going to pass away, and that all Doc Putnam can do is put him on bed rest—which he doesn't have time for. But I think, more than anything, he's too ashamed that we have no money to pay the bill."

"Let me tell you something about men," Leah said. "They're all little boys trying to act like grown-ups. And their idea of being grown-up is to show how tough they are."

Pat smiled. "That's about right," she said. "But Will's kept us going, no matter what. I think he's afraid if he spends a day in bed, he won't be able to get back up. It's a hard thing to watch." Pat's eyes went shut for a moment, the lids blue and papery. Leah suddenly felt stupid about what she had said about men being boys. These two were doing everything they could to keep their heads above water.

"Honey, how are *you* holding up?" Belva asked. "You look pale as a ghost."

Pat was wearing a gray apron that might have been white once, and her face seemed almost the same color. "Oh, I don't know," she said. "I'm doing my best, but I'll be glad when the weather cools a little and the kids are back in school. They wear me out some days. I sent 'em all out-side a little while ago. I told 'em, I didn't care how hot it was, they weren't going to be in here under my feet all day. They didn't like it much either, but that's how I've been lately—grouchy as an old bear. I don't think my mother ever once talked to me the way I do to my kids. I hate to imagine what they think of me." Tears filled her eyes.

"You're just forgetting, honey," Belva said. "There never was a mother who didn't get out of patience with her kids once in a while."

"Will tells me I ought to keep them working more, but sometimes it's just easier to do things myself—and not have to fuss with them. Kids nowadays don't think they should have to do as many chores as we did."

Belva chuckled. "I'll tell you what I think. Every generation thinks the one behind it isn't amounting to much—and doesn't work as hard as the one before. I used to say the same thing about my kids, and they're all quite a bit older than you now."

"I know. That's probably right."

"Everything's magnified right now," Belva said. "It's hot, and Will's not feeling well, and we aren't getting any rain—and you're tired right to the bone. When the heat lets up, I have a feeling you and Will will both start feeling better."

"I just want to send the kids off to school. Me and little Billy do all right when it's just the two of us around here. It's having all five in here together that bothers me."

Leah thought she had heard enough. It was hot for everyone, and every mom got tired of her kids sometimes, but she wasn't sure it did a lot of good to sit around and talk about it. Belva could chat like this for two hours, and maybe Leah should do that too, but there was another woman they wanted to visit that afternoon. So Leah said, "Pat, is there anything we can do for you?"

The question sounded too abrupt, too businesslike, and Leah saw the effect on Pat. She sat up straight and said, "We're fine, Leah. We'll get by all right. I'm sorry to complain so much."

"Now, tell me the truth," Leah caught herself saying, even though it sounded impatient. "We could get some men out here to help on the farm if Will is falling behind on things."

"No. He wouldn't like that. We're okay. We're not going to have as much from our garden to put up this year, so things might get awful lean this winter, but who is there around here who won't be in the same situation?"

"Well, I know, but be sure to let us know if Will gets down and does need some help with this second cut of hay—if we get one. And if you do run low on food this winter, let us know. Don't go hungry. We can keep you in flour and potatoes—things like that."

"Thanks. That's good of you to offer."

She was sitting up straighter now, maybe a little offended, but certainly showing some steel in her back. Leah thought that might be good, but she could also see what she had done to the woman—challenged her, in so many words, to buckle down and make the best of things. Leah wished she had used a different tone of voice. The bishop had told her to show the women how to get by—to mend and garden and bottle things for the winter—but little Pat had been doing all those things all her life. Leah had no idea what she could offer the woman—except food, if it came to that.

"Honey," Belva said, "you're scared, aren't you?"

"Sure I am. I don't know what's wrong with Will. For all I know, it might be something serious. But I guess a woman has to get by, even when something happens to her husband." She looked at Leah. "I guess she just has to face what comes." Her face was losing its firmness again, her lips and chin beginning to shake. She put her hand to her mouth, though, and stopped herself.

Belva usually didn't move quickly, but she did now—crossed the room in a second, it seemed, and pulled Pat up into her arms. "Oh, Patty, it's going to be all right. Sickness comes, but it goes. And these hard times can't last forever. One of these days you'll be traveling down to the temple to see your kids get married, and you'll be doting over your grandkids, thinking they're a miracle—just perfect, even coming from those ornery kids you've got under your feet right now."

"I shouldn't say those things. I—"

"No. It's all right. It's just the way life goes. We all pass through good times and bad times, and it comes out all right in the end. One day you'll be old like me, and you'll look back and think how good it's all been, even the worst times."

"But I watch Will every day out there in that sun, working himself into the grave, and he's only just turned forty-five. I don't know what I'll do if I lose him." She finally let go. She sobbed against Belva's plump shoulder.

"It won't happen, Patty. I know it won't. He's too strong to die. He'll fight his way through this, and you'll make it through this winter. Maybe next year we'll get more rain. It's just that way with farming. Some years it rains and some years it doesn't, but you look back at it all, and there's no better life than you and Will have out here."

"I know. It's what I've said myself."

"You've got sweet kids, too. Every one of them is just as pretty as a little picture, just like you, and they're nice as can be. I've watched how polite they are at church, and how they sit there so quiet in opening exercises at Sunday School. It's all going to be all right. You just trust me on that."

"Oh, I know. We'll come out all right. We always do, somehow."

Leah finally stood up and approached the two. But she didn't know what to say or what to do.

"We love you, sweetie," Belva said. "We pray for you all the time.

And we pray for Will. You're a good, righteous family, and God knows that. The Lord always takes care of his children."

Leah felt like an intruder, standing behind the two, about twice as tall as Pat, constructed of too much bone and muscle, a head too filled with reason. She wanted to be able to do this—give Pat what she needed—but she found little sense in most of what Belva was saying, even if it was what Pat needed to hear. Leah actually wanted to slip out and wait at the car, but instead, she said, "I'm sure things *will* work out. And you be sure to let us know what we can do."

Pat stepped away from Belva immediately. "Thank you," she said. "And if I can help any of the sisters in the ward who have it worse than we do, I want to do that."

"All right. Good. That's the spirit we all have to have."

Everything had become awkward again, but Belva gave Pat another hug, and then Pat walked with them to the door. She thanked Leah for having come by. "I'll bet you could fry an egg on that old car out there," Leah said. "I hate to get back in the thing."

"I'm sorry you had to drive clear out here. Don't do it again. I'll let you know at church how things are going for us. And I'm sure we'll be fine."

"I didn't mean it that way," Leah said. "I was just . . . I don't know. Just talking. My mouth takes off before I give it permission about half the time."

Pat smiled a little—and then she shook Leah's hand again. Leah knew it was time to give the woman a hug, but she still didn't do it.

It wasn't until Belva and Leah were sitting in the car—which was as hot as Leah had predicted—that she said, "I'm sorry, Belva. Maybe you should make these visits yourself and just report back to me what you find out."

"Why do you say that?"

"Because I don't know how to do this."

"That's not true at all. You're a great strength to the women of this ward."

"Belva, don't do that. Don't try to invent me. You know what I ought to be and you get that confused with what I am."

"I don't think so. Not at all."

Leah backed away from the house and turned the car back up the lane to the main road—another dirt road. Leah was sick of red dirt, sick of it blowing everywhere, collecting in her house, clogging up her throat. By afternoon, her head ached every day. The sun beat down in the afternoon so hot that it pulled the strength out of her. And always she wondered the same thing: What in the world did God have in mind, just letting things go on the way they were going? People needed him, had for a long time now, and no matter what Belva said, he didn't seem to care.

Belva was talking, telling her that she felt good about the visit. Pat was strong and she would be all right. Leah loved this dear old lady, but her self-assuredness was annoying at times. Leah didn't say that, though; she just drove to their next visit, back in town. Grace Wallace had her own worries. Her husband, Henry, had been laid off his job over at the Gilsonite mines. Since then he'd been doing day labor when he could find it, and so had their older son, Hank. The two were pulling in a dollar or two here and there, but without food from the church, they would have been in big trouble these last couple of months.

Grace had told Leah the week before that Henry's pride was hurt by his having to take handouts. She said that on days he couldn't find work, he was almost beside himself trying to kill the time. He'd walk over to the Whitehorse Café once in a while to talk to some of the older men who liked to sit there and drink a little coffee—the ones who didn't worry much about the Word of Wisdom—just to pass the time. Henry wasn't above having a cup himself, but he didn't think he ought to be spending a nickel for something like that, and when the other men had offered to pay for him, it had embarrassed him so badly that he'd stopped going. So now he put some time into the garden early each day, and then checked on some of the places he'd worked before: mostly farms, where they sometimes needed an extra hand. But until the next cutting of hay started, there wasn't much to do, and with the drought, maybe there wouldn't be anything to cut.

When Leah and Belva knocked on the door, Henry opened it, invited them in, and called for his wife. But then he disappeared out the kitchen door and into the backyard. Leah knew exactly why. He was like a lot of men. He wouldn't stop Grace from saying they needed food, but he didn't want to ask himself—or be there to hear his wife do it. Grace did admit what they needed, and Leah wrote it down and was about to leave, but Belva took hold of Grace, the same as she had Pat, and she told her, "Listen, Grace, this will pass. I promise you it will. I hear talk every day that after this election, whoever wins is going to have to do something to make things pick up again. I have a feeling we only have one more rough winter—and don't worry, we'll stand by you until Henry gets back to work."

"I'm just so ashamed to ask for help," Grace said. She was a thick-waisted woman with fleshy arms and a strong, almost masculine face, but she was slumped now, like she was carrying a weight on her back. "We've always paid our tithing—we do even now. Up until this year, we paid something for budget, too, and I always paid my dues to Relief Society. I can't tell you how hard it is to be the ones taking, not giving."

"Well, now, think about that," Belva said. "If there never was anyone in need, how would we *learn* to give? You'll do the same for someone else when the day comes that you can."

"We sure will. I don't want you to think we're not thankful."

"I know you are. And I know something else. You keep paying your tithing and the Lord is going to open up the windows of heaven and bless you beyond anything you can imagine. You remember when times get better that I told you that, because I know it's going to happen."

"Well, thank you. I think you're right."

Grace glanced toward Leah, as though she thought maybe she would hear something else to cheer her. But Leah said, "I'd be careful about accepting too many promises from Belva. She's so old, she could kick the bucket any day now, and then she won't be around to answer for what she's promised."

It was a joke, of course, and Grace tried to smile, but Belva was the only person who actually laughed. "That Leah, she's something, isn't she?" Belva said. "I don't know anyone who makes me laugh so often. And she's right about me. I could slip away tonight in my sleep. But if I do, I'll talk to the Lord and tell him to make good on my promises— because I don't want you to be mad at me."

Grace did laugh a little this time, and Leah made her way to the door, even though Belva was still finding things to say. It was out in the car that Leah finally expressed what she'd held back after the first visit. "Belva, you're a big help to these women, but don't you think we have to be just a little careful about what we promise? Sometimes things go bad and stay bad—at least for a long time. It might not be the best thing to tell people that their troubles are almost over."

"But they need hope, Leah. Hope's what it takes to keep going. I've learned that lots of times in my life."

Leah had cranked the old engine and it had caught, but it was still sounding sick as she fiddled with the throttle—and then it died. She reset the lever on the steering wheel, then got out and cranked again. The engine coughed, quit, and then started on the next try. This time she got back in and managed to get the choke set right. She waited, though, for the sound to smooth out a little. "But here's what I'm trying to say, Belva," she said, glancing over. "You told Pat that her husband won't die, and you don't know that."

"I think I do, Leah. I really think I do."

"But how can you? People die young sometimes. You don't know what he might have going on inside him. Maybe something *is* wrong with his kidneys. Maybe he has cancer."

"My husband got *very* sick once when he wasn't much older than Will, and the doctor said he might not make it. But he did. The bishop gave him a blessing and he pulled through. He lived almost thirty years after that."

Leah knew she ought to let it drop. Belva never seemed to see the holes in her reasoning, and maybe it was just as well that she didn't. But some of these promises were going too far. "Your husband lived, Belva, but mine died. He was a healthy young man one minute, and a horse— one that knew him well—kicked him. It was the last thing in the world you'd ever think would happen. Two days later the doctor was calling the undertaker for me—because I was too numb and confused to make the call myself."

"I know. I was just thinking about that—after I said what I did. But there are reasons for things. Look what you've learned, and what you can do now with all you've experienced. You wouldn't be able to serve so well now if you hadn't been taught some hard lessons."

Leah took a breath, decided to quit, but then tried one more time anyway. "Maybe that's what Pat's going to have to go through, Belva— the same thing I did. If we tell her that Will won't die, and then he does, how's she going to deal with everything?"

"Well, you just deal with it when you have to. That's what we do in life."

"I know. But you're saying he won't die, and then you're saying, if he does, Pat will have to deal with it. You can't have it both ways."

"Sure you can. Life's just full of contradictions."

"But . . ."

"The thing is, he isn't going to die. That's what we have to keep in mind. And that's what Pat has to know. She just needed someone to help her through her worries."

Leah shifted the old car into gear. As it started to roll, she took a long breath of dusty, hot air. She tried to stop herself again, but her mouth was saying, "So you *know* he's not going to die?"

"Well, no. He's going to die someday. But it won't be over this thing he's dealing with right now."

"You *know* that?"

"Oh, Leah. No one ever knows anything for sure. But what I know as much as a person *can* know is that he's going to get better."

Leah turned onto Main Street and drove past the bishop's garage. She felt like stopping in right then and there and saying, "Bishop, make Belva the president. She knows things and I don't," but the thought made her smile, and then she began to chuckle.

"What are you laughing about?" Belva asked, and she was laughing too—for no reason.

"Oh, Belva, I do love you," she said. "And you know what? I don't say that to anyone. I've tried, and I can't do it."

"I know you love me. I know it whether you say it or not. But I'm glad you said it. It makes you feel good, doesn't it?"

"Actually, it makes me feel stupid, if you want to know the truth."

"Well, I know that feeling. I feel stupid about half the time." Leah laughed, and then Belva did again, probably for different reasons. But Belva added, "I certainly hope you tell your kids that you love them."

Leah didn't laugh about that.

Chapter Eight

IN EARLY SEPTEMBER Leah finally cut her second crop of hay, but there wasn't much to cut. The summer had remained dry and the alfalfa was sparse. This would be one more year to survive and then, as usual, to hope for better conditions next year. Franklin Roosevelt was becoming more specific about what he intended to do to get the country back to work, and Leah was finding that she liked the man. It was easy to believe that he really would make a better effort than Hoover. It was almost the only thing to create a little optimism these days, and she found that more and more people were feeling the same way.

Leah was still worried about the state of her Relief Society, but she wasn't sure what to do. It wasn't just that some of the women wouldn't attend; there was a loss of spirit that Leah could feel in the meetings. At work and business meeting Belva had taught the women some of the skills that they needed—ways to cut expenses and make do with fewer resources—and they had quilted the two quilt tops that had already been pieced, but little more had been done. Leah had finally told the women there wouldn't be a bazaar that year, since no one could afford to donate material and she didn't think anyone was in a position to buy the items they might make. No one disagreed with her, but she had seen in their faces that she had taken something away from them.

Still, Leah didn't know what else she could do. She tried to concentrate on the problems she saw in front of her. She was helping the bishop keep a lot of families going when their crops were so meager and so many were laid off their jobs.

Leah also worked hard to salvage what she could from her own land. Wade helped her with the hay, worked hard, and enjoyed his days on the farm. Leah liked the way he was taking responsibility, working well with the horses, milking all the cows, showing that he was now as strong as she was, maybe stronger. He loved to tease her about the way he could outwork her, wear her down—and the truth was, she was finding that he could do it. What worried her, however, was that he never said anything about going to college. One afternoon, when they were finishing up after a long day of work, she told him, "I hate to work this hard and then, at the end of the season, figure I'm lucky to get enough out of our turkeys and what grain we can sell just to pay the taxes. There's just no way for a farmer to come out ahead."

This time of year, she let the turkeys free range across their property, eating from the fields, but she would soon have to fatten them as much as she could and hope she could get a decent price out of them.

"I figure this can't go on forever," Wade told her. "The government can't let all the farms in the country go broke. People have to eat."

"But we've been saying that for a long time. What I look forward to is the day when you've gotten your education and you can take a job as an engineer or something like that—work that pays you what you're worth, and doesn't work you to death."

Wade was lifting a collar off old Betty's head. He patted the horse, rubbed her lathered neck, and told her what a good job she'd done, but he didn't reply to his mom.

Leah had things she needed to do, but she wanted to talk to him for a few minutes. "Wade, what do you think you do want to study when you get to college? Have you thought any more about that?"

"Not really."

"Maybe you ought to get a degree in business, work your way up in a company for a while, and then get enough ahead to open some kind of business of your own."

Wade laughed. He was carrying the collar over to hang in their little equipment shed, a lean-to on the back of their house. He turned back. "You've always told me how cocky all the people are who run their own stores in town. What do you want—*me* to be like that?"

"No. But I want you to make a good living so you can give your kids what they need. I don't want my grandkids to go without things, the way you and Rae have."

"Yeah, I guess. But I don't want my kids to think they're better than other people, either."

Leah was wearing her old straw hat with the wide brim. She pulled it off and wiped her forehead with the palm of her hand. She wondered when the heat was ever going to let up. "You don't have to be like that— even if you do well—and your kids don't either."

"Maybe not. But that's how rich kids seem to turn out." He walked on into the shed, but when he came out, he added, "Tommy Evans thinks he's the cock of the walk, just because he lives in a little nicer house than most of us." Wade pulled off his battered straw hat and ruffled his hair with his fingers, shaking loose bits of hay that twirled into the shafts of light that were angling across the roof of the shed.

"But the Evanses are coming down a few rungs these days. Clark is barely getting by. They could end up losing that house. He told me so himself."

Wade set his hat back on his head. "Well," he said, "you wouldn't know they were having a hard time if you talked to Tommy. He still thinks he's the king of the school. He'll be giving me a hard time again this fall."

"Is it still this business about you not playing ball?"

"Sure. According to him, I'm letting the whole school down. But that's stupid, if you ask me. There's more important things in this world than playing sports."

"But you know what? You ought to go out for some of the teams. I hate to see you working all the time. I can get by if you want to play football this fall."

"Oh, sure you can." He laughed. "You can just run this place all by yourself and serve as Relief Society president at the same time. There's no problem there."

Wade crossed back to Barb and released the leather lines from her harness. "We're going to let you rest tomorrow," he told the horse, patting her on the neck. "You just take it easy for a little while."

There was something really lovely about Wade's attitude, the way he treated the animals and his willingness to put in such hard days, but she worried about him giving up all the fun of high school, always working. "I could quit," she said. "I could tell the bishop it isn't working out for me to serve as president. The truth is, Belva and Marj would be better off without me anyway."

"Don't do that, Mom. This is the best thing you've ever done, working in the Relief Society."

"Do you really think so?"

"I do. You seem . . . a little different. You don't talk the way you used to."

"Hey, I've got my foot in my mouth half the time, the same as I've always had. I don't think I'm any different."

Wade was unhooking the harness, but he turned and looked at Leah. "It seems like you're not so mad at everyone as you used to be."

Actually, Leah knew that; she'd felt the change too. "You're the one talking about people you don't like, Wade. Tommy Evans must have at least a little of his dad in him. And if he does, he couldn't be too bad of a boy."

Wade was walking to the shed now, carrying the harness, but he glanced back, as though he were surprised by what she had said. Leah was embarrassed. She thought Clark was a nice fellow; that was all she had meant.

"I didn't say that *I've* changed," Wade said. "I said that you have."

"Well, if you think it's a good change, maybe you should stop being so hard on the town kids. I'll bet you'd like some of them if you got to know them better."

"See. You've changed your tune. That's not what you've been telling me all my life."

"I know. But I've always said too much. I was mostly talking about people I didn't even know."

Wade walked on into the shed. When he came out, he said, "There's a car coming down our lane."

Leah turned to look. Her breath caught when she saw that it was a Model A. "Uh-oh," she said. "That looks like the bishop's car." She walked around the house and waited for the car to stop. Wade followed and stepped up next to her. By then Leah could see that it *was* the bishop. As he got out of the car, she saw in his face exactly what she feared: Something had happened.

"What is it this time?" she asked.

He walked toward her and pulled his hat off. "Do you think this heat is ever going to let up?" he asked.

Leah didn't answer. She just waited.

"It's young Millie Wilson. Her baby died."

"Died? What happened?"

"I guess it's that crib death, or whatever they call it. Millie went in to check on her this morning and the poor little thing was cold as ice.

She died in the night—just for no reason. She'd had some sniffles, but she wasn't sick."

"How's Millie doing?"

"She's going all to pieces. It's her first baby, just eight months old, and she keeps saying that it's all her fault. She thinks she should have checked on her in the night."

"But the baby's been sleeping through the night lately. I talked to Millie at church last week, and she told me that herself."

"I know. But you know how you'd feel—just finding her like that."

Leah nodded. She thought she did know.

Bishop Bowen had that look on his face she had seen a time or two before: a kind of boyish, scared look, as though he suspected he was in over his head with the job he'd been called to do. "I tried to call you, but you didn't answer. I guess you've been outside all day."

"Yeah. Hauling hay."

"Do you think you can get away long enough to drive into town and spend a little time with her?"

"Sure." Leah glanced to see the sun hanging pretty low over the western mountains. She had wanted to sit down for a little while this evening. She really needed to. But she had to gather her strength now. This would be a hard night.

She looked at Wade. "Can you and Rae fix yourselves something for supper?" she asked.

"Sure." Leah heard more emotion in his voice than she expected. Wade was looking at the bishop. "I took a math class from Mr. Wilson last year. He sure was proud of that baby of theirs."

Leah saw something that surprised her. Wade had tucked his hands into his pockets, and he ducked his head now, but just as he did, she saw tears glistening in his eyes. It was more than she had done. She reached her arm around his shoulders and said, "I don't know how long I'll be there. I might have to stay the night."

"That's all right," Wade said, and stepped away from her. She knew he was embarrassed by his reaction and didn't want her to notice it.

"I have to clean up," Leah told the bishop, "and then I'll drive in."

"All right. Her mother won't be here until tomorrow. That's what Millie needs right now—a mother to put her arms around her."

The words sounded like advice, as though the bishop were saying that she shouldn't be too hard on Millie. Leah felt bad that he thought that was necessary.

Leah didn't have time to take a bath, as she needed to do, but she undressed and washed, and then she put on her tan dress. In her car, on the way into town, Leah tried to think what she could do or say, but she knew there was nothing, really. She just needed to be there.

Leah had known Millie since she was a little girl; she wasn't much more than one now, probably still not twenty. She had gotten married right out of high school, two years back, to a new young teacher who had come to town.

Leah knew Millie's mother and father: Bud and Louise Boyd. They had given up on their farm the year before and moved to Price, where Bud had taken a job in the mines. Since then, he'd been laid off, according to Millie, and that had been her biggest worry. Now she had this to face. Millie was a red-haired little thing, still skinny as a stick even after the baby, and not really very pretty. But she thought Roy was the best man who ever lived, and she had told Leah, not three weeks back, that she didn't know how a girl could be any happier, even though teaching school didn't pay much and the two of them had done nothing but scrimp since they'd gotten married.

Millie would grow up now. Leah couldn't teach her how to do that, but life would. Life always did.

Sometimes Leah wondered whether all the troubles in town had only started in the last few months, but the bishop had told her, "I guess we've had a few more things come up just lately, but it seems like there's always something going wrong. Pretty much every family has its problems. I don't think I knew that until I was called to be the bishop." And that was what Leah was finding. She'd been out there on the farm, making do, and she hadn't had any idea what so many people had to deal with. The week before, she'd found out that Fran Hopkins had cancer in her breast. She was only fifty-five, and the doctor she'd gone to see in Salt Lake had told her she'd never hold out another year. Garfield Mackie had cancer too. It had started in his prostate and then spread all through him. He was a lot older than Fran, it was true, but he was so full of pain he couldn't stand to have Edith, his wife, even wash him. Phyllis Walker had had a baby boy the year before, and he had seemed just fine at first, but it was turning out that the little guy wasn't right. He couldn't crawl yet, and his eyes wouldn't focus on anyone. Phyllis was just heartsick to think he might be retarded. She'd had a terrible time giving birth to him; she wondered if maybe his brain had been damaged.

A lot of people were doing okay. It wasn't that. It was just that, if you talked to a woman long enough, or even a man, you'd find out they had a child who had gotten into some trouble or a daughter who had married out of the Church and maybe the fellow wasn't treating her right. Or she'd married *in* the Church, and the same thing was going on. The bishop had told Leah that too many men were worried to death, and they were losing their tempers and beating their kids or their wives. Leah knew some of the women who were putting up with it, trying to make the best of things. The stake president had cut one man off from the Church for acting that way, and still, his wife hadn't left him.

Some nights Leah asked the Lord why things couldn't ease up a little. Maybe it was the Depression, and maybe it was just life, but it seemed as though people carried around more burdens with them than ought to be necessary. Life was supposed to be a test, but did babies have to die for no reason? And why did girls, just barely grown themselves, have to go through something like that?

Leah knocked softly on the door when she arrived, but she told herself she couldn't indulge Millie *too* much. The girl had to recognize that her life wasn't over because of this. Roy came to the door, looking pale and tired. "How's she doing?" Leah asked.

"Not very well. She's stopped screaming, but she won't get off her bed. She just cries and cries. I don't think she's stopped for more than a few minutes all day."

"Well, it's hard. But we need to get her thinking about the future. You two have a lot of good things ahead of you."

"That's what I told her. I keep saying, 'We'll have Catherine Ann in the next life. We'll still have a chance to raise her.'" But the words seemed desperate more than sure. Roy was a little man with light, thin hair, already receding a little, and a bit of fuzz on his upper lip that he seemed to think was a mustache. He was almost colorless, at best, but now he was white and thin, as though he'd lost weight since that morning.

"Will she come out of the bedroom, or do you think I ought to go in there to talk to her?"

"I don't know. She said she didn't want to see *anyone.*"

"Well . . . I'll go in. Maybe she won't mind. Has she eaten anything?"

"I made some soup for her, and she had a spoonful or two, but that's about all."

Leah heard the fear in Roy's voice. She knew what he was thinking: *Millie won't ever be herself again.* "Are *you* doing all right?" she asked.

She saw his face change. She knew he had been trying to keep Millie together all day, and he hadn't given in to his own grief. But now his eyes brimmed over, and she saw him begin to shake. He was only about twenty-two himself. He'd gone two years to the Weber Academy, in Ogden, and had gotten his teaching degree, but he was probably only four years out of high school. "I loved that little girl so much," he said, and suddenly his knees went out from under him. He caught himself before he sank all the way down, but he stepped back and dropped onto the couch, covered up his face, and sobbed.

Leah had no idea what to do. She couldn't take him into her arms; he wouldn't want that. And there was nothing to say. He'd said it all, all day. So she only bent and touched his shoulder. "It's okay, Roy. You need to cry. I'll see what I can say to Millie."

"I'm sorry. I'm sorry," he was saying. He stood up, tried to get his shoulders back. All Leah could think was that the world asked too much of men—that they stop crying as little boys, that they "buck up" no matter what they had to face. "She's in there." Roy pointed to a door on the side of the little front room. The whole house wasn't more than four rooms.

So Leah opened the door softly and stepped inside. But what she saw wasn't what she expected. Millie was curled up, her knees almost to her chin, and she was asleep. Leah slipped over and sat down in a chair that Roy had apparently kept by the bed all day. Millie had never dressed, was still wearing the cotton nightgown she had apparently had on when she'd found her baby.

Leah watched her, breathing softly, looking the way Rae used to look when she was three or four, curled up the same way. And then she realized. If she had lost Rae as a baby—found her cold in bed—it might have been more than she could have taken. And Leah had been much older. The thought took the air out of her. She sat down by Millie, trying not to make a sound, and decided not to tell Millie anything when she finally woke up—just to hold her, if that was what she needed.

So Leah waited and let Millie sleep. After twenty minutes or so, Roy peeked in. Leah got up and walked to the door. "Let's let her sleep," she whispered. "I'll sit with her. You get some sleep too, I guess on the couch."

"I don't need to sleep, not yet."

"All right, then. But you take some time for yourself, and let me sit with Millie. She'll wake up sometime, and her mother won't be here yet. I'll do what I can." She stepped away, but then turned back. "Do you have a blanket I can put over her?"

"No. Just what's under her, on the bed. Except . . . the quilt. Catherine Ann's little quilt."

"That'll be good. Let's put that over her."

Roy left and came back with the quilt, which he placed over his young wife. Millie squirmed for just a moment and then pulled the quilt close around her face and settled into sleep again.

Roy looked at Leah; he seemed a bit relieved. He left, and Leah sat down again. She watched Millie, tried to sleep a little herself, and once, late in the night, told Millie, "It's all right, honey. I'll sit here with you, but you sleep some more."

Millie looked wide-eyed in the light of the small lamp Leah had turned on. She seemed confused for a moment, and then, obviously, remembered. "What time is it?" she asked.

"I don't know. One or two—something like that."

"I can't sleep anymore."

"Just rest, then."

"Leah, my baby's gone," she said, her voice tiny as a baby chick's.

"I know. But rest. Don't think tonight. God gives us sleep to heal us." Leah slipped to her knees and ran her hand over Millie's forehead and hair, then touched her cheek with the back of her fingers.

Millie looked scared, lost. But she didn't cry. She curled up again, pulled the little quilt tight around her, and in only a few seconds was breathing deeply. Leah sat in the chair, thought about Rae and Wade, thought about what she needed to say to them, thought about what she knew tonight that she didn't always remember.

Leah also wondered about her dream again—the one she had had after the bishop had first called her as president. Maybe it was little Millie she had seen that night—the face she couldn't remember. But she had wondered, too, if it hadn't been Mary Dibble. She didn't want to think like Belva, but it seemed to her that she had been called to help someone, that God had needed her for that. Maybe this was the time when she could do something to justify the bishop's faith in her.

Leah dozed at times, but she never left the chair. When she noticed the first hint of light in the window, she guessed that it must be after five o'clock. She felt numb and her body ached. She stretched her arms but tried to keep her silence. Then she heard a whisper. "Leah, we have to figure everything out."

"All right. You mean about the funeral?"

"I guess."

"We'll do that."

"Roy says we'll have more children, and we'll have Catherine Ann again after the resurrection."

"That's right, honey."

"I can't just cry and cry. I have to think about Roy. I scared him bad, the way I acted yesterday."

"It's okay. You needed to cry. And you'll cry a lot more. But that's all right."

Millie's face was a faded yellow in the light of the lamp. Her eyes were closed. "But I need to make him some breakfast. Where is he?"

"I heard him in the kitchen just now. I think he's already fixing something."

"That's right. That's what he would do. But *I* need to take care of *him*. He's sad too. He loved her so much, Leah. He's the best daddy you ever saw."

Millie was getting up. Tears were coming again, but she was looking about, trying to think what she needed to do. "Go and check on him," she said to Leah. "I'll get dressed."

"Okay. I'll tell him you're doing better."

"Yes. Tell him that. He's so worried about me. I could see that yesterday, but I couldn't stop crying."

"It's all right. I'll tell him you're getting up. That'll make him feel better."

"Tell him not to make breakfast. I want to do it."

"Okay."

So Leah went out to the kitchen, still groggy and yet feeling blessed. Changed. She'd seen what God could do, what Millie could do.

Roy told her, after he'd heard what Millie had said, "You go home, Leah. We'll be all right. Thanks for staying over. Millie's mom will be here before the day's over."

"She wants to talk about the funeral," Leah said.

"I talked that over with the bishop. He had some ideas. Millie and I can figure out the rest."

"We'll have meals brought in," Leah told him, "and we'll help out with any family members who'll be coming."

"I know. It's always the Relief Society that keeps people going when something like this happens."

The words struck Leah. Maybe she had never known what the Relief Society was, or even the Church. When Wayne had died, the sisters had come, had helped, but she had thought it was what they had been instructed to do. She hadn't known it was this—this closeness. This holy night she had just experienced.

Leah patted Roy on the shoulder, and then she went out to her car. She drove home and got Rae and Wade up. Rae was grouchy and mad that it wasn't even time yet—twenty minutes before she usually got up. Wade told Rae, "Quit your complaining. I get up earlier than this every morning."

"That's because you're so *wonderful*," Rae said. "You'll be taken up into heaven any day now, translated before our very eyes."

"Just be quiet. Okay?" Wade said.

Leah was sitting at the kitchen table, waiting. She didn't say a word, and the two finally seemed to notice that something was different this morning. They sat down at the table with her.

"Wade told you about the Wilson baby, didn't he?" Leah asked Rae.

"Yes. But what happened exactly?"

"She just died. That happens sometimes."

"How are they doing?" Rae asked, and she seemed chastened, maybe by the softness in Leah's voice.

"They'll be okay. They've already worked through some of it."

"Have you been up all night?"

"I slept a little."

And then Rae and Wade waited, seemingly aware that Leah wanted to say something.

"Last night," Leah said, "I was sitting by poor little Millie, and I thought, what would I have done if I had lost one of you when you were babies—or ever—and I thought, I couldn't have borne it. Millie has to get through it, but I'm not sure I could have, especially after I had lost your father."

Rae was staring at Leah, looking more confused than pleased. Wade was nodding, as though he thought he understood.

"I love you two, and I'm afraid I never tell you."

Rae was staring back at Leah, and Leah could see the doubt in her face.

"I feel like I've done a lot of things wrong with you kids," Leah said. "I've complained too much, been way too harsh with you. I've also been way too hard on some of the women in town. I know that now that I'm getting to know them."

"Well, you haven't been too hard on their daughters," Rae said. "They've been colder than ever toward me since you've been Relief Society president."

"I riled things up too much. That's why. I'm sure some of the mothers have said things that have gotten the daughters upset with me—and they take it out on you."

"Well, then, don't tell me to be more *understanding* with them. LuAnn Willis asked me what happened to the bazaar this year. I told her what you told me, but she said, 'Oh, that's too bad. Your mother must feel awful.' She acted like she was being sweet, but she was gloating and both of us knew it."

"Maybe. Maybe not. But we've got to let some of that go—and I've got to mend some fences." She waited, but Rae didn't say anything, and Leah felt as though she'd failed one more time. "Rae, I'm sorry I got you up early. I just wanted a minute or two to tell you that I really do love you. I don't think you know how precious you are to me."

Rae took a long look at Leah. She didn't say whatever she was thinking, but Leah saw no sign of acceptance or of any softness. Rae waited for a time, and then, without saying a word, got up from the table and walked back to her room.

"Thanks, Mom," Wade said. "Don't let Rae bother you too much. Right now, it seems like she doesn't want to be happy."

"I know."

Chapter Nine

LIFE FOR LEAH WAS quieting a little with winter not far off. Morris Burton, a local slaughterer, had come to her farm and helped her kill and dress four of her hogs for the winter, and she had bottled applesauce, green beans, beets, and pickles. She had also stored potatoes, carrots, turnips, and parsnips in her root cellar. She had killed a number of her turkeys and sold them to a fellow who came to the valley every year from Salt Lake. Rae had had to work hard to pluck turkeys and help with all the bottling—and still leave time for Leah to do her Relief Society work. The girl hadn't been excited about the extra burden, but she had done it.

Wade had decided to play football that fall, with Leah's encouragement. But he had worked hard alongside some hired help to cut and thresh wheat, then haul it to the gristmill to have it ground into flour. There had also been corn to harvest and store, and he had taken a few days off from school when the work had been heaviest—which he didn't mind at all. Lots of boys did the same, and even football practice was set aside with so many of the players busy on their farms.

But Leah had enough cash to pay her taxes and water assessment, and even though all the crops had been sparse, she felt she would have enough food for the winter if she were careful. Not holding a bazaar that fall had lightened the load for Leah and the other sisters, but the whole ward had taken notice, and that surprised Leah a little. Some of the sisters had told her, "Let's have it next year anyway. I just think we should." Leah was beginning to think those who said that were right.

Most of the women had become more comfortable with Leah, and some who hadn't come to meetings all summer had finally returned. Still, a handful of town women who were members of the Relief Society weren't coming, and what Leah now knew was that some of them were the ones who could make things happen. They were also the ones who had felt most attacked by Leah's comments in that first meeting of hers—and the ones who probably felt they would lose face by showing up.

Belva told Leah, "You need to bring Nadine Willis back. She's always been such a spark for us—and she used to donate most of the material we used to make quilts."

That was the kind of thing Leah had been learning about Nadine, but she told Belva, "I'm not going to beg her." The truth was, though, Leah knew she had to make another attempt to set things straight. Now that the full program of Relief Society, with weekly meetings, had started up again for the fall, it was probably time to do something.

The presidency was sitting in Belva's kitchen, seated at a little pine table. Belva had built a fire in her woodstove and had stoked it up as soon as Leah had arrived. Leah could feel sweat breaking out on her forehead, and she worried she would soon be sweating under her arms into her tan dress. "Holy cow, Belva," she finally said, "I think you're trying to bake us."

"Oh, my," Belva said. "I'm always so cold this time of year, when the weather turns. I'll crack a window, and that fire will die down in a minute."

"Well, wait a minute. Maybe I'm the only one hot in here. I get these danged hot flashes now. They almost cook me in bed at night." She looked at Marjorie. "Are you as hot as I am?"

Marj laughed. "It is a little warm in here," she said.

"Do you get hot flashes, or are you still too young for that?"

"Well, I . . ."

"Never mind. You don't have to answer. I'm always the one asking what I shouldn't. But I'll tell you, I've been going through the change for a couple of years now, and maybe that's why my kids hate me. One of my milk cows kicked over my bucket the other day and I stood up and punched her square in the ribs. She felt it, too. She gave me a look like she wanted to kill me."

Belva was trying to open the kitchen window, reaching over her sink, but she wasn't having much luck, at least partly because she was laughing so hard. Leah stood up and helped her, but when she turned back to the table, she was surprised to see Marjorie shaking her head and laughing. Betsy was grinning too, with all her little teeth.

"I don't think the president of the Relief Society is supposed to strike innocent animals," Marj said.

"Innocent? There's nothing innocent about Geraldine. That cow lives to torment me. She knows *exactly* what she's up to. She does something like that, and then she puts on her big ol' cow-eyed look, like she's not quite sure what just happened." Leah tried to imitate the look, making her chin droop and staring blankly. "I know that cow's heart. She's evil."

The sisters laughed hard, especially at the face Leah had made, and something occurred to Leah. They liked her. All three of them did. Belva *loved* everyone, but she also *liked* Leah. And Marjorie, who had been so distant in the beginning, clearly enjoyed being around Leah. Betsy was so quiet that it was hard to know what she thought about things, but Leah could see in her eyes that she found Leah fun.

Leah sat down at the table and smiled, not laughing, but just trying to say to them, "I like you too." She soon felt her own embarrassment, though, and she ducked her head. She really did need to be a little more dignified. "Well, anyway," she said, "I tried my best with Nadine that day I visited her, but she put the worst possible interpretation on every-thing I said. You'd think I was trying to steal her silverware or something the way she talked about me coming into her house *uninvited*."

Leah watched Marjorie. She knew this was a sticky subject with her. But Marj spoke gently when she said, "Leah, I think Nadine *has* been pretty hard on you—and I know she's made comments to other women in town. That has probably kept this little feud going. The women who aren't coming don't know you very well, really, and I keep telling them your heart's in the right place. But you know what? You *were* hard on them at that first meeting—at least the way they interpreted what you said—and I don't think you know *them* well enough, either."

"I've gone by to see some of them, and they won't give me a chance to mend fences. They're cold as ice. Doris and June were at least polite, but Glenda and Suzanne wouldn't even let me through the door. Suzanne had a hundred excuses about how busy she was."

"She is busy, Leah. She does more volunteer work in this town than anyone I know."

"And more chit-chatting and putting on fancy little teas."

Leah saw Marjorie react, saw her stiffen. "There's really not much of that going on anymore, Leah. Suzanne keeps the library going almost by herself. If she quit going down there, we'd have to close the place, and the kids in town need a library. We all do."

Leah could hear the hint of impatience in Marjorie's voice—the defensiveness. And she knew why. She remembered now what Suzanne had told her that day she'd called on her—that she was on her way to the library and would be there most days that week. Leah had suspected her of exaggerating, but apparently, she hadn't been.

Leah sat back and took a breath. The air from the window was blow-ing on the back of her neck, a little too cold, but she was still thankful for it. "I don't know what to do, Marj," she said. "I could make another round of visits, but I'd probably make things worse. Evelyn told me she was busy working for the Republican party, and I told her she was doing the devil's work. I was just joking with her, but her face wrinkled up like a dried apple. If I call on the sisters often enough, I'll drive them *all* away."

"You can't tell us that anymore," Belva said. "We've seen how much you've helped some of the families in the ward."

"I think you should go see Nadine again," Marjorie said. "But telephone her first, so she knows you're coming. And then ask her to help you. She could change a lot of women's minds, if you could change hers."

"That's just exactly what I've been thinking," Belva said.

"I know. I've thought about it, too," Leah said. "But last time I told her to get off her big rear end. By now, she might think I was right about getting out of bed. But I doubt she's forgotten the 'big' part—even if I was right about that, too."

Belva was giggling again. "It's one thing," she said, "to call a spade a spade, but I think you went a little too far that time."

"No, I didn't. I should have said *huge*."

Belva ducked her head, obviously *sure* that Leah had gone too far, and Marjorie said, "Leah, that isn't funny. It's that kind of thing you have to stop if you want the sisters to accept you. You've never had to worry about your weight so you—"

"Because I work."

Marjorie stopped and stared at Leah.

This time Leah knew she had crossed a line. She took a breath, and then said in a softer voice, "I'm sorry. But whenever I say anything really awful, just remember, that's the *real* me speaking. It's when I seem like a nice person that I'm playacting."

"No," Belva said. "It's the other way around."

"I wish," Leah said, and she meant it. She had described herself that way mostly to be clever, but her own words had struck her hard. She knew she *could* be nice, but she wasn't very often—and she needed to be. "I'll go see Nadine," she said, "but I think someone ought to go with me."

"Take Marjorie," Belva said. "She knows Nadine best, and if all three of us go, she might feel like we're ganging up on her."

"Okay. That sounds good." Leah could see out the kitchen window. Only a few yellow leaves were still hanging onto the old cottonwood tree out front. She hated to think about winter coming on and things getting worse for a lot of families. She had to swallow some pride and do what was necessary to get the sisters working together. "Will you go with me, Marj? I promise not to say anything about Nadine's . . . anatomy."

Marjorie smiled just a little. "And I won't say anything about you looking like a *beanpole.*"

Leah was taken aback. Marjorie had taken some teasing from Leah, but she had never returned any of her little insults. Leah liked that Marj felt able to do it, finally. "A *fireman's* pole. That's what I am," she said. "I'm the ugliest thing in this town. I don't have any padding at all on my fanny. I'm sitting on bones." She squirmed on the wooden chair, exaggerating her discomfort. Belva giggled again.

Two days later Leah and Marjorie were sitting in Nadine's living room, or receiving room, or whatever it was called. It crossed Leah's mind that the woman hadn't started selling anything off yet. "Nadine," she was saying, "I think we got off to a bad start when I came over here last time. I shouldn't have walked right in like that, but I'd heard you weren't feeling well, and . . . I don't know . . . I wasn't quite sure what a Relief Society president was supposed to do. I guess I still don't know."

Marjorie was quick to say, "Nadine, I saw Alice this week. She told me to say hello."

Nadine nodded. Leah realized she was supposed to beat around the bush for a while—since that's what Marjorie wanted to do—but she never had been good at that, and she had no idea what to say. She certainly didn't know anyone who wanted her to tell Nadine hello.

"I don't see people much anymore—unless they come into the store," Nadine said. "I practically spend my life down there."

This was said to Marjorie, but Leah knew it was meant for her— Nadine's way of saying, "You told me I should go to work, and that's just what I've done."

"Have things picked up at all, down at the store?" Leah asked, but that seemed to be the wrong thing to ask, too. Marjorie changed the subject before Nadine could answer. So Leah let the two of them talk. She didn't know these games.

But Nadine had obviously kept the question in mind, and after a time, she said, "No, Leah, the store isn't doing any better, but at least it's no worse. What I feel bad about is that we've had to lay almost everyone off. Jim and I work long hours—and we can stand that—but we used to feed a few families in this town, and now we don't. I'm sure you know Irvin Watts, who used to work for us. It breaks my heart every time we see him and his wife at church. I know they're just barely scraping by."

This, of course, was a way of answering Leah's accusation from the time before, but it was an answer that struck home with Leah. She hadn't thought what it had meant to others when Nadine had taken over their work. "The Wattses *are* having a difficult time," Leah said. "I guess that is hard for you to think about."

Leah was thinking that Nadine might have more substance to her than she had ever imagined. She had meant what she'd said, and Nadine and Marjorie seemed to hear her sincerity.

"It's the ones out of work I feel the worst about," Marjorie said. "It hurts their pride so much."

"That's right," Leah said. "I've seen what it does to them."

"But Leah, your life must be hard, too," Nadine said, "being out there on your farm all alone."

Leah heard something in her voice: a kind of declaration of peace. "I've gotten used to it," Leah said. "I guess that's what we all have to do—accept what comes."

But Leah hadn't spoken with her usual protectiveness, and Marjorie seemed to notice. "Do you get lonely?" she asked, as though she understood that Leah needed to say something to Nadine that came from deeper inside herself.

Leah rubbed her hands along the velvet arms on the chair she was sitting in. She hesitated, but then she said what she was thinking. "Sure I do. But I was lonely long before Wayne died. He'd come in from the fields tired, and he worked 'til dark more often than not. After supper, he never did have much to say."

"That's how so many men are," Nadine said.

"I'm sure that's true. And I knew Wayne was quiet when I married him. But I guess I didn't realize what a hard time I would have with that. He was a good man—dependable and all those things—but I don't think he could have told me how he *felt* about things, even if he'd tried. Life, for him, was a job to do—not something to think about."

"How did you two meet?" Nadine asked. She was sitting in a chair with a high, ornate back, like a throne. She looked something like old Queen Victoria, with her double chin and such a serious face.

"We didn't exactly meet. Not that I remember. We saw each other at church all the time, and he was in his thirties and still single. I was single, too, and older than a lot of the married women in the ward. I think for Wayne, it was just the logical thing. He bought me dinner a few times, down at the Whitehorse Café, and we went to some picture shows together. He never did take me to a dance, and I found out why. The poor man couldn't hear a beat if the drummer had been pounding him on the head. But he asked me to marry him, and I didn't know whether I'd ever get another offer."

This brought on some silence. Leah knew what they were thinking.

"I'm not saying that I had no feelings for him. He was strong and good—and he wanted me when no else ever had. But I'm just saying that there wasn't a lot of romance involved. I'd been reading novels all my life, and I guess I'd been hoping that Mr. Darcy would show up—but maybe that only happens in fiction."

"Was it hard to go from teaching to farming?" Marjorie asked.

"Hardest thing I've ever done."

"Except for losing him."

"No. Not really." Leah had been looking at her lap for a time, but she looked up now. "That's something I've admitted to myself, but never to anyone else. The hardest thing was giving up teaching and going out to that quiet house. I wanted to teach another year, but it wasn't allowed. They make a woman quit teaching when she gets married. So I tried to keep house and cook and garden, bottle fruit and all the rest, but I was like a fish out of water. I'd wait all morning for Wayne to come in for dinner, and then he'd eat hard and fast and head back out. I'd ask him how his morning had been and it was like asking him what he thought of a painting or a piece of music; he had no idea. 'All right,' he'd say, 'but old Jack threw a shoe and now I'm way behind where I ought to be.' Then he'd be gone again. I can't tell you how many times I cried the minute he walked out, just because I knew I'd be alone until dark again. And then he still wouldn't talk to me."

"Did you ever tell him how you felt about that?"

"I did finally, and he said, 'What is it you want to talk about?' How was I supposed to answer a question like that?"

"I know that story," Nadine said. "If I tell Jim what I'm thinking, or even just tell him what I did all day, he teases me about 'prattling on.'

He's not as quiet as you say Wayne was, but he says what needs to be said and then he can't imagine why he ought to say anything else."

Leah looked at Marjorie. "Clark's not like that, is he?"

"No," Marjorie said. "Clark thinks about everything, and he likes to talk about things. But he thinks deeper than I do." She looked down at her hands, tucked together on her lap. "To tell the truth, I think I'm a disappointment to him. I see him get excited to tell me something, and then I give my opinion and he gives me a look like I'm too thick to catch on to what he's saying, and he lets the matter drop. He needs someone more like you, Leah—a schoolteacher, or at least someone who reads a book once in a while. I try to read, but I fall asleep every time. People at the library tell me about all the books they like, so I try some of them, but so many are just stories, and that's not what interests me."

"But you're an actress, Marj," Leah said. "How can you not care about stories?"

"I like to be someone, and I like to be on the stage, but when I come home from a play, Clark wants to tell me what it all meant, and I think, 'I suppose. But it seems like someone just made up something. It didn't really happen.'"

"Oh, Marj," Nadine said. "Life is all stories. We see what happens and then we tell ourselves what it means. It's the story that's real—not what actually happens."

Leah was astounded. She had thought the same thing so many times, had even told her students something like that, and as often as not, they hadn't understood. It was hard to imagine that Nadine, of all people, would know that. "What a storyteller does," Leah said—to Nadine, although she was looking at Marjorie—"is *see* more than most of us. We say he's making up his stories, but he—or better yet, *she*—watches more carefully, and then tells us what we would have seen ourselves if we'd just stopped to look."

"I suppose. But I'd rather do something than read about it."

"That's fine," Nadine said, "but if you do it, and then can't think what it means, it's never much of a memory. Life has more to do with memories of the past and longings for the future than it ever does with *right now.*"

"Nadine, you're a philosopher," Leah said. "That's the most interesting thing I've heard anyone say in a *very* long time."

Nadine laughed, and Leah was surprised by what she was seeing. Nadine was prettier than Leah had ever recognized. She had lovely eyes, bluer than she'd noticed before, and peaceful, even when squinted with laughter. She also had wonderful color in her skin now, her spirit seeming to gleam, maybe fired a little by the fun of some good thinking. "It comes from doing very little all my life, and then making what I can out of it," she said.

"What do you mean? You and Jim have done so much."

"No. Jim has. When I was a young woman I wanted to go places and see things—take trips around the world and see all the countries I'd read about. But Jim brought us out here and he worked night and day to build up his business, and all I could think to do was make my house as pretty as I could—just spend his money. And now we don't have the money coming in, and I'm down there at the store every day." She hesitated and looked at Leah. "You were right, though. I needed to get out of that bed and go to work. I knew it long before you told me. But I also knew that once I did, I'd never have another minute to think about anything other than the price of a yard of fabric. And that's how it's turned out, too. I work in that store all day, just keeping things in order when no one comes in—and watching women pinch their pennies to buy a broom or an eggbeater—but I don't have time to feel anything. I'm only home today because I told Jim I needed to be here long enough to meet with you."

"Well, I appreciate that you would take the time. I've felt bad about the way I handled things last time."

"But you don't know why I was so mad that day, do you?"

"Well, I have a pretty good idea."

"No. My old bottom *is* big. It wasn't kind of you to mention it, but that's not what got my goat."

"That wasn't the worst of what I did," Leah said. "It wasn't my right to tell you what you ought to do. I can tell, now, you had more things on your mind than I ever considered."

"Well, yes. I didn't like you telling me the obvious. But more than anything, I looked such a fright, and I didn't want *anyone* coming into my bedroom to look me over." Nadine was smiling. She sat up straighter and extended her jaw a little, as though to tug in her double chin. "It was my vanity."

"Oh, my," Leah said. "I didn't really think about that. I have no vanity because I have absolutely nothing to be vain about."

"No. You're a pretty woman. You don't do one thing to pretty yourself up, but you have a nice face, and such a statuesque figure. I've always wished I could look like that." She looked at Marjorie. "Or like you, Marj, with your beautiful eyes and your pretty hair."

"You know, Nadine," Leah said, "I used to think about things like that. But I've been out there farming so long, I hardly know what I look like, or notice much about anyone else. I think I've become a beast of burden. I haven't had any stories—and nothing to long for. I live in the *right now,* and, as you said, that's the least interesting part of life. It's Relief Society that's making me feel again, and I hear lots of stories— almost more than I can take sometimes."

"But you've had your kids to think about," Marjorie said. "You do everything you can for them."

"I do." Leah leaned forward and put her elbows on her knees, even though she knew that was hardly a ladylike pose. "But I'm not sure they care. I want them to go to college, but it means more to me than it does to them. I'm mostly an annoyance to Rae, always chewing her out about something, and grouchy most of the time. It's knowing that that eats on me—that I'm just not a very good mother. I feel at times like I never should have married, and never had kids. I was a pretty good teacher, and maybe I should have stuck with that."

Leah was embarrassed. She had said too much, and now everyone was quiet.

"Every mother feels that way sometimes," Marjorie said. "I don't see you at home, but I see you with the sisters, and you're helping them. And the truth is, I never thought I'd say that. You make me nervous the way you go about things, but you've helped women who needed someone as honest and straightforward as you are."

Leah wasn't sure that was true, but even more, she was embarrassed. She didn't like this kind of "women's talk."

"Well, anyway," she said, "Nadine, we came to invite you back to Relief Society. Do you think you could forget some of the 'straight-forward' things I said—and my barging into your room—and come back?"

"I'm at the store all the time, Leah. That's been the big problem."

"No. The problem's been with me."

"Well, I'll admit, I'm not sure I would have come, even if I hadn't been working. But that doesn't change the fact, I'm usually at the store when you hold Relief Society on Tuesday afternoons."

"Could you take some time off, the way you did today? If you came back, I'm pretty sure some others would. And we need your help. The sisters missed having the bazaar this year. We need to have it next year, and we need to get started on it early. Could you help us with that?"

"Jim would shoot me. He tells me the bazaar competes with the store."

"Oh. I hadn't thought of that."

"Well, I don't care about that. We sell some thread and a few things, so we come out all right. And the bazaar is important—more than I think you realize, Leah."

"Apparently so."

"I was just thinking," Marjorie said. "Nadine ought to be the chairwoman of the next bazaar. She knows what people can buy now—and what they *will* buy."

"They won't buy much, and that's why you have to have simple little things, so a woman can spend a dime, or a half dollar at most, and feel like she's donated to something good—and bought something she actually needs at the same time."

"That sounds right. Would you chair the committee?" Leah asked.

Nadine hesitated, took a long look at Leah, and then said, "I told some people I would *never* go back to Relief Society until you were released. It's going to make me look a little foolish if I go back on my word."

"I wouldn't worry about that too much. I spend my whole life looking foolish."

Nadine laughed. "All right. I guess I could do it. But when I get up a head of steam, you won't want to get in my road. I like to do things my own way."

"That's fine with me. You can just have at 'er and I'll stand back and watch what happens."

"And don't start calling on me here at home without giving me warning."

"I won't. I learned my lesson about that."

Nadine laughed and waved her finger at Leah. "And keep your opinion about the size of my *rear end,* as you called it, to yourself."

"Sure. Any woman with a bony behind like mine should never bring up the subject."

Nadine laughed hard. "Oh, Leah. You do have a way with words."

That evening, when Leah was getting ready for bed, she realized she felt relieved, happier than she had in a long while. She had liked opening up to Marjorie and Nadine, and she'd liked *them*. Nadine was much more interesting than Leah had ever imagined, and Marjorie, in her honest admission, had seemed so much easier to understand.

Leah read from her Book of Mormon for a time, and then she picked up her *Relief Society Magazine,* which she had intended to get to for quite some time. She read an article by Louise Robison about coordinating relief efforts with county agencies. It was good advice and the sort of thing Leah was just starting to understand. She also loved the advice she found in another article about the need for libraries in all the ward buildings. Women should spend less time with "pies, pickles, and preserves," it said, and more time with "poems, paragraphs, and paper."

There was also a list of women who were achieving things, stepping forward in the world to do things that only men had once done. Leah liked hearing those things. Relief Society had fought for women's suffrage earlier, and now was involved in the women's peace movement, joining leaders of the National Council of Women and the International Congress of Women in raising their voices against war. In Utah, the sisters were being called on to fight the repeal of Prohibition. Leah knew that bootleg liquor was widely available, and she wasn't sure Prohibition would hang on much longer, but still, she liked that Relief Society worked for the right things—and wasn't afraid to speak out. Never in Leah's life had it occurred to her that she was part of something big, but she was feeling that now. She liked the idea that she was more than a lone woman, stuck away on a farm. She was part of a sisterhood that was making a difference.

Leah prayed that night. She prayed every night these days. She prayed that things might go better in the world, that the Depression might end before much longer, but especially, she prayed for her sisters.

Chapter Ten

LEAH CAME IN FROM milking one evening later that week. "Rae," she called, "are you going to fix supper tonight? I've still got a couple of things I've got to do outside."

Leah heard no answer, so she walked to Rae's bedroom door and knocked. "I'll do it," Rae said, but her voice was muffled.

Leah opened the door a crack. "Are you all right?" she asked.

"Yes. Do what you have to do and I'll fix supper."

But Leah could hear the emotion in her voice. "What's wrong?" she asked. "You sound like you've been crying."

"Just go ahead. I'll see what I can cook."

"All right," Leah said. She was tired of Rae's little dramas. "There's some of that fried chicken left over. You can boil some potatoes and open a bottle of green beans—or whatever you can find in the cellar."

Rae didn't answer, and she didn't get off her bed.

"Rae, did you hear me?"

"Yes. I heard you. People *miles away* heard you."

"Well, then, get up and get going." Leah decided she'd better get out of there before she said anything else. She walked out to the corral and threw some hay over the fence to the cows and then checked on the other animals. With Wade playing football this fall, it wasn't easy to keep up with everything, but he was doing well on the team, and he seemed happy. She thought he was getting a little sweet on Gloria Deaver, a girl in the ward, so maybe that was part of the reason. Leah had noticed how all the girls flirted with him. He had always been handsome, but now he was a halfback on the football team, and that seemed to mean something. Leah had never really understood much about sports—and why girls should care about things like that. But what surprised her most was that Wade's broken tooth, which Leah hated to look at, didn't seem to bother the girls.

Leah was worried that she didn't see Wade putting in much time with his books. He could read a chapter from a textbook once and remember it better than Rae ever could, so he got by all right in school, but she almost wished she'd never told him to play football. She loved to see him feeling better about his life, not so cut off, but in another couple of years his grades would be a lot more important than anything he could get from sports.

Leah wished that she didn't always have so many things to worry about, but she *had* felt a little less lonely all week. There had been a time in Leah's life when she'd had friends—especially in college. She'd expressed her opinions then and revealed some of her personal concerns, even to some male friends. She hadn't been pursued by a lot of men, ever, but she'd had some friends who liked to pal around with her. Above all, she'd had roommates who would sit up late with her on weekends. She'd told them things she had never admitted to anyone, and heard things just as personal. Conversations like that had brought her close to young women she hadn't even liked at first.

There was something about getting past the surface with people, knowing what they worried about or feared, or what they hoped, that seemed more meaningful than almost anything else in life. For so many years she'd lost all that, but since she'd talked to Nadine and Marjorie, Leah had run the conversation through her mind dozens of times. She'd told them things about herself that she'd never expressed to anyone, and yet it had all come out rather naturally. They hadn't been shocked or unkind; they had accepted what she'd said with interest and empathy.

What Leah was thinking about for the moment, however, was what she had just said to Rae. She really should have asked Rae what was upsetting her. She had developed a habit of responding harshly to the girl, and she knew she had to stop doing that. So she left a few things she had thought of doing and walked back to the house. She found Rae in the kitchen peeling potatoes, looking gloomy. "Let me do that," Leah said. "Do you have a bunch of homework you have to get to?"

"No."

"Well, let me help you. I'm sorry I was so . . . whatever I was before. Abrupt, I guess."

Rae continued to peel, looking down at the potato in her hands. She was sitting on a kitchen chair, but she had slid the chair back and was holding a pan on her lap, letting the peelings fall into it. She had changed out of her school dress and had on a faded housedress that Leah sometimes wore herself. The two of them were built alike, and Rae was even catching up to Leah in height. That was something Leah had hoped wouldn't happen. She didn't want Rae to be as gawky as she had always been.

Leah got a knife from a kitchen drawer, and then she pulled a chair out from the table and angled it toward Rae. She took a potato from the bowl Rae had set on the table, shifted closer, and began to peel into the same pan that Rae was using. "Tell me what's wrong," she said. "Did something happen at school today?"

"Just the same old stuff," Rae said.

"With the girls?"

"I don't want to talk about it, Mother. I really don't."

"You're calling me 'Mother' now? It's as serious as that?"

"I mean it. I *don't* want to talk about it."

"Okay. It's a deal. We'll just talk about potato peeling." She peeled for a time, and then said, "So, Rae, what do you think of these spuds? They're nice big ones, but they seem a little wilted to me. I guess they've been in the cellar too long. But how long *is* too long? It's a great question, don't you think? I do think about *deep* things. I went to college, you know."

Rae didn't respond.

"Of course, potatoes just naturally lead to profound questions. It's my opinion that they still boil up all right, even when they're getting a little old, but they don't mash as well, perhaps due to the loss of moisture content. But here's a thought. We might consider frying these, saving the time of boiling them and, at the same time, adding variety to our lives. What do you think, Rae?"

"Stop it, Mom. I don't think you're funny."

"At least I'm 'Mom' now. That's an improvement."

"Not really. I told you, I don't want to talk about it."

"What? Potatoes?"

But this time Rae didn't say a word, and Leah could see that she was way too upset to be teased out of her mood. So Leah let some time pass. They were almost finished with their peeling before Rae finally said, "You think the town girls—and their mothers—are changing their attitudes about us, but they're not."

"Do you want to talk about that, or do you want me to leave you alone?"

"I'm just warning you. You may think those town women are your friends, but they talk behind your back. And don't tell them what you really think about things, because it just might get back to your kids."

Leah lifted the pan off Rae's lap and set it on the table, and then she took the knife and potato from Rae's hand and set those on the table too. "Okay, look at me. If you want to say something to me, say it."

"All right, fine. But if you wish I'd never been born, just tell me; don't go to town and tell your 'friends.' They love to gossip."

"Wait a minute. What are you talking about? I never said such a thing."

"Don't lie, Mom."

Leah stood up and grabbed Rae by the elbows and pulled her to her feet, so the two were standing close. "I did *not* say that I wished you'd never been born. Who said I did?"

Leah wasn't sure whether she was angry at Rae and her little games, or angry at the person Rae had been talking to—but she was getting angrier every second.

Rae tried to turn away, but Leah still had hold of her arms, and she held her fast. "Who told you that?"

"LuAnn."

"What in the world was she talking about?"

"She said that you and her mother had a big heart-to-heart talk, and you told her that you had made a mistake to get married—because you never really loved Dad. And you shouldn't have had kids because that meant you had to quit teaching—and you would have been happier as a teacher."

"Rae, that's nonsense. Nadine took something I said, all right, but she twisted it all around and made it come out so there's no truth in it. Or maybe LuAnn did the twisting. Why would she say something like that?"

"She was mad at me—that's why. She was cheating on our math exam today and I watched her. She was copying off Harv Burton's paper and he was letting her do it. I told her after class that if I saw her cheating again, I'd report her, and then she lit into me. She told me I was hateful and she knew why. Then she told me all those things—that you didn't love Dad and only married him because no one else had ever taken any interest in you."

Leah's anger suddenly hit the flash point. She spun toward the telephone, lifted the receiver, and cranked the handle. When the operator answered, she didn't wait for her to ask for a number; she barked into the phone, "I want to talk to Nadine Willis. You know her number. I don't."

"Thank you, Leah," the evening operator, Janice, said rather tersely, and then Leah waited. She didn't have any words in mind yet. But she wasn't going to let Nadine get away with this.

"Don't do this, Mother. It'll just make a bigger mess."

But Leah paid no attention. "Hello. Willis residence," a female was saying.

"Nadine?"

"No. I'm sorry. This is her daughter. Would you like to speak to my mother?"

"First, I ought to wring *your* neck, you conceited little prig, but I guess I'll start on your mother."

"Sister Sorensen, I know I shouldn't have—"

"Just put your mother on the phone." But Leah had heard something in LuAnn's voice, some tone of regret, or maybe just of fear.

Leah heard LuAnn say, "Mama, it's Sister Sorensen. I can tell she's upset. I need to explain to you what I said to Rae. She made me mad and I . . ."

Her voice trailed off, and then in another couple of seconds, Nadine was on the phone. "Hello, Leah. I'm not sure what this is all about."

"It's about you being a *snake*, Nadine. A *rattlesnake*. I said things to you in confidence, and I guess before I hardly got out the door, you started turning it into gossip for all the lovely ladies in town. If you're going to talk about me behind my back, the least you could do is tell the truth. I've got a daughter here who thinks I told you that I never should have given birth to her."

"Leah, wait a minute. Calm down. That's not what I told LuAnn."

"Well, then, you two get your story straight. Maybe it's your daughter who's the snake. Either way, I don't want anything to do with either one of you. I'll take care of my own bazaar." She slammed the receiver back on the holder and spun toward Rae. "I didn't *say* that to her," she shouted.

"Then what did you say?"

Leah felt her anger collapse. How could Rae understand?

"You must have said something like that. Maybe they twisted it, but she wouldn't just make all that up."

"Oh, Rae, how am I supposed to explain this to you?"

Rae didn't respond for a few seconds. She merely stared at Leah. "I think you just did," she finally said. "And you know what? I don't really feel like eating anything tonight. Why don't you fry your own potatoes?" She walked to her room and shut the door, hard.

Leah sat down at the table and tried to think. Her rage was gone now and she knew a couple of things. First, whatever hatchets had been buried with her sisters were all dug up now, and there was just no way for her to continue as Relief Society president. And second, there were things she had felt for a long time—things she had tried to explain to Nadine—that she had never expected to discuss with her children. But now she would have to. So she stood up again, and this time, in a much more subdued voice, asked Janice to ring up the bishop. But she couldn't resist saying, "I have no doubt you listened to that whole conversation, Janice. Have a good time telling everyone you know about it."

"Leah! You know I don't do that."

"Oh, do I? Things get around in our dear little town, and I think you and Brenda help as much as anyone." Leah didn't even know whether that was true, but she'd burned most of her bridges; some spirit of self-destruction told her that she might as well burn any that were left.

"That's just not true, Leah. I can't believe the way you're talking. I didn't think you took that tone with people anymore."

"Don't worry. I'm not going to be Relief Society president much longer. I'm calling the bishop to quit—the way I should have done a long time ago. You can announce that and save the bishop the trouble."

"Leah, you really ought to hang up right now, count to ten and cool off, and then get down on your knees and ask the Lord to help you. You're going to tear down everything you've built up this last year if you fly off the handle this way."

Leah didn't count to ten, but she did take a long breath. She knew that Janice was right. "I'm sorry," she said. "I don't mean to take this out on you. But do put me through to the bishop."

"He's not home."

"How do you know?"

"A couple of people have tried to call him, but his wife said he wasn't there. Glade Jenson died, and my guess is, the bishop is over with Mae, making the funeral arrangements."

"He didn't call me about that."

"He tried. You didn't answer. That was a couple of hours ago."

"Okay. Look, don't tell anyone what I said. But I do have to talk to the bishop. I'll call him back later."

"But don't resign. We need you, Leah."

"Oh, Janice, I just need to get out of this job. I'm a terrible mess. You know that." She had heard the front door open a moment earlier, and now she turned to see that Wade was standing in the kitchen doorway, looking surprised, probably at what Leah had just said.

"Only at your worst," Janice was saying. "And we're all a mess at our worst. But you've been at your best lately. Why would you want to go back the other way?"

"I don't know, honey. I can't think right now. But thanks." She was still watching Wade, who shrugged, as if to ask what she was talking about. But Leah asked Janice, "Did Glade really die, or were you just trying to keep me from reaching the bishop?"

"Leah! I wouldn't make up something like that. Maybe you ought to head over there. Mae's going to need you. Glade's old and he's been dying for weeks now, but when the time comes, it's still not easy."

"I know. I guess I will go over, but I've got one thing I better take care of first."

She hung up the receiver and said to Wade, "Sit down in the front room for a minute. I need to talk to you and Rae." Then she walked to Rae's bedroom, opened the door, and walked in. "Rae," she said, "I know you don't want to talk to me, but I have to say some things. Come out to the front room."

Rae hesitated, didn't speak, but then slowly rolled off her bed. She wiped her hands across her cheeks and in the same motion pushed her hair away from her face, which was blotched and red. Leah waited for her to walk ahead and then followed her into the living room. Wade was there already, and Rae sat down next to him. "What's going on?" Wade asked.

Leah sat down on the faded overstuffed chair that matched the equally faded couch, where Wade and Rae were sitting. "LuAnn Willis said some things to your sister—supposedly things I'd said to Nadine. I just want to see if I can explain what I really said."

"I know what it is," Wade said. "At night, when the moon is full, you turn into a vampire. I've seen the blood on your lips some days, early in the morning."

"You're not funny," Rae said.

"I think I am. Listen. I'll laugh." Wade started saying, "Ho, ho, ho," and bouncing like a drugstore Santa.

"Wade, this is serious," Leah said.

Wade shrugged. "All right. All right. I'm listening. But I hope this doesn't delay supper too long, because I'm starved."

"Just listen. We'll eat in a few minutes." Leah tried to think where to start. "I visited Nadine Willis a couple of days ago, and we got talking about some personal things. Nadine asked me—or maybe it was Marj— whether it wasn't a lonely life out here without a husband. I don't remember everything that was said, but I know I told her I was lonely even before your dad died. I wasn't meaning anything bad about him, but he *was* a quiet man. I told them how I would sometimes be in the house all alone all day, and then, when he came in, I wanted to talk a little. You kids were so young, you probably don't remember, but he didn't ever have much to say. And that was always hard for me."

"He used to play with us," Wade said. "I remember him down on his hands and knees on this floor right here, playing with a little toy truck and horse trailer I got for Christmas."

"I know. He did lots of nice things, but if you asked him how he *felt* about things, it was hard to get anything out of him. That's all I was saying."

Wade let his legs extend across the rug as he hunched down on the couch. "Women always want to talk about their *feelings*. Men just don't say much about things like that."

"Some do, Wade."

"So that's what you had against Dad?" Rae said, her voice full of accusation. "That he didn't tell you enough about how he *felt* about things?"

Leah told herself to be calm. She gripped her hands together, waited a few seconds, and then said, "Rae, I'd been a teacher. I'd been with students all day every day, and before that, in college, with lots of friends to spend time with. And suddenly, here I was, out here on a farm. Your dad was working outside most of the day, and when he'd come in, he was tired. I'm not blaming him. And I'm not saying that most men wouldn't be the same way. I'm just saying, I was alone—and lonely—and it was a hard adjustment at first."

"You told Sister Willis you didn't love him. You said you only married him because no one else asked you."

"No. I didn't say that. I said something that might sound pretty close to that, but that's not what I meant. I said that there wasn't a lot of romance in our dating—that our courtship wasn't like the stories you read in novels. Your dad was single at an older age than most, and so was I, and we knew each other from church. He asked me out a few times, and then he asked me to marry him. Your dad just went about things in a very practical way."

"So why did you marry him?"

"He was a good man. I knew he would be a good husband. And I wanted to have a family."

"But you didn't love him?"

Leah looked away. How could Rae possibly understand? "I don't know, Rae. Marriage doesn't always start with *passion*. A lot of the pioneers married people they hardly knew. Two people join their lives together and try to support each other. Love comes from shared experience, going through things together, raising kids—and all the rest."

"I think this explains a lot," Rae said. "You got married and then started to wish you'd stayed with teaching, where you weren't so *lonely*. But you couldn't go back because of me—and you've resented me ever since."

"Oh, brother," Wade said. "What's this supposed to be? *Psychology?* Mom's always loved us."

"Tell the truth. She's always loved *you*. I'm the one who stole her life away from her."

"Rae, I don't know how to prove it to you," Leah said, "but that just isn't true."

"It's why you've always been so full of anger and hatred. You hate the way life turned out for you."

"Rae, lay off," Wade was saying.

But Leah felt Rae's dart strike a little too close to the target. She leaned over and put her elbows on her knees, then rested her head on her spread fingers. "Rae, I know what you're saying. I do get mad, and I've said hateful things about people. And maybe some of that comes from all of these years of working so hard and not being part of anything but the farm. It hasn't been easy. Your dad died early, and that's been hard for you, too, but we've made the best of it. Everything I do is for you kids."

"That's just another way of saying you would have been better off without us."

Leah raised her head. "Oh, Rae, think about it. Life is hard, that's all. When you have kids someday, you'll find out that you do things more for them than for yourself—but you don't blame your kids for that. I don't regret that I have you two. That's the last thing I'd regret. You're my whole life."

Rae stood up. She put her hands on her hips. In a resolute voice, she said, "I don't plan to get married—and one thing's for sure, no one *plans* to marry me. But maybe that's better. I've learned too much anger from you. I don't think I ought to pass that along to another family."

Leah nodded, slowly, time and again, and then she said, "You're right about one thing, Rae. I'm not a kind person. I told you that. I haven't told you that I love you—not nearly enough. And I've been way too judgmental about people. I *have* passed that on to you, I'm afraid. But I'm trying to change. I really am."

"I'm not. I'll hate LuAnn Willis as long as I live. And I'll wish just as long that you hadn't married Dad when you didn't love him. You feel so sorry for yourself, but I wonder what it was like for him. I know what it's been like for me."

Rae walked back to her room and shut the door again.

"She's just being dramatic, Mom," Wade said. "She loves big scenes like this."

That was true. But so were some of the things Rae had said, and Leah was trying to think what she could do to make things right.

"Don't quit your job in Relief Society," Wade said, as though he could read her mind.

"I was just starting to get a few things straightened out with the sisters, Wade, and now I've ruined any chance I had of working with them. I'll have to quit now."

"At church last Sunday, Sister Johnston told me you were her favorite Relief Society president ever. And she's not the first to tell me that."

Leah knew that. Some of the sisters did feel that way. But she'd gone too far this time, and she and Nadine could never patch things up again. Leah was also sure she wasn't wrong about one thing: That woman *was* a snake, and so was her daughter.

Chapter Eleven

CHRISTMAS WAS ONLY a couple of weeks away and Leah was still Relief Society president—even though she had tried to quit back in November. She'd gone to see about Mae Jenson, whose husband had died, and she'd caught up with Bishop Bowen there. The two had left at the same time, and Leah had told the bishop what she'd said to Nadine Willis on the phone and advised him to replace her. He'd looked at her with tired eyes that seemed to ask, *Don't you ever learn?* But he hadn't said that. He'd said instead, "Leah, Mae needs your help right now. Spend some time with her—especially around Christmas—and just let her know that a woman can make it through after she loses her husband."

"I'm not the only widow in this valley, Bishop," Leah had told him. "Belva could help Mae more than I ever can."

"Leah, I'm sorry," the bishop had said, "but I don't want to hear this. I don't know what Mary Dibble would have done without you these last few months, and the same with Pat Hyatt and quite a few others. Last week Millie Wilson told me you've been like a mother to her, calling on her two or three times a week. I've never seen a Relief Society president work as hard as you have—and you've had the good sense to stay close to the women who need you the most."

"Bishop, I know what you're saying. There are some women in the ward who've gotten so they depend on me a little. And I could keep visiting them. But what about all the ones I've offended?"

"I'm not saying you don't need to watch your tongue—but some of them ladies need to be a little slower about *taking* offense. What I'm worried about right now is that I've got a woman whose heart is broke. She needs someone to show her how to put one foot in front of the other. I've seen you help women like that, and I know you can do it again."

So Leah had turned her attention to Mae, and she'd dropped her request to be released. And part of the reason was that she knew what would happen if she gave up on her calling. She would also be giving up on herself.

Since then Leah and Rae had established an uneasy truce. The terms were that Rae remained moody, distant, and quiet, and Leah left her alone. As it turned out, when she did that, Rae was just as likely to prepare supper or sweep the kitchen floor as she had been when Leah was nagging her. It was something worth learning. Still, with every broom stroke Rae seemed to be making a statement: *I'm doing this even though you don't love me.* Or worse: *I know I'm the hated child, and I know you love my brother more, but I'll give you nothing to blame me for—and then I'll get out of here.* Rae didn't talk a lot about her goals with Leah, but she did refer to the future, always as, "After I leave for college . . ."

What Leah knew was that this year was her last chance with Rae. She needed to put her arms around her, open up to her, find some closeness. But she didn't know how to do that, and Rae clearly resisted any overtures that Leah made. So the cold truce continued.

Leah had never taken such a careful look at herself—had never been forced to. She talked often with Belva, and the two did a good deal of soul-searching together—actually, both of them searching Leah's soul.

What Leah found there was an emptiness that she didn't fully understand.

But Belva couldn't see it: "Oh, sweetheart, I liked you the first time I met you, and I've liked you all the better as we've worked together this last year. I see you growing about an inch a day, your best self coming out exactly when it's most needed, whenever the women turn to you for help."

"I don't see that at all, Belva."

The two were sitting in Belva's kitchen, each with a cup of Postum. Leah had taken a couple of sips, but she couldn't stand the stuff. She longed for a cup of coffee.

"You're too hard on yourself," Belva said. "You've made some mistakes, but who doesn't?"

Leah thought about that. But a mistake seemed an accident, a slip, and her problems ran far deeper. "Do you know Rae's real name?" she asked.

"Sure. It's Rachel. You used to call her that when she was little."

Leah was watching the window. Light snow had been falling when she arrived, but big flakes were coming down now, dropping fast. She knew she had to get going before the lane to her house was snowed in. Snow had come early this year, and it was piling up at the farm. She'd had to use her horses a couple of times already to plow the lane open.

But she wasn't ready to leave just yet. There was something on her mind—something she had never told anyone—and she wanted to tell Belva.

"When I was eleven or twelve, something like that, I heard Mom say that my name was from the Bible. So I looked up the story—and didn't really understand it very well. But I did understand that Jacob worked all those years for Rachel and then got stuck with Leah. I asked my mom why she hadn't named me Rachel. Rachel was the pretty one. All the

Bible said was that Leah was tender-eyed, and that sounded like maybe she cried all the time or maybe had pinkeye."

"No. It means she had pretty eyes—the same as you do."

"So why didn't Jacob want her?"

"He saw Rachel first, and he'd fallen in love with her."

"Well, whatever the reason, Jacob didn't want her, and it made me mad that Mom would name me after someone like that. My mother said she liked the name, that was all, and she hadn't thought about the story, but as I got into high school and the boys wouldn't ever ask me to the school dances, I always thought, 'I'm the *other* sister—the one no one wants.' I didn't even have a real sister, but that was still how I thought about myself."

"So you named your daughter Rachel. The one Jacob loved."

"I did. Because it was the name I'd wished for. But Rae figured that out eventually. People would notice the two names and bring up the story. I think she liked the idea when she was still in grammar school. But then I think she saw things were going to turn out for her the way they'd been for me, and she started telling Wade and me to call her Rae. It was what we'd started calling her sometimes anyway."

Belva reached across the table and put her hand on Leah's hand. "So you both consider yourselves the unloved sister? Is that what you're saying?"

"I guess so."

"But the sisters you look after, they all love you. That ought to tell you something."

"But every time I make a little headway, I slip backwards, and I'm the same old Leah again—too quick to speak. Nadine had no business telling LuAnn the things she did, but I never should have called her when I was so hot under the collar."

"Well, I know how bad you feel, but I'm betting Nadine feels the same way. You're both such lovely women, and—"

"Don't start that again. If Nadine isn't a snake, she's first cousin to one, and the truth is, a cedar fence post has more love in it than I have."

Belva smiled, her cheeks puffing into little circles, and she said, "You're like a coconut, Leah. You look rough on the outside, but crack you open and you're nothing but sweet meat and milk inside."

Leah laughed at the comparison—didn't believe it for a moment—but still liked that Belva thought so.

"Look what you did for the Fillerups," Belva said. "I think you're the only one who could have done it."

Recently a man in the ward, John Fillerup, had broken his ankle at the sawmill and had been unable to work. Leah had gone into the home, Belva at her side, had sat down at the table with John and his wife, Berta, and had calculated their savings and the time he would be off. Then she had written down a list of commodities they would need to make up the difference. When Leah and Belva had first arrived, John had been staring at the wall and Berta had obviously just wiped her tears away, her cheeks and eyes still red. But Leah had told them that there was no need for worry, the Church wouldn't let them go hungry.

Berta had spoken quietly but with a hint of resentment. "It's easy to write things down on a sheet of paper, but this could get a lot worse. John was worried about a layoff even before he got hurt. These bosses like a good excuse to get rid of a man once he's past forty, so they can hire in some boy with a strong back—someone who's willing to work for next to nothing."

Leah had looked at Berta, and then over at John, and said, "So do you want to make a list of all the terrible things that *could* happen, or do you want to deal with what *has* happened?" The mood had changed after that, and the planning had gone well.

"I know you were blunt with Berta," Belva told Leah, "but I need to be more that way, too. I'd probably start crying with her, and leave her and John more downhearted than ever. You're not mean; you just say it like it is. And that's what people need to hear sometimes."

"But I need those tender eyes Leah had. It might be good if I *could* cry with the sisters at times." She looked out at the snow again, the whiteness filling the window, the flakes falling in single, driving motion. She had to go, but she took another sip of Postum and then said, "I used to force myself not to cry. But now I don't have to. I don't *feel* things the way I should."

"Don't tell me that. I've watched your eyes. You may not cry, but the women know you care about them."

Leah wanted to think that was true, but she was still remembering what she had said to Nadine on the telephone. And maybe worse, she was still feeling bitter toward the woman. How could Leah show up at her house now and say, "I guess I spouted off too much *again,* and even though I can't stand you, let's bury the hatchet *again.* I want you to run our bazaar *no matter what I said on the phone.* Let's work together *even though I'd rather punch you in the nose.*"

Leah had talked the whole thing over with Marjorie, and Marjorie had agreed to stay on in the presidency, but she admitted that lots of women in town had heard Nadine's side of the story, and no one understood Leah's ugly attack. Marjorie admitted that Nadine had given LuAnn dangerous information, and probably shouldn't have, but she was convinced that Nadine had actually been trying to help LuAnn understand Leah, and especially Rae, who—in the Willis version—had been hateful toward LuAnn for years. Leah was willing to grant that there might be something to that, but she still didn't understand Nadine—or LuAnn—reaching conclusions that Leah hadn't reached. Leah had wished many times that she might have spent her life as a teacher instead of a farmer, but she had never once wished her children away.

Of course, that last interpretation might have been Rae's—not Nadine's *or* LuAnn's. Leah wondered, maybe she really should go back to Nadine and take the full blame for everything that had happened between them, both times. But that wouldn't be honest and she knew it. Nadine might not be as bad as Leah had once thought, but she was still a socialite, and Leah was sure she would love nothing more than to get these Depression years over so she could go back to feeling superior to everyone in town.

Marjorie had told Belva—who had then told Leah—that she had seen Leah at her best that day at Nadine's house, and she had known that Leah was someone she could admire and respect as president. But then she had said, "If Leah would just try to be that person more often, the two of us can still work together." That sounded like a warning to Leah—and something Marjorie could report back to her friends in town who were taking Nadine's side—but Leah, once again, knew that Marjorie had a point, and she made up her mind she was going to try to be her best self.

So Leah's Relief Society work had continued, and on a cold evening, December 18, 1932, she and her counselors were out making calls on sisters who weren't likely to have much for Christmas if the Relief Society didn't help. On their last call, at a farm south of town, they'd had to park Marjorie's car on a country road and hike down a snow-packed lane to the house. According to what the bishop had heard, Jack Peckham was about to lose his farm. Glen Whiting, the banker in town, had told Bishop Bowen that he had no choice but to foreclose on Jack before spring.

Irma, Jack's wife, opened the door when the sisters knocked, but she stepped out on the porch rather than ask them in. "Sisters, I know you mean well," she said, "but it's better if you don't come in. Jack's saying he don't want a dole from nobody, and when you knocked he guessed who it probably was. He said, 'Send 'em off. We don't need a handout ham for Christmas. We'll make do on the beans we got left.'"

"Let me talk to him," Leah said.

"No, Leah. He's not going to listen to you."

But Leah was already pushing past Irma. She walked straight to the kitchen, the only lighted room in the house. She found Jack at the table, just sitting, a coal-oil lamp in front of him. He was wearing a shabby pair of bib overalls, and he hadn't shaved in a few days. The skin around his eyes looked rough as a grindstone and just as dark.

"Look, Jack," Leah said, "you can eat beans for Christmas dinner if that's what you like. But we're going to bring in some dinner—and some little gifts—for your kids. It's just plain wrong to let your pride stand in the way of that. Those kids need to have Christmas, no matter what's happening in your life."

Jack stared at Leah for a long time. Finally, he said, "I guess maybe they do. But I'll figure something out. I don't want charity."

"Oh, come off it, Jack. Get your bottom lip off the ground and try to show those kids what a man does when trouble comes his way. There's nothing wrong with taking help when you have no other choice."

The other women had followed Leah into the kitchen, and now Irma stepped ahead of Leah and said, "That's about enough, Leah. That kind of talk ain't going to help anything. Maybe you don't know what we've been through."

"I know plenty. I've been farming around here as long as you have."

"But you ain't been kicked off your farm in the middle of winter, with noplace to go."

"You haven't been kicked off yet."

"No, but it's coming," Irma said. "Glen told us that this week. He said we could stay for Christmas, like he thought he was Santa Claus."

"Well, then, it's time to figure something out."

"That's easy to say, but it's—"

"No, that's all right," Jack said. "Leah's right." Leah was taken by surprise. Jack stood up, as though finally conscious that he was facing four women and was sitting down while they stood. She saw him draw in some breath, as though he meant to stand tall. "I know what we got to do. I just don't like it."

"Look, Jack," Leah said, "I can only imagine what you've been through lately. I didn't mean to sound so hard."

"No. You said it right. A man has to handle what comes. I got a brother who says we can move in with him. I just haven't wanted to face up to doing it."

"But let us give you a little help for now."

Jack looked past Leah. "Hi, Belva," he said. "Marj." He pointed toward the front room. "Why don't you ladies sit down and talk to Irma a little. She's needed that. I been feeling down for a couple of days, and I guess I been licking my wounds. I ain't been easy to be around."

"Where does your brother live?"

"Down in Bountiful. He said we can come and live at his place for a while. But he's got six kids hisself. With our five, I don't know how we'll all fit in."

"Is there any work around there?"

"Not anyone hiring. He's still working, though, and he said he wouldn't let us end up in the street. I was hoping Glen would work with us one more season, but now he says he ain't got a choice. His bosses are telling him, right after Christmas, to start the foreclosure papers going through. I don't blame him."

"But it doesn't make sense. This farm's just going to sit idle."

"No. There's some folks with money buying up these little farms that go broke. They figure once the drought lifts, and these hard times ease up, they'll have their hands on all this land for near nothing. It ain't right, but Glen says a bank's gotta stay afloat. If it goes down, it'll take a lot of folks with it."

"How much would he have to have to keep you in here another year?"

"He said two hundred. But he might as well say a million. Or a nickel, either one. Because I don't have a nickel."

"I'll tell you what. I know Glen pretty well. I'll talk to him and see if there's some way to work this out."

Jack shook his head. "Leah, you ain't *that* good of a talker. The only talk he wants to hear is, 'Here's your two hundred bucks.'"

"All I'm saying is that I'll talk things over with him. But I'd say this to you: Enjoy Christmas. Hold out some hope. I might be able to say something that will change his mind."

"What you got up your sleeve, woman?" Jack actually smiled just a little.

"Who knows? Maybe I know something about Glen's wicked past. I can blackmail him."

Jack chuckled. "Well, I can tell you right now, there's nothing you can do."

"Look at me, Jack." Leah stepped closer to him and knocked her finger against his chest a couple of times. "I'm telling you I'm going to do something. I'm tired of what's been going on. This nation can't destroy all its farmers and then expect to eat. Things have to change. I'm going to see to it you stay on this farm. I don't know about you, but I think Roosevelt is serious. When he takes office in the spring, he's going to set right off to get us rolling next season. I'm going to talk Glen into giving you another year to try. You plan on being here—and we'll help you make Christmas as nice as possible for your kids."

Leah knew she was saying more than she ought to, but she was sick of what had been happening for such a long time. She still had money in her bank account, and she couldn't let it get away from her, but she suddenly felt how wrong it was to let it sit there when lives were being ruined. She was going to see Glen tomorrow and pay that back interest.

"Well, I don't know, Leah. I think you're barking up the wrong tree."

"I'm not just barking. I'm promising. I'm going to do something."

Leah knew she couldn't say any more than that. She would come back when she could tell Jack and Irma something definite. But she wasn't going to let those kids eat beans for Christmas, and she wasn't going to let them move away in the middle of winter, with no prospect for work.

Afterward, when the women were walking back up the lane, Leah wasn't surprised when Marjorie said, "Leah, you always tell Belva not to give people false hope. I don't understand why you told Jack what you did. I doubt Glen Whiting is going to listen to you any more than he did to Jack—or the bishop."

Leah crunched along through the snow for a time, her breath billowing before her eyes. But the cold wasn't reaching her; she felt too happy with what she'd decided to do. She knew she had to be careful what she said, but she didn't want Marjorie to think it was false hope. "I think Glen will listen to two hundred dollars."

"And where are you going to get the money?"

"Never mind about that. I know a way."

On Christmas Eve, in the afternoon, the presidency stood on Jack and Irma's porch again. The day was just as cold as the last time they'd been here, but Leah couldn't remember feeling this good in a long time. She knocked, and in a few seconds the door came open. The Peckhams' oldest daughter, Beth, who was probably sixteen now, was standing there, looking expectant. Leah had stopped by a couple days before to let Jack and Irma know that a Christmas dinner would be coming.

Beth let the women in, and each carried in a cardboard box. Leah could see that Jack must have made a trip to the mountains. He'd cut a piñon pine, and the kids had decorated it with rings of colored paper. It crossed Leah's mind that she should have thought to bring some popcorn to pop and string.

The rest of the family was in the kitchen. Another daughter, fourteen or so, and three boys—the youngest one only about four—were all standing, waiting, looking excited. The boys had all had baths and their hair was still slicked down. Their faces looked polished, and their clothes clean, but all three boys were wearing overalls that had been patched many times. The oldest boy, Carl, wore overalls that were too tight on him, and the little one, Max, was wearing some that were much too big—surely handed down. The middle boy, Davis, had on boots that were cracked in the folds across the top of his feet. Leah wondered whether he could walk through the snow without filling them up.

But all the kids were grinning. "Smells good," Carl said, the room already filling up with the smell of roasted turkey.

"It tastes good, too," Belva said, and she laughed in that billowing way of hers, one burst seeming to build on another. "I've been tasting everything while I cooked this afternoon." She looked at Irma. "I'd put that turkey in the oven for maybe half an hour, just to brown it a little more. And don't worry, I brought a few chunks of coal to keep your oven hot for a while."

The kitchen was already warm, but Leah knew that the Peckhams hadn't had any coal for a long time. Jack cut and hauled wood, but the only heat they had was from the kitchen stove.

The sisters set the boxes on the kitchen table and started lifting things out: hot rolls wrapped in a Christmas-red cloth; a big bowl of mashed potatoes; sweet corn; Jell-O salad; cranberry sauce. Marjorie had baked two big pies, apple and pumpkin. When she set them out on the table, the boys moved closer to look—and smell.

Leah glanced to see that Irma was standing near the stove, her hand to her mouth, her chin quivering. "Thank you," she whispered. She lifted her apron to her face.

"We had some coats stored at the church," Leah said. "Ones that others have donated once their kids grew out of them. I thought your kids might be able to use some better coats. See if these fit."

The kids dug through the coats, Leah showing them which ones she thought would fit each child. They tried them on, all laughing, clearly thrilled, and not caring that the fit wasn't always just right.

In another box were packages wrapped in red and green paper. "Oh," Leah said, as though she'd forgotten about the gifts. "You'll want to put these under the tree. We ran into Santa Claus, who was about to get his work under way, and he asked us if we could bring these things out here. That poor man is overworked, trying to get to so many houses."

She handed the box to Beth. With the packages was a little sack containing one orange for each member of the family. Leah knew that the gifts were small. Nadine had given Marjorie some toys for the little boys. They were things that had gotten scratched up a little at the store, but Jim had repaired them as best he could. The girls each had a dress, newly sewn by sisters in the ward.

Beth took the presents to the tree, and the boys followed to watch her put them out. While they were gone, Leah finally took a good look at Jack. He was standing back, looking stolid. She knew this was hurting his pride. Leah had to be careful the way she handled what she was about to do.

When the kids returned from the living room, she said, "There's one more thing. I talked to Glen Whiting. He's willing to let you stay here for another growing season."

Leah had expected a cheer from the family, but the reaction was almost the opposite. Jack's head popped backward as though he'd taken a punch. Everyone was staring, as though they couldn't quite comprehend what Leah had said.

"Are you sure about this?" Jack said. "What did you tell him?"

"I told him he's got to stick with the farmers around here. They've been his bread and butter for a long time. It's just plain wrong to give up on them."

"But that interest will just build up another year. I'm not sure I can—"

"No, it won't. It got taken care of. I know someone who cares about us farmers. He paid the interest, for now. You can pay him back someday, but it won't come due next year. Just whenever you can pay it."

"Who is it?"

"It doesn't matter. He didn't want his name to be known. He just wanted to help out—because he knows what a good man you are, and he knows you'll pay him back in time." Leah looked around at the kids. "He told me that your dad knows this land about as well as anyone around here, and he's a good farmer. It's not his fault things have gone the way they have—with the drought so bad this year."

"That's right," Irma said. "It isn't Jack's fault. No one works harder than he does."

"No one would make a loan like that unless he knew that Jack was good for it," Leah said, looking at the kids again. "Your dad's a respected man in this town."

The girls were nodding, the boys, staring. "Do we get to stay here and not move?" Carl asked. He was standing stiff, his arms at his sides. He seemed afraid, as though he didn't dare trust good news after all the other kinds they had had.

"That's right. You do."

"What if it don't rain again next year?"

"We'll all worry about that when we have to. But right now I'd be thinking more about a turkey dinner, with stuffing."

"And we'd better get out of here," Marjorie said. "I've got my own turkey roasting back home. I've got to check on it."

"What do you say to these good ladies?" Jack said.

"Thank you," the children whispered, still seeming more in awe than excited. The daughters came to Leah and Belva and Marjorie, hugging each in turn, both of them breaking down now in their joy. Irma was trying to keep control, but she was awash in tears herself. She hugged the sisters too, and then Jack, clearly not knowing what do, came forward and shook their hands.

"We'll get through this thing yet," Leah told him.

"Do I have to sign some papers, or—"

"No, it's a handshake-and-a-promise kind of loan. When the day comes that you can pay some back, just give the money to me and I'll hand it over. That's all there is to it. And there's no interest expected on the two hundred dollars."

"It's hard to understand. No one's got any money right now."

"Well, that's not quite true. But don't worry about who did it. It doesn't really matter."

"We've been praying so hard," Irma said. "And it just seemed like the Lord wasn't listening."

"He's always listening," Belva said.

Leah was watching Jack. She was pretty sure it was Irma who had done all the praying. But she could see that he was feeling blessed right now. "Leah, I don't know quite what to . . ." Unable to get any more words out, he stood in front of Leah, nodding, and then gave her another pat on the shoulder. He swallowed a couple of times and then said, "I gotta bring in a little more wood for the night." He turned quickly and walked to the back door, grabbed an old wool coat from a peg on the wall, and headed on outside.

"He'll go out to the shed and cry," Irma said. "But he won't do it in front of all of us."

"I know."

"Leah, you saved us. You gave us another chance."

"Don't thank me. I just knew the right people to talk to. And you know I'm a smooth talker, if there ever was one." She laughed at herself.

But outside, in the cold air, Marjorie asked, "How did you get the money, Leah?"

Leah looked away. She could see heavy clouds out to the northwest.

Another storm was coming. "I did it with my charm and good looks," she said.

"It was your own money, wasn't it?" Belva said.

"My money? Where would I get money?"

"I don't know. But no one's going to loan money to a farmer right now—especially one who's already defaulted on his mortgage."

"You don't know that, Belva. There are good people in this town. And they don't want everyone else to know the good they do."

"I think Belva's right, Leah," Marjorie said. "I think it's your own money. But I won't tell anyone that. The last thing we'd want is to have a rumor get around that you're a nice person."

"I swear, you two don't use the brains God gave you—*if* he gave you any. I don't have any money to be passing around." But when they got back to the car, Belva and Marjorie hugged Leah as though they still didn't believe her. Leah found herself amazed to think that they would suspect her of doing such a thing—even if they were right.

Chapter Twelve

ALL DURING 1932 LEAH had heard that the Depression had finally "hit bottom." But things got worse during the early months of 1933. Roosevelt wouldn't be taking office until March 4, and he was promising to make some big changes in his first hundred days, but the whole nation seemed to be waiting, and, as it did, the economy worsened. Banks had been failing for years, but Leah was hearing on the radio now that a lot more were closing. Some were announcing "bank holidays" to stop bank runs that were usually started by the panic that a rumor could set off.

For all these years Leah had been hanging on to her money, knowing that it would take quite a bit to send Rae and Wade to college. Tuition, whether they went to Brigham Young University or one of the state colleges, was almost a hundred dollars a year, and room and board would cost at least twenty dollars a month. There would be books to buy, too, and clothing. Leah had let her kids get by with worn clothes in high school, but when they did finally leave home, she wanted them dressed well enough that they wouldn't feel embarrassed.

In spite of all that, Leah was finally realizing that she had enough. Even after paying the interest on Jack's farm, she still had almost a thousand dollars. If Rae and Wade would work part-time while they were in college, they could pay for most of their room and board, and Leah was beginning to believe they *should* work, so they would appreciate their opportunity to improve themselves. Or at least that was the reason she gave herself when she gave away some more of her money.

Another farm family—the Gardners—hadn't been able to pay taxes on their farm and were looking at foreclosure. She paid the tax anonymously—a sum of about seventy dollars—and then told Lawrence Gardner, the same as she'd told Jack, that there were people in town who didn't want to see local farmers go broke. Leah didn't mention such things to anyone else, but a rumor got around that someone had stepped in and helped Jack Peckham and Lawrence Gardner. The speculation about that was actually a good thing in some ways, since people were suspecting almost everyone else of being the generous donor. But it led to Leah helping out one more farmer, Randall Pete, who was also behind on his mortgage payments.

Leah helped out with some smaller amounts, too. It was hard not to when she saw the kinds of trouble some people had. She was aware, from things Sister Bowen had said, that the bishop was struggling just to keep his shop open. He was fixing way too many cars for people who couldn't pay. Others were leaving their cars at home rather than having them repaired. And no one was buying much gasoline. Part of that was because the winter had continued unusually cold, with more snow than anyone could remember. Lots of cars wouldn't start in the cold, and those that did often couldn't get around in the deep snow. Leah hadn't seen so many teams and wagons in town for years.

Ben Estes ran the little Whitehorse Café in town, and people just weren't eating there as often as they once had. Now his truck had broken down and he couldn't make his run to Vernal to pick up the wholesale food items he needed. His wife had told Leah that Ben wouldn't ask the bishop to fix his truck, not when he couldn't pay the man, but she was worried sick.

So Leah asked the bishop to walk over to Ben's place—when she knew Ben wasn't home—and he had gotten the old truck sputtering enough to drive back to the shop, where he had installed a used fuel pump and changed the spark plugs. Leah had paid the bishop $7.50 for the parts, and she had tried to pay him something for the labor, but he hadn't been willing to take it. Leah had driven the truck back to Ben's place and then, when she'd seen him later that day, told him a lie. She said she'd heard his truck wasn't running, and, having learned to tinker with cars over the years, she'd gotten it going for him. She wasn't sure he believed her, but the truck was running, and there wasn't much he could say.

There had been a number of other small matters of that sort, but each time Leah paid for something, she told herself she would do no more. Then she told herself she had to hang on to $800—never go below that mark. Now she had only $770, but she had vowed that was it. It was time to remember her own family. The truth was, she didn't have enough to get both kids through four years of college now. She was relying on the idea that she could get Rae through, if she worked while in school, and by then, things really *would* get better.

She did shell out another $20 for fabric after that, when the Relief Society supply ran out entirely, but that made a good round figure: $750. She would stop there.

Leah had rarely spoken to Nadine all winter. She certainly didn't come to Relief Society meetings on Tuesdays, but she did come to church. Leah didn't exactly try to avoid her, and she had nodded and said hello a couple of times when they passed one another in the hallway, but neither was about to break the ice. Leah knew she had been way too ugly in what she'd told Nadine on the telephone, but Nadine was continuing to say things that were getting back to Leah. According to what some people reported, Nadine was claiming—and she talked to everyone in town at the store—that the bishop was having second thoughts about Leah serving where she was. Another change in the presidency was probably not far off. No one ever seemed to have heard the words from Nadine herself, but they had heard them from someone who had talked to someone who had heard her. Still, it was exactly the kind of thing she probably would say, and where would the rumor start, if not from her?

Leah knew the Relief Society would never be unified with that kind of talk going on, so she finally told herself she would have to be the one to take the first step. But rather than visit Nadine at home again, Leah decided to stop by the store to see if she could say something that would soften things between them. When she tried, though, Nadine was busy, or maybe got that way when she saw who had walked through the door. Leah was able to approach Nadine only as she was bustling down an aisle, striding ahead as though she aimed to knock Leah over. Leah said quickly, as she stepped out of the way, "Nadine, I've been wanting to thank you for the help you gave the Peckhams for Christmas."

"I was glad to do it," Nadine said, not even looking back as she kept going down the aisle.

Leah told herself that she had made an effort but Nadine was still being snooty. She headed for the front door. Along the way she heard someone say, "Hello, Leah."

Sue Sessions was standing by a clothing rack nearby. She was holding up a dark blue dress, looking at it. A young woman, maybe sixteen or so, was with her. "Hi, Sue," Leah said, and walked over to her.

"Leah, this is my niece from Salt Lake—Victoria Farrell. She's come out to live with us for a while. She's going to help me with my brood of kids."

"Oh, really? Well, that's nice." Leah extended her hand to the girl. "Are you going to go to the high school while you're here?"

"Not right now," Victoria said. She was a pretty girl with curly hair and round eyes, very blue. Her face colored, as though she were a little embarrassed by her answer, but she looked directly into Leah's eyes in a way that most young people didn't, and she grasped Leah's hand with a firmness that felt like confidence. Leah wondered what would bring her out here. The Sessions family had seven or eight kids, but they certainly didn't have enough money to pay for a helper. Even an extra mouth to feed would be a burden. Maybe her family in Salt Lake had fallen on hard times, but Victoria's dress was nicer than anything the local girls wore on a weekday.

"Leah's our Relief Society president," Sue said. "She's a good one, too." Sue laughed. "She's a breath of fresh air."

"How so?" Victoria asked, again sounding more self-confident than most teenagers.

"She speaks her mind, whether it's something people agree with or not."

"Yes. But I've got to quit that," Leah said. "Everything I say is right, of course—but some people haven't figured that out yet."

Victoria laughed. "Well, that's their problem. I like people who say what they think." She shook her head, flipping her curls, and Leah caught a whiff of perfume. The Emporium had its own smell—a kind of oiliness, maybe from the treated hardwood floors, or from something Nadine used to scrub the place—but the scent Leah was noticing was subtle, probably expensive.

An awkward little pause followed, and then Sue, who seemed rather self-conscious today, said, "Vickie's mother sent a little money with her. We're trying to pick out something she can wear around the house, and maybe something for church."

"Well, that's good. I'll let you—"

"Wait just a second. Vickie's going to try this one on. We can't decide what we like. Why don't you give us your opinion?"

"Hey, listen, I'm the last person to ask. I'm an expert on horse blankets—not dresses."

"I don't believe that," Victoria said. "Just wait long enough for me to slip this on." She headed to the back of the women's section, where there was a dressing room. She swished through the racks of clothing, taking longer steps than most girls ever did.

But Vickie hadn't shut the door before Sue was saying, "Oh, Leah. This is such a tragedy. You need to know about it."

Suddenly Leah knew what was going on. "She's pregnant, isn't she?"

"Yes, she is. And they've sent her out here to stay until she has her baby. But I'm the one who has to live through this with her—and watch everyone in town stare at her. I don't know *what* I'm going to say to my own kids."

"What's she going to do with the baby?"

"Give it up for adoption. She's only fifteen." Sue was a sturdy woman, with sizable hips and big shoulders, but she looked frail today, her face red—probably from the cold weather—her hands nervous, her eyes jumpy.

"Doesn't the father want to marry her?"

"Oh, Leah, my sister would never let that happen. He's a good-for-nothing boy, four years older than she is. He goes to the university and he's known more for his drinking habits than for anything he's done in his classes. His dad has money, and he's paying for the doctor and every-thing, but he doesn't want anything else to do with the whole thing."

"The father or the son?"

"Both. This isn't the first time the father's bought this boy out of trouble, from what we hear."

"Vickie doesn't seem all that worried about the situation."

"She hasn't really faced anything yet. But she's starting to show, just a little, and that's why we're buying her dresses. I don't know how she'll deal with this once people start to notice." Sue folded her arms in front of her. She was wearing a wool coat that had obviously been made to last one winter too many. Leah saw something she had seen so much lately: Someone who had very little was still willing to do what she could for someone else. She must have longed to buy a dress for herself.

"Sue, these things happen. People understand more than you might think. Once people know the truth, there's not much more to say. And I'll tell you what. I know the sisters in this town a lot better than I did a year ago. They won't be cruel. Some of the daughters might do some giggling about it at first, but most of them will be good to her."

"Once she shows, I don't see how I can walk into church with her. I'll be too ashamed."

Leah put her hand on Sue's shoulder. "Look at me," she said. And when Sue looked back, she told her, "Don't hide her away. This town's too small for that. If I were you, I'd come to Relief Society and tell the sisters what's going on before anyone has to figure it out. Just say, 'This young girl needs your love and support, and so do I.' Our sisters will respond to that."

"But Vickie acts like she's not even embarrassed. What kind of example is that to the girls in our ward?"

"My guess is, she's just trying to keep her head up. And I think she should. This happens more than you might think. Most of the girls just marry quickly and hope people don't count the months too carefully."

"But she *needs* to experience some shame."

"She'll get her share of that. But we don't have to rub it in. How would you like to have a baby and then give it away?"

"I couldn't, Leah. I just couldn't."

But now Vickie had opened the dressing room door. She stepped to a mirror on the wall and looked at herself. Leah could see the reflection of her face, and she watched as the girl's countenance changed. She was seeing what Leah could see, that the dress didn't hide what was happening to her. She turned around, all the bright roundness gone from her eyes.

Leah walked toward her. "Vickie, you're *so* pretty," she said.

Victoria hesitated, her jaw tightening, and Leah could see that she was fighting her emotions. "Not as pretty as you think," she whispered.

Leah wanted to take the girl in her arms, but she didn't know her well enough—didn't actually know how to do something like that. Instead, she said, "Don't say that. You're beautiful. I see it, and so does the Lord."

But that brought the tears. Victoria turned quickly. "I'll take it off," she said, hurrying back into the dressing room.

Leah turned around and looked at Sue. "We need to help her," she said.

"I know. Thanks for saying that to her."

Leah worried on the way back to the farm. She worried first about Victoria, and how the presidency would deal with her situation, and then she worried that the sisters might not be quite so generous as she had promised—and that Sue might not be so open as she needed to be. But she worried most about Rae. And some about Wade. She wasn't sure what she had told them, what they knew. She wondered whether Rae could be taken in by the first boy who paid attention to her, whether her moral principles really ran deep enough. Leah had always meant to say more to her than she had. They had talked about periods when Rae's time had come for that, and Leah had made certain she understood what that had to do with babies, but Leah had never really said anything about boys who might "try things" with her. And she had never told Wade not to be that kind of boy. He was so good-looking, the wrong kinds of girls might throw themselves at him. She wondered what the boys on Wade's basketball team said about girls, what kind of behavior was acceptable to them.

Leah had told Sue not to hide Victoria, to be open, but she was rather shocked to realize how old-fashioned her own behavior had been when it came to talking to her own children. These were modern times, and Leah had always trusted that open discussions led to the best results. So why hadn't she had the courage to follow up on her theory?

After supper that night, Leah asked her kids to stay at the table, and she said, "There's something I need to tell you. But you can't say anything to anyone else for now."

"Uh-oh. The vampire story finally comes out," Wade said.

Rae rolled her eyes at him. "Just be quiet and listen for once," she said. Rae had never again brought up her accusation from the previous fall—that her mother didn't really love her as much as she loved Wade—but she always acted as though she believed it, and she had little patience with Wade. Wade didn't seem to care. What worried Leah was that he really didn't take things seriously—even important things.

Rae had cooked dinner and had spilled gravy onto the coal stove. There was a bitter smell in the air now, and still a little smoke. Rae hadn't wanted to open a window because she said it was too cold in the house already. The girl was always cold. But Leah got up and opened the door to the closed-in porch, trying at least to let some fresh air circulate into the kitchen.

When she sat down at the table again, Leah said, "A new girl recently moved here from Salt Lake. She's living with Sue Sessions and her family for a while. She's pretty as a picture, and she seems to be very nice."

"Okay. I promise not to tell any of the guys," Wade said. "How old did you say she was?"

"She's fifteen, and—"

"Did you want me to make her welcome? I'm happy to help out."

But this was all talk, and Leah knew it. Even though girls paid attention to Wade, he had never taken a girl to a school dance or a picture show. For all his confidence at home, he was shy around girls.

"Be still a minute," Leah said. "This is serious."

"She must be expecting," Rae said.

Leah was taken by surprise. "What makes you say that?"

"Because you're acting like there's some sort of scandal, and I know what Salt Lake families do when a girl gets herself in trouble. They send her out of town."

"Where did you ever hear that?"

"It's happened before. A couple of years ago there was a girl staying in town with the Petersons. She even went to high school for a while—before they hid her for the rest of her time. All the kids knew about it."

"Not me," Wade said. He grinned. "I didn't know a single girl could have a baby. Does the stork get mixed up or something?"

"Yes," Rae said. "He drops the baby off in the wrong cabbage patch."

"Well, then, you better keep an eye out for storks and stay out of cabbage patches." Wade looked back at his mom. "I'm glad we're having this talk. I need to know about these kinds of things."

Leah leaned back in her chair and took a long breath—her way of saying, *Let's all stop here and I'll start over.* So far, this hadn't gone the way she had planned. "All right," she finally said. "She is pregnant, and before long that will be obvious." She shot a quick warning glance at Wade to stop him from any more of his facetiousness. "Please don't say anything to *anyone* for now. I think Sue Sessions will tell the sisters at Relief Society meeting before long—just so things will be out in the open and people won't have to speculate."

"Maybe she kissed a boy," Wade said. "That's how you really get babies—from kissing. That stork story is a big lie."

Leah cast him another displeased look. Then she said, "The only reason I even bring this up is that I got thinking while I was driving back from town that I haven't said enough to you kids about the kinds of situations that can come along."

"Oh, good. We're finally going to get 'the talk.' I've been waiting for this for years."

Rae slapped Wade across the shoulder, but she was actually smiling a little.

"Wade, don't," Leah said. "I'm serious."

"I am too. If the girl kisses *me,* am I the one who gets pregnant?"

Rae's smile was getting bigger, even though she was trying to act disgusted. "Go out and watch our rabbits," she said. "They'll teach you everything you need to know."

"Actually, that *is* everything I know," Wade said. "I've gotten my education from watching all the animals around here. But they seem to figure everything out for themselves without ever getting 'the talk' from their parents."

"So you know all about it. Is that what you're telling me?" Leah asked.

"Yes. Rae should never be alone with a boy in a rabbit hutch."

"Or if he has long ears and wiggles his nose a lot," Rae added. She let out a little laugh and then stopped herself.

"Kids, come on. I need you to be serious for a few minutes."

"Okay, Mom," Wade said. "Go ahead and tell us *all* about it. Tell us about those little sperms that swim around like tadpoles—and everything else we don't know."

Leah was shaking her head now, and Rae was still trying her best not to laugh. "We do take biology at school, Mom," she said.

"I know you do. And I know you've grown up on a farm, and you've watched animals being born. But I'm not talking about all that. I'm talking about making a decision about what's right and wrong. We've never talked about chastity and self-control, and not getting yourself into compromising situations."

"Okay. Here's what they told us at MIA," Wade said. "Don't kiss. Don't hug. Don't sit in a car and neck."

"Well, I think that's pretty good advice," Leah said. "I don't know that a goodnight kiss is wrong, once you've been dating someone for a while. But when two young people go a little too far and start getting all excited, they can make really bad judgments."

"Tell us about the 'getting all excited' part," Wade said. "Is that when the rabbit's nose starts to wiggle?"

Rae bent over the table, dropped her forehead on her arm, and finally let herself laugh. Meanwhile, Wade was still grinning, and Leah was thinking she might as well give this whole thing up.

"I'm sorry, Mom," Wade said. "But you did wait an awful long time to say anything."

"I know. I'm sorry about that. But I do think that you have to imagine yourself in that situation, and—"

"Don't worry, I do, Mom. All the time."

"Okay, never mind. You're on your own." Leah stood up. The truth was, she was humiliated.

"No, no. I really am sorry."

"Mom," Rae said, "when I saw what that last girl went through—the one who was out here a couple of years ago—I told myself I would *never* let anything like that happen to me."

"But honey, it's not just the embarrassment and the difficulties of having a baby. It's a matter of obedience to God's law. He's told us . . ." She hesitated, but then decided she really should use the word. "He's told us that sex is only for marriage."

"I know. We talk about that in Gleaners. Sister Gardner's been really honest with us about all those things."

"As opposed to your mother?"

"Yes. But that's okay. It's more embarrassing to talk about with your mother."

"Mom, I don't know what you're worried about," Wade said. "Rae and I don't even go on dates."

"I know, but you will."

"I doubt I ever will," Rae said, and Leah heard her usual seriousness return.

"You will, honey. You're built too much like me—taller than most of the boys. I think that scares some of them away. But you'll find some lanky fellow like your father, and he'll decide you're just what he's been looking for."

They both knew the next step in the logic: . . . *and you'll marry him because no one else will ever ask.*

Leah wanted to take all those things back, to never have Rae believe that she had "settled" for Wayne even though he wasn't the kind of man she had dreamed of finding.

"I'm not waiting around for some guy to *choose* me," Rae said. "I'm going to go some places and do some things. If I ever get married, it won't be until I've had some adventures of my own."

Rae didn't really sound convincing, but Leah tried to take her words seriously. "What adventures?"

"I want to travel, see some of the world. And I want to live in a bigger town for a while. Maybe in California, or somewhere more exciting than this. And I want to have some money. I'm going to start a business or something like that, and I'm going to make so much money I can buy what I want and do what I want to do. I don't want to be tied down to some man who just works for a living—or runs a farm."

"I've never heard you say any of this before."

"I know. But it's what I've been thinking about a lot lately. I'm going to major in business at college—and I don't mean secretarial work. I don't care if they tell me I have to be a teacher or a nurse. I'm going to do what I want."

"Hey, let's not get off on all that stuff," Wade said. "We're supposed to be talking about S-E-X."

"You ought to be thinking about your own future," Rae told him. "You don't want to live the way we do, do you?"

"It wouldn't bother me. There's a lot going on around here. Especially back there in the old rabbit hutch."

"Okay, that's it," Leah said. She stood up and began to gather up the dishes. But she was still thinking about Rae. The girl was searching around for an answer, for some way to feel good about herself, and Leah worried where that could lead her. She almost wished her kids were little again and she could go back and try to do her mothering better this time. Rae was not far from leaving home—and Wade too, for that matter—and Leah was not at all sure they were ready.

Chapter Thirteen

THE WINTER OF '32–'33 didn't want to end. In all the years Leah had lived in the Uintah Basin, she'd never seen anything like the cold that winter. She had no thermometer, but she heard talk of thirty, even forty below zero. All she knew was that milking a string of cows every morning, out in that cold, was an ordeal. She and Wade would shovel their way to the corral lots of mornings, throwing the snow higher and higher until they seemed to be pushing forward through a tunnel. And then they would lean their heads against the flanks of the cows to get just a little warmth, and they would milk fast, the splashing milk sometimes freezing around the top of the bucket.

Keeping animals watered was almost impossible, as ponds froze and troughs turned into blocks of ice. Lots of farmers lost animals when they simply couldn't get to them. Leah and Wade hauled heated water to pens and troughs, working constantly to keep up.

The house, all winter, had seemed impossible to keep warm, the kitchen the only room that wasn't uncomfortable. Leah put sadirons on the woodstove each day, and at night wrapped them with towels and tucked them into the feet of the beds for extra warmth. That helped a little, but she and Rae and Wade all slept piled in quilts.

There were weeks when Leah couldn't get out of her lane for days at a time. During one blizzard, after she conferred with her counselors in town, they called Relief Society off, but somehow Leah managed to open her lane on all the other Tuesdays, and she made it to her meetings. Her old Model T fought her some days, and she hurt her wrist a couple of times when the crank jerked backward, but she usually got it started. She found it necessary to walk to town only a couple of times.

But now it was a Sunday morning in late February, and she couldn't get the old "Tin Lizzy" going. The engine would turn over, seem to catch, but then kill again as she was jumping back in the car. She figured the battery was finally dying and she wasn't getting enough spark. She'd prayed—and sometimes cussed—that battery this far through the winter, but now it had apparently given up the ghost. She supposed she ought to be thankful it had lasted as long as it had. But she wasn't thankful. She was mad. The bishop had asked to meet with her on a Sunday morning at 7:00, and it was probably her attempt to start the car so early, when the temperature was still below zero, that had been the death blow.

She didn't have to think much about what she would have to do. She had allowed some time, half expecting this to happen. So she tromped back into the house and yelled, "You kids will have to walk to church. The car won't start. I'm walking in now to meet with the bishop."

Silence.

"Did you hear me?"

"Yeah. Okay." It was a deep, husky voice.

"Tell your sister."

Silence.

"Did you hear me? Tell your sister."

"I can hear you, Mom," Rae shouted. "Everyone in the western states can hear you."

Leah thought of some things she could say to that, but she didn't. She marched to her bedroom, found a stocking cap in her bottom drawer, and pulled it down over her ears. Then she strode back to the front door and pulled on galoshes over her shoes and buckled them up. She stepped outside but immediately thought better of it. Her legs were going to freeze.

So she started over. She hurried back to her bedroom, pulled off her gloves and coat, galoshes and shoes, grabbed her overalls off a chair by her bed, hiked her dress up around her waist, and then pulled on the overalls over the top of her dress, with the skirt bunched up in the middle. She could just imagine how wrinkled it would be by the time she pulled off her overalls, but that was better than getting frostbite. She put everything else back on, pulled her cap on again, and started out. "I'm really going this time," she yelled as loudly as she could, just to bother Rae—and to let out a little anger.

Once outside she glanced at the heavens and mumbled, "I don't see why you couldn't have started that old car just *one* more time." But she actually sort of liked the idea of walking to the church on a morning like this. God could toy with her if he wanted, but she would make it to her meeting anyway. If ol' Job could get knocked down a half dozen times and keep getting up, so could she.

She had plowed the lane with the horses earlier that week, and there was no new snow, but the thin layer that remained was hardened and slick. She found herself skating in a few places, but the work was good for her. It warmed her up. And then, when she reached the main road, the pavement was dry. She tromped along hard, her face stinging a little but her body getting warm. The sun wasn't up yet, but the snow in the fields was picking up light from a waning moon, and the scene was magnificent—the fences gone, all covered over with crusted snow, and the limbs of spreading willow trees making dark lines, like spiderwebs, above the glimmering white. Leah didn't tell herself it was beautiful—

she'd seen this scene too many times before to fuss about it now—but a comforting calm was coming over her.

The mile into town did seem more like two this morning, but she made it to the church four minutes before seven, and the bishop's car still wasn't there. She tried the door and found it locked, and she mumbled to herself about the bishop being late, even though he wasn't, not quite. But she had thought maybe he would get there in time to get the furnace stoked up. Now she would have to wait for him to do that while she froze.

But she decided she could use this time to shed some of her excess clothes and at least look a little more like a Relief Society president. She unbuckled her galoshes and pulled them off, took off her coat and hung it on the door handle. She was just removing her overalls when the bishop pulled into the parking lot. The overalls were halfway off, as though she'd been caught with her pants down, and she wasn't quite sure what to do. She decided to make it quick. She jerked the overalls to her ankles, making sure her skirt came with them.

She stepped out of the overalls and was putting her shoes back on when Bishop Bowen got out of his car. He was grinning. "That's one I never saw on the church steps until now," he said. The sun was not far from rising, and there was enough light to see his big ears, glowing red. She wasn't sure if it was from the cold or from embarrassment.

"Don't tell me about it. Tell the Lord. He stranded me out at the house with a car that wouldn't start. I wasn't going to walk all the way here in a dress—and freeze myself to death."

"What's wrong with your car?"

"I think the Lord finally gave up on my battery. I asked him to point with his finger and send down a charge, but he told me, 'Sorry, Sister, you're on your own. I got more important things to do this morning.'" By then, she was pulling her coat back on.

The bishop had his keys out. He was still smiling big enough to show his missing tooth. He opened the door and stepped in, then held the door open for Leah. She stepped in with her overalls draped over her arm and her galoshes in the other hand. "You should've called me," the bishop said. "I would've run out there and hauled you in."

But Leah was noticing that the building was already warm. "Who got the furnace stoked up this early in the morning?" she asked.

"This time of year I always come over about six on Sunday mornings. I get a good fire going and then I run back home for some breakfast."

It was a simple thing, but it struck Leah. It was like Bishop Bowen to take on something like that himself and not bother the custodian early on a Sunday morning. She felt warmed by that thought as much as by the furnace. "Come in and sit down," he said. "The heat reaches my office pretty direct. It's the warmest place in the building."

She followed him down the hall and stepped into the office behind him. It *was* warm. Her face felt hot now, and tingly. She pulled off her stocking cap and gloves and ran her hand over her hair. She knew she looked a mess, but these meetings were his idea, not hers.

"This is about the only hour I can find time to sit down with you, Leah. Sunday always gets so busy. But maybe we ought to figure something else out."

"No. It's all right. I'm used to being up early, and used to the cold. As you can see, I know how to dress for it." She dropped the overalls on a chair but decided to keep her coat on for now—mostly just to cover up her wrinkled dress.

"Brother Badger will be here any minute. He comes in and works on the records and finances on Sunday morning."

Leah understood what he was saying. She knew he would think it improper to be there with her alone. He had left the office door open a little, too.

"Listen, I think I have a used battery down at the shop—one that will still take a charge. I'll run out to your place in the morning and stick it in your car."

"No. You keep that for someone who needs it worse than I do. I'll come in and buy a new one from you. I've stretched faith a little past the breaking point, relying on that old thing so long."

"But you might as well use that one I have at the shop. It should keep you going for quite a while."

"No, that's all right. I can find a few dollars when I have to."

But the bishop was watching her, seeming to study her face. "Leah," he finally said, "you've been doing a lot for people. And that's good. But once in a while, maybe you're the one who needs a hand. Let me be the one to help you this time."

Leah almost said yes, but she just didn't like the idea. She had fought her way through a lot of things, and she could manage this. If the bishop had any idea how much money she still had stashed away in the bank, he'd be shocked. "No, that's all right. It's time I have a new one. Have you got one on hand?"

"Sure I do, but—"

"I'll have Wade stop by for it after school, and there's nothing to putting one in. I can do it."

"Leah, at least let me bring it out to you. That's a long way to lug a battery."

Leah nodded. "Wade's a strong boy."

"You're an independent woman, Leah, and I guess that's good." He hesitated and took another long look at her. "But don't you think it's just a little prideful to resist so hard against anyone giving you a hand now and then?"

"Probably so. But I told you from the beginning, I'm not one of your nice church ladies."

"You did tell me that. But you can't get away with that kind of talk anymore. I know too much about you now."

"Well . . . let's talk about the sisters and not use up all our time talking about me."

Bishop Bowen leaned back in his chair and folded his arms over his chest. "I'm going to bring that battery out," he said.

"All right. That's fine. I certainly don't want to be prideful." She smiled. The prophets on the wall behind the bishop were looking solemn this morning in their beards. She was glad Bishop Bowen was willing to laugh with her. The poor little guy really wasn't much to look at, but he was wiser than she'd ever suspected, even smarter, and what she knew now was that he was as good as anyone she'd ever known.

"How *are* the sisters doing? It seems like things just keep getting harder and harder for most of our folks."

"Some are doing a little better, but it seems like the problems *are* worse right now. Winter's the worst time. Farmers have more time to think, and worry, and men out of work have fewer places where they can catch on for a day or two of pay."

"What about Irma Peckham? And Jack? Do they have enough to eat?"

"Oh, yes. Irma canned a lot of things in the fall, and they're getting by. We've given them flour a couple of times, and a few other commodities."

"It's never been clear to me how Jack managed to hold onto his farm."

"He may not. If things don't go better this year, he might lose it yet."

"I know. But you said someone paid the two hundred dollars on his mortgage interest, and I can't think who in the world was willing to do something like that." The bishop was watching her again, and she had the distinct feeling that he suspected her.

"I promised I wouldn't tell, Bishop. But there's people in this town who are surviving all right. And some of them hate to see what's happening to our farmers."

Bishop Bowen nodded. "But it's not just the farmers, is it? Have you learned to feel anything for the people who've had it pretty good and now have to cut way back—maybe face the prospect of losing what they have?"

"I guess I have, Bishop. But when I was in Nadine Willis's house, all I could think was, Go ahead and sell some of this stuff, lady. Don't cry poverty to me when you've got your house filled up with Chinese vases and fancy oil paintings."

"Let me tell you something, Leah. She has sold off some of her things—some furniture, for one thing. And I think she'd sell some of that other fancy stuff if she knew anyone who could afford to buy it."

"Well—maybe she wants too much for those things. She might find out, sooner or later, you can't eat knickknacks."

Bishop Bowen sat forward and laced his fingers together. He said softly, "You still don't like her, do you?"

"I guess I wouldn't invite her over for Sunday dinner. And I guess she wouldn't come if I did."

"You don't know that."

"I think I do."

"Leah, Nadine does a lot more good in this town than you'll ever know about."

"No. I do know that. She's done a lot through the Relief Society—giving us material we can use for our quilts and things like that."

"You don't know everything she does. She's a better woman than you think she is."

"I think she's flat-out *wonderful*. In fact, I think she ought to be the Relief Society president. Put her up for it and you'll see my hand go up."

"Why can't you two work things out?"

"I tried, Bishop. You know I did. And you also know what she did to me."

The bishop was shaking his head, still looking down. "Leah," he said quietly, "you've done a lot of good, but I'm not sure you understand what Relief Society is. I think it's what you still have to figure out."

"Actually, I've made some headway on that. The problem for me is not in understanding. It's in not living up to what I understand."

"But I wonder if you *do* understand—fully. A lot of women in the Church join Relief Society, but even more of them don't bother. I think some just think it's something extra, like one of these garden clubs or book clubs. But there's more to it than sharing recipes and studying liter'ture. When Relief Society is strong, the Church is strong. It's like it's the beating heart of the Church—the feelings behind everything. The problem is, in our ward, we still have quite a few women who've quit coming and haven't joined back up this year—like they don't understand what they're part of. And the trouble is, most of that comes from this feud you and Nadine have going."

"I don't know anything about a feud. All I know is that I told her something in confidence—something very personal—and the first thing she did was tell her daughter. Between the two of them, they made the whole thing worse than it was, and then LuAnn told Rae, and Rae's been mad at me ever since. I don't like the situation, but I also don't like what she did."

"What about the things you said to her on the telephone?"

"She ran straight to you and told you her side of the story, didn't she?"

"No, she didn't. Actually, someone else told me."

"That just means she blabbed it around town."

"Leah, the point is, you said some awfully hard things to her. I've given you some time on that, because I figured by now you'd let your heart soften and you'd go back to her and take some of that back, but you haven't done it."

Leah sat up a little straighter and folded her arms. She hadn't thought she was coming in for a lecture. "I said hello to her in the store here a while back and she came at me like a bulldozer. If I hadn't moved out of the way, someone would have had to scrape me off the floor—just a skinny streak down the center aisle."

The bishop smiled a little at that one.

"Bishop, you don't have to say it. I know I'm not in the right on this. And Nadine isn't either. We do need to work something out."

"Leah, I need to have not just you two, but all the sisters working together. I'm not so sure the worst of this Depression is over."

"Can't the Brethren up in Salt Lake step in and help? The federal government gives relief here and there, but it's never enough to keep a family going. We're helping people out as much as we can, but our stores are running out, and we're getting less coming in all the time."

"I've talked to Church leaders. It's too much for them to handle too. There's been some work going on in one of the stakes in Salt Lake. The stake president is trying to get some kind of program going so that getting help to people is more organized. Maybe we'll see the Church do more with that in time, but right now, I only have fast offerings to work with—and like you said, not much is coming in now. Let's hope Roosevelt's as good as his word. He keeps saying he's going to get people back to work."

"Maybe he will. But it won't happen overnight."

"I know that. And that's where I rely on you so much. Welfare work is still mostly Relief Society work, and some of the women who can do the most aren't having much to do with Relief Society right now."

"Bishop, I told you. I tried to say something to Nadine, and she almost—"

"Leah, I'm asking you to go back to her again. I know you can settle this thing—if you want to bad enough."

Leah shut her eyes and took a breath. "All right. I'll see what I can do."

"There's something else I'm worried about."

Leah opened her eyes.

"We have a young sister who's come to stay in our ward."

"Sue Sessions's niece, Victoria. I know all about that. She's expecting a baby."

"Well, I'm glad you know, but I'm afraid a lot of other people do too, and one of the girls in the ward made a comment to her that has hurt her feelings. Now she feels like everyone is talking about her."

"Bishop, I told Sue to stand up in Relief Society and tell everyone what the situation was—just be out in the open about it. But she didn't do it. I know darn well things would have been all right if she'd just done that." Leah wiped her hand across her forehead. "Is it way too hot in here or am I having hot flashes again?"

The bishop's ears moved—seemed to rise—as he grinned. "It is a little warm," he said. He started to get up, but Leah could see where he was going, and she got up quickly and pushed the door open a little wider. That did bring in some more air. She noticed, too, that Brother Badger was working at his desk now.

The bishop sat down again, his smile fading only gradually, but he said, a little more quietly, "I think you're right. Sue should have said something. But it was Vickie who didn't want her to do it. She wanted to come to church for a while before everyone found out what was going on. Now she's saying she won't ever come back, and Sue's all upset about that. But maybe that would be the best thing until the baby comes."

"Why do you say that?" Leah asked. She hoped Brother Badger couldn't hear them.

"I'm thinking it's just as good if our young people don't see her coming around like that. If you could visit her some, and maybe—"

Leah's temper flashed. "If she has to stay home, what about the nasty little creature who hurt her feelings? Maybe she should hide away in shame too."

"Well, Leah, I know what you're saying, but—"

"Vickie did something wrong, no question, and she's living with the consequences, but anyone who would want to kick a girl like that, when she's already down, maybe she ought to be sent away so we won't see her in *her* condition." Leah tried to stop herself, but her other thought spilled out. "And I'll bet a silver dollar that it was LuAnn Willis, that hoity-toity little . . ." But Leah heard the hatred, and she let her sentence die.

"It wasn't LuAnn. And just maybe you shouldn't be so hard on *her*, Leah. LuAnn's grown up a lot lately. She's been a conceited kid, but hard times have made her see things a little different than she used to."

It was hard to imagine, but Leah told herself that maybe it was true. She took a deep breath and said, "I'm sorry, Bishop. Now I'm the one pointing fingers. You're a better person than I am."

"No, I'm not. But I'm in a situation where I sit down and talk with people, and they open up to me lots of times. When something like that happens, you just see people different."

"I know. I've just got to remember that it's true for *everyone.*"

"So tell me this. Does it set a bad example to the other young people to have a girl coming to church when she's gotten herself in trouble that way?"

"We believe in forgiveness, Bishop. That's what people ought to learn from her coming."

"Maybe the kids would get the idea you can do the wrong thing and get away with it."

"She's not *getting away* with anything. She's a little girl trying to keep her head up, but she's aching inside. If you've taken time to talk to her, you ought to know that. And it might be good if our kids do see what happens when someone makes a mistake like that."

The bishop was nodding. "Well . . . you might be right," he said. "And I know what you're saying. I have talked to her. But she's a little bit cocky when you first meet her. Maybe that's the only thing some people will ever see."

"I think Vickie needs a friend right now. I've considered asking Rae to spend a little time with her—just so she won't feel so all alone. She's not going to school or to MIA activities. I'm afraid she's going to be stuck spending every day with that big herd of kids at the Sessions's house."

"That might be good. Do you think Rae would want to make friends with her?"

"That's a good question, Bishop. Rae's awfully wrapped up in herself right now. It would be good for her to think about someone else, but she might turn me down flat."

"Well, think about it. I do feel sorry for the girl. She broke down and cried like a baby, and she kept saying, 'No one will ever marry me now. I've ruined my whole life.'"

Leah had known that was what Vickie had been thinking. She'd even planned, quite a while back, to ask Rae to make friends with her, but then Rae and Wade had started all that joking and Leah had begun to think that Rae wasn't the right one to do it.

"Well, listen," the bishop said, "our time's getting away from us, and I have a pretty good-sized list of people I want to ask you about. In a lot of cases, you know more than I do."

Leah wasn't sure that was true until the bishop started to name the people off. It turned out she did know more, but she also learned something about herself. Each name seemed to call up feelings of concern. She really did care about the families in the ward, especially the women she had gotten close to.

At the end of the meeting, Bishop Bowen said, "Leah, I sure do appreciate what you're doing. I know some sisters are mad at you, but others keep telling me what a good job you're doing."

"I guess Nadine Willis didn't tell you that."

The bishop laughed. "Well, no. But you already told me, you're going to work a little harder on that."

Leah *had* told him that. She just didn't know how she'd ever do it. "I think I'll step outside and slip these overalls on," she said. "I think it's still pretty cold out there."

"Let me run you home. I have another meeting, but I can be a few minutes late."

"No. I'm fine. I can use the fresh air—and a few minutes to think." She laughed. "According to you, I've got to figure out what Relief Society is."

He grinned again. "But are you going to walk back for Sunday School and then again for sacrament meeting?"

"I'll pray a little harder. Maybe that battery will pep back up for one more day."

"It just might."

But Leah didn't pray about the battery again, and when she got home and tried the crank a couple more times, nothing happened. So she and her kids did walk to church twice more that day. The fact was, though, the day warmed considerably, and the air was pretty nice, especially for sacrament meeting. Rae complained a little, but not as much as Leah had expected. Maybe she was growing up a bit. Or maybe she had seen the look on Leah's face when she had started to moan. But Leah still wanted to think a little more before she asked Rae to befriend Vickie.

Bishop Bowen showed up at Leah's farm about noon on Monday and put a new battery in her car. He told her to pay him when she could, that it cost six dollars. That had to be the wholesale price, she figured, and she told herself she would pay him today, and pay him $8.50. She'd checked in the Montgomery Ward catalog and knew that was what it should cost. She knew she would have to take a few more dollars out of the bank. So later in the day she drove into town, parked in front of the bank, and had just stepped out of her car when she saw a sign across the front door: "Bank Holiday."

Leah's breath stopped. She knew—everyone knew—what that meant. Leah saw a couple of men she knew on the sidewalk talking to another. She walked over to them. "Walter, what's going on?" she asked.

Walter Moss was the only lawyer in town. She knew he was in on any decision the bank owners had made. "Well, it's nothing to get too worried about," he said, but that was what she would expect him to say.

"Has the bank failed?"

"Not exactly." Walter was a man in his late sixties, white-haired, with deep creases in his cheeks. His face seemed almost skeletal, always had, but he looked grim now, no matter what he was saying. She glanced at Garth Welker, the man Walter had been talking to. He owned a feed store in town and probably had dealings with the bank. He looked more than worried, maybe scared.

"Walter, just be straight with me," Leah said. "What's happening?"

"I guess you could say that they've come up short and can't pay out all the savings people are demanding. But there's work going on to sell out the holdings to a bank in California. Those people have more resources, and they hope to make good on the accounts—at least to the degree they can. If you've got money in the bank, you might not get it all back, but in time, you should get . . . some of it."

"Some? How much?"

"There's no way of saying, Leah."

"When will they know?"

Walter looked down toward his feet. Garth mumbled a good-bye and walked away. "It could be months, Leah. I don't know."

Leah took a breath and looked away. She could see some teams of horses, with wagons, tied up next to automobiles. This could be the most crushing blow yet to farmers as well as townspeople—anyone who had managed to get a little money ahead and had tried to start a nest egg. "I could lose everything, couldn't I?" she said. "All of us could."

"It's possible. I won't tell you that it isn't."

Leah thought of Rae graduating in June, planning to go to college in the fall. Maybe all that was gone now. Maybe everything was gone. Leah walked away from Walter and got into her car. She needed to set the spark and then get out and turn the crank, but she just sat there. Her first worry was paying the bishop for the battery. Maybe she ought to take it back to him. But a blackness was coming over her, and she couldn't think what to do. She wanted to pray, but she thought of her prayers Sunday morning. Batteries lasted only so long, no matter how much God loved you. And bad things happened to people no matter how much they prayed. She wanted to cry, but so did a lot of other people in this town—all the people she had told to buck up and keep going. Now she finally knew how lost they had felt.

Leah got out and started her car. She drove home, sat in a chair in her front room, and stared straight ahead. She had to send her kids to college somehow. It was the one clear thing she had lived for. She felt the way she had on the day Wayne had died, too numb to feel, too scared to hope.

When the telephone rang, Leah thought of not answering, but she got up and walked to the kitchen and picked up the receiver. "Hello."

"Leah, it's Belva. Have you heard about the bank?"

"Yes."

"You had money in the bank, didn't you?"

"Yes. Some."

"You've been paying it out, giving it to people, haven't you?"

Leah didn't answer. She didn't want to lie, but she didn't want to say anything about that.

"Oh, Leah, what can I do to help you?"

"Nothing. I haven't used it to live on. I can get by without it. It's just that I wanted to send Rae to college this fall." But she was breaking down, and she couldn't do that. She gripped the phone hard and didn't—couldn't—say anything more.

"I'm coming out there, Leah. I'll be there as soon as I can."

Chapter Fourteen

TWO WEEKS HAD GONE by and it was now March, but the bank was still closed. What had changed was that Franklin Delano Roosevelt, the new president, had declared all banks on holiday. He had started his presidency by stating at his inauguration, "So first of all, let me assert my firm belief that the only thing we have to fear is fear itself—nameless, unreasoning, unjustified terror which paralyzes needed efforts to convert retreat into advance." He had promised a whole series of changes that were to come immediately. Among other things, he wanted to pass legislation that would secure the nation's banks by giving them federal support. The only trouble was, the bank in Richards had closed before the president's action, so it was already too late—unless someone bought it and managed to keep it going. Leah, along with a lot of people in town, kept asking what was going to happen, but no one could offer any answers.

So far, Leah had decided not to say anything about the money to her children. Rae was going about life as though she would be gone to college that fall, and it was clear that she could hardly wait. Rae clearly wanted to get away from high school, the farm, and especially her mother, and Leah felt sick every time she thought of telling her that she couldn't go.

Leah had also decided not to ask Rae to befriend Vickie. She had started a conversation that had been heading that direction when Rae had shown that she didn't feel much empathy. Leah had hoped that Rae could act as a sort of big sister. That part might have been all right, but Rae had never spent much time with boys, and she seemed to have almost no concept of how a young girl could let herself "do something like that," as she had put it.

The fact was, Leah was going about life in a kind of daze. She didn't want to burden anyone with her worries. Only Belva knew about her loss. Leah was plagued by the possibility that her children's future had been lost with the closing of the bank. She didn't know what Rae would do. She would have to look for work in a town that had no work—either that or leave and try to find something somewhere else. She could stay and help Leah on the farm, but if she did, she would be devastated and, surely, hard to live with. It seemed unlikely she would find a husband here in Richards, where no one had ever taken enough interest to ask her on a date.

But Leah worried just as much about Wade. The boy had so much ability, but he was easily pleased and would probably like nothing better than to take over the farm, marry some girl from the area, then scratch out a living the same way Leah had done. What kind of life was that? Wade was smart enough to study almost anything, and likable enough that he could do well in business. He would make a wonderful doctor, a smart lawyer—*anything,* if he ever got motivated to work for it.

Leah had told herself so often this last year that she ought to pull her money—or at least a big part of it—out of the bank, and just hide it somewhere on the farm. She had heard of so many bank failures across the nation, but Walter had always told her that the bank was on solid ground, and the bank president, Glen Whiting, had reassured her as well. She now realized that banks stayed in business by selling confidence. It was fear that caused bank runs, and no bank could suddenly deliver all its savings into the hands of its customers.

What she hadn't known was that a few days before the "holiday" had been announced, a rumor had started in town that the bank was in trouble, and lots of people had withdrawn their money. They were the ones who had broken the bank, and yet they were also the ones who had gotten out in time. It seemed unfair, and Leah was especially upset when she heard that even Walter had saved himself by pulling out most of his assets just before the doors closed. It was hard not to believe that people like Nadine Willis, and even Marjorie, hadn't heard the rumors and done something too. But she had no proof of that.

Leah had one hope. President Roosevelt—"FDR," people had started to call him—had promised that in his first hundred days in office he was going to take action to get the nation going. On his first Sunday evening in office, he had spoken to the nation by radio, held what he called a "fireside chat," and he had reassured the people. One of his first attempts, he'd promised, would be to improve conditions for farmers. He had proposed a new Agricultural Adjustment Administration and legislation to pay farmers for not planting one-third of their acreage and for cutting back the size of their herds. Farmers would get the sure income for not planting, and the overabundance of farm products would be reduced. That would force prices up. Some were calling the idea communistic, and others were shouting that it was wrong to cut back on food production at a time when many were going hungry, but Leah saw the idea as a hope that she would receive some income this year. If prices were up, and if the bank reopened, even if she had lost much of her money, she might be able to put together enough to get Rae started at college, and maybe the following years would be even better.

It was what everyone seemed to be feeling—that maybe the worst was over. Roosevelt was intent on making something happen, and everyone was talking as though things were changing already, just to hear a little optimism. It was true that some people were worried about the techniques the new president wanted to try. He wanted to take the country off the gold standard—which had always required paper dollars to be backed by actual holdings in gold—and thereby allow a gradual inflation to stimulate the economy. Some thought disaster would come of that, but most had no idea how those things worked; they only hoped that jobs would open up and the country would begin to move again.

For now, Leah was trying to hold steady, keep going about her work, and hope that she wouldn't have to break any bad news to Rae. And she was trying to do the same with Relief Society—keep up with all those who needed help and carry a little of this new national mood to them. What she hadn't done yet was what the bishop had asked of her. She hadn't gone to see Nadine. She knew she would have to do it one of these days, but she just didn't know how to handle the situation. She supposed she needed to humble herself and say she was sorry—and she *was* sorry in some ways—but she hated to give Nadine the satisfaction of believing that Leah had been the one entirely in the wrong. She knew very well that she'd been too harsh on the phone, but she still wasn't sure that anything she'd said had been inaccurate.

Still, she had to do what she could to make things right, and she was trying to think of the right way. That was how things stood one morning when she woke up knowing that her alarm would go off any minute, but the room was still dark and cold and she longed to stay in bed a little longer than usual. She had gone to bed plenty early the night before, but she had not been able to go to sleep with all her worries running through her head. Now she shut her eyes, drifted halfway back into sleep, then reached for the clock when she heard it ring. Then she realized that it wasn't the clock ringing but the telephone, out in the kitchen—and it was her ring. She jumped up quickly and hurried out to answer it.

What she heard was a shrill voice, full of panic. "Leah, my baby! He's having fits. I don't know what to do."

Leah recognized the voice: Roylene Dobbs, from the farm next to hers. "What are you saying, Roylene? Is he having convulsions?"

"I guess. I don't know."

"Does he have a high fever?"

"Yes. He's burning up."

"Okay. Listen to me. Get his clothes off. Wash him in lukewarm water—not cold. Is Monte there?"

"No. He's out at his dad's place, working for him on the farm."

"I'll be there in five minutes. Get started washing him." Leah hung up the phone and yelled, "Kids, I've got to run to Roylene's. I might not be back for a while. You'll have to get yourselves up for school."

She heard nothing, didn't worry about it for the moment, but hurried to her bedroom. She pulled on the shirt and overalls and slipped on the socks she had worn the day before. Then she stepped into her boots and tied them loosely.

She was at the door in two minutes, no more, and yelling again. "Did you kids hear me? I've got to run right now!"

"I heard you," Rae said. She had come to her bedroom door. "Can you get out the lane in the car?"

Leah was surprised Rae would bother to get up, bother to ask. Sometimes lately the girl had seemed almost human. "I don't know. The mud's bad. If I get stuck, I'll just leave the car. Be sure to get Wade up."

"What's happened?"

"Roylene's baby has gone into convulsions. I've got to go."

As Leah stepped out and shut the door, she heard Rae ask, "Will he be all right?"

But Leah had no time to answer questions—especially that one. She got the car started on the third crank. She drove toward the lane and then gunned the gas and hit the deepest mud hole going as fast she could. The car slithered. Just as it seemed ready to bog down, it broke onto drier ground. From there, she just kept plunging ahead. She made it to the road, turned right, drove the quarter mile or so, and then skidded through another muddy lane. She stopped out front, jumped from her car, and ran in, not bothering to knock, but yelling, "Roylene, I'm here."

"I'm in the kitchen." She still sounded panicked. Leah hurried into the kitchen, the only room with a lamp on. Roylene was standing at the sink using a cloth to wash water over the baby's chest and arms. He wasn't convulsing, but he was far too limp. Leah didn't like the way he looked.

"He's stopped jerking," Roylene said, "but he won't cry or anything. He won't even open his eyes. What should I do?"

Leah didn't know. She stepped up next to Roylene and felt the baby's head. It was still hot. "We better get Doc Putnam out here—that, or go to him."

"Monte told me not to call the doctor. We don't have any money."

"It doesn't matter. Grab a blanket for the baby. I'll call the doc and tell him we're coming. That'll be faster than waiting for him."

She spun the crank of the telephone, then told the night operator to get the doctor on the phone. Seconds were ticking by and the phone was only ringing, but finally Doc Putnam's voice came on the line, saying, "Yes?"

"Doc, it's Leah. I'm driving Roylene Dobbs's baby in. He's been having convulsions and now he's not responding."

"What do you mean? Is he breathing?"

"Yes. But he won't wake up."

"All right. Bring him in. I'll be in my office by the time you get here."

As Leah hung up the receiver, she heard Roylene crying. Leah turned to see that she had laid a blanket on the table and was wrapping the baby in it, but she was saying, "I don't know how I'll pay him."

"Roylene, stop that. We'll worry about that later. Come on. Let's go."

So they hurried back to the Model T, which Leah had left running, and they made another slick run to the road. The drive to town was short, and once Leah hit the road, she pushed the car as hard as she could. Leah wanted to tell Roylene that the doctor's bill would be paid, that there was no reason to worry, but she couldn't tell people that anymore. She couldn't pay for it any more easily than Roylene and Monte could.

"I should've gone to him before this—two days ago," Roylene said. "But Monte kept saying, 'It's just a cold. A doctor can't do anything about that.' I told him and told him—Roger was sicker than that. He just kept saying, 'And where's the money going to come from?' But I should've done it—just brought him in anyway, or at least called the doc to see what I should do."

"You can't blame yourself, Roylene."

Roylene was holding the baby too close, keeping it too warm, and all the while talking. "Wake up, Roger. Please, please. Just open your eyes."

"Give him room, Roylene. Unwrap him a little."

"But it's so cold in the car."

"It doesn't matter. Give him some air."

"Okay." She pulled the blanket open and Leah got another glance at the little boy, gray as putty and not moving at all. "Roger, can you hear me?" Roylene said. "Wake up." She looked over at Leah. "Leah, you can't believe how Monte yells at me if I do things when he says not to. He's going to be so mad about this."

"For heaven's sake, Roylene, do you want your baby to die? What's Monte going to say if we let that happen?"

"I don't know. He'll blame it on me, either way. That's what he does—no matter what I do." Roylene began to cry again—had never really stopped—and she pulled the baby to her chest. "Oh, Roger, you've got to get better," she was saying. "You've just got to. I can't live without you."

Leah braked to a stop in front of the doctor's office, and sure enough, a light was already on. The doctor lived behind his office. It was all one building: his office, a few rooms that served as a hospital, and the house where Doc Putnam lived with his wife.

Roylene hardly waited for the car to stop before she had the door open and was sliding out. Leah jumped out too, and she hurried around the car to catch up. The office door was locked, so they knocked, and in a few seconds Doc was there, fumbling with the lock and then pulling the door open. He had put on some trousers, with suspenders, and a wrinkled white shirt, but he didn't have on his usual suit and tie, not even any shoes. He looked like he hadn't shaved in a couple of days either, a shiny gray stubble sprouting on his cheeks and chin.

"Come in, come in," he said. "Has he come around at all?"

"No," Roylene said, her voice trailing into a sob.

"Well, let me take him. What have you done for him so far?"

"We got him in some water," Leah answered for Roylene. "He's cooled down some."

"That's the right thing." He looked intently at Roylene. "Now calm down. You did exactly what you should have. Tell me how long he was so hot, before the convulsions set in?"

"I don't know," she whimpered. "When he finally went to sleep last night, after crying for such a long time, I fell asleep too. I should've checked him more, but I was so tired, and I guess I thought . . . oh, I don't know what I thought."

"It's okay." The doctor walked to a little table in the center of the office, set little Roger down, and opened up the blanket. "Have you noticed him pulling at his ears at all?"

"I don't know. He might have."

"Well, they don't always do that. But these high fevers start with an ear infection most of the time." The doctor reached for his stethoscope, hanging on a peg on the wall, and he listened to the baby's chest.

"I wanted to call you. I should have."

"Don't worry about that now." But Leah heard a little too much concern in Doc Putnam's voice. He was well over seventy now, and he must have seen plenty of these situations turn out badly. He had told Leah a while back that if he could find a young doctor to move to Richards, he would retire—but that was not likely to happen soon.

"Is he going to be all right?"

But the doctor didn't answer. He put his stethoscope aside and used an instrument to check Roger's ears. Roger was limp as death. Leah felt her own fear rising.

"That's what it was, all right," Doc Putnam finally said. "He's got a bad ear infection. The eardrum has broken through."

"Will he be deaf?"

"No. But . . ."

"What?"

The doctor wrapped the blanket loosely around the baby and picked him up with a gentleness that touched Leah. He was a handsome man in his way, with depth in his dark eyes, even his wrinkles seeming to lend him dignity.

"Roylene, sit down a minute. There's not a lot we can do for him right now. We'll keep him from getting hot again, but mostly, now, we're just going to have to wait."

"Something's wrong, isn't it? It's bad."

Leah finally paid attention to what the poor girl looked like. Her feathery hair was a mess, and her eyes looked crazed. But she looked, more than anything, like a child. She *was* a child, with way too much of a burden on her shoulders. She didn't sit down. She was dressed in a thin cotton housedress—something she must have grabbed just to cover herself. When she wrapped her arms around herself, folding them around her middle, Leah could see how thin she was, her ribs making ridges under the cloth.

"Here's Bonnie coming up the walk," Doc Putnam said. "I called her to come over and help."

He waited for Bonnie, his nurse, to come through the door, and then he told Roylene, "We're going to see what we can do for a few minutes, but I want you to calm down and put this in our hands—and the Lord's—for a little while. You sit here with Leah, and don't think too much. Worry's not going to make this baby better."

By then, little Bonnie, who had worked for the doctor only a year or two and was about the same age as Roylene, stepped to her, hugged her, and whispered, "We'll take good care of him." Then she took the baby from Doc Putnam and walked through the back door of the office.

All this was worrisome to Leah, and obviously terrifying to Roylene. "Let me go back with you," she said. "I can help, or I can . . ."

"Not yet," the doc said. "Just sit down. I'll come and talk this over with you in about five minutes—ten at most."

He followed Bonnie from the room. Roylene turned toward Leah, looking angry now. "If he dies, or if he's deaf, or if his brain is all burned up—I'll hate Monte as long as I live. I should have called the doc. He'd be all right now if I'd called when I wanted to."

"You don't know that, Roylene," Leah said. "And don't think of the worst. Just do what the doctor said." Leah sat down in one of the office chairs. She patted the seat of the chair next to her. "Sit down and wait until he can tell you a little more."

"No. I'm going back there."

Roylene turned toward the door, but Leah was up immediately. She grabbed Roylene's shoulders, held firm, and turned her around.

"Roylene, stop this. You can't fly off the handle. You're a mother, not a little girl. Get yourself under control."

"I *hate* Monte," Roylene hissed. "I hate him. He bosses me around. He thinks he's always right, and he isn't. Since he lost his job, the only thing he thinks about is money. He didn't even care about Roger, and now he's—"

"Roylene, stop it. You don't hate your husband. He's a good boy. He's just scared, like all the rest of us. He thought Roger had a cold, and he didn't want to spend the money. It's what lots of people do these days."

"But I told him Roger needed—"

"Stop it!"

"Leah, I don't want my baby to die!" She was screaming now, trembling.

Leah took a breath, softened her voice, and held Roylene by the shoulders. "I know, honey. But don't say things you won't be able to take back. This is real life. You've got to grow up, right now. Don't blame Monte—*or* yourself. Just do what you have to do."

"I can't. Not if my baby dies." And suddenly she was sobbing again.

Leah took the girl in her arms. "Oh, Roylene, I know how you feel. But don't decide what you can't do. You don't know that yet."

"Is he going to die?"

"I don't know, honey. I don't think he will—but I can't promise you that. Sometimes hard things happen, and we have to be strong enough to face that."

"You don't cry, Leah. You don't ever break down."

"I don't let myself cry, honey. That's my way. But there's nothing wrong with crying. Just don't say you hate your husband. Those are words that do too much damage."

Roylene grasped Leah tighter and cried hard, her skinny body quivering against Leah's chest. But Leah felt her calming after a time. Leah sat down and pulled Roylene into the seat next to her, then wrapped her arm around her shoulders and pulled her close.

"Should we say a prayer?" Leah asked, a little surprised by her own words—as though they had come from her mouth before she had thought of them.

"Yes, please. But you say it."

So Leah prayed. She asked the Lord to help little Roger and to bless Doc Putnam to know what to do for him. She also asked for a blessing on Roylene—and Monte—to give them comfort and strength. After she had prayed, Leah thought that she knew something, that she had an answer. But she didn't trust such feelings enough to make any promises yet. She merely held Roylene and waited.

The sun was coming up, natural light gradually filling the room. Doc Putnam was gone at least twenty minutes, not five or ten, and when he came in, he didn't look confident. He stood by the table, leaned back against it, and crossed his arms. "Roylene, we've got the fever under control now. You did most of that yourself. But there's no telling yet what that fever has done. Right now, he's still not showing much sign of coming around, so it's hard to say just how serious this might be. He might wake up soon and be fine. And if he does, that eardrum will heal up all right. For now, we just have to keep watching him."

"What should I do?" Roylene asked, and Leah knew she was trying to sound grown-up.

"Go back and sit with him. We'll make sure the fever doesn't come back." He rubbed his hand over his chin. "I need to go clean up and get ready for the day. I've been going almost steady for two days. I don't think I've slept four hours."

"I'm sorry, Doctor."

"No, no. Don't take it that way. I'm just saying, I need to let you and Bonnie watch him for a while, and I'll get myself shaved, at least."

"You look better than I do, Doc," Leah said. "I look like a farmer, not a farmer's wife."

"You look fine, Leah," the doctor said. "As far as I'm concerned, you're the finest-looking woman in town."

"What?"

"I'm an old man. I've learned how to look at a woman and *see* her. I always liked you, my dear, but I've watched you soften this last year. I see it in your eyes."

For once in her life, Leah didn't say anything, but another sense of knowing passed through her.

"Roylene, you watch Leah and learn from her," Doc said. He walked to the door. "Bonnie's going to let me know if she needs me, but mostly we have to let the little fellow rest for now. He might have some swelling in his brain, but if he does, that will go down over the next few days. If I had to predict, I think he's going to be all right. I don't think the fever was high enough—or lasted long enough—to do serious damage. So let's hold that thought for now." He stepped out and shut the door.

"Roylene," Leah said, "if you can tell me where your father-in-law's farm is, I'll drive out there and get Monte."

"Not yet. I don't want him to know yet."

"He's got to know."

"He'll think I did the wrong thing."

"No. You look him in the eye and tell him what you did, and how you did the best you could. Don't blame him, but don't let him blame you either."

Roylene nodded, and Leah guessed that she was trying to picture herself doing that, maybe resolving to do it. Finally, she said, "Don't leave me yet. I need you to keep telling me to think right."

"Okay. But I'll use the doctor's telephone and call Belva. Maybe she can make the drive out to get Monte. He has to know."

Roylene nodded, and Leah called Belva, who knew exactly where the Dobbses lived. She said she would head out there right away.

So Leah and Roylene went to Roger, and they sat by him, touched him often, and watched him sleep, looking peaceful and not so limp. In time the office opened and people with their illnesses and injuries started coming in.

It was almost ten o'clock when Monte finally arrived. He looked at little Roger, touched his head gently, and then he took Roylene in his arms. There were tears in his eyes. Leah heard Roylene try to sound confident as she explained to Monte what the doctor had said, and what had been happening. So far, there had been little change, but Doc Putnam had said, not half an hour earlier, that Roger's heart was sounding stronger, and his breathing was better.

Monte held Roylene with one arm and shoved the other deep into the pocket of his overalls. "This is my fault," he said to Leah. "Roylene wanted to call the doc and I was too dad-burned worried about the cost of it. If he doesn't make it, it's all on my shoulders." A little sob broke from him.

"No, no," Roylene said. "Don't say that. I should have seen it was getting worse and brought him in sooner. But we can't blame ourselves. Things happen sometimes. No one can be right all the time. Leah's been talking to me about that."

Monte turned and took Roylene in both arms again. "But I'm sorry," he said. "I'm so sorry. You're the mother, and you knew something was wrong. I should've listened to you."

"Listen, you two," Leah said. "I'm going to leave. You'll be all right now. Just let me know if anything changes."

Leah walked to the outer office in her overalls and saw a couple of Relief Society sisters sitting there. She thought of apologizing for the way she looked, but she didn't. She could see that they both had sick kids, and both looked worried. She asked about both situations and promised help, if needed. And then she went home and sharpened the blades on her plow. She longed to get started with spring planting. She thought of a year ago, just a little later in the spring, when she had been plowing and the bishop had come along. But that was the other Leah—who was now a little hard to remember.

When Leah came in from her work that afternoon, she was tired, not so much from the work, she supposed, but from the long, worrisome day she'd put in. Rae was in the kitchen. She was frying slabs of pork in a frying pan, the grease making a sizzling noise. "Roylene called," Rae said. "Her baby woke up, and the doc said he's going to be all right."

"Good." Leah felt air flow back into her lungs.

"She said she never could have got through it without you. She wanted me to tell you that."

Leah nodded, but she couldn't really say anything at the moment.

"You're a good Relief Society president," Rae said.

"Is that what she said?"

"Yes." She looked away, avoiding Leah's eyes, and added, "But I'm saying it too."

The two finally looked at each other for a moment, but Leah couldn't think what to say. She wasn't sure what was going on. So finally she said, "Well, I need to clean up. I'm a mess." And then she added, "Thanks for getting supper going."

"Yeah. It's not much, but it's edible, I think. We don't have much left to cook."

"I know. But anyway, thanks." Leah wanted to say more, but she figured she'd better just let that be enough for now. When she started talking, she usually only made things worse.

Back in her bedroom, though, stripping off her dirty overalls, she admitted to herself that she had said the right thing a couple of times that day.

Chapter Fifteen

Leah had another dream—maybe the same dream. It was full of confusion, rambling into tangents, and when she awoke she couldn't remember much of what had happened. There had been a kind of plot, it seemed, but she didn't know what it was. Still, that face had come back. Leah had known the young woman, but she couldn't see her now, couldn't remember who it was. She wondered whether it was Roylene, but she didn't think so. She was almost sure she would have remembered if it had been her.

Leah had kept in touch with Roylene over the last month, since the day little Roger had been sick. He was doing fine now, seemed to be entirely back to normal. Doc Putnam had told Monte that he could pay him later—whenever he could. Monte and Roylene thought they could manage it when Monte's dad finally paid him—whenever *he* could pay.

"It'll work out," Leah had told Roylene. "But you two be kind to each other. No more blaming."

"I know. I never should have said some of them things."

"You were upset."

"I was. But Monte is different lately. He told me he's done some things wrong with me sometimes—trying to act like he's my boss and everything."

That sounded good to Leah, that Monte had recognized some things in himself. She hoped everything would be all right. She knew that people sometimes vowed to change and then slipped back into old patterns, but Monte was young and good, and she had believed his sorrow when she'd heard him express it.

What Leah was feeling was that *she* wanted to do a better job. She had come a long way in a year, but she hadn't humbled herself, not the way Monte had. It was way past time for her to do something about Nadine and the town women; she needed to bring the sisters together. The trouble was, she didn't know what to do, and the burden of her spring planting was upon her again. So she tried to get as much done as she could one Tuesday morning, and then, before Relief Society meeting, she drove into town early enough to talk with Marjorie.

Sitting on Marjorie's porch, the sun feeling good on the south side of the house, she told Marj, "I think it's time I say something to Nadine, but I don't want to make things worse."

"You had a nice conversation with her that day I was with you. I would just talk to her the same way."

The leaves on the willow tree near the porch were budding out, still gold, not having deepened into green yet, and the tree was glowing in the sun. There was something about light in the spring, the clarity of the air, that always made Leah feel restored. And today she felt unusually mellow. "But I trusted her, Marj. I told her all those personal things—things I never imagined she would repeat to anyone. You can't imagine the damage that did to my relationship with Rae."

"But here's what you don't know, Leah. Nadine's worried sick about LuAnn. She knows the girl grew up having too much, and she can see what that's done to her. Rae's not the only one she's mistreated. And my

Sharon's not so different. She and LuAnn get along fine at times, and then they're mad at each other for a while. Sharon can be a trial, too."

"Bishop Bowen told me that LuAnn's changing."

"I think she is. Nadine hopes so too. But she still worries about her, the same as I worry about Sharon."

"Rae's resentful toward lots of the girls at school. She used to be thick as thieves with Nedra White, but even those two don't spend much time together anymore. I'm not sure Rae knows how to be a good friend, and maybe that's what she's learned from me."

"We've all made mistakes, Leah. No one ever does everything right when it comes to raising children."

Leah was looking across the street at Lily Placer's house. She was one of the women who hadn't attended Relief Society meetings for such a long time. The truth was, Leah hardly knew her. Her husband was another of the men who ran big sheep herds in the area. He'd built his wife a beautiful house in town, and they seemed to be surviving the Depression just fine. Leah had often seen Lily early in the morning, pruning the rosebushes around her house. Those roses would be coming on soon now, in lots of colors, the way they did every year. Lily also collected glassware—which Leah had only heard about—and she loved music. She directed the ward choir. Leah had nothing against the woman, and yet Lily was one of the people she had inadvertently insulted—one who claimed she wasn't coming back to Relief Society so long as Leah was president.

"Marjorie, I need to bring everyone back. The bishop told me when he called me that I had to teach the women to be strong—and I guess that's what I thought I was doing—but he's also warned me that I have to soften my voice. I want to do that, but every time I try, I only seem to make things worse."

"You've made a lot of things better. I've watched what you can do for women who think they're at the end of their rope. They grab on to your strength, and it gets them through."

"I guess they do, Marj. The truth is, though, I'm not as strong as they think I am. I've found that out lately."

"What makes you say that, Leah?"

Leah watched Marjorie's eyes, those pretty round eyes. She wasn't a complicated person, Leah thought, just a woman who had hoped for more out of life. She had married a dentist, thinking she would always be secure, and she'd come here, far from the people and places she loved. And then things hadn't been as easy as she had expected. But she was a much nicer person than Leah had imagined.

Suddenly Leah was saying what she had told herself not to say. "I've made some big mistakes, Marj. All these years I've sent my kids to school in ragged clothes, and I've held back on some of the things I could have done for them. I had some money, but I held on to it so I could send the kids to college."

"That was the right thing to do, Leah. College will get them ahead in life more than *anything*."

"But I lost the money. It was in the bank."

"Oh, Leah. I didn't know."

"No one knows." She sat for a moment, still looking across the street at Lily's pretty white house, the rosebushes, the groomed lawn. "Well, that's not quite true. I told Belva—or actually, she guessed it."

Marjorie certainly knew that Leah was closer to Belva than to her, but at the moment, Leah felt surprisingly attached to Marjorie, too. They had been through a lot together over the last year.

"We had a little money in the bank too, Leah, but it wasn't enough to make a lot of difference." She laughed. "I guess that was the advantage of doing so poorly these last couple of years."

"There's still talk that we might get some of our money back. Every week they tell me we'll know something by the next week. I've been hoping it would be enough to get Rae started in college, but I'll be running out of time before long, and I still haven't told her. If I have to tell her she can't go, I don't know what she's going to think of me. All these years she might have dressed nicer and had a few more things, and I took that away from her."

"Let me tell you something, Leah."

Leah looked back at Marjorie, saw tears fill her eyes. "We all do things we regret. I've spent so many years driving my husband away from me, I don't know whether I can ever get him back."

Leah must have let her surprise show.

"I don't mean that way. We're not going to divorce. Clark would never do that to our kids. But I've berated him for not collecting the money people owe him, and I've pushed him to bring in enough to keep us from going bankrupt. He's done his best, and I've learned to manage on less, but even if times ever get better, I don't think I can pull him back close to me. He doesn't love me. And I don't blame him."

"I doubt it's really that he—"

"He *doesn't* love me, Leah. He would never say so. He probably doesn't even admit it to himself. And he would never want to hurt my feelings that much. But he's a gentle man, and I've tried to make him into something he isn't. Now he just does what he has to do and stays as far from me as he can. In every way. Do you know what I mean?"

"Sure." There was so much pain in this world—so many heartbreaks. Leah was always surprised to find out that every woman, once Leah got to know her, seemed to be suffering in some quiet way. She supposed every man probably was too. "Things happen in marriage, Marj," she said. "I told you about Wayne. I just wanted to talk sometimes, and it wasn't that he didn't want to—he just didn't know what to say. He didn't understand talking for the sake of talking. We were just different, that's all, but I struggled with the difference—probably more than I needed to."

"Clark knows that if he talks to me, I won't say anything worth saying—nothing intelligent—so he's stopped trying. I know he'd love to talk to you. He's told me before how smart you are."

Leah couldn't look at Marjorie. She felt "found out." It seemed that she had hurt Marjorie merely by sharing a few thoughts with Clark—and holding close the memory of those conversations.

"Life's hard, Marj," Leah said. "No matter how good things look on the surface, we all seem to have our burdens to carry."

"I know. But I want to make things better. I've been borrowing Clark's books from him lately and trying to take interest. I've even tried to talk to him a little about some of the things I've read. I just wish I'd started trying a long time ago. I was pretty when I was a girl, and that seemed enough. It was all boys seemed to care about—even Clark, back then. I didn't know being pretty wasn't enough."

"And I was never pretty. Reading and thinking were all I ever had."

"You're pretty now, Leah. As a woman gets older, a good mind seems to show through in her face."

Leah laughed. "And what about a sharp tongue? That shows through, too, and isn't pretty at all."

"You just need to talk to the women the way you've talked to me today. Go back to Nadine and get all the hard feelings behind you. And then call on the other women who aren't coming."

Leah hesitated as a bee buzzed around her head and then flew off. She was glad to see bees out again, searching for the year's new blossoms. "Apologizing to Nadine again just seems so empty," she said. "I doubt she would even believe me."

"Don't even talk about that. Just show her you want to be friends. Once you get talking, you'll end up saying the right things."

But Leah wasn't sure about that. That evening she tried to imagine the conversation, how she would get it started, and everything felt so awkward that she put off calling Nadine for another day. When she did call, Nadine sounded hesitant and formal but agreed to meet the day after that. By the time the two sat down together, Leah had practiced at least a dozen little opening speeches, but sitting in Nadine's fancy living room once again, not one of them came to her. She *had* come up with a kind of "excuse" for visiting, and she started with that.

"Nadine, I wanted to ask you for a favor," Leah found herself saying.

"A favor?"

"Actually, it's something I was hoping LuAnn might be willing to do, but I wanted to talk to you about it first."

Nadine looked skeptical. Maybe she was wondering what Leah was up to, but Leah really did have an idea. "There's a new girl from Salt Lake in town staying with Sue Sessions. She's her niece. Her name's Victoria."

"Yes. I saw her at church for a while. I notice she's stopped coming."

"Yes. I know. I don't know what you've heard, but I'll just say that she's gone though some hard times."

"The rumor is, she's pregnant. LuAnn came home from school with that story. Is it true?"

Leah wasn't surprised that word was getting around even if Vickie had decided to start hiding out. "Yes, she is. I promised Sue I wouldn't say anything. But she's showing now to the point where it's hard to hide, and people are going to see her."

Nadine nodded. Leah didn't like the firmness she was seeing. Nadine was waiting for her apology, it seemed.

"I just thought that LuAnn might be willing to be a friend to Vickie. She's actually a fun girl. I think she was very popular in Salt Lake."

"Sounds like it."

"I didn't mean that. I just think she's someone LuAnn would like. The poor girl is really all alone and she needs a friend."

"Why don't you send Rae over to see her?"

"Actually, I thought about it. But Rae doesn't seem like the right person."

"I guess I don't see your thinking. I'm not sure this Vickie is going to be a good influence on any of our girls. Why should I put LuAnn in such an awkward position if you won't ask Rae to do it?"

Nadine was using that authoritative voice she took on sometimes, sounding slightly irritated, slightly superior, and entirely too regal in her high-backed chair. Leah wondered whether she had done the right thing in coming here at all—and especially in asking for a "favor."

"That's a good question, Nadine," Leah said, as calmly as she could, and then she took another breath. "But I wasn't thinking of it that way. I don't think Vickie will change our girls. I was just looking for someone who could help her get through this time she'll be spending out here. LuAnn is outgoing, and she knows everyone. If she was friendly with Vickie, all the other girls in the ward would accept her too."

"And what about Rae?"

"Rae has a lot of problems, Nadine. She doesn't feel accepted herself, and she's resentful about that. She's so wrapped up in herself right now that I don't think she knows how to reach out to anyone else."

"And there's no one Rae resents more than LuAnn."

Leah gave up. This was not going to go well. She told herself she wouldn't get angry, no matter what; she would just end the conversation and get out. "Rae is way too much like me, Nadine," Leah said. She slid to the front of her chair. "She's prickly with people, and then she takes offense when they act the same way toward her. She hears insults in anything anyone says to her, whether it's intended that way or not. Maybe someday she'll be all right, but for now, I don't think she can be of help to anyone. Lately, I see some signs that she's starting to grow up, but she's got a long way to go."

Nadine seemed to think all that over. As she continued to watch Leah, the folds around her eyes smoothed a little. "Those insults are not all imagined, Leah. I've heard LuAnn say things about Rae's old dresses. There's not a doubt in my mind that she's said things to Rae that were *intended* to hurt her feelings."

Leah could breathe again. "I don't know, Nadine. I don't want to think the worst of the girl. I did that once before—about both you *and* LuAnn—and I'm not going to do it again. I'm sorry for the things I said to you on the phone that day."

Nadine nodded. "Leah, I was trying to soften LuAnn toward Rae. I thought if she understood a little more about some things Rae had been through, that might help LuAnn be kinder. But LuAnn can be nasty. All I did was put a dagger in her hand. I should have known she would use it."

"But I've seen LuAnn be very sweet. I stopped by at Primary the other day, and she was helping with the little kids. She was really having fun with them."

"That's true. The bishop called her to that job, and it's been good for her. But she can be a terrible snob. I don't know where she ever learned to be like that." Nadine smiled and let her eyes drift upward. "Apples don't fall far from the tree, do they?"

"Sometimes I feel like Rae's picked up on my very worst qualities, and now she's working to make an art form out of them."

"That's exactly what I see in LuAnn," Nadine said, and for a time she sat and chuckled. "I don't *really* think of myself as a snob. And yet I know that Jim's money—when he had it—hasn't always been good for me. I grew up poor as a church mouse, Leah, and I remember what it was like. But when a person starts to get a few things, it's easy to forget. In that way, it's been good for me to go through the things we've experienced lately. But what do I do about LuAnn?"

"I was thinking it might be good for her to think of someone else. I'm not exactly sure how it will work. But Vickie is aching, and she doesn't want to show her feelings to anyone. Maybe LuAnn could learn something if she shares some of what Vickie's going through."

"My guess is, she'll be curious enough that she'll want to find out what she can about the girl. My fear is that she'll blab it all over town."

"I don't think so, Nadine. I've only had a few glimpses of Vickie's pain, but when I saw it, I knew what a sad little soul she was, and I felt like there was no way I could have added to what she's going through."

"What do you want her to do? Just call on her, or—"

"Vickie's not going to be involved in MIA, but she could come back to church. I'm sure she's feeling too embarrassed right now, but she shouldn't feel that way. If LuAnn would invite her to come, and sit by her in church, I think the other kids would follow the lead."

"All right. I'll talk to LuAnn. I'll ask her to be her best self—and see what comes of it. But I can tell you right now, there's an excellent chance that LuAnn will sneak behind the girl's back and tell tales."

"The tales are already out there. I have a feeling that LuAnn's going to respond all right to this."

"Thanks, Leah. It's nice to have someone believe in her."

Leah nodded and stood up.

"Are you holding up all right, Leah? I know how hard you have to work to keep that farm going and to do all the work you do for the sisters."

"I'm busy, that's for sure. But that's how I've always been."

"Did you ask anyone else to be in charge of the bazaar?"

"No. We might just let that go again this year."

"I think we should have one. The sisters need it more than ever."

Leah watched Nadine, trying to read her.

"I'll get going on it, if you want me to," Nadine said. "I'd like to do that. I've been thinking for weeks about coming to see you, but I've been too proud to do it."

"I know what you mean. I've been the same way. But I'll tell you,

Nadine, if you *could* take over the bazaar, that would take a big load off my mind."

"It's about time we all stopped acting like high school girls ourselves. Let me say something to some of the other women who haven't been to Relief Society lately."

"Should I call on them, or—"

"Yes. Give me a few days, and then I think you should. Don't try to talk them into anything. Just be yourself."

"You mean a porcupine looking for a hug?"

Nadine laughed. "You *can* be thorny. I'll grant you that. But even a rose has thorns."

"I suppose. But no one hugs a rose either."

Leah had chosen her words on purpose. She felt as though it might be time to give Nadine a hug, but she didn't think she could do that—and didn't think Nadine was ready either. So she did some more nodding and laughing, worked her way to the door, and then she escaped.

When Leah got home, she had a water turn to take. She put her overalls on and walked to the west side of her fields to turn a head gate. She walked along the ditch after that to make sure the water was getting to her pasture and to her vegetable garden. This time last year, the fields had been too wet, but the season was setting in dry so far this year.

Leah was still in the pasture when Wade got home from school. He disappeared into the house and came out a few minutes later, having changed from his better overalls into some older ones.

"I'll feed the animals," he said as he walked toward Leah.

"Come here a minute," Leah said. She leaned on her shovel and waited for him to reach her. He stopped, smiling for no reason, the way he always did. He pushed his old straw hat back and waited.

"Did you have a chance to meet Vickie Farrell when she came to church?" Leah asked.

"Sure. She was in my Sunday School class a couple of times." Something in his eyes seemed to say that he'd paid some attention to her.

"Are the kids at the high school talking about her?"

"They know about the baby now. But it's not hard to tell. When she came to church, she had on a dress that was loose in front, but I could still see that she was starting to bulge."

"So what was your impression of her?"

"She didn't act like she was all that upset or anything." He grinned. "I think she should have had that talk with you—the one where you told me and Rae all about the birds and the bees and the rabbits."

"I'm serious, Wade. Are the kids going to be cruel to her?"

"I don't know." Wade looked serious again. "I haven't heard anyone say anything too bad. Some guys have said how good-looking she was, and how, you know, they could see how it would happen."

"What's that supposed to mean?"

"Just that she would get the attention of guys." He shrugged. "And then, you know, the kinds of things guys might say."

"No. I actually don't."

"Well, even if they go to church and everything, sometimes they like to act like they've been around."

"But I don't think she's a loose girl, Wade. I think she made a mistake."

"Yeah. That's what I'd guess too."

"Will you be nice to her?"

Wade shrugged. "Sure. I talked to her for a while at church that last time she came, and she was telling me about her big high school in Salt Lake. She kind of likes to flirt around a little, if you want to know the truth."

Leah was taken by surprise, but she said, "Some girls, when they're really pretty, get so they thrive on the attention they get from boys. That's probably what got her into trouble in the first place."

"I guess."

"She probably wants to feel, more than anything right now, like she's still herself, still pretty—that her life isn't over before it ever got started."

"What's she going to do with the baby?"

"Don't talk about this with the other kids. Let Vickie say what she wants to say about it. But she's going to give the baby up."

"That's what I figured. That's got to be hard."

"I don't think she has any idea how hard. But she just needs some friends—some people who will treat her like she's not *ruined* for life."

"Sure. I'll just do what I did before. You know, talk to her at church—if she comes again."

"And at school, if the boys are talking about her like she's a little tramp, could you tell them she's a nice girl?"

"I guess. They'll just say, 'Oh, yeah, she's *really* nice,' or something like that. You know how boys are."

"No. And I don't think I want to."

Wade grinned again. "We don't *want* to be so stupid. But when we all get together, we can't seem to help it."

"Especially the boys on the teams. Right?"

"Naw. All of 'em."

"Be different. Okay?"

"Hey, I didn't say anything about her. I did think she was nice. And when I heard what was going on, I felt sorry for her."

Leah nodded. Raising kids by herself had never been easy. But now that she was starting to see how things were turning out, she liked to think that Wade would be okay. She hoped Rae would be too.

Chapter Sixteen

Each Sunday Leah watched for Vickie to show up at church. Leah had visited her a couple of times and invited her; the girl had been vague in her answers, clearly fearful of coming. But one Sunday in May, just as the opening hymn was starting, Vickie walked in with LuAnn. They joined Nadine and Jim Willis in the pew where they always sat, toward the front. All during the singing LuAnn and Vickie kept talking, as though they were old friends—and they continued to whisper through most of the meeting. Leah wasn't sure that LuAnn was having the influence that Leah had hoped for, but Vickie did seem animated as she talked.

After the meeting, as Leah was leaving, she had a chance to approach the girls at the back of the chapel. There was no mistaking now that Vickie was pregnant. She made eye contact with Leah, and then she looked away, seeming embarrassed.

"Hi, Vickie," Leah said. "How are you?"

"Okay."

It was LuAnn who said, "She's a little crazy; that's what she is. She's been telling me stories about all her funny friends in Salt Lake."

Vickie took another quick look at Leah, even more embarrassed, Leah thought, and maybe apologetic, but she didn't say anything. She and LuAnn walked out together. Leah followed for a minute and then waited in the entrance for Sue to come out. When she did, Leah pulled her aside and whispered, "How's Vickie doing?"

"Oh, Leah, she's having such a hard time," Sue said. "I almost had her talked into coming to Sunday School this morning, but she backed out at the last minute. When I got back, she looked like she'd cried the whole time I'd been gone. But LuAnn's been coming by to see her two or three times a week, and the two are getting to be pretty good friends. LuAnn stopped by this afternoon, and they talked for a long time. Then Vickie got dressed and said she was coming to sacrament meeting. The two of them walked over together. I know how Vickie acts when she's around people—like she doesn't have a care in the world—but it's just her way of hiding what she's really feeling. She's sure that everyone in the ward thinks she's worthless."

Leah was amazed by the difference between appearances and realities. She had seen the same thing in lots of other families in the ward: things people were ashamed for others to know. "Well, Sue, she came. That's the important thing. Next time it won't be quite so hard."

"I know. But people must think she's a hard little nut—laughing and whispering like that when she's in her condition."

"We're all in some condition, Sue. And we all hide it the best we can."

"I know. And thanks for saying that. But really, I'm not sure Vickie is going to make it through this. She's told me twice now that she'd rather die than have to face all this shame here, then turn around and go back to Salt Lake to face the people in her own ward—and at her high school. She knows the story has gotten around back home by now."

"And what about giving up the baby? How is she dealing with that?"

"I don't think she's faced it yet. But she's feeling life now, and she's starting to understand—it's not just an embarrassment; it's a child. The more she thinks about that, the harder everything is going to be."

"I'm hoping LuAnn can be a help to her."

"She already is. Vickie can hardly believe that such a popular girl would have anything to do with her. And I'll tell you something. LuAnn's a nicer person than I ever thought she was."

That was good to hear. And it made Leah wonder whether she had actually ever seen the world before. She had been looking at surfaces—like the reflections on water that hid all that lay beneath.

On Tuesday Nadine came to Relief Society, and so did Lily Placer and Pearl Street. They slipped into the back row of seats as though they didn't want others to take much notice of their having returned, but everyone did notice, and lots of the sisters greeted them. And then Suzanne Oberg came in at the last minute and sat in the same row. The chatter in the room seemed different, the faces more natural and happy, as though everyone sensed that a bad time had passed.

Leah stood before the women, feeling awkward, as always, and still self-conscious about her appearance. She greeted everyone, without mentioning the women who had come back, but then, after a hymn and a prayer, she asked Nadine to say something about the bazaar.

Nadine stood at the back. "Yes," she said in her big voice, "it's time we get going on the bazaar for this fall. I've brought fabric and patterns today, and some of you have said you want to start piecing quilt tops. If you can do that, we'll be able to set up our frames before long—but I've got some new ideas this year. Be sure to come to work meeting next week and I'll show you some things we're going to make—things that should sell well. You'll have some fun making them, too."

She lowered herself back into her chair, still smiling, seeming pleased to be back.

Leah thanked her, and then she said to the sisters, "I don't know about you, but I think most people in this country are starting to feel a little more optimistic, with President Roosevelt taking action the way he is." She stopped. Folks were expressing a little more hope these days, but some people didn't like what Roosevelt was doing, and as often as not, it was the people who ran businesses who were complaining about the federal government moving toward regulation, trying to set wages and prices. The last thing Leah wanted to do was offend the sisters who had returned today.

"But the thing is, times might be hard for a while yet, or they might get better. We don't know. The important thing is that we all work together to do what we can for those who really are down on their luck. It sounds like there's going to be some government work projects, but how soon we'll see any of that reach us out here is hard to say."

"That's all just talk anyway," Sister Oberg said—without raising her hand. "These feds want to pay farmers to kill their pigs. People are going without food, and now they want to butcher newborn pigs and bury them. Something's gone crazy." Her eyes were buried under heavy cheeks and thick, black eyebrows, but Leah could see that she was watching closely, ready to be insulted all over again.

Leah took a breath. For well over a decade farmers had been producing so much food that prices had been forced downward to a level that made farming unprofitable. Roosevelt wanted to stop the overproduction, and for this first year that meant killing pigs already born. By next year, the government would merely pay for cutting the size of herds, not for killing live animals. It did sound cruel, but the hope was that in the long run it could change things for farmers all over the country. So this was something Leah had accepted, and the old Leah would have told Suzanne that she didn't know what she was talking about.

But the new Leah said, "I know what you mean, Suzanne. It *is* sad to kill animals when so many people could use that meat. But those are things politicians decide. What we have to do is make sure the families in our ward have enough to eat."

"I know that," Sister Oberg said, her voice less intense. "It just seems a shame to me." Leah watched the tightness leave those hunched cheeks.

"Yes. I'm sure we all agree with that." Leah looked around at the group, all these ladies so varied in background and education and opinions. And she was the one who had brought up politics—just about the last thing in the world she should have mentioned. It was not yet June, but the last few days had been warm, and the heat in the Relief Society room was building this afternoon. A few women had been fanning themselves, but they had stopped now, as though they were tense, probably worried what Leah was leading them into again.

"I think the bazaar can do a lot more than just help the ones who are sick or out of work, or something like that," Leah said. "A lot of why we do it is just to get together and work side by side. We really need to know each other a lot better. If there's one thing I've learned this last year, it's that every single family is affected by this Depression, and it only looks like some are not. I used to have the idea that life had turned out hard for me, and that the rest of you had gotten off pretty easy. I've found out that it only looked that way because I was hiding away and peeking out through a knothole in my hiding place. The fact is, we all have struggles. And the best thing we can do is think the best of each other, not the worst, the way I've had a tendency to do. Ol' Will Rogers likes to say, 'I never met a man I didn't like,' and I guess I don't feel exactly that way. I've met a few women I didn't like so much—and even more men— but . . ."

Some of the women laughed, softly, and most everyone smiled, as if to say, *Yes, I can think of some I don't like.*

"But you know what? That's just *meeting* them. It's when I get to know a woman's heart, understand what she's feeling and what burdens she's had to carry—that's when I find out that I like her after all. I know that I'm one person who's not that easy to like. I'm rough as a cob, and if there's a way to say the wrong thing, I'll find it every time. But I've gotten the feeling from you sisters that you've accepted me pretty well. And I'm going to say something to you that I usually don't say."

Leah stopped. This was harder than she'd thought it would be when she'd planned it out. She looked over the heads of the women, not at them, and she said, "I love you. All of you."

Leah heard a little sniff. She looked around at Belva, who was using a white handkerchief to dab at her eyes. Leah didn't think she would ever get emotional in front of these women. She hated it when people stood up in testimony meeting and started blubbering and wiping their eyes. But she found herself fighting her feelings now. So she laughed and added, "Let me put it this way. I love you just like family. Of course, I've got one brother who rubs me the wrong way and always has. Do you know what I'm talking about? But I do love him."

That got a bigger laugh. She liked the way they were still looking at her now, seeming to know how to take her—better than they would have last year if she had said something like that.

"We really do need to stand by each other," she said, being serious again, "and help where we can. But it doesn't start with a bazaar or a government program; it starts in the way we think about each other. It's like we're crossing the plains together and we are *not* going to leave anyone behind—and not just because it's our duty. It's because we're sisters."

Leah saw a lot of nodding, and then Belva said, "Leah?" Leah turned and nodded, and Belva stood up, the way some of the older women had apparently learned to do. Belva was wearing a little white hat and, of all things, white gloves, on a day that was getting hotter by the minute. "If you live long enough, you find out, sooner or later, everyone has a turn at being the one who needs a little lift," she said. "I know it's hard for those who need help right now. We'd all rather be the one giving a hand than the one needing one, but if we have the right spirit about it, we don't think of it as reaching backward; it's all a matter of linking arms and everyone moving along together."

"That's right, Belva," Sister Oberg said. "That's exactly right." And that seemed her declaration. She wanted to get along.

Leah nodded to her, thanked her. And then she noticed that Sue Sessions had raised her hand. "Yes, Sue."

Sue stood up. She was a masculine-looking woman, with her big shoulders and big jaw, but she seemed to have aged five years in the last few months. There was a weariness in her face that Leah had never seen before. "Sisters," Sue said, "I'm sure you know about my niece. Everyone has seen her by now—or heard what's going on. I wanted to say something sooner, but Vickie asked me not to." Sue was in the middle of the group, but she was looking straight ahead as though she didn't want to look into anyone's eyes. "All I want to say is that Vickie's going through a terrible time—worse than you might think, just from watching how she behaves. I'm not justifying any of the mistakes she's made, but I do want to ask for your understanding—and a friendly word to Vickie would be more helpful than you could ever know. I know you worry about the example she's setting for our kids out here, but you need to understand, she really is sorry about what's happened. She—"

From the back of the room, old Sister Christensen spoke up. "Sue, you don't have to say another word. There's not a family here that's not had something of that sort happen. It's always been that way. The girl needs support now, not blame, and I don't think there's one person here who wouldn't agree with me."

There was a little murmur in the room, other women saying, "That's right, Ruby."

Tears were suddenly running down Sue's hard cheeks. "Thank you," she said. "I should have known you'd feel that way." She sat down.

Leah only added, "I've talked to Vickie, and I can tell you that what

Sue just told you about her is true. This is a good chance for us to be as good as we're supposed to be—and also to help our children treat her right."

Again, Leah saw lots of nods of agreement.

It was a good meeting. This was the week the sisters discussed theology, and Wanda Baird led a discussion on the period of peace after Christ appeared in the New World. The sisters talked about the traits that could bring such good feelings. It was just the right thing to talk about today, Leah felt. When the meeting ended, lots of the sisters came to Leah and hugged her, whether she liked it or not, and as best she could, she pretended she didn't mind. Lily and Pearl and Suzanne didn't hug her, but they thanked her for what she'd said, and that seemed to mean they were going to keep coming.

So Leah felt good when she was getting her things together, ready to leave. It was then that Marjorie came to her. "That's the best meeting we've had," she said. "You have to feel good about it."

"I do," Leah said. "I got through a whole meeting without putting too much shoe leather in my mouth. Of course, next week I'll probably get it wrong again and send half the women home mad."

Belva was not far away. "Now, now," she said. "Don't say that. The sisters are getting to know your heart. Your words won't matter much if you've got that part right."

Leah had heard about as much sweet talk as she could take in one day. She thought she needed to head back to the farm and get the good smell of manure back in her nostrils. But Marjorie said, "Leah, walk down to my place for a minute. You too, Belva. I made us up a little something for an early supper."

"You know, Marj," Leah said, "I really need to get home and get some work done before the day's over."

"I knew you'd say that, but you'll have to eat anyway, and I've got something ready. I've also packed up a little box you can take home to feed your kids, so you won't have to cook tonight."

"Oh, Marj, you shouldn't—"

"Leah, I'm not taking *no* for an answer. You don't have to stay long."

Leah was still worried how long this all might take—and even more, how much more sweetness she could tolerate—but she knew better than to turn Marjorie down. The two were feeling good about each other these days, and it was no time to step away. So they all walked over to Marjorie's house, and Marj set out some sandwiches she had made earlier and some lemonade. It was quick, and good, and Leah was glad she had come over. But as she was getting ready to leave, Clark walked in. Something about the timing made Leah feel that his arrival had been planned.

"Leah, I'm glad to see you," he said. "There's something I've been meaning to talk to you about."

Leah had no idea what that would be, but when she glanced at Belva, she got the impression that Belva knew about this and was expecting whatever was coming.

"Remember last year when Wade broke his tooth and you came in to see me about getting it fixed?"

"Sure."

"There's something I know now that I didn't know back then."

Leah slid her chair back from the kitchen table and stood up. She had a feeling where this might be going. "What do you mean?"

"Do you know how he broke that tooth?"

"In gym class. He said he bumped into someone."

"He did. Sort of. He bumped into our son Tommy's fist. The two of them got into a fight, and Tommy slugged him in the mouth."

"Boys!" Leah said. "They never change."

Clark was standing with his hands tucked into his back pants pockets, the way he did so often. Marjorie had stepped over next to Clark, and now the two of them were between Leah and the door to the living room, as though they wanted to block Leah's way out of the house.

"The thing is, boys do get into these kinds of tussles when they're playing ball, but we found out more about it. Tommy came clean with us here a while back."

"Clark, it wasn't Tommy's fault. Kids just—"

"Just hear me out for a minute."

Leah glanced at Belva again. She could see that something was coming, knew what it was, really, and she also knew she couldn't accept it.

"Tommy likes Wade now. But he was mad at him last year. I guess he was trying to pressure Wade into playing on the varsity teams."

"I know a little about that. And I know that Wade's been a lot better accepted this year, since he's been playing."

"Well, then, you see what I'm saying. This fight was Tommy's fault, not Wade's, and Tommy is the first to admit it now. He told me the other day, every time he sees that broken tooth, he feels bad about it."

"No, Clark. I know what you're going to say, but we'll get it fixed one of these days, and when we do, I'll pay full price for it. You've done way too much charity work already. You have a profession, and you need to be paid for your work."

Leah stepped forward, but Clark and Marjorie didn't move out of the way, and now Belva had hold of her arm. "What about the things we said in our meeting today?" she asked.

"That's fine. We *should* go back for those who might be left behind. But those who *can* keep up, *should* keep up. That's part of how it all works."

Marjorie reached out and put her hand on Leah's arm. "Leah, we know how much money you've given to people this year. You saved the Peckhams from losing their farm. And you helped out Lawrence Gardner and Randall Pete."

"I think you gave a lot more than we know about," Belva said, "and then the bank closed and you lost the rest of what you had. So let Clark do something for you."

"Someone else was willing to pay for the materials," Clark said. "The only thing I'm offering you is my time—and unfortunately, I've got plenty of that."

"Don't try to lie to me, Clark. I—"

"No, it's true. I'm not paying for the gold. Someone wanted to do that for you."

"Then it was Belva." She turned and looked at Belva. "Old lady, you don't have money to be throwing around like that."

"I know I don't. So don't accuse me."

"Well, you're all in on it, and I appreciate the offer, but really, I'm going to be fine. Even if my money's gone, it looks to me like I could make something off my crops this year. Wade wants to do some extra work on some other farms this summer and save some money of his own. And I think that's good for him—to earn his own way."

"But if he's willing to work that hard to get that tooth fixed, that shows how much he hates going around with it broken like that."

"He does. I know. But those things are learning experiences. He'll appreciate it more if he has to work for it. And he'll think before he starts throwing punches at somebody again."

"Look, Leah," Clark was saying, "we're doing a little better now. We've seen some improvement lately, and . . ."

But Leah was getting forceful. She made her way around Clark and Marjorie and on into the living room. "I really do appreciate the offer, Clark. I honestly do, but let's take care of the ones who are down and out. I'm not in that bad of shape yet. A broken tooth just isn't that important right now."

And she left.

Afterward, in the car, she wondered about herself, wondered why she had felt so angry. She hoped they hadn't been able to see that. But it was embarrassing—insulting, really—for them to see her as desperate. She would get that tooth fixed—maybe sooner now, to show them they had no reason to worry—but she would pay her own way. She had kept up for eleven years since that spring her husband had died, and she wasn't going to fall behind the wagon train and force someone else to come back to get her.

Rae was happy for the sandwiches, so she wouldn't have to cook as she usually did on Tuesdays after Leah's meetings. Once Rae had finished eating and gone off to her bedroom, Leah told Wade, "I've been thinking about that tooth of yours. The broken one. You never say much about it, but I know it bothers you."

"Not that much."

"It's mostly the poor kids who don't get their teeth fixed. Right?"

"Who's not poor? Walker Hopkins has a missing tooth right in front. He's not all that poor. But he got it knocked out sleigh riding two winters ago, and how's his old man supposed to buy a whole bridge to put in there?"

"So you two have talked about it?"

"Yeah. We just said, you know, things happen."

"How did you get yours broken?"

"I told you."

"Was it Tommy Evans who poked you?"

Wade's face reddened—and he wasn't one to blush. "Who told you that?"

"Was it?"

"Look, Mom, I didn't tell you what happened because you always say you don't want me fighting. But me and Tommy are good friends now. That's all forgotten."

"I'll try to get the tooth fixed this fall, after the harvest. I don't think it will be much of a problem to do that this time around."

"I told you, I'm going to earn the money this summer. I won't leave you high and dry, but if I can get some extra work once in a while, I'll take it. I'm not a little boy anymore. I can take care of some of my own needs."

Leah thought she heard herself in his words, and she didn't know whether she was proud of Wade for his independence or ashamed of him for his pride. "But you're okay with Tommy now?"

"Sure. We're the best players on all the teams. He's pretty much the star, but without me, we wouldn't have been near so good as we've been."

But Leah had heard something in Wade's voice. "Does it bother you that he's the star?"

"Look, Mom, for as long as I can remember, Tommy's been the guy everybody at our school pays attention to. I don't care about that anymore. But the day's going to come when I'm the one who goes out and makes something of myself. Tommy thinks he can just ride along—the way I've always done. But I've made up my mind. I'm going to work hard in school next year, and I'm going to go to college—just like you've always told me. Someday, when I have my own business or something like that, and I'm pulling in the big money, ol' Tommy will still be talking about how good he was at sports in high school. A lot of good that's going to do him by then."

"He's a smart boy. He'll get serious about school sooner or later."

"Maybe. I don't know. But I'll tell you one thing. I'm a whole lot smarter than he is. If he can bluff his way through, he's all right, but he's not much in math, where the right answer is the right answer. I plan to come back here someday and see what he's been up to—and I've got a feeling that *I'll* be the star that day."

"Wade, you've never talked like that before. You always said you wouldn't mind being a farmer."

"I know. But I told you, I'm growing up. I'm starting to see what I want."

"And mainly, it's not playing second fiddle to Tommy—is that what you're saying?"

"No. I've just decided I want to do something with my life. That's what you've always said to do."

"Does this have anything to do with the girls at the high school?"

"What?"

"Is there some girl you want to impress? Is that what's got you fired up to make something of yourself?"

"No. Why would you ask that?" But he was blushing brighter now.

"Wade, you and Tommy aren't in competition with each other—for girls or anything else. That's not what life's all about. You do your best, and he'll do his, but you can hope for him to do well at the same time you're trying to get ahead."

"Tell *him* that. Since we were in grade school, he's been showing me up and then letting me know about it."

"But you just said it—you're growing up now. That stuff shouldn't matter."

Wade grinned, showing that tooth. "It *doesn't* matter that much, Mom. I just like the idea of him having to look up to me someday and tell himself, 'That's the guy who used to go around in patched-up clothes, but now he's got a lot more money than I have.'"

"Wade, I know I've talked that way at times. But I don't think it's the best way to look at things. Tommy's mom used to bother me a lot, but it turned out, she didn't have as bad an attitude toward me as I thought she did."

"I *know* Tommy's attitude. It's: 'Wade's my buddy as long as he helps our teams win—and doesn't show me up too often.'"

"I don't think that's true, Wade. Marjorie says he likes you."

Wade was smiling again. "Hey, we're best buddies. But he's still going to envy me someday."

Leah felt sad to hear Wade's tone of voice. But she told herself not to be surprised. He was only expressing what she'd been teaching him all his life.

Chapter Seventeen

IT WAS JUNE NOW, 1933, and Leah was finally feeling comfortable in her calling. The town women were coming to Relief Society, Nadine was moving ahead with the bazaar, and some of the families in the ward were starting to manage a little better. There was a lot of talk of better times, and even though few actual jobs had been created in rural towns yet, the promise of federal work projects was raising hopes. Governor Blood had announced a road project from the basin out toward the Colorado line—that would mean jobs too. So a little spark of optimism seemed to be causing people to buy some of the things they had long gone without. That was causing business to pick up a little in Richards. Jim had hired back one of his employees part time, and Nadine was not putting in quite so much time at the store. Marjorie said that a few people were finally getting dental work done—false teeth, more often than not.

Relief Society work and business meetings were better attended than they had been in a long time. With the fabric Nadine had furnished, the women had pieced three quilt tops and worked on other items for sale.

On a warm morning—the meetings now switched away from the hot afternoons—the sisters gathered to begin quilting. Nadine and Leah had set up three frames in the recreation hall at the church, and women had started coming in soon after they had finished breakfast and gotten their men out of the house. The day promised to be hot, but with the windows open in the rec hall, the temperature was pleasant so far, and the breeze felt good.

Leah was better at setting up frames, stretching the fabric, and supplying the women with thread and needles than she was at doing the actual sewing. She knew that the sisters judged the quality of a quilt by the size of the stitches, and hers always looked three times as long as the tiny stitches Belva could make. So Leah fussed around getting people started, and then she stood behind Belva to see whether she could learn anything. "I don't know how you do that," she told her. She rested her hand on Belva's shoulder. "How do you work so fast and still keep your stitches tiny?"

"Practice," Belva said. "As you often remind me, I'm a *very* old woman." She laughed. "I started stitching when I was a little girl."

"Did you make a lot of quilts back in those days?" one of the women asked.

"We made our share," Belva said, "but not such fancy ones, and not for bazaars. We needed them for warmth. We didn't have much when my family first came out to this basin—not much of anything. We had to make everything by hand."

Women were sitting all the way around the rectangular blanket, which was stretched tight on the frame. Two other frames were set up, and women were gradually filling the chairs around them. Their clothes weren't quite as fancy today. Some were wearing housedresses, and most had taken off their summer hats and set them aside. This was a day to work—but what Leah loved was that it was also a day to talk. Many of the women had small children who were playing in the back of the recreation hall. The Relief Society also owned some playpens, and little ones were sleeping or playing in those—demanding attention from time to time. There would be lunch at noon, but most of the women would stay longer. It was a nice change for most of them, a day away from their farms or homes, one day of the month when they could sit and chat and get something worthwhile done at the same time.

Women did visit one another, of course—especially in town. Visiting teachers also made their rounds, and people chatted over fences while they were out hanging up the wash or working in their gardens. But this was the one time they had to talk at leisure and share some of the things they had been thinking about. It was especially a good time for the farm women, who spent many days alone.

Millie Wilson was sitting next to Belva. Since Millie had lost her baby, Belva had called on her often, and Millie seemed to think of her as a grandma. What Belva and Leah knew was that she was expecting again, and that was healing her. Irma Peckham was on the opposite side of the quilt, facing Belva. She had been through a tough winter, but the weather had been better so far this spring, and her husband had his crops in. Their hope was that they would be able to meet their payment this fall. Grace Wallace was chatting with June Lewis, seeming happier than she had been in a long time. Belva had promised her that things would get better for Henry, and that had happened. The sawmill had hired him back, at least a few hours each week, and the boss was saying that the mill would be using him more before the summer was over. Mary Dibble was getting by so far, with the help of her sister and brother-in-law, and with lots of visits from her visiting teachers, who had arranged for her land to be farmed by some of the men in the ward. Glen Whiting, at the bank, was holding off, letting her try to work things out to stay at least another year. Pat Hyatt wasn't there today—probably too busy at home—but Will was getting stronger each month, even though it never had been clear what had been wrong with him. Belva liked to remind

Leah that she had known all along he would be all right, and Leah always laughed at that, but it was hard to argue with Belva's "prophecies." Leah had learned not to.

The trouble was, of course, there were new problems. Jean Watkins had lost a baby grandson to the flu. He was up in Idaho, and she couldn't even make it to the funeral. She was worried about her daughter-in-law, who was sick herself. And Virginia Hanks had fallen on her back stairs and broken her hip. Her husband wasn't well enough to help much, so the sisters were taking turns going over to bathe Sister Hanks and to bring in meals. And there were lots of other things, including some new men out of work since the Gilsonite mine had cut back its operation. Still, Leah knew something now: Troubles came, but troubles did pass. Belva wasn't so wrong as Leah had once thought she was. The Lord did seem to look over his children and help them through their hard times.

Glenda Poulson was sitting at a corner, close to Doris Berg. It was the first day back for both of them, after they had stayed away all last year. The market that Glenda and her husband operated was still struggling, but the Poulsons also owned the local movie theater, which had stayed surprisingly busy. *Gold Diggers* was playing there right now, and everyone seemed to be going to see it. Leah had no interest, but she had heard the song from it on the radio: "We're in the Money." She caught herself whistling it at times and then laughing at herself.

Leah had visited Glenda recently and they had talked about the store-bought bread. Leah had admitted that she didn't like the stuff, but she knew lots of people preferred it. She explained that she hadn't meant to accuse the Poulsons of selling anything they shouldn't.

Glenda had already been talking to Nadine—and seemed softened. She had clearly been waiting for her apology but, to her credit, seemed prepared to accept it. And she admitted something Leah hadn't expected. She said that she had sometimes felt guilty that she hadn't had to sacrifice much during these hard years, and she probably hadn't done enough to help those who were in worse shape. "It's hard to know where to start," she had told Leah. "And then Harvey always says that people get used to the dole awfully fast, that we shouldn't be handing money over to just anyone. He doesn't like it that the government wants to give out assistance to every Tom, Dick, and Harry—even the ones who've been lazy."

Leah thought of many things she could have said about that, but she only said, "Well, we each have to decide what we can do. It's not easy to know sometimes."

"Well, I want to do more," Glenda said. "I know you think I'm hard-hearted, but I'll tell you, I meet everyone from this valley down at our store. And I know what they're going through. We've extended a lot of credit—more than we should—and we could still go broke. But I want to do a little more to help out in other ways." And then she had promised to come back to Relief Society.

Leah had also brought Rae to work meeting. She was out of high school now, but she hadn't found a job. She was helping Leah, as she had done in summers past, but Leah knew she wanted to prove herself a little more and show she could raise some of her own money.

Rae had not been overly thrilled about coming into town to quilt with the "old ladies," as she had called them, but she did like Belva—and actually, Rae had more of a knack for stitching than Leah did. Leah kept watching her, and she saw her relaxing into the mood of the day, chatting with women she had known only as the mothers and grandmothers in her ward. Leah liked to see that, her little girl taking up her role as a woman, becoming part of the sisterhood. "It's not just quilting to be quilting," Leah had told her that morning. "We'll sell these quilts, and the money we make will help keep people eating this winter. We're not out of this Depression yet—not by a long shot."

"I know," Rae had told her. "You've told me all that before."

Leah wasn't sure that Rae really understood. And yet, there she was, fitting in, doing the work. Maybe this would be the beginning of her accepting some of the women in town—and, Leah told herself, maybe it would be the beginning of her seeing a little beyond her own nose.

"Belva, what was it like when you first settled out here?" Liz Bowen asked. The bishop's wife was in her late thirties, Leah thought, a few years younger than her husband. She and the bishop had a big family to look after, but Liz had left her children with her fourteen-year-old daughter and come over to be with the women.

"It was all cactus and lizards out here," Belva said. "I wanted to turn around and go back to Hennifer, where I was raised. That was such a pretty, green place."

"Were you just a little girl when you first came out?"

"Oh, no. I was thirty by then. Thirty-one, I guess. I had four kids and one on the way." She laughed. "Although we never said that in those days. We did our best not to show our bellies, and when it was time to deliver, we used to say that a woman was 'taken sick.' We all knew what that meant."

"It's what I still say," Gwen Olavson said, and she chuckled to herself. She was a woman over seventy, widowed for many years. "It still seems better to me than talking so loud about things that are private. But I know I'm old-fashioned about that."

"It's what we grow up with that seems natural," Belva said. "But I never did understand why having a baby was anything to keep quiet. We surely don't hide our babies once they're born."

Gwen was chuckling again. "Well, like I said, it's just the way I was raised."

"So what brought you out here?" Liz asked Belva.

"Free land. My husband's brother came first, and he said the land wasn't bad, once you cleared it, and we could homestead. My husband was working on farms, trying to get enough money together to buy a place, and this seemed like the best chance to get started. But I'll tell you, we paid a higher price than money for that piece of ground we got. Blood, sweat, and tears, as they say."

"What kind of house did you have?"

Belva laughed again. She continued to stitch, her fingers moving with a deftness that astounded Leah, who was still standing behind her. "When we got to our place—it was over on what they called 'the bench' in those days, close to where Vernal is now—we stopped our wagon in the middle of the sagebrush and Reid wouldn't let the kids get off the wagon until he cleared a little patch of dirt. He didn't want them stepping into all those prickly pears. It was spring, and still cold at night, and I slept in the wagon with the girls. Reid and my older son, Johnny, slept out on the ground. I was scared to death of snakes and scorpions—even though there weren't that many, really." She looked up and laughed. "Do you really want me going on about all this?"

"Yes, I do. I asked, didn't I?" Liz said.

Some of the other sisters said the same thing. Leah looked around at them, their heads down except when they stopped to stretch or glanced up to say something. She liked this better than their meetings when they had lessons. She liked the idea of working together, making things, and just talking of things that came up. The morning breeze was dying down, and the heat was getting a little worse all the time, but no one seemed to notice it the way they did in the Relief Society room. Maybe they just didn't pay as much attention.

"We built a cabin that summer," Belva said. "Reid had to cut logs over toward the mountains and haul them down, and we had ground to clear and plow and plant. I don't know how we did it all." She hesitated and snipped off a thread, and then she added, "But we didn't get by without help. Reid's brother helped us build the cabin, along with some of the other men. Once they had the logs ready, they put it up pretty much in one day."

"People pulled together in those days," Gwen said.

"Yes, maybe a little more than now. But lately, I've seen more of that again."

"Did you have Relief Society back then?" Millie asked.

"Not right at first. We just barely had church. We'd all meet together on Sundays—just out in the open. The men would take turns preaching, and that was nice. But to me, it always seemed like they talked longer than they needed to—you know, with little kids to keep track of."

"Some things don't change," Glenda said, and everyone laughed.

"The church built up pretty fast, as more and more came, and we built a school building and used that for church. Reid's brother was the branch president, and Reid served with him as a counselor. Later on we got organized as a ward, and Reid was called as bishop. That's when we started holding Relief Society. I was president for a long time in those early days—fifteen years or so. What we did most was look after the new families that were homesteading. We'd see to it they had quilts, right off. No one could bring enough when they first came. So quilts to us were a matter of protecting life, keeping our kids from getting sick. Still, we wanted them to be pretty. It's what made things nice at home in those little cabins."

"It's the best thing we do," Liz said. "I hope we never stop making quilts."

Leah looked out across the quilt top. It was a "Crown of Thorns" pattern, done mostly in greens and reds and white. Leah knew that some people could paint landscapes or write poems, and all that was fine, but nothing she had ever seen was more beautiful than a fine quilt.

"But Relief Society is more than just helping people out," Belva said. "New sisters would arrive, some of them having just left their families for the first time, maybe newly married, and they were lonely and scared. There had been an Indian uprising in Colorado just a few years before we came out, and we all lived in fear of a war with the Utes—although that turned out never to be a problem. Those poor souls were worse off than we were, even then."

She straightened up for a moment, arched her back, and drew in a deep breath. Leah wondered whether she shouldn't take a rest soon.

"The loneliness was terrible. But we saved each other; that's what we did. When we called each other 'sister,' we knew what the word meant. It was so nice to gather together, sing and pray, and teach the gospel to each other. And then we'd work together to make things a little nicer in our homes. It was such a blessing to us."

Leah heard the emotion in Belva's voice. Everyone did, and things got quiet for a time.

"But this is a time just about as hard. Different, because we mostly live in nice houses now, but maybe more full of worries. And I have to say to all of you, I've been lonely again, you know, since Reid passed away, and this work in the Relief Society, making visits and all those things—well, it's saved me again. There's not a sister in this ward I don't love with all my heart."

Leah had always been annoyed by flat statements of that kind—the clichés Mormons used. But she didn't doubt Belva. She *did* love every sister—and brother—she knew. Leah had watched her show that she did.

But Belva had begun to laugh. "Of course, I'll admit, the same as Leah, over the years I've met a few that I didn't *like* so much. I guess I still loved them, though."

This brought a big laugh, and Leah said, "Those of us who are hard to like need the most love, Belva. It's good we have you."

"Oh, no. You're easy to like—and love."

But Leah was pretty sure some of the others were thinking Leah was right.

"I guess you learned plenty about making things stretch back in those days," Liz said.

"Well, yes. Nothing went to waste. We made our soap, of course, and we sewed everything ourselves. We all had chickens and a cow, and we kept a big garden. But all those skills are still the same. I see almost everyone going back to them now."

For a time the women talked about the things they had gone back to lately, the ways they could stretch their dollars. Liz said she had found she didn't need as much sugar in her bottled fruit as she had always used, and LaRae said she had learned to take an old coat, turn it, and cut a smaller one from the worn cloth. She'd done that for her younger daughter the winter before, and the coat had looked almost new.

After a time, Leah moved to the other quilts and listened to the women talk and laugh. *They're saving each other,* she thought, *the same as those early sisters did,* and she was amazed at the joy she felt. She had resisted women's clubs all her life and had even preferred to sit and talk with men at church events, just so she wouldn't have to hear all the jabber about recipes and "women's problems." But these women were funny, it turned out, and smart. Marjorie, at one of the quilts, was talking about the production of *Hamlet* she had performed in when she was in college—the challenge of playing Ophelia. All the women seemed to know the play well.

Nadine was stitching at times, but she was also moving about, threading needles, turning the quilts and retightening the frames as the sewing progressed. She walked over to Leah and said, "It's such a perfect morning. This last year or two I think we've almost forgotten how to be happy, but everyone seems to be enjoying themselves today."

"That's what I was thinking," Leah said. "I've worked so long and hard out on that farm. I've needed this, and I didn't even know it."

"You're going to turn into a sweet church lady, Leah."

"I'll never be so sweet that you'll want to spend a whole lot of time around me."

Nadine smiled, and Leah wasn't sure whether she was denying the assertion or agreeing with it, but Nadine said, "You know what pleases me more than anything?"

"That I've not been sewing too much and ruining these quilts?"

"No. Not at all. A Relief Society quilt should always have bad stitches mixed with the good ones. That way, we know it's made by real hands." Leah was about to say something about that, but Nadine didn't let her. "What I'm talking about is LuAnn. She's taken little Vickie under her arm, and she's shown more understanding for another person than I've ever seen from her. She comes home sometimes and just sobs about it. She says that Vickie's starting to feel so much for this baby inside her, and it's breaking her heart to know she has to give it up."

"I know. I've spent time with Vickie too. There's a lot more to that little girl than I thought there was at first. She's so lonely out here, and she looks ahead and doesn't know what to expect from life."

"That's what LuAnn says. At first I think LuAnn thought it was just something new to get to know a 'bad girl' from Salt Lake. But she doesn't think about it that way now. She keeps asking me how she can do something for Vickie to make her life turn out all right. She's planning to go to college down in Salt Lake this fall, and she wants to stay friends with the girl."

"I wish I saw more of that kind of change in Rae. She's grown up a lot this last year, but she still holds back from just about everyone. She always tells me she can't wait to get away from here."

"I've talked to LuAnn about Rae. She claims that she's tried harder lately to be friendly to her. I think she knows that she was one of the ones who made Rae feel lonely when they were younger. But now she feels like there's too much water under the bridge—that Rae wants nothing to do with the girls her age in the ward."

"LuAnn's right about that."

"Well, Rae at least seems to be happy this morning. Look how she's laughing with all the ladies. I couldn't get LuAnn to come. And by the way, I'm not saying all of LuAnn's problems are over. She's been good to Vickie, but she's still a spoiled kid in a lot of ways. And she's as lazy as ever. I have her working at the store this summer, but she doesn't come in until noon because she likes to sleep away most of the morning."

"I just don't know when these girls are going to turn into the *fine* examples of womanhood we two are, Nadine. Do you think it will ever happen?"

Both women laughed, and they moved back to the quilts. For a time Leah sat by Rae and stitched. Rae was slow, but she concentrated on her stitches and kept them small. Leah decided to try that. And then it occurred to her that she ought to tell Rae what she was thinking.

"You do this better than I do," Leah said. "I try to go too fast."

Rae looked up, clearly surprised. "I thought you were thinking I'm too slow," she said. "I've been trying to hurry faster since you sat down."

"I'll give you a good motto for life," Leah said. "Try, in every way, to be as unlike your mother as you possibly can."

All the women at the quilt laughed, and Rae said, "Oh, trust me, Mom, that's already my motto."

After the laughing stopped, Belva said, "But that was exactly the answer your mother would have given. You two have the same sense of humor. You're really two peas in a pod. You just don't know it."

Leah glanced at Rae. They both shook their heads, but they laughed, too.

The morning passed quickly, and the lunch was nice, but early in the afternoon some of the women had to leave, and by three, most were gone. Leah knew that she too needed to wind things up and get back to her farm. She was starting to put supplies away when she saw Nadine, who had taken some materials out to her car, return to the rec hall. She walked directly to Leah, and it wasn't hard to see that something was wrong. "Leah, I just saw Jim outside," she said. She took a hard breath. "He said the negotiations to sell the bank have fallen through. The bank will have to close for good unless someone else comes through with an offer."

"Does that mean people are going to lose *everything* after all?"

"It's not for sure. But Jim says he's afraid that's what'll happen. I guess the word is spreading through town, and a lot of people are feeling knocked off their feet again."

Leah felt as though all her strength had drained away. Everyone had had such a nice day, and now this. She glanced at Rae, who was still sitting by Belva, laughing and chatting. How would she react when Leah told her she couldn't go to college?

Leah had thought all this through many times. She had considered selling out and moving to a city where there was a college. But she couldn't get much out of her farm, and if she tried to sell off her animals and equipment, she'd have to sell them for next to nothing. And where would she get work in a city? Salt Lake was so full of destitute families that a bunch of them were camped out in shanty towns and eating at soup kitchens. She'd read that in the newspaper.

"Well, it's good we have most of our money tied up in the store," Nadine said, and she tried to smile. "We didn't lose as much as we would have—back when things were going better. I doubt very many people did lose a lot—except for a handful who can afford to lose a sizable sum and keep going."

"I think more have been hurt than you might think," Leah said. "Lots of people had only fifty dollars or a hundred, but it was the only nest egg they had. I've been talking to plenty of the sisters who are scared to death. When you don't have so much as a dollar stuck away somewhere, it makes you feel like you're one step from a cliff, ready to fall off."

Nadine seemed to hear something in that. "Leah, did you lose some money?"

"Not enough to fuss about."

But Nadine was still watching her closely. "Will you be all right?"

"I always get by."

Now Marjorie was coming. "Did you hear the news?" she asked. Leah could see that the word had been moving through the hall.

"Yes," Nadine said. "And I think Leah lost more than she's admitting."

"I'll be fine."

"Oh, Leah," Marjorie said. "It isn't final yet. The bank still might find a buyer."

"Sure. But even that doesn't guarantee we'll get any of our money back."

"I know," Marjorie said. She was nodding, obviously thinking. "We need to check on people. Some of them are going to be set back hard by this."

"Things went so well today," Nadine said. "And now it feels like we're right back where we were last fall."

But Leah couldn't stand there and talk about this. It all hurt too much. She was suddenly too worried about herself to feel compassion for anyone else. So she finished up what she had to do and carried out the things she had brought. Rae helped her, but she had heard the news too, and when she tried to talk to Leah, she seemed to sense that now was not the time.

Leah was just shutting the car door when she saw old Brother and Sister Riddle walking down the street. She saw the look on their faces and knew that they had to have had money in the bank. Leah went to them, shook their hands. "Are you two doing all right?" she asked.

"We don't have a thing in the world," Brother Riddle said. "Everything I worked for is gone. I don't know how we're going to live."

"There's still talk that—"

"There's lots of talk. But what does it mean? It don't seem right that a man can work all his life and stick every penny away so when the day comes that he can't work, he and his wife will still have a little something."

And then all these lawyers and bankers and crooks figure out some way to take it. Someone's got my money. That's for sure. I don't know how they can say they don't . . ." His voice broke and he stopped.

"We'll manage somehow," Sister Riddle said. She was patting his shoulder. "We still have our place. We'll . . ." But she couldn't finish either.

"Listen, you two," Leah said. "Don't think this town will abandon you. No one's going to go hungry. And President Roosevelt is doing things to save the banks, and to help farmers. I really think we're going to be all right. All of us. But it's maybe like the days when you two first came out here. Sometimes we all have to get together and build houses for one another."

"People don't do that anymore," Brother Riddle managed to say.

"Yes, they do, Brother Riddle. We will. I promise you. Don't give up hope in people."

Sister Riddle was saying, "That's right, Arvin. That's how we have to think. We'll be all right."

Leah patted Brother Riddle again, promised him again, and then let him and his wife go. She got back in the car and looked at Rae. "I was feeling pretty sorry for myself, but those two remind me what we have to do—depend on each other."

"We lost some money, didn't we?"

"Well . . . yes."

"I can't go to college now, can I?"

"I don't know, honey. You might have to wait a year. We might get some of the money back yet, and we might have a better year. The government is trying to get people working—and the weather might be better this year. There's plenty of ways we can manage this yet."

But Leah could see what was happening to Rae. She was giving up, realizing that she had to face another year here, another year of life being the same—the life she hadn't been happy with for a long time.

"How much did we lose?"

"It was quite a bit, honey." She didn't want to admit what she'd had, but she knew that the time had come; she had to. "Seven hundred or so."

"*Seven hundred dollars?* What are you talking about? Where did you get that kind of money?"

"From insurance. When your dad died."

"You never told us that. You said you had a little, but you never said it was so much."

But Leah knew what she was really thinking. They had lived as poor people so long when she had all that money in the bank. "It was for your college, honey. We could have spent it all and lived a little better, but then, the rest of your life, you'd still be scraping to get by. I wanted you to get an education and have something better in your future."

"I know." But she was broken, and Leah didn't know what to say.

"I did it for you and Wade, honey. I wanted things too, but I kept that money for the two of you."

"So we'd come out better than the kids in town."

It didn't sound like an accusation, but it entered Leah's chest that way. "Well . . . yes. I know that's part of it. Part of what I always thought."

But now the silence did sound like an accusation.

Chapter Eighteen

THE SUMMER OF 1933 turned out worse than the year before. Everyone in Utah—in much of the nation, for that matter—prayed for rain, and none came. Crops dried up in the fields, reservoirs emptied out, and irrigation water, if there was any, had to be rationed. It helped some that farmers were being promised money for not farming some of their land, and prices did rise some—but everything died in the heat, so there was little to sell. Animals often had to be sold off for next to nothing because farmers couldn't feed them. The new Civil Works Administration was promising to put many men to work on various projects, and that would help, but it was designed as a temporary program, and was nothing anyone could expect to rely on for long. The Civilian Conservation Corps set up a camp in the basin that summer, too, and that put some young men to work, but Wade wasn't old enough to qualify. Workers had to be eighteen.

People around town also prayed that an investor would be found to reopen the bank, prayed that they might receive some percentage of what they had lost. But that didn't happen either. Sometimes Leah told God what she thought of all that, but she also told herself that she was still eating, and lots of people across the country were in worse shape than she was. She finally had to plow her dried-up cornstalks under the ground and watch her alfalfa die down so low that she got only one meager cutting.

The one good thing about that summer was that she spent so much time encouraging people that she filled her head with an attitude of survival. The worst thing was watching Rae dry up with the hay and the corn. She continued to seek work in town, and Nadine did have her come in and work at the store once in a while, but Rae worked so few hours that her paychecks hardly made a difference. Leah actually tried to sell her car, thinking she could walk into town and get some help from Marjorie when they had to make visits, but she couldn't find anyone who wanted the old thing, or at least anyone who could come up with $100 for it. The truth was, that probably was more than it was worth, but it was maybe half of what Leah felt she needed to get Rae started. If the girl could work on campus and help with board and room, $200 would cover tuition and books and some of her living. But Leah's ad for the car in the paper met with offers of only $50 or so, and that wouldn't even pay tuition.

One evening in August Leah finally told Rae, "Honey, I think we might as well face it. We can't get you into school this fall."

"I know that," Rae said. "I've known it all summer." She was sitting on her bed. Leah was standing in her doorway, leaning against the door frame.

"I guess I did too. But I kept hoping we'd get some rain and I could end up with a little income this year. We've never had a summer quite this bad."

Rae's bedroom—the whole house—was filled with heat, the way it had been for a couple of months now. Leah opened her window at night to try to get a little air, but there wasn't any. When a breeze did blow, it filled up Leah's head with dust, closing up her sinuses, making her head throb.

"It doesn't matter. I had college all built up in my mind. But things probably wouldn't be any better there than they are here."

"What was it you were hoping would be better?"

Rae's head slowly came up. She looked at her mother for a long time before she said, "I guess I was hoping some boy would finally think I was worth asking out, but that's not very likely, is it?"

"Oh, Rae. Don't say that. You're just coming into your own. You're like me, long and lean and not very curvy, but you're prettier than I ever was, and you're smart. Your face has cleared up so much this last year, too. Some fellow will—"

"Don't, Mom. Okay? I don't want to hear it." She looked down again at her hands in her lap. She was wearing a housedress so old, so washed out, its blue had paled to gray and the fabric was thinning down to nothing.

"I'm sorry," Leah said.

"Don't be sorry. I know you mean well. I just know how things are."

"Honey, I feel so bad about building you up for this and then letting you down." Leah walked over and sat on the bed next to Rae. "I've always thought about you kids making a success out of your lives—but I know I wanted to prove something about myself. You know, that I could manage without a husband and still do right by my kids."

"Every mother wants her kids to do their best. There's nothing wrong about that."

"I know. Up to a point. But I had my mind made up that you were going to outdo those town kids, and that seemed important. It was the wrong way to think."

"Mom, I was too hard on you about all that. I've thought a lot about it this summer. I've asked myself, if I ever did get married, would I be willing to work as hard for my kids as you have for us?"

"I just did what had to be done."

"No. You've been strong as iron. You never let us feel sorry for ourselves, and you never gave up. I don't know many women who could run a farm the way you have."

Leah could hardly believe what she was hearing. She had hoped for a long time that Rae would someday feel better toward her.

"Sometimes I think now, what if someone finally asks me to marry him? I guess I'd probably accept, whether he was my dreamboat or not. I never should have said those things I said to you last year—about you not loving Dad."

"But I did love him, honey—more after a few years than I did at first. It's just that he was so silent, and I was lonely out here. I think you can understand that."

"Oh, yes. I understand loneliness."

"I'm sorry, Rae. If I had it do over again, I would buy you nicer clothes, make you feel better about yourself, and then let college take care of itself."

"I don't know, Mom. You did what made sense to you, and I'm not going to blame you for that."

Leah heard the front door open and knew that Wade was coming into the house. She heard him shed his boots, and then he appeared at the bedroom door, saying, "Hey, do we get any dinner tonight?" But he obviously saw the gravity of the mood. "Is anything wrong?" he asked.

"Nothing new," Rae said.

"We were just talking about college. I don't see any way that Rae can go. School starts in just a few weeks, and there's no sign the bank is going to open."

"Listen, I've been thinking about all that. I didn't get much work, with the farmers giving up on their crops halfway through the summer, but I saved up twenty-nine dollars. That could be part of fall tuition. And I might get some more work this fall. If you've saved a little, and

Mom can come up with a little, maybe we can still pull it off. Isn't FDR going to pay us a little for not farming some of our acres?"

"I doubt it would be enough," Leah said. "And I don't know when it will come."

"The money you earned is for your tooth," Rae said.

"I know. But what's another year? I'll get it fixed someday."

Leah glanced to see that Rae was staring at Wade, tears in her eyes, and then she looked back to see that tears had come to Wade's eyes too. The pain was almost too much to look at, but it was a good moment, too—for all three of them. It suddenly struck Leah that someday she would tell the Lord thanks for the miserable drought, for the bank failure, for Wayne's death, and for everything else that had brought them to this single moment. But it was a little soon to feel that thankfulness just yet, and she prayed again that somehow she could still send Rae to college.

The sisters in the ward had continued to show up for work and business meeting. As the summer had worn on, it had become clear that suffering would continue and needs would be great again. Businesses had picked up a little—only to flatten out again—and the drought would make things harder than ever for farmers. Even their gardens had been much less productive than usual. But a successful bazaar could raise money to help some people get through another winter.

Leah knew that some of the members would come to the bazaar and spend a dime or maybe a quarter, but the ones who would buy the quilts were the ones who had donated the fabric, and then they would return the quilts to the Relief Society to give to needy families. That had seemed silly to her last year, but now she saw how it got everyone involved, gave everyone a chance to give something—if only their time in stitching the quilt. Leah also understood the sacrifice of those who were worried about losing everything, but still recognized that they had more than most, and kept giving. And Nadine was the one giving more than anyone.

So the sisters had worked hard at their quilts and other projects, and they had continued to enjoy each other, but most of the optimism of the early summer had died in the drought, the same as the crops.

After the work meeting during the third week of August, Marjorie and Belva and Nadine, along with Leah, swept the rec hall and put things away. Leah saw Belva walk over to one of the chairs that ringed the room. She sat down and began to fan herself with her open hand. "Are you all right, Belva?" Leah asked, walking over to her.

"Oh, yes. Sometimes the heat just tuckers me out. It's been such a hot summer."

"You go on home. I'm afraid I work you too hard."

"Oh, no. Work is what I thrive on." She smiled. "What are you accusing me of—being old?"

"I never think of you as old anymore, Belva. You have as much energy as anyone I know."

"Well, no. I don't. But I like to keep busy. It's better that way—always has been." She had worn her favorite dress—a soft periwinkle color. It was embroidered with flowers on the shoulder and had a trim white collar. She usually wore it only to church. Maybe she had wanted to cheer herself up—or maybe she was tired of wearing the same old things, the same as most people were. Leah was still wearing her own ugly dress, maybe now out of pride, just to say that she wasn't going to worry about such things. One dress was enough.

But Belva looked drained, her skin pale. Leah worried that she was being taxed a little too much. Marjorie and Nadine had taken some things to their cars; they came back into the hall together and walked over to Leah and Belva. They asked Belva whether she was all right, and

Belva said she just wanted to rest for a few minutes before she walked home.

"You're not walking home. I'll drive you," Nadine said.

"Well, that would be nice."

"You have a lot to do, too, Leah," Marjorie said. "Aren't you sending Rae off to school next month?"

"No. She's decided not to go."

"What do you mean?"

"We just can't do it, Marjorie. This drought has been the last straw."

"But this is what you've worked for all these years."

"I know. So one more year won't matter. By next fall, maybe we can figure something out." Leah sat down next to Belva. Leah had a little notebook in her hand, and she used it to fan Belva, who let her own hand drop, shut her eyes, and seemed to draw in the breath of air.

"There's more talk this week that the bank might reopen," Nadine said.

"There's always talk. But tuition is due right away. And I can't help her with her board and room, even if she worked and paid part of it herself."

"Couldn't you get a little loan?" Nadine asked.

Leah smiled. "From the bank?"

"There are other banks—and savings and loan places. Maybe down in Provo or Salt Lake, you could apply for something."

"And use what for collateral? A worthless farm with taxes coming due?"

"How much would you need?" Marjorie asked.

"I don't know. I was trying to get $200 together—even $150 could get us started—but I can't even come close to that."

"Oh, Leah," Belva said. "That breaks my heart. I have a few dollars I could let you have. Couldn't we all—"

"No. Listen, I've got to get back out to my place. I've got lots to do."

But the truth was, she had very little to do. The sun had burned up most of her work, and she had had way too much time to think lately.

"I wish we could have given Rae more work," Nadine said.

"I know. We appreciate what you were able to do. If you can use her some more this fall, maybe before Christmas, that would help. Maybe she can save more this year, and . . ." Leah laughed. " . . . as we always say, maybe we'll have better weather next year. Maybe we'll have better prices. Maybe things will start to pick up. It's the same old song, isn't it?"

But all this was hurting more than Leah wanted it to, and when she glanced at Marjorie she saw that she had tears in her eyes. "I'm so sorry," Marjorie said. "This is all you've ever wanted."

Leah felt the words harder than she wanted to. She felt her throat tighten, her eyes burn. But she wasn't going to do this. "Well, anyway, let's scoot out of here and I'll lock the door. I really do need to get going." But they had all heard it, the thickness in her voice, the shakiness—Leah knew that.

Leah walked out first, took a deep breath of the hot air, and waited for the other women to follow her outside. Marjorie said, "Leah, let's think about—"

"Marjorie, I've thought about it every way there is. It's okay. Rae and I talked it over, and she understands." But Leah was losing control, and she could not, would not, do that. Marjorie was still talking when Leah locked the door and walked away to her car. She drove home and then she found work to do, things she had been intending to do for a long time: oiled the hinges on the shed doors, repaired a broken board in the chicken coop, and spliced a harness line. She did it all in the heat of the afternoon, and she sweated with the effort, but she kept herself going until well into the evening. She didn't want to go back to the house and look at Rae, who was merely going about the motions of life, broken.

But it was Rae who finally came out and told her that supper was getting cold. So Leah walked to the house, ate, and then filled up a tub with water as cool as she could stand to sit down in. She swabbed herself with the coolness and then put on an old cotton housedress. But the house was still stifling, so she carried a kitchen chair outside and sat down on the little porch. A breeze had picked up out there, a warm south wind, but at least the air was moving.

The sun was almost down now and the sunset was coming on, only faint yellow so far, with a couple of thin clouds to give substance to the color. For so many years Leah had pictured this time when she could tell Rae that she had saved for her college, that money was not going to be a problem. She had thought of sitting there on the porch, offering Rae advice about study habits, about living with other girls, and . . . everything else. Life. Everything was going to make sense then. They had lived a spartan life, but Rae would have had her chance to go to college even though lots of kids couldn't do that.

A car turned into the lane, and Leah watched the dust rise behind it, a hint of orange now in the air, filtering into the blowing dirt. It wasn't the bishop; she knew that. And then she realized it was Nadine and Jim's car: a Pierce-Arrow, probably the fanciest car in Richards, but very old now. Nadine had never visited the farm before, and Leah wished she wouldn't come now. She could almost guess what this would be about.

The car pulled up in front of Leah's porch and Marjorie got out on one side, Nadine the other, and then LuAnn slipped out of the backseat. "Hi, Leah," Nadine said. "Getting a little air, are you?"

"Yes. *Very* little. But it's like an oven inside."

"We just wanted to talk to you for a minute. Is Rae in the house?"

"Nadine, I hope this isn't about—"

"Just be still for once. Let us tell you what we've been thinking."

Leah didn't say anything, but she stood up and held her ground. She didn't call for Rae. Nadine took care of that. She stepped to the door and called out, in her booming voice, "Rae, come out to the porch for a minute."

Rae soon appeared at the door and stepped out. "Let's talk out here," Nadine said. "Leah says it's hot inside."

But there was only the one chair on the porch. Rae said, "Let me get some more chairs from the kitchen."

"No. That's all right. We'll only be a minute. We have a little proposal."

"Nadine, I—"

"Just listen to us, Leah," Marjorie said. She was standing with her arms to her sides as though she were up in front of a group, about to make a speech. LuAnn was standing back a little, behind her mother, mostly studying the old boards in the floor of the porch. Leah could see that this was awkward for her. But Nadine pulled LuAnn alongside herself, and the little group ended up standing in something like a circle, the town ladies all in housedresses themselves, and no hats, not looking as elegant as they did at church or at Relief Society meetings.

"Here's something you may not know about your mother," Nadine said, looking at Rae. "Before the bank closed, she was spending your college money anyway. She was throwing it around, all over town."

It was clear from Nadine's tone that she was joking, but this was not something Leah wanted Rae to know. She had often thought that if she hadn't helped anyone in town and had stuffed that money in her mattress, money would not be a problem now. She still could have sent Rae and Wade to school without much problem. It all seemed like extravagance now that she had nothing, and certainly Rae might see it that way.

"You didn't know that, did you?"

Rae laughed a little. "No, I guess not," she said, but she clearly didn't believe it.

"She was giving your college money away."

Now Rae was looking more curious. "I don't think I believe that."

"She gave money to people who needed it, Rae. She kept some

families from losing their farms. We think it might have been four or five hundred dollars—maybe more. Wouldn't you like to have that now?"

"Nadine, if it had been in the bank, I would have lost it anyway," Leah said. "And you don't know how much it was. You're making that part up."

But Nadine was still looking at Rae. "The truth is, she wasn't throwing it away. She was investing it. This whole town knows about it. Things like that finally do get around, and everyone knows she helped people when some of the rest of us could have—and didn't."

Rae nodded. "That *doesn't* surprise me."

"Well, it's coming back now. It turns out, you won a scholarship. We just created the first annual 'Richards High School Outstanding Student' scholarship, and you won it." Nadine turned to Leah. "Don't say what you're thinking of saying. This isn't a loan. It isn't a gift. It's a scholarship, and we can give it to anyone we choose. And we chose Rae. It's an award of two hundred dollars."

"Nadine, we can't take this," Leah said. "You can call it what you want, but it's money a lot of other people need more than we do. Rae can put college off one more year."

"I'm not talking to you, Leah. I'm talking to Rae. There's another part to this." LuAnn had gradually slipped back a little, and now Nadine pulled her closer again. "We know that board and room can amount to quite a bit, but I have a brother in Salt Lake, and he owns a little house he sometimes rents out to students. He's told LuAnn that she can live in it this year—for no rent at all. And LuAnn has something she wants to say to you."

LuAnn spoke softly. "Yes," she said. "I know you were planning to go to Provo to college, but if you'd like to go to the University of Utah instead, you could live with me. Sharon Evans will be living with me. We'd love to have you, too."

This all sounded memorized and awkward. Watching Rae, Leah could see how conflicted she was.

"So what do you say, Rae?" Nadine asked. "Wouldn't Salt Lake be all right—with the scholarship and a place to stay?"

Rae glanced at Leah, and Leah could see that she wasn't sure. So Leah said, "It's very nice of all of you to think up something like this, but it's still not right. I may have helped a couple of people, but they were about to lose their places. We're not in that kind of drastic condition yet."

"This isn't your decision, Leah," Marjorie said. "What do you say, Rae?"

Before Rae could answer, LuAnn said, "Do it, Rae. We'll have fun."

But the words still didn't have a natural ring, and maybe that was what brought Rae to say, "No. I think my mother's right. We can manage all right. You should give the money to people who need it more."

"Honey, don't think of it as charity," Nadine said. "We really do want to start helping some of our kids get to college. We want to offer this scholarship every year. It's just as important as food to hungry people. Our kids here in town need to have the chance for an education."

"But I wasn't the best student at the high school. There are others who deserve it more."

"We chose you, Rae. You've always planned on college, and most of the kids at the high school haven't. You deserve the opportunity."

"Not really," Rae said, and tears came into her eyes. "But thanks. It's really nice, what you're trying to do." She turned to the door, still open, and walked inside.

Nadine turned to Leah. "You can't let this happen, Leah. This town wants to send Rae to college, and a lot of people donated just a little to put this together this afternoon. They were happy to do it, and a lot of it is because they've come to love you so much. Don't stand in the way of people trying to do something that's good and right. It's making sure no one is left behind—the very thing you talked about."

"I also said that those who could walk, should walk. We only go back for the ones who've lost their strength."

"Leah, this is wrong. Really wrong," Marjorie said.

"Well . . . maybe it is. I don't know. Maybe I've taught Rae the wrong attitude. And I want you to know, I *do* appreciate your intentions. But you heard what Rae said."

And there they stood, everyone looking dismayed. "Leah, please," Nadine finally said, "talk this over with Rae. The scholarship is still hers. We could even set this up so that she would pay the money back someday and help other students in the future." When Leah didn't respond, she added, "Please think about it."

"Sister Sorensen," LuAnn said, "I felt funny—because I know Rae doesn't like me—so maybe I didn't say it right. But I did mean what I said. We want her to come and live with us."

"I know. That was nice of you, LuAnn. But I can't see her changing her mind."

"If you said the right things, I think *you* could change her mind," Marj said.

"I'm not going to tell her to—"

"Leah, I'm serious. You're doing the wrong thing, and I think you know it. We're not going to accept your answer until you've thought some more. And if I were you, I'd pray about it, too."

The three women walked back to the car and got in. The sunset was mostly gone by then, but Leah watched the car bounce up the lane, turn onto the highway, and head back toward town. Only the blowing dust was left in the air. Leah knew she had to go inside and talk to Rae, but she hardly had the heart to do it. Then, as she stepped inside, she realized there was someone else she needed to talk to first.

She walked to the telephone in the kitchen, rang for the operator, and asked for Belva. When Belva answered, she said, "Hi, this is Leah. How are you feeling? I've worried about you all day."

"Oh, I'm fine. I think I just got a little warm today. But we all did."

"Are you feeling sick at all?"

"Not exactly. Just a little tired. I think I'll go to bed pretty soon."

"Can you sleep in this heat?"

"I *never* seem to sleep too well anymore." Belva laughed. "One more problem of old age."

"Have you talked to Nadine or Marjorie today—since our meeting this morning?"

"Of course I have. Have they been out there yet?"

"Yes. Are you the one who put up the money they wanted to give us?"

"No. Of course not. Everyone wanted to get involved. It's the easiest money we ever had to raise. And it's such a good idea, to give a scholarship to one of our kids every year."

"Is that what it really is, Belva, or were they just trying to give us some money and not make us feel embarrassed?"

"Leah, you ought to be ashamed of yourself. You're the one who told us that we all ought to be looking out for one another."

"I know, but—"

"But nothing. I hope you're not thinking about turning the money down."

"I did turn it down. Or actually, Rae did."

"Well . . . you're going to change your mind about that. I won't let you do it. You're a good woman, Leah, but you're stubborn. And you're prideful sometimes, if you want to know the truth."

"I guess maybe I am. But I can't take that money. Rae and I already decided that."

"Then un-decide. You're teaching Rae the wrong thing this time. Don't stand in her way. Give her this chance."

Leah laughed. "Well, I'll think it over, but like you said, I'm pretty stubborn."

"I love you, Leah, but sometimes you need a mother to cut a stiff switch and give you a darned good spanking. That's what I'd do if I wasn't so old and decrepit."

Leah laughed. "Like I said . . . I'll think about it. But at this point, I don't think I can change Rae's mind."

"Then I'll have to do it. I'll talk to her."

"Let me talk to her first—and see what she's thinking."

"You won't do it right, Leah. I'm coming out there in the morning and I'm going to set this thing straight. She's going to take that scholarship—that or I'm going to camp in your living room until I wear both of you out."

Leah laughed. "Come out if you want, but I've got to tell you, Rae's just about as stubborn as I am."

"That's all right. I'm going to change her mind."

Chapter Nineteen

AFTER LEAH HUNG UP the phone, she walked back out to the porch. She knew that she ought to have a good heart-to-heart with Rae, but now she was confused. She didn't know what she should say. She understood what had happened. Rae had actually considered accepting what the women had proposed. But she had picked up on Leah's concerns—and, even more, LuAnn had bothered her. Maybe Leah and Rae *were* prideful about things like that, but when Leah thought of trying to change Rae's mind, she knew she couldn't do it. She had been telling herself for years that she was a woman who could have walked across the plains, and she still believed it; no one had to take pity on her just yet. Maybe that was stubborn, or even prideful, but she didn't know how to be any other way. And the truth was, she had felt some satisfaction when Rae had told LuAnn no.

Still, she kept hearing Belva's voice telling her she was wrong, and she had learned to trust Belva's heart. Maybe the woman was right.

So Leah kept thinking. She stayed on the porch long after dark. A dim moon was casting a little texture on the land—the fence lines, the row of Lombardy poplars along the west side of her property, even the distant mountains. Leah tried not to think about the future, but it was still there, like all that dark, and it felt about the same. It was true that she had changed in the last year, and she was glad for it. She understood people better than she had, felt better about them, and liked the women she had worked with. She wasn't sure she would be happier with a husband at this point in her life, and didn't think much about that, but she still felt what she always had: that if her kids never got a leg up, never made it beyond this farm, she would feel bad about her life. She supposed God loved his children for their efforts more than their results, but right now, he seemed to be knocking her down every time she tried to get up on her feet, and she really didn't like to tell herself how she felt about that. The walk across the plains was long, she figured, and a woman made it by tromping forward all day long, every day. She would just have to keep doing that.

She put off talking to Rae, and then, when she finally did peek in, she saw that Rae was on top of her bed, asleep. So Leah went back to the porch and sat down again. She didn't want to go to bed, not in that hot bedroom, so she stayed up late, and finally Wade came out to the porch. "Are you still up?" she asked.

"Yeah. I've been trying to sleep, but I've been tossing and turning in there. I didn't think I ever heard you come in. I was just wondering if something's bothering you."

Leah could see in the dim light that he had nothing on but his pajama bottoms, the slick skin of his chest picking up the glimmer from the moon. He was such a powerful boy, made strong from all the work she'd put on him. Whenever she looked at him, though, she thought of that tooth she'd never fixed. She'd used her money to help other folks and hadn't looked after him.

"Rae told me what those ladies wanted to do," Wade said.

"What did she say about it?"

Wade hunched down next to Leah. She could feel the heat from his arm next to hers. She took hold of his hand. "She said LuAnn put on an act, like she wanted to be friends with her—but Sister Willis probably made her do it."

Leah knew she'd thought the same thing at the time, but she didn't like hearing it. "I don't know, Wade. Maybe we take things that way too much. The girl was trying to do the right thing. Maybe we have no right to say she was wrong to do it."

"LuAnn's like a house cat. She prowls around and rubs up against your leg, but if you try to pick her up, she scoots away."

"Did she ever rub up against your leg?"

Wade laughed. "No," he said, "I'm too young for her. But she likes every boy to look her over. Then she plays with them, like how a cat plays with a toy."

"How do you know all this?"

"The guys on the teams all talked about her last year. They said that was how she was. And she's the same with the girls. She has to be in the middle of everything. She plays up to one and then the other, and they all compete to be her best friend."

Leah had seen that, just in the way she acted around the ward, but she had seen some other things, too. "Don't you think a young girl can grow up and change?"

"I guess. I don't know. Do you think that's what she's doing?"

"She's been nice to Vickie, and I didn't know whether she could do that."

"Vickie's a little like her, though. I think she was the popular one in her own school, just like LuAnn is here."

"So what are you saying? LuAnn's just hopeless?"

"I don't know. I'm just saying that's how she is—you know, from what I hear and what I've seen myself."

Leah let go of Wade's hand and stood up. She stepped to the front of the porch and looked across the distance to Richards. She could see lights from town making a bit of a glow. The sky was filling up with stars, too. "I've started to wonder if LuAnn's not quite the little peacock I used to think she was—you know, not so conceited as Rae always said she was. LuAnn has grown up with money, and that's a hard test too, the same as not having any."

"I think I'd trade if I got the chance."

Leah laughed. "I know what you mean. But don't you understand what I'm saying?"

Wade stepped up next to Leah and looked off in the same direction. "Sure. I think Tommy Evans had things too easy, and then, when times got tougher, he's had to buckle under a little. It's probably been good for him."

"Has he changed?"

"I don't know if he's changed. But I like him a little better. Lately, we've been more like real friends. We've talked about trying to play for the same college, maybe get scholarships to play, and get our education that way."

"I thought you said he wasn't going to college."

"That's what I thought—just because he never bothers much about his school work. But lately, he says he wants to go. I think it's mostly so he can play some more ball—and be a big hero for a while longer."

"If you played together, would he still have to be the star? That's what you always say about him."

"Sure. He'd like it better that way, but I guess I'd like to get so I'm better than him. That's just how we all are."

"But you like him all right?"

"I'll tell you what it is, mostly. It seems like everyone has things about them that you don't like all that much. But I'm the same way. A girl at school told me that I make a joke out of everything and she doesn't like that about me. And it's true, I do that a lot. So . . . you know . . . if you look around for friends who are just the way you want them to be, you'll never find any."

"I think that's right." Leah stood for a time, still looking toward town. It was hard not to wonder what life would have been, had she lived in Richards, single and still a teacher. But she would have missed this, Wade growing up. "You're turning into quite the guy, you know that?"

"What are you saying? That I wasn't up to much until now?

"There you go, turning everything into a joke."

"I know. It's just *terrible* when I do that."

"Do you like that girl?"

"What girl?"

"The one who said you make a joke out of everything."

"I'm not telling you."

"Don't start liking girls yet, okay? I still think you're my little boy."

"Okay, I'll quit kissing her, too."

Leah turned. "Now you're joking, aren't you?"

Wade was the one laughing now. "Afraid so," he said.

Leah stepped back to her chair and sat down again. Wade turned around and leaned back against the porch rail.

"I probably *would* kiss her if she liked me—but she doesn't."

"Life. It goes like that." Leah had heard a lot more emotion in his voice than she had expected, and she felt sorry for him, but she was still glad he hadn't been kissing that girl. "Let me ask you something else. What if Dr. Evans told you he wanted to do something nice for you and fix your tooth for free? Would you let him do it?"

"No. We told him before, we'd pay for it when the time comes—and pay full price—and I'm not that far from having the money now."

"What if he said he'd do it for what you have right now?"

"I'd wait until I had it all."

"Are we too prideful about that?"

"I don't know. But we try to do for ourselves. That's what people ought to do."

"I guess. But if we all supported each other, and didn't wait until someone was desperate, we'd all be better off, wouldn't we?"

Wade crossed his arms over his chest and stood in the dim light for a long time, his face dark to her. "I don't know," he finally said. "I'd just rather raise the money myself. I feel better about that."

"Well, that's how I think about it, too. But maybe we're wrong about feeling that way."

"Better that than someone always with his hand out, looking for the world to give him a living."

"That's for sure." But Leah wasn't quite satisfied with Wade's conclusion. It didn't seem quite the whole story. "Let's see if we can't get some sleep," she said. "If it's cool in the morning, let's sleep in a little late, okay?"

"That sounds good. But usually I wake up anyway."

"I know. I've got the same problem."

They walked in, and Leah lay on the top of her bed, convinced that she wouldn't sleep much. But she did drift off, and deep in the night she had the dream again. She saw lots of faces: all of the women in the Relief Society, it seemed, one after another. She did wake up early, as usual, but she didn't get up. She lay in bed and thought about the dream. Maybe *all* the sisters had needed her; maybe God had called upon her because she was the right one for the time. But that hardly seemed right. It seemed more likely that she needed all of them. And she still couldn't see that one face she had seen before. She didn't know who it was. One thing was certain to her, though; she was glad she had gotten to know Nadine and Marjorie. She told herself they had been kind to offer the scholarship, and she hoped she hadn't offended them. She needed to talk to them and tell them she hadn't meant to be so stern with them.

Leah got up. She longed for a cup of coffee, but she didn't have one, knew she never would again. She put on her housedress, not her over-alls, and she walked out quietly, slowly, the moon gone now but the first light of the sun tinting the eastern sky. She fed the animals, listening to the sounds of her farm and smelling the smells. This was home, no matter whether it had been dropped on her or not. If life was supposed to be a training ground, maybe this was a pretty good one. And the bishop's calling had been an important one, too. This morning she felt blessed that she hadn't just hidden away out here, that she had crossed the gap and gone into town to learn what she could.

Leah gathered some eggs and went back to the house. Wade was still sleeping, and she was glad he could get some extra rest. She broke some eggs and stirred them up for scrambling. In a few minutes, Rae stepped into the kitchen. She looked drained and tired, still wearing her cotton nightgown. "Did you sleep okay?" Leah asked.

"Not really."

"I know. It's just too hot. But the weather is going to break before long."

"I know." But that was all she said, and then she walked to the out-house. When she returned, she went to her bedroom, dressed, and then came back to the kitchen. "Is Wade outside already?" she asked.

"No. I told him to sleep in this morning if he could. He had trouble getting to sleep last night too. I'll milk the cows."

"I can fix breakfast," Rae said.

"Sit down a minute. I've got some eggs ready to cook. But let's wait until Wade gets up. We'll have breakfast together."

Rae nodded and sat down, but Leah could see how lost she was.

"Did we do the right thing?" Leah asked.

"You mean about that so-called scholarship? That's their name for giving us a handout."

"They meant well, Rae."

"Oh, sure. LuAnn and her 'we'll have fun.' If I lived in the same place with her, she'd never have anything to do with me. Before long she'd move into a sorority house with the popular girls. Then I wouldn't even have a place to live."

"Are you sure?"

"I know LuAnn."

Leah wasn't going to have that conversation again. It was the wrong time. "I just don't want you to mope around all winter," she said. "Let's see whether you can't get more work somewhere. Let's figure every way we can to put some money aside. If the government comes through with something, the way they promised, maybe we can pay taxes and still have some money left over. Maybe you could even start school winter quarter, down at the BYU. Let's just do this as soon as we can, and not feel too sorry for ourselves."

"Who said anything about feeling sorry for myself? I told you before, I'll work hard and save what I can. It just makes me mad that those 'fine ladies' from town had to come out and make us feel like we're beggars."

"I don't think we have to think about it that way, honey. Remember what Belva told us about the families that first settled out here? They all got together and helped build each other's houses. No one was a beggar. They just supported each other. That's all Nadine and Marjorie wanted to do—give us some support. They'd seen me helping people and they wanted to do something for you."

Rae looked confused. "Then why did you say no?"

"Were you wishing I wouldn't?"

"No. I'm just saying, if you're so sure it was all right, why didn't you say, 'Sure. Hand over the money'?"

"I just . . . I guess I felt like other people needed it more."

"And they do. So that settles that. I want to have breakfast. I have some things I need to do today."

"Okay. I'll—"

But Rae had already stood up from the table, looking so tall, so much like Leah that the image was almost frightening. "I'll cook some eggs for myself. I'll leave the rest for you and Wade."

The voice was the same, too. And the attitude. "Wait just a minute," Leah said. "Let me say something to you."

But Rae didn't sit down. She crossed her arms and waited. Leah could see that she was working up some anger again.

"You know why I named you Rachel."

"Yes. You told me that. Jacob loved Rachel, not Leah."

"But I don't think you know how I felt about that. The first time I heard that story, all I could think was, *I'm Leah; I'm not the pretty one.* It made no sense. It was just my name, but it felt like my mom had known ahead of time what my life was going to be like."

"You should have passed the name on to me. *Rachel* was sure the wrong one for me."

"But that's what I want to say. I got something into my head, and I made too much of it. I see you doing the same thing. Don't make up your mind about yourself. We'll get you to college in time, and if you feel good about yourself, others will too. You're getting so pretty now, and—"

"Mom, I know you're trying to help, but I don't want pity any more than I want charity."

"It's not that. Really. I just see you cutting yourself off from people." But the telephone was ringing, and it was Leah's ring. She got up and walked to the phone. "Just a minute," she said. "I'm not finished with what I want to say." She picked up the phone and said hello.

She expected to hear Nadine or Marjorie, but someone said, "Have I called too early?"

"Oh, no. We get up early out here." Leah didn't recognize the voice.

"This is Catherine Moody. Belva's daughter."

"Oh, yes. Is she feeling all right? She seemed a little sick yesterday."

"Leah, I have some bad news."

She hesitated, and Leah's breath held. She already knew what was coming.

"I came over to check on her early this morning and she was still in bed. But Leah, I could see as soon as I looked at her, she was gone. She died in her sleep—the way she always said she wanted to do."

Leah couldn't speak.

"It's not such a bad thing when you think of it. She was almost eighty-two, and she died peacefully. She's missed my dad all these years and today she's with him."

"But I . . ." Leah meant to say, *But I need her,* but she couldn't say it. She couldn't say anything.

"I thought of you first, Leah. You were her favorite. She always said you reminded her of herself, back when she was young."

"I . . . I . . ."

"What's wrong, Mom?" Rae was asking, but Leah couldn't answer her either.

"Listen, I know this is a surprise. Why don't I give you a minute? Maybe you could call me back a little later. We'll have family coming in, and I know the Relief Society usually—"

"I will. I'll call you. I'll come into town. I . . ." Leah couldn't do this. She hung the receiver up and turned toward Rae. "It's Belva," she said, but she had to get away. She hurried to her bedroom, and she tried to kneel by her bed, but her knees gave way and she collapsed on the floor. "Lord, not this," she said. "You can't do this to me, too. I need her. I need her." And then Leah let go. She cried, sobbed as she hadn't done in many years, and all she could think was that this was one blow too many. Belva was her support—was her mother, more than her own mother had ever been.

And then Leah realized Rae was there, kneeling next to her. She touched Leah's hair. "I'm sorry," she said. "I'm so sorry."

"It's okay," Leah said. "It really is. She's with Reid now."

But Leah was still sobbing, and Rae pulled her head onto her lap. "I know how you love her," she said.

Leah let herself cry for a time. All the while, she was remembering Belva's phone call the night before. "She was coming to see you this morning, Rae," Leah finally said. "She wanted to talk to you about the scholarship."

"I'm sure she wanted me to take it."

"She said that I was teaching you the wrong thing. We were being prideful."

"But LuAnn only—"

"No. Let's not say that right now. Belva would never think of it that way."

Leah hardly knew what she was saying, but it was the last thing Belva had told her, that she needed to reconsider. She turned her face back against Rae's leg and cried again, but, after a time, she wanted to tell Rae the rest. "She said that we're too stubborn. She said she would camp out here until we changed our minds."

"I wish we could have seen her one last time," Rae said. "I wish I could have talked to her."

"Rachel, we've got to talk about this some more. We really do."

Rae didn't answer. But she tightened her grip on Leah, and Leah cried again.

Leah stood at the podium in front of her ward—or actually, people from both wards, and from all around the valley. Everyone knew Belva and loved her, and they filled the Second Ward building to overflowing. It was Friday now, but on Wednesday Catherine had told Leah, "We found a note she wrote and put in her top drawer. She'd written 'Funeral' at the top, and then she'd written, 'song: Maria Jones, There is a Green

Hill Far Away,' and 'speakers: Leah Sorensen, Bishop Bowen.' We don't know if she wrote it down just lately or months ago. The only thing she ever said to me was, 'It'll be a nice thing when I can pass away. So don't make a big fuss at my funeral. Have a nice time, and don't preach too long.'"

Leah couldn't imagine that anyone would ask her to speak, but she couldn't say no to Belva. And now she was standing in front of all these people, wishing she didn't have to do this. She cleared her throat and gripped her hands together, pressing them hard, trying to make them hurt. "Belva told Catherine that she didn't want anyone to preach very long at her funeral," Leah said. "She didn't want us to make a big fuss about her going on to where she was ready to go. I think that's why she thought of me for a preacher instead of some of you long-winded men. She knew I couldn't give a sermon, even if an angel was whispering it in my ear—or, in my case, probably a devil." Folks laughed, but she didn't wait, just pushed on. "What I'll say I'll say pretty quick, and then I'll sit down, the way she wanted me to."

But Leah was hearing too much emotion in her voice. She had to get herself under control. So she did it the way she always did. She laughed and said, "I'll try not to cuss during this talk, but I won't promise a thing. I've spent too much time around plow horses. I speak their language. But I'm always . . . well, I'll say *darn* sorry about it after I do it."

This got a bigger laugh.

"I think if we took a vote, we could all agree, we never met anyone quite so good as Belva. If she doesn't make it to the celestial kingdom, all the rest of us are in big trouble."

Leah tried to laugh again, and some were smiling, but just as many were nodding. "I've never liked funerals where people stand up and say the dearly departed was perfect in every way. Belva had eighty years to practice, and she got very good at being good, but I have a feeling there was a little devil on her shoulder, too, just lurking around, maybe held over from her childhood. It's the only possible explanation for why she would find it in her heart to like me. She liked to giggle a little when I said things I shouldn't, and I think it was that devil telling her not to be quite perfect.

"Leah came out here fifty years ago, dragging along four kids, and then she had four more. And all the while, she helped her husband break this hard ground and get a farm established. So she must have said 'heck' a time or two, even though I never heard such strong language come from her mouth. She wasn't a big woman, like me, but she could plow, and she did. Maybe I've got the wrong idea, but I kind of think every woman still ought to plow some ground once in a while, just to harden up a little. Life isn't easy, and we need some steel in our backs for it. Plowing gives you some of that.

"I knew Belva pretty well before I asked to have her serve with me, but I got to know her a whole lot better this last year and a half, and I'll tell you one of the reasons I needed her. She had to help me see what Relief Society is. The bishop helped me with that too. I thought Relief Society was women getting together about like they do in a social club: chatting, getting the latest gossip. I went to Relief Society at times, skipped it more often, but I never did understand what Joseph Smith had in mind when he formed the organization. This year I read a statement of his in our handbook. He said that the Church wasn't fully organized until the Relief Society was formed. Think about that."

Leah took a few seconds and did let them think. They needed to do it, too, she was sure. Some of the men liked to make fun of the "old ladies" in the Relief Society—even women did, at times—but Leah had grown weary of that. "Joseph told the women in Nauvoo to prepare the members for the temple when they hadn't even finished building it. He told them to teach and admonish. And then he said to look after the people, to feed the hungry and bless the poor. I know we quilt and we like to gab a little while we do, but if the priesthood is the soul of the Church, we're still the heart.

"Belva told us in our meetings that out on the plains the Saints made sure no one was left behind. More often than not, though, when someone had to be nursed and fed, or when a baby was born out there, or someone broke down from all the work and strain, it was a sister who gave them not only sustenance but the will to go on. I've met some fine men in my life, but I never knew one with both the will and the spirit of someone like Belva. It's mothers who make this world work, and they pull us all along.

"Brothers and sisters, Belva taught me more this last year or so than I'd learned my whole life." But now it had happened. Suddenly Leah was not just weeping but gulping to hold back the emotion that had struck her. She stood there for half a minute at least, tears streaming down her face. It took all her strength not to collapse again, not to cry out loud.

Finally, she managed to get out, "I've said enough. You know Belva. She's the best of what a mortal can be. She's what we all *ought* to be. She looked around her and saw goodness in all of us, and we were all better for having felt her eyes upon us."

Leah had a few other things in mind to say, but she didn't say them. She knew she was about to break into sobs. So she closed in the name of the Lord and sat down. The congregation was silent, and Leah looked to see what was in their faces. They were as moved as she was, surely by their memories of Belva.

Leah was sitting on her porch again, and she wasn't surprised when she saw the Pierce-Arrow coming up the lane, this time at an earlier hour, but the red dust still rising and rolling the same way. At the funeral, Leah had told Marjorie, "Why don't you and Nadine come out again and talk to Rae. I don't know whether we did the right thing that last time."

So the Relief Society had fed Belva's family and then washed the dishes, and Leah had only been home about an hour when the car appeared. She stood up and walked to the door. "Rae," she said, "come out here. The sisters are back, and I think they want to talk to you about that scholarship again."

Rae came to the door. She didn't say anything—and she didn't seem surprised.

As the car stopped, Leah said, "Honey, let's listen better this time."

Rae nodded. She stepped onto the porch, and Leah saw something new in her face. It changed even more when LuAnn, who was with them again, said, "Rae, I know how I've acted sometimes, but we're not little girls anymore. I really would like to have you live with us in Salt Lake. We should have been friends all these years."

Rae didn't say anything, but she nodded, ever so slightly, and that was that. She was going to college in another month, and her face showed that she was more excited than she wanted to let on.

"This is the right thing," Nadine said.

"Yes, I think it is," Leah said. "I'm glad you gave us another chance." But then she did something she had never thought of doing—and wouldn't have done if she'd thought about it longer. She stepped forward and wrapped her arms around all Nadine's thickness. There were words she thought of saying, but she held those back, and just let her long arms speak for themselves. Then she did the same with Marjorie, and even LuAnn. Then Rae followed her example. By the time it was all finished, Leah was more or less humiliated, but she wasn't sorry she had done it.

So the town ladies got back in the car, and Leah turned to Rae, and she hugged her, too. "I'm glad for you," she said. "This is a good thing."

"I hope so," Rae said, and Leah understood why Rae still had her doubts. She'd known plenty of disappointment already in her life.

But Leah was excited for her. She did feel certain it was the best thing, even if she feared the loneliness that was coming. Still, she had a lot of sisters, and that was what she'd lacked all her life.

The weather had cooled a little that day, the worst of the heat having finally broken, it appeared. So Leah went to bed earlier that night, and she slept well. But the dream came again, and when she woke up in the morning, she remembered this time what she had seen. She finally recognized the young woman in the dream. She realized it was Rae—Rachel—looking a few years older, and looking pleased about something, maybe about her life. And now Leah understood why the bishop had called her to serve—why God had.

Author's Note

DON'T TRY TO LOOK UP RICHARDS, UTAH, on a map. It doesn't exist. I wanted to deal with certain aspects of life during the Great Depression years—such as bank failures—and I couldn't find a rural town in Utah that fit all my historical requirements. So I invented a setting. Still, I tried to create a sense of the early Depression years and the adjustments that people in small communities had to make. My details about Relief Society and the way the LDS Church functioned at the time, along with the regional, state, and national backdrop, are factual. The story, of course, is fictional.

For those who would like to do further reading about America in the 1930s, some of the best resources are: *The Great Depression, America 1929–1941,* by Robert S. McElvaine (Random House, 1984; Times Books, 1993); *The Hungry Years: A Narrative History of the Great Depression in America,* by T. H. Watkins (Henry Holt, 1999); *Daily Life in the United States, 1920–1940,* by David E. Kyvig (Ivan R. Dee, 2004); *Down and Out in the Great Depression: Letters from the Forgotten Man,* ed. Robert S. McElvaine (University of North Carolina Press, 1983); and

Rethinking the Great Depression, by Gene Smiley (Ivan R. Dee, 2002). I also found helpful John Steinbeck's essay "A Primer on the '30s," published in his collection, *America and the Americans* (Penguin, 2002).

A first-rate history of the LDS Relief Society is *Women of Covenant,* by Jill Mulvay Derr, Janath Russell Cannon, and Maureen Ursenbach Beecher (Deseret Book, 1992). I also used the *Handbook of the Relief Society,* published by the General Board of the Relief Society in 1931. *Pure Religion: The Story of Church Welfare since 1930,* by Glen L. Rudd (Church of Jesus Christ of Latter-day Saints, 1995), is another useful resource.

One delightful experience was to read the *Relief Society Magazine* from the era. The history of women in the Church is one of strength, independence, intelligence, and forward thinking, and nowhere is that more obvious than in the *Relief Society Magazine.*

Max B. Rasmussen, a wonderful family friend, has lived in the Uintah Basin most of his long life. I interviewed him and his wife, Patsy, about life during the Depression years. Much of my firsthand information came from them, and they also allowed me to use their copies of some valuable books : *A History of Uintah County: Scratching the Surface,* by Doris Karren Burton (Utah Historical Society, 1996); *Builders of Uintah: A Centennial History of the Uintah County, 1872 to 1947* (Daughters of the Utah Pioneers, 1947). They even let me take their original copy of the 1930–31 *Montgomery Ward Catalogue.*

I also have William D. Hurst, my wife's father, to thank for the long and helpful account he gave me of his memories. Over ninety now, he vividly remembers small-town life in Utah. Whenever I had questions about cars, farming, prices—all kinds of things—I called him.

In the spring of 2007 my wife, Kathleen, was released as a member of the Relief Society general presidency. She served for five years with Bonnie D. Parkin and Anne C. Pingree. Bonnie and Anne became not only her dear sisters but mine, and we became equally close friends with their husbands, Dr. James L. Parkin and Dr. George C. Pingree. This book is dedicated to them because of that friendship, but also because of the truths this presidency taught me. Bonnie and Anne, along with Kathy, recognized that Relief Society is not only an inspiring organization for LDS women but also a powerful force for good in our world. They constantly asked the members of the Church, especially young sisters, to embrace the organization fully and to realize both its current value and ultimate potentiality. What my fictional character Leah learns in this book is what I learned while my wife served, and this book is my tribute both to Relief Society and to the work of Bonnie, Kathy, and Anne.